Will obesity—the enemy within—destroy America?

Will terrorists succeed at using our nation's gluttony against us, so that they can take over?

Or can a journalist, a Special Ops soldier, and a renegade surgeon stop the terrorists and save America?

The Enemy Within

TWO SISTERS
WRITING & PUBLISHING™

For more information about this title or to order other books
and/or electronic media, contact the publisher:

Two Sisters Writing and Publishing
18530 Mack Avenue, Suite 166
Grosse Pointe Farms, MI 48236
www.atkinsgreenspan.com

ISBN
978-1-945875-23-6 (Paperback)
978-1-945875-24-3 (eBook)

Printed in the United States of America

Cover and Interior design: Van-Garde Imagery, Inc.

The Enemy Within

Michael H. Wood, MD

Elizabeth Ann Atkins

Prologue

As KING DAEMON LED his 10 Royal Brothers through the long, dark corridor, his angry heartbeat pulsed so hard that his eyes were bloodshot.

"Come, quickly," King Daemon ordered as moonlight shooting through the skylights cast a silvery glow over his red silk robes that fluttered around his long legs and velvet slippers.

He strode faster, squeezing his eyes shut as his thoughts thundered with memories that triggered an ever-constant hunger for revenge. These thoughts inspired his life's mission to crush America and rule the world. Yes America, whose soldiers had slaughtered young Daemon's parents before his very eyes, causing the blood of his screaming mother and father to spray across his face and into his mouth.

That horrifying moment had made him hunger for the blood of those who bullied the world under the bogus glory of red, white, and blue.

King Daemon sped up, and his men followed. His mind flashed with the image of an American flag patch on the uniform of the killer-soldier who slayed his parents. The same assassin who, now as US Army General, was leading the charge to dominate Royal Tricqua.

I am allowing him to live long enough to witness the deadly vengeance I will wreak on his beloved country, his wife, and his daughter…

Now, King Daemon squinted, trying to see past the violent visions in his mind's eye that were blinding him to what was happening right before him.

"Almighty, we enter here," said one of a half-dozen, armed guards surrounding the men. The guard waved the biochip implanted in his wrist over an invisible panel in the ornately tiled wall; double doors opened onto a large laboratory aglow with fluorescent lights.

Inside stood Dr. Milo Braza, the Kingdom's Minister of Science, wearing a white lab coat and wireless eyeglasses over the hairless, beige oval that was his slim face. He bowed.

"Almighty King Daemon," he said, "welcome. The demonstration is ready for your royal viewing." Dr. Braza led King Daemon and the men to a large, stainless steel table on which sat three glass cages containing white lab rats.

"I will show you exactly how your genius vision will wreak sickness and death on gluttonous Americans," Dr. Braza said, nodding toward the cages, which contained eight rats each. "How we will literally become the enemy within the greedy, blasphemous mouths of Americans."

King Daemon squinted at the rats, envisioning them as American men, women, and children.

Dr. Braza's eyes sparkled with the brilliance that made him one of the world's foremost experts on chemical warfare and genocide. He had studied the human extermination policies and procedures implemented in Germany, Cambodia, Rwanda, and Armenia. Now he had devised a strategy with unprecedented stealth and efficiency to ensure victory and dominance for the Global Kingdom of Royal Tricqua.

"We are ready," King Daemon declared. His entire being shivered with the euphoria of that day in the near future when he would stand on the lawn at 1600 Pennsylvania Avenue in Washington, DC and raise his arms to almighty God in gratitude for granting him the global dominance that was his birthright.

"Almighty King Daemon and my Royal Brothers," Dr. Braza said, pointing to the first cage, "you will notice that the rats in cage number one are healthy, energetic and slim, eating only on normal cycles of hunger."

The rats were scurrying around, ignoring a bowl containing food pellets alongside pieces of hamburgers, French fries, pizza slices, and candy bars. None drank from the side-by-side bowls of water and orange, fizzy soda pop.

King Daemon and the men nodded in observance. The room was silent except for the hum of monitors attached to the cages; each had a digital display showing the individual rats' vital signs, body fat composition, size, and weight. Dr. Braza gestured toward the second cage.

"Here is where the magic begins to happen," he said. "You will notice that the rats in cage number two are overweight and have low energy because they are sickly." He paused as the rats ate the same food offered in the previous cage. Some slept. One rat wobbled as if in a drunken stupor, then bumped into the glass. "That one is blind due to diabetes. Its feet, as you can see, are purple, and beginning to rot with gangrene."

King Daemon's spirit leaped with excitement as his mind's eye envisioned his enemies suffering the same fate. He was especially eager to watch the soldier-assassin who robbed him of his parents, suffer with America's agonizing defeat. After many years of research, King Daemon's men had identified his parents' killer as General William "Wild Bill" Brewster. At this very moment, Royal agents were monitoring his every move, while the General lived and worked in the downtown capital of Trykka, so stupidly believing that under his leadership, the Americans were achieving victory here by imposing their bogus democracy.

King Daemon balled his fists and glared at his own reflection on the glass cage; his bloodshot eyes glowed against his almond complexion that was tinged reddish with anger. His entire being hummed with the urge to kill that man with his own hands.

Soon…

"And finally," Dr. Braza said, stepping in front of a third cage. "You will notice that these rats are morbidly obese and cannot stop eating."

Four rats—so fat that they looked like pink cantaloupes covered in white fur—were eating in a frenzy from a pile of hamburgers, French fries, pizza slices, and candy bars. They also guzzled the orange, fizzy soda pop.

"The rats in all three cages are being fed varying levels of the elixir that I have created and injected into the food,"

Dr. Braza said. "It is an exponential obesity multiplier called OC-8, or Obesity Catalyst 8, with the number eight representing Infinity."

With a piercing, threatening stare, King Daemon said, "Tell me that you obeyed my order that OC-8 be non-detectable during autopsies."

Fear flashed in Dr. Braza's eyes as he nodded. "Absolutely, your majesty. Our trusted comrades in the United States have provided the exact specifications that enabled me to formulate OC-8—and the even more potent OC-88—to strictly adhere to the US Food and Drug Administration's guidelines for a safe 'flavor enhancer' that will be marketed and sold to restaurants and food manufacturing companies."

King Daemon crossed his arms. "Tell me how it works."

As the men watched the rats eat, Dr. Braza explained: "OC-8 is to the taste buds and other senses what opium is to the brain. When added to foods, OC-8 enhances the eating experience in a way that is as overwhelmingly pleasurable and as addictive as heroin or cocaine. So much so, that the person becomes insatiably addicted to food, as fiendishly as a drug addict craves more drugs, consuming them to the point of overdose and death."

Commotion in cage three drew the men's attention.

"Gentlemen," Dr. Braza said, "I believe we are about to enjoy the pleasure of witnessing the grand finale."

The men were silent as one obese rat keeled over and became still. A monitor beeped. A red line extended across the screen. A second rat waddled around in a stupor. Its pink feet turned purple, then black, and fell off. The rat let out a squeak, then rolled on its side, dead. Six other rats were clawing and chewing a cheeseburger on a bun and a slice of pizza. Their frenzy made their mouths and feet appear as if they were in a video playing on fast-forward.

Suddenly one of the rats convulsed, then collapsed with its face in the tomato sauce. The others suffered a similar fate. The lone living rat continued eating for a few minutes. Then its eyes widened. A red crack, dripping blood, appeared under the white fur of its huge pink belly. It had eaten to the point of splitting open.

"Yesssssss," King Daemon declared, his eyes widening as if in a trance. "America, take a look at your future. Eating like a fat rat. And dying like a fat rat. Because your enemy is within. It is your gluttony for food, and it is killing you by your own hand."

Chapter 1

SOMEONE'S FOLLOWING ME...

A quick burst of adrenaline propelled Jeralynn Brewster's track-star legs to pump faster over the black tire marks on the cement. A few days ago, she'd watched Indy cars roar along this street during the Detroit Grand Prix.

But now on this sunny Wednesday morning, the race cars were gone, as were the pit crews, party tents, and cheering crowds in the grandstands. And Jeri was loving her usual morning lap around the nearly six-mile perimeter of the island park of Belle Isle. Her mother was always warning her not to run alone out here. But she was neither scared nor unprotected.

I dare somebody to interrupt my run this morning. I just dare them...

She coolly glimpsed back while dashing around the first curve of the one-way, three-lane road. To her left was the huge, white marble Scott Fountain, spraying water up toward the cloudless sky. To her right, past green grass, breeze-rustled trees and the bright blue Detroit River, rose the gleaming downtown skyline. And yes, about five yards behind her—a man in a dented green Pontiac Grand Prix, was driving slowly, wearing mirrored aviator sunglasses, watching her…

Just try something, jerk.

Jeri kept running to the hip-hop beat in her wireless earbuds; her iPhone was tucked in a small, black canvas pouch attached to a band around her left arm. And thanks to her breakfast of steel-cut oats and a green vegetable smoothie, she felt powered up to run all day. Or handle any problems that might suddenly arise from a random guy with bad ideas.

It was 8:00 a.m. She was alone, aside from a couple sipping coffee on a blanket under a willow tree by the water, and a few people sitting in parked cars along the road. She inhaled the fresh air, loving the solitude and freedom of running outdoors on a beautiful summer morning. This was her best "think time," as her legs kicked into autopilot in synch with her breath, and her mind sparked with new ideas.

But she resented the intrusion of some sinister creep. Her run took exactly one hour from the time she left her loft apartment near downtown, sprinted over the ornate white Belle Isle Bridge, circled the island, then ran back home. It always revved up her mind and body for a full day of reporting and writing as part of the lifetime mission she'd declared at age five: to help people be healthy and safe.

That included women, who were so often viewed as vulnerable targets for whatever scurrilous intentions might be spinning in the twisted brains of guys like the one following her right now.

I'd be happy to set the record straight for him, on behalf of all of us...

Just like she did every day as a journalist. Today she had a big story due about the latest obesity rates. After a shower, she'd head into the downtown Detroit bureau of the *American Daily News,* where she'd been covering the health and wellness beat, with a Midwest angle, for the past two years.

"Good morning!" a man said, zipping past with a *whirr* amongst a half-dozen others on racing bicycles.

"Hi," she called. Her female friends who always told her she shouldn't run alone here would have felt comforted by the presence of other fitness devotees; Jeri felt nothing but a burst a cheer about the greeting, and the sight of other people living healthy lifestyles as their muscular legs pumped them forward.

Her phone rang just as a souped-up Monte Carlo with giant silver tire rims sped past; inside were four African American teenagers. One leaned out the window, whistling over the deep bass rumble and graphic lyrics of rap music blasting on the car's stereo. "Hey, blondie! You *wearin'* them shorts!"

Jeri smiled and kept running while her phone flashed *Mom.* The bass music continued to *boom-boom-boom,* and the guy tailing her was still slowly coasting in her peripheral view.

"Jeri, don't tell me you're on Belle Isle alone," her mother snapped with a fretful tone.

"Then I won't tell you," she said, breathing normally as she sprinted around the curve and beheld the beautiful scenery.

"Jeri, it's dangerous! A woman out there alone!"

"Mom, you're forgetting I can kick anyone's a—" Jeri started. "Anyone's butt. I run here almost every day. Please don't worry about me—"

"It's the other people, people with guns, that I worry about—"

"You don't think I came out here naked, do you?" Jeri asked playfully, gripping the metal outline in her black pouch. She also wore her hair twisted up in a bun as opposed to a ponytail or braid that someone could grab from behind.

"Jeri, honey, I'm going to my book signing and your dad is on the other side of the world—"

Aggravation—at her mother and the guy behind her—made Jeri quicken her pace, pounding her feet on the weather-beaten cement. She leaped over a pothole with the kind of strength that had enabled her to win the state high school championship in the low hurdles.

"Exactly, Mom! I'm 28 years old, trained by the best of the best—Dad! How can you be married to the most awesome Army general *ever*, and fear your own shadow? I didn't inherit your paranoia genes, thank goodness!"

"Jeri—"

"Seriously, Mom, I'm fine. I'll text you when I get home, okay? And I'll see you at your book event tonight."

Jeri hung up, then ran faster. She adored her mother, but the overprotectiveness was so tiring.

What did she think Dad and I were doing all that time with the Navy Seals in San Diego? Or at the gun range? Did she forget that I went to Basic Training?

"Hey, G.I. Jane!" a woman said as Jeri dashed past a vacant playground. The woman, who had long black dreadlocks, was sitting on a bench, slipping into rollerblades. "Cool shirt, girl!"

"Thank you," Jeri said, smiling as she glanced down at her camouflage-patterned tank top that said *G.I. JANE* across the front. It was a gift from her father; that had been his nickname for her since, as a toddler, she'd been making her Barbie dolls zip around in toy tanks and trucks he gave her rather than the pink Corvette that her Aunt Katie had given her for Christmas.

Jeri ran past three obese women. Wearing bright T-shirts, caps and leggings, they were speed-walking and talking.

"I've lost 34 pounds," Jeri overheard one woman say, "just by giving up fried foods and pop, and comin' out here. But I can't even tell you how much I hate exercise. I only do it so I can get this weight off and get my blood pressure under control."

"Good morning," Jeri said.

"We'll be runnin' as fast as you pretty soon," another woman said playfully.

"I hope!" another said.

"Then we'll run together!" Jeri said, smiling, as she sped past them. She loved to see people actively trying to slim down and get healthier here in one of America's fattest cities. She was so grateful for her lifelong passion for physical fitness that had inspired her to become all-state in track and captain of the swim team, breaking state records in the 200-

meter butterfly and freestyle. During the off-season, her sport was soccer. And she did judo, karate, and kickboxing year-round. Her biggest thrill was when Dad let her go with him to the Naval Base in San Diego for a summer, when she trained with the Navy Seals.

She'd also loved healthy food since birth; every picture of her as a baby in a high chair and as a little girl at the big dining room table showed her eating individual beans—kidney, garbanzo, pinto—with her fingers or scooping her hand in a bowl of quinoa or black rice by the handful.

While growing up, her straight-A success at the private Worthington School had enabled her to graduate magna cum laude, two years early, as valedictorian. Her classmates had voted her "Toughest Girl" and put a caption under a photograph of her in the senior yearbook that said "*G.I. Jane. Don't mess with me: I'll crush you!*"

She'd maintained her commitment to physical fitness at Columbia University's Graduate School of Journalism in New York. And now here she was—still being trailed by a creep. Jeri kept running, conscious of the car behind her, almost excited to see what the guy might try. One thing was for sure, he would not make her late for work.

Today she would receive the latest obesity statistics released by the US Centers for Disease Control and Prevention. She would write a story and include insights from today's live coverage of the Congressional hearing for the American Obesity Eradication Act. Testifying in support of its passage would be Detroit bariatric surgeon Dr. Michael

Wise, who helped craft the act with Michigan legislators, based on aggressive policy proposals that he outlined in his bestselling book, *Till Death Do Us Part: A Battle Plan to Win America's War on Obesity.*

Unfortunately, the American public seemed to be moving in the opposite direction, as a much-hyped new chocolate restaurant would be opening in Metro Detroit today. Jeri had already done a hard-hitting preview story about it last week, in the context of it being yet another terrible trend for America's health. In her article, she had used a word she'd learned during several interviews with Dr. Wise: "obesogenic." The word described how fast food, modern conveniences, and high-tech, sedentary lifestyles had created a world that seemed programmed to make people fat.

Today she would also learn from her editor whether her proposal was approved to travel to the Republic of the East, the former Tricqua, where her father was on a mission for the US Army. Jeri wanted to do an in-depth story about how American intervention to defeat the rebels and install a democratic government had also brought fast-food restaurants, processed food, and a rising obesity rate in the once-healthy nation.

Jeri could never fall prey to the ever-worsening, global epidemic as sweat dampened her skin and the quick pace of her pulse kept her resting heart rate low and her weight in a healthy range. And she planned to keep it that way. In fact, she'd chosen journalism as a vocation in middle school because it provided a platform to educate and inspire people to make positive changes in their lives.

Now, as the guy behind her crept closer, it looked like she might have to do that for him as well. She discreetly unzipped her black canvas pouch for easy access, if necessary.

She ran fast along the straight stretch of road past the Belle Isle Casino, where several overweight teenagers were posting signs with arrows that said GOLDEN HARVEST HEALTH FAIR TODAY at 10:00 a.m. The signs were stamped with sponsors that included Heavenly's Burgers and, of course, Golden Harvest, the nation's biggest food manufacturing company.

Jeri had written many stories about how this corporation contributed millions to college scholarships, health fairs, and nutrition education. But she'd also written about how it was doing just as much harm as good, if not more, by owning and promoting a franchise of Creamy Dream Chocolate Shoppes. They also franchised Doughnut Delite and French Fry Cafés, having recently opened all three in Detroit within the last few months.

Jeri found it maddening that companies like Golden Harvest, which didn't offer a single healthy option at any of their fast food franchises, hosted health fairs to allegedly counter the illness and obesity that resulted from the food they sold. Golden Harvest held the distinction as dominating the top three spots in the "fastest-growing restaurants chains in America" year after year.

Now, as she jogged past an ornate Chinese footbridge, she remembered a rumor she was trying to confirm. Golden Harvest CEO Douglass Golden was allegedly working behind the scenes in Washington, DC, to fund a federal program that would give the company exclusive rights to open its fast food restaurants inside schools to replace cafeterias and provide lunch and snack programs, as well as after-school and weekend programs. As other companies with healthier options were vying for that coveted privilege to help cash-strapped schools feed more children with shrinking budgets, Golden Harvest was considered a done deal because it wielded so much power and influence on Capitol Hill.

A convertible Mercedes driven by a dark-haired man in a business suit, sipping coffee, passed her, blaring the morning news on the radio: "Breaking news in the Republic of the East. A suicide bomber kills a dozen women and children in a busy market, just a week after insurgents burned an effigy of the US President—"

Jeri's steady heartbeat quickened as she thought of her dad. She had Skyped with him this morning. He'd told her that these were examples of why he'd be staying in the Republic longer than originally planned, and that it wasn't a good time for Americans to visit.

If my trip is approved, he won't be happy...

Now running past woods to her left, and the river to her right, Jeri was alone—no parked cars, no bikers, no Rollerbladers, just the stalker, who was now approaching on her right.

"Hey," the guy said through the open driver side window. His skin was smoker-gray, like a dead fish, and his straight brown hair hung around his shoulders. His forearm, hanging out the window, was tattooed with a red heart stabbed with a sword and coiled by a snake. The center was scrolled: "Debbie, R.I.P." Scratches on his arms were so fresh they had not scabbed over. Had he just been struggling with someone?

Cigarette smoke billowed from the window; Jeri held her breath and kept running, her mind fast-forwarding over the possible scenarios that could arise. She hadn't practiced her moves in awhile. This creep might provide a good drill and add an extra *umph!* to her workout.

"Looks like you got a long way to go," he said, revealing several rotten teeth. "Need a ride?"

"No," she said firmly, seeing her toned, bare shoulders and arms reflected in his sunglasses. "You should keep driving." Jeri was mad, not scared. Even when the man suddenly sped up, stopped the car about two yards ahead of her, popped the trunk, let the engine idle, and came around back toward her.

"Come here!" he ordered.

He thinks he's gonna grab me, throw me in the trunk and drive away... No chance!

She shot past the right side of the car into the middle of the road. He lunged at her. She sprinted faster; he chased. His pudgy physique under a grungy T-shirt and jeans gave her the impression that he'd be slow, but he was surprisingly fast for someone who looked so out of shape.

Still, Jeri outran him. But she tripped on a pothole. Flew forward on her knees. And her black pouch skidded a few feet out of her reach, along with her phone. He put his foot on the pouch. Staring down at her, he said, "Shoulda listened when I said, 'Come here.'"

He tried to grab her, but Jeri shot up like a shark surging from the ocean. Her two fists rammed his solar plexus. He flew back onto the cement, his sunglasses flying off.

"You fuckin' bitch!" he shouted. His eyes, devoid of emotion, shot pure evil at her, sending a chill down her spine.

Her black pouch was just a few feet from his hand; the silver handle of her .22 caliber pistol glimmered in the sun. He flashed a wicked smile as he reached for it. She jumped forward; her foot smashed down on his wrist. His skin scraped into shards of crumbling cement. With his other hand, he tried to grab her ankle, but she kicked it away with her other foot.

"You're interrupting my run, you stupid motherfucker," she yelled down at him.

"Let go of my wrist!" he shouted, squirming like he was about to kick her.

"I do have the unfair advantage here," she said, grabbing his other hand. She yanked him upward to his feet, and he struggled to get his balance. As she glared at him, all the anger that she had ever felt in her 28 years over the fear that women have of exactly this happening—to themselves or their loved ones—came surging out through her fists.

Whether she'd been training with soldiers or just doing a good kickboxing workout on the bags at the gym, her fists had never pounded so hard as when they hit this punk's flabby body. He grunted with every blow. Jeri's arms felt like turbo-charged pistons with an endless fuel supply: her thoughts. One-two: left-right jabs to the kidneys. One-two: two punches to the chest. One-two-three: right knuckles in the nose, left fist in the cheek, right upper cut in the jaw.

His groans were a wheezy mix of pain, shock, and desperation. She kept pounding, bending to the left, cocking back her right leg, and blasting her foot into his crotch.

He reeled back, doubled over, clutching his groin.

Jeri—her heart pounding, her chest rising and falling—smiled.

Dazed with a crazed look in his eyes, he lunged toward her. But Jeri bashed his left and right ears with her fists.

"You stupid motherfucker!" she shouted, pounding him everywhere with double- and triple- punches. "You're done!" She kicked him again, shouting, "This is for whoever scratched you this morning."

"Stop, you crazy bitch!" he shrieked, his nose and lip dripping blood as he cupped his crotch.

She came at him; he tried to grab her wrists. But she gripped the sides of his arms, yanked him up, then body-slammed him so hard on the cement that he bounced slightly. As he gasped for air—yelping, "You broke my fuckin' shoulder!"—she grabbed her phone and dialed 911.

"Detroit Police, Belle Isle station," an officer answered. "What's your emergency?"

"A guy just tried to attack me near the Dossin Great Lakes Museum," Jeri said, aiming her .22 down at him. His body froze, but his face twisted with pain.

"Are you in a safe place, ma'am?"

"Oh, yes. I have the guy subdued."

"We'll be there shortly," the officer said.

"Thank you." When Jeri hung up, the guy groaned: "Man, I fucked with the wrong chicks today."

"Oh, so you do this often?" Jeri asked, her mind spinning with horrific images of what might have happened if he'd snatched her, and of other women he may have attacked.

"You a cop?" he demanded.

A crunch sound made her turn to the right. The dreadlocked woman on rollerblades was running over his sunglasses.

"Looks like you got this under control, G.I. Jane," the woman said with a smile. "I've seen this asshole out here, watchin' me." The woman rolled over to him and glared down. "I woulda done the same thing to your punk ass."

A police siren wailed; red and blue lights flashed on the guy's pale face as the squad car came to a stop. The officers jumped out and quickly handcuffed the guy. "You Larry Van Gluten?"

"Yeah, why?"

The officer turned to Jeri. "You just caught a serial rapist. Attacked a woman jogger near Chene Park just this morning."

"Is she okay?" Jeri asked.

The officer shook his head. "Fortunately, she got away, but the three other women before her didn't. Raped, beaten. You just protected a whole lot more women from this guy."

Jeri glared down into his hateful eyes. "Glad to help," she said.

"You ain't seen the lasta me," he threatened, glaring at Jeri as the woman on Rollerblades aimed her iPhone at the scene.

Then, after the other officer took a report and reviewed Jeri's permit to carry a concealed weapon, she finished her run. And she was not late for work.

Chapter 2

A COLLECTIVE GROAN OF disgust rumbled through the United States Congress in Washington DC. All eyes were transfixed on the enormous projection screen showing video of a substance that few had seen in its gruesome, raw state.

"Ladies and gentlemen, you're looking at public enemy number one!" exclaimed Dr. Michael Wise. "You have the power to stop this weapon of mass destruction that is already unleashing World War III right here on American soil!"

The surgeon's testimony resounded in the stunned silence. The previously recorded video showed the details of a bariatric surgery he performed a dozen times each week, as he maneuvered tiny metal clamps and scalpels around the interior of an intestinal cavity during the robotic procedure. A murmur of groans and repulsed commentary filled the room.

"Behold the most insidious weapon of mass destruction the world has ever seen!" he nearly shouted. "Every day, I am on the front lines of our losing battle against this poison." Dr. Wise bellowed, pointing a red laser beam at video images of glistening, yellow-orange gunk streaked with blood-red lines. Like a huge glob of melted cheddar cheese, the fat formed a vast sea in which smooth pink objects—organs—occasionally bobbed up, yet remained mostly submerged.

Dr. Wise studied the faces of lawmakers, their staff members, the public gallery, and reporters whose television cameras were broadcasting this hearing around the world. Even the President of the United States, and the health-promoting First Lady, had vowed to watch the hearing, which they had expressed in a certified letter to Dr. Wise's office back in Detroit. In the letter, President Thomas Alexander and First Lady Mrs. Faith Alexander had also praised his book after he sent them an autographed copy.

Now, the 48-year-old surgeon's entire being welled with desperation and hope that the country's top leadership would finally take aggressive action by implementing the life-saving strategy that he'd outlined in his book. A hardcover copy sat on the long table before him. As he was waiting for a response, emotions and adrenaline surged through his body.

I did all the thinking and work for them. Now all they need to do is launch the attack. Either they decide that today is D-Day… or I will wage guerilla warfare against the billionaires who are killing American men, women, and children…

He felt relieved and encouraged as he glimpsed tears streaking down the face of US Senator Cheryl Simpson of Michigan. She had sponsored the bill that prompted this Congressional hearing. But the chairman of this committee, who sat dead center on the tier of decision-making lawmakers, was covering his face and shaking his head.

Damn him!

Senator Brace Buxton III of Alabama was nothing but a whore to the billionaire industries that were inflicting sickness and death on Americans. Rumor had it that he—the fourth generation of his family to hold this seat—was just as crooked as his forebears, and that he pocketed millions from the food industry to pass or block legislation in their favor. It didn't help that he was movie-star handsome, with the slicked back hair, a clean-shaven face that was suntanned year-round, and the super-fit body that enabled him to post newsworthy finish times in the annual Marine Corps Marathon.

The media had tried but failed to substantiate rumors that he was linked to a sex ring providing high-caliber call girls to powerful men in Washington. He was a known adulterer, but even during the #metoo era that brought sexual harassers to justice, smooth Buxton's well-known, behind-closed-doors behavior always evaded substantiation in the media and in courtrooms.

That man was wickedly shielded from punishment while pursuing his mission to pursue profits and power at any cost. When Dr. Wise was a young boy in Alabama, the name Buxton was synonymous with Jim Crow segregation, and an especially deadly climate for black men. Dr. Wise recalled many occasions as a very young boy, hearing his father and uncles speak in hushed tones about men who'd disappeared or gotten killed, often with some connection to the Buxton name.

Besides the plantation that their family had owned

since the 1700s, the Buxtons assumed a lot of powerful—appointed and elected—positions, including a handful of county sheriffs across the state, two judges, and owners of the general store in Dr. Wise's hometown. Not to mention that the patriarch of the family was the governor; so, while Dr. Wise watched his father endure the humiliation of racism, the Congressman, now glaring down at him in this hearing, had been a boy the same age, living a privileged life in the governor's mansion with his parents and siblings.

Governor Buxton's segregationist rhetoric had emboldened the Klan to escalate beatings and lynchings of black men after Dr. Martin Luther King, Jr., was assassinated in Memphis in 1968. That summer, the Wise family moved to Detroit, where Dr. Wise's father earned a good living as an assembly line worker at the Ford Rouge Plant while putting himself through law school. At the time, Mom took care of home and the three kids. As a grown man, Dr. Wise was not intimidated by whatever power Brace Buxton thought he could wield. Didn't he know that by helping the food industry poison Americans, he was crippling the workforce and the economy?

An equal mix of rage and determination shot through Dr. Wise as he thought about his family back home in Michigan and in rural Alabama where many relatives still lived. His younger brother, Leroy, was a ticking time bomb of the same heart disease and diabetes that had claimed their mother's life. Adding insult to injury, Leroy and his wife, Darlene, were raising their three kids with the same bad habits that could only lead to the sickness and early death that would make new generations have a shorter lifespan than their parents.

Why hadn't Leroy learned from watching Mom's bad eating habits catch up with her and send her to an early grave, while Dad set the example for health and longevity?

The issues of fat and failing health split the family, as both Dr. Wise and his father were outraged by Leroy's reckless behavior for himself and his family. As a result, Dad rarely came to Detroit. And though the brothers lived just miles apart in Detroit, they rarely saw each other because Dr. Wise could never refrain from warning his brother to stop poisoning himself and his family with their obesogenic lifestyle.

Now Dr. Wise's heart ached as he thought about how so many of his relatives were already dead, blind, or immobilized by fat and disease. He'd all but given up on morbidly obese Aunt Lucille. Sure, she made the second-best peach cobbler in town next to his mother. Mom's pie was the best, with that perfect, golden-brown crust on the top and bottom, served with a double-scoop of vanilla ice cream melting from the pie's heat on the plate.

Thankfully, his father had always been health-conscious, eating an abundance of vegetables, fruits, and grains, with little meat, while the rest of the family enjoyed a traditional African American diet that included too much fat, sodium, and calories. Back when Dr. Wise was growing up, his mother stayed at home, but she had a side job, running numbers in their working-class neighborhood.

This contrasted sharply with Dad's respected position

as a law professor at the Wayne State University School of Law. Shortly after arriving in Detroit, he started law school while working at the factory. Now he spent his days teaching America's rules of justice, and his nights writing about the injustice that the system inflicted on women and people of color, prompting them to engage in tactics for economic survival such as "illegal" lotteries that actually created the blueprint for government-run lotteries. Professor James Wise, who retired to his study each evening and weekend to write bold books about racial injustice, made a national name for himself that resulted—after raising the kids in Detroit—in his highly coveted, current position at Harvard.

While still in Detroit, Dad's mornings always included a brisk walk around the neighborhood, followed by a breakfast that he brewed up in the blender with wheat germ, green vegetables, and all kinds of things that created a sort of swamp-water-colored beverage that his father chugged with enthusiasm while standing beside the kitchen table as Michael and the rest of the family ate bacon, sausage, eggs, and pancakes.

At dinnertime, Mom served pork chops, fried fish, baked or fried chicken, and her special beef tacos that she'd perfected with the help of her Mexican friends who lived down the street. Daddy ate in moderation, and always included extra vegetables and salad with his meals, along with a piece of fruit for dessert. Daddy never drank or smoked, and he always got seven to eight hours of sleep each night.

During dinner, only his father wanted to hear young Michael talk about how he'd learned in high school biology class that being overweight was bad for the heart and every other organ, and that overeating caused insulin problems that led to disease and death.

Dad was constantly warning Mom to cook and eat healthier food. But Mom's own kitchen had made her obese, and sick with diabetes and hypertension. One day while Dr. Wise's father was lecturing at the law school, he received a call. Mom was gravely ill. Dad excused himself from the auditorium, rushed to the hospital, and arrived too late. As he had warned her so many times, she died from complications from diabetes and hypertension. Mom never survived to see Dad recruited to share his theories as a scholar at Harvard Law School. There, his left-leaning theories sparked spirited debates and a deep friendship with a more right-leaning lecturer who would become the current President of the United States of America.

Now, Dr. Wise wished his father were here with him in Congress to witness this hearing, but Dad had been adamant about not wanting to risk ramifications at Harvard by being seen in what he deemed an exercise in futility.

Dr. Wise was pleading for radical change rooted in what he'd witnessed at his own family's kitchen table. But some of these powerful leaders were just as reluctant to hear his grave warnings as his own relatives. The person who gave him the most lip about his dinnertime lectures was Aunt Lucille, who was notorious for making an entire meatloaf or cobbler or pan of macaroni and cheese for herself, then serving everyone else from a second pan.

She devoured whole trays of buttered biscuits with her platter of fried chicken as her body expanded and her hospitalizations for her "sugar" grew more and more frequent. Witnessing this self-destruction had inspired Dr. Wise to become a physician, then a bariatric surgeon. His father was proud of him, but had passed on the opportunity to attend this hearing because he wanted nothing to do with his son's "rabble-rousing in Congress;" his father believed that the Act would be defeated, and that would propel his son into a revolution.

He's right. I've been preparing for this my whole life…

The pain of being a chubby child himself—nicknamed "Little Fatty Michael" by his brother, sister and cousins—had also spurred him onto this mission. Thankfully, playing basketball and running track in school, plus imposing the kind of portion control that he'd learned about in library books, had enabled him to drop the childhood chubbiness. In fact, while he'd earned straight A's in school, he had enjoyed a growth spurt that led to a height of a lanky six-feet, three inches.

But he was infuriated by his baby sister, Evelyn, who seemed to grow upward and outward at a disturbing rate. Now 40 years old, you couldn't tell her she wasn't the finest thing walking around with that huge behind and hips. Half the time she was showing it off—or so she thought—in tight white pants and even cheetah-print leggings.

She claimed that her behind attracted compliments and attention from a steady stream of male admirers. Dr. Wise hadn't seen her since Christmas at Aunt Lucille's house, when he'd been unable to stop himself from scolding her about allowing her 10-year-old daughter to develop type 2 diabetes from eating so much junk and believing that "big is beautiful."

Now, as Dr. Wise pled his case to the US Congress, he felt emboldened by all the anger and pain that obesity had inflicted on his own family. Multiplying that by every family in the nation of 350 million people made his voice rise with indignation.

"Obesity," Dr. Wise shouted, "is the enemy within! And we must stop it! We must stop it now, before it crushes America's status as a global superpower!"

Senator Buxton let out a sound that was suspiciously like a reflexive laugh, which he quickly covered with a cough.

"Excuse me, Dr. Wise," he said with his lilting Alabama accent. His gray eyes flashed in a mocking way. "Got a little tickle in my throat there."

Dr. Wise cast a hard look at the slippery senator who had, for a full decade, voted down every bill that even hinted at imposing government regulations on big business. He spoke forcefully that it was nobody's business how a company marketed, advertised, or sold food and beverages.

Glancing at other lawmakers on the committee did little to encourage Dr. Wise. Samuel Addams of Massachusetts had spoken out in the media against any government controls over the food industry. His beauty-queen wife, on the other hand, had her heart in the right place by helping inner-city kids start vegetable gardens and learn about nutrition.

But Dr. Wise's blood boiled when he looked up at Congressman Raymond Samuels, the ultra conservative from New York City. The man was African American in pigment only, as one of America's staunchest opponents of affirmative action. Dr. Wise hoped that his wife, Mabel Samuels, who was the US Surgeon General in attendance here, had talked enough sense into him to support the Obesity Act. Chances were, since obesity and its related diseases impacted African Americans disproportionately and more severely than whites, they both had relatives who were suffering and could be helped by the passage of this Act.

Dr. Wise's mood went from bad to worse when he glimpsed slickster Richard Blane in his periphery. The chief marketing strategist for Heavenly's fast-food restaurants was sitting in the front row; he'd been all over the media in recent weeks, calling Dr. Wise a "radical socialist."

Despite his many opponents, Dr. Wise forced his voice to stay steady and strong as he looked each lawmaker in the eye. "My aim is that every citizen watching this right now will flood your offices with calls and letters of support to pass the American Obesity Eradication Act."

But the sad reality was that millions of citizens across the country had already given up hope that leaders in Washington would do anything to stop this crisis. That's why hundreds of them were gathered outside Congress right now, rallying for action. And if the lawmakers failed to act, the crowd would wait on standby for Dr. Wise to secretly announce that the revolution was *on*! Dr. Wise cast a defiant stare up at Senator Buxton.

I don't care how many billionaires are backing you, or what position you hold in Congress, or how much access you have to the President. We, the people, will win the battle....

He did not blink, even as Senator Buxton's eyes fired a shotgun blast of malice down at him.

Chapter 3

US Army General William "Wild Bill" Brewster watched the television in his office in downtown Trykka, the Capital City of the Republic of the East, formerly known as Tricqua. On the screen, Dr. Wise and Senator Buxton glared at each other during a Congressional hearing.

"Looks like they're about to go to blows!" the General exclaimed, standing beside an American flag and a large wall map of the Republic of the East. "That hearing looks more like a showdown for a boxing match!"

"Put my twenty bucks on the doc," said Calvin "Bullet" Alvarez, wearing desert camo from head to toe, along with a flak jacket, and a high-powered assault rifle. His tough but playful personality glowed in his brown eyes and across broad face, now bristled with a few days' beard growth during his mission. His six-feet, four inches of brawn made him look giant as he sat at the conference table.

"Wild Bill, I gotta tell ya, the doc's got fighting spirit in his eyes," Bullet said. "But the pampered Senator looks like he couldn't fight off an alley cat 'less he paid somebody to do it for him."

"You're right on, as usual," the General said, glimpsing the gold watch that Maggie had given him for their 25-year wedding anniversary. He had precisely 44 minutes before he would leave his office here in the US Embassy, ascend a flight of stairs to the roof, and board a military helicopter bound for a US Navy destroyer in the Bay of the Republic of the East, where he would participate in a briefing with the Joint Chiefs.

"Bullet, as much as I'd love to watch the Congressional fireworks on TV, I need an update from you," he said.

The three-star General wished his father were alive to see him now. Dad's dedication as a Special Forces Marine had inspired him to attend West Point and climb the military ranks. From the start, he had a reputation as a rising star. As a young Marine commander, he had led a NATO group that eradicated a dangerous terrorist cell in the former Tricqua. He had been praised for his ability to orchestrate the stealth operation with soldiers from the US, Great Britain, New Zealand, France, and Germany.

While they had wiped out the entire terrorist cell and gathered valuable intelligence, he had created a lot of enemies, including the King, whose parents and relatives were killed when he was 11 years old. Prior to becoming President of the Republic of the East, the King had named the General on his hit list of most hated Americans.

"I don't trust the King," the General told Bullet. "He's going along with our democratic song and dance, but hatred runs deep. I need to hear what you got."

"Much more than anybody at the White House or the Pentagon is bargaining for," Bullet said. "This war ain't over." He laid his gun across the conference table then grabbed a cold bottle of water from the mini refrigerator and chugged it.

After working together for a dozen years, the General knew that the anxious glint in Bullet's eyes meant that his mission had revealed something far more sinister than anticipated.

"Tell me if you confirmed my hunch," the General said. "I'll bet a million bucks those bastards have a plan to use the democratic leaders as puppets to make us think everything's on the up and up, while they're working behind the scenes to scheme against us."

Bullet nodded. "Add my million bucks to the bet and somebody's gonna get rich. Soon as our guys decipher the files on those hard drives we took this morning, we can report back to the powers that be, and get clearance to blast the Presidential Palace and stop those motherfu—"

"Hold on, hold on, we're done blasting," the General said. "Now I know they don't call you 'Bullet' for your warm and fuzzy side—"

Bullet smiled.

"But the situation is too fragile right now," the General said. "I guarantee the Joint Chiefs will want diplomacy first—"

"Diplomacy my ass!" Bullet pointed to the TV. "All those fancy lawmakers are so busy talking about obesity, they don't have the balls to heed the doctor's warning. Meanwhile it's killin' us! If we don't watch our step over here and blast the shit outta all these people who hate America, they're gonna creep up on us just like obesity did, right under our noses!"

Shaking their heads, they both turned back to the TV.

Chapter 4

Sitting at her desk at the *American Daily News* office downtown Detroit, Jeri was enthralled by Dr. Wise's testimony as she watched the television in her cubicle. But she was even more excited to call her father to report the good news. She speed-dialed him, grinning as she heard his deep voice: "How's America's best investigative reporter doing today?"

"Dad, I'm coming to the Republic!" Jeri exclaimed, glancing out the window 30 stories above the city. "My editor said yes to my proposal."

Silence.

"Dad?"

Her father sighed, then said, "I can't say that's a good idea right now, even for you, G.I. Jane."

"Dad! I got the story idea from you—"

"Which one?"

She took a deep breath. "How democracy is bringing fast food and obesity there. My angle is that we've been there to help the country, but the Western diet is actually hurting them."

"That's a relevant and worthy story," he said, "but the bigger story here is the rebels who want America—our food, our values, and our high-tech lifestyles—out altogether."

"Dad," she protested, "if I can beat down a thug in Detroit during my morning run—"

"You scared the living daylights out of your mother," Dad said. "She saw video of you on the news and called me."

Jeri smiled, thinking of her mother's panicked call this morning after the local TV stations reported that Jeri had helped catch an elusive serial rapist. The rollerblader had apparently sent video from her phone to Channel 3. "She called me, too, but—"

"Jeri, I don't call you G.I. Jane for nothing," her father said. "You're tough, but this is no place for you right now. If things get any worse, I—and the State Department—would warn against your coming."

As he spoke, Jeri turned to her laptop computer and typed an email to the travel coordinator at the *News* offices in New York.

I'll be leaving in about two weeks, staying about 10 days. I'll need accommodations both in the capital city and in the rural town of Mora.

As she typed, her father said, "Jeri, I have reason to believe that all Americans who enter the Republic, especially journalists, are monitored constantly, even after you leave. Phones, computers, Devices, people you see, what you do. Somehow they've obtained military-grade tracking technology that uses satellites, bio chips, and other methods that make Big Brother look like a Boy Scout."

Jeri glanced at the photo of herself and her parents on her desk. Taken just a year ago at the Pentagon when Dad was celebrated for spearheading the stability and democratization of the Republic, it showed Dad in his full uniform. Beside him, Mom wore one of her usual flowy linen dresses. Jeri sported the same type of slim black pantsuit with a simple blouse and stylish-but-comfortable heels that she wore today.

Now, her father's caution made her pause. It was quite uncharacteristic; that meant things over there truly were worse than most people believed.

"Dad, you shouldn't have let me train with Navy Seals and sharpshooters if you didn't want me to act like one," she said, "even though my weapon of choice is the written word."

He chuckled. "Ah yes, the pen is mightier than the sword. You are your father's daughter, so it's pointless to argue, once you make up your mind. But I can tell you right now, your mother will be none too pleased."

Jeri exhaled. "I'm going to her book event tonight; I'm sure I'll hear about it. Dad, are you watching Dr. Wise testify at the obesity hearing?"

"You better believe it," her father said. "In fact, I've got an autographed copy of his book right here in my office. He's got a brilliant vision that could work. Unfortunately, he's talking to folks who tend to do what's best for business, not what's best for people."

Jeri glanced at her TV monitor. She marveled at the intensity in Dr. Wise's eyes as he spoke about his plan to save Americans from obesity and early death.

"It really is public health threat number one," Jeri said, glancing at her computer's display of the shocking statistics that the CDC had just released about America's worsening obesity epidemic.

"Daddy, I'd better get back to work," she said. "I love you."

"Soldier on, G.I. Jane," he said playfully. "I love you more than the desert over here has sand."

Jeri stared down at today's paper lying on her desk. Her byline was under the lead story on page one with the headline: CONGRESSIONAL HEARING COULD REVERSE 'OBESOGENIC' CULTURE IN AMERICA—OR FAIL TO STOP THIS DEADLY TREND. The story included a sidebar about the opening of the Creamy Dream restaurant that epitomized this problem.

Shareese Smith, Jeri's editor, appeared in the entrance of her cubicle, looking excited and holding a stack of printed-out emails.

"Check out this huge response to your story today about the chocolate restaurant," Shareese said, as she entered in a tailored business jacket over skinny black leggings with patent leather flats. "These are just a few of the emails, and Golden Harvest wrote this *scathing* letter to the editor. Says your story is a 'bitter hatchet job!' But we're also getting an avalanche of letters and emails from health advocates like this one." She read: "'I want to praise Ms. Brewster's hard-hitting perspective and refusal to jump on the food company's promotional bandwagon, like most media.'"

Shareese, who had short-cropped black waves and a

radiant, caramel-hued complexion, smiled. "That's why we hired you. Everybody else is getting caught up in the hype, but our Jeri Brewster sees the big, bad picture, and has the balls to write about it."

Jeri clicked her TV to a local news channel—showing live coverage of the restaurant's opening—and exclaimed with disgust: "United States of Carbohydrates in full effect! Look at that!"

"Insanity!" Shareese shook her head as they watched a traffic jam and mob of people of every age, race, and size in front of the restaurant designed to look like an enormous, candy-covered gingerbread house.

"This may be the sweetest spot in the world right now," said Channel 3 reporter Ryan Jenkins, speaking live in front of the crowd that included many obese people—some using canes and riding on motorized scooters. "Hundreds of chocolate lovers lining up right now to get a taste of what's inside." The reporter inhaled deeply. "And if the scent in the air is any indication, their taste buds are in for quite a treat."

The camera panned police officers directing heavy traffic off 10-lane Woodward Avenue in Royal Oak. Ryan said, "Notice license plates from surrounding states, like Ohio, Indiana, and Illinois, as folks flock to one of the most hyped events in recent Metro Detroit history."

Jeri said, "It's so disturbing that they chose Detroit as their test market. And if this crowd is any indication, Golden Harvest is probably already building more restaurants like this in every state."

The reporter smiled. "I hate to admit it, but what kid or adult wouldn't want to go into a gingerbread house with treats like this?" He held up the menu. "Just listen to this sweet stuff—"

"No, let's not!" Jeri muted the TV. "I love that quote in my story, where Dr. Wise says people are 'committing slow suicide, bite by bite.'"

"True," Shareese said.

Jeri switched to Global News Network, where reporter Pat O'Shea was standing in front of Creamy Dream and said: "Hundreds of people gathered here are seemingly oblivious to the health risks of eating such a sugar-laden diet. Later I'll have a report about the latest scientific findings that show, chocolate contains ingredients that are as addictive as cocaine. And the CDC has just released the latest obesity statistics—"

"Jeri," Shareese said, nodding at the TV as Jeri switched back to Dr. Wise testifying.

"He's such a trailblazer," Jeri said. "I love his courage, and that he doesn't care that some people call him an Uncle Tom or a militant radical or just plain crazy."

Shareese nodded. "Depending on what happens with the Obesity Act, I see a long list of follow-up stories for you."

The way Senator Buxton was glaring down at Dr. Wise, the future of the Act didn't look promising.

Jeri said, "I want to substantiate the rumors that there's an underground movement forming around his work. If this goes down, I hear they're planning to wage their own war against obesity. I mean, does that mean guerilla gardening on vacant lots in the 'hood or does that mean a real militia network smuggling guns and attacking places to disrupt the junk food supply chain?"

Shareese nodded. "Let's find out!"

Just last week Jeri had grilled her most secretive, informed sources about this, but they'd all continued to claim ignorance of any details to confirm such an underground movement. Maybe the outcome of the hearing would inspire someone to talk.

"Meanwhile," Shareese said, "let's do a piece about why the powers that be are allowing the obesity epidemic to spiral out of control, as Americans blatantly reject healthy eating. Especially if the Obesity Eradication Act is defeated, we need to follow the money to show how citizens are helpless against this money machine of big business."

Jeri felt chilled by the sober reality of America's worsening health. "I've been thinking about a hard look at how the medical industry benefits from rising rates of cancer, obesity, hypertension, and diabetes. Maybe that could be my next book."

Jeri glanced at the hardcover book on her desk entitled AMERICA: SHAMELESSLY FAT AND GETTING FATTER! by Jerralyn Brewster with a Foreword by Dr. Michael Wise. His contribution had resulted from her making a positive impression on him when she interviewed him about his life's work.

"I want you to interview him as soon as he gets back to Detroit," Shareese said, "as part of a bigger series that we can do on this subject." She crossed her arms and scowled. "Like I said, follow the money. These big companies, and the lawmakers who're making it easy for them, are fattening their bank accounts, while their addictive, manufactured food is worsening the obesity rate and sounding the death knell for millions of people."

Chapter 5

AN UNCOMFORTABLE MIX OF pride and shame tugged at Leroy Wise as he stood with his wife, Darlene, and watched their three children speak to a television reporter. All five of them wore the same sky-blue T-shirt, emblazoned with the words: I GOT MY CREAMY DREAM™ TODAY. GET YOURS!

Leroy crossed his thick arms over his distended belly as his kids answered the pretty, young journalist's questions about the new restaurant. A guy stood a few feet away with a big camera on his shoulder, and the kids were surrounded by a dozen or so kids and their parents, all wearing the shirts that were given free—along with dessert—as a promotion for everyone who came to the restaurant.

Leroy's pride at the kids' excitement quickly turned to shame. The whole world was about to see his and Darlene's children in front of a giant gingerbread house on Global News Network. He had helped them become just like himself and their mother: fat.

"I love French fries," says thirteen-year-old Leroy, Jr., "so I'm getting chocolate-covered fries! Salt and sugar mixed together is my favorite flavor!"

The reporter turned to Keisha, who said with her sweet, five-year-old voice, "I know I'll like it here 'cause I like chocolate on everything, especially my fingers. I always get it on my face, too!" She giggled.

The reporter asked 18-year-old Kenya, "What about you, big sister? What's on the Creamy Dream menu for you?"

She flashed a big smile with silver braces and said, "My mom and I love melted chocolate, so I'm definitely going to join the Chocolate Fountain Club." She held up her phone, showing a colorful image of the gingerbread house inside a white cloud with a sky-blue background. "They've got this app where you get points and win a free birthday party here if you come at least once a week."

A chubby, blond teenage boy standing beside her held up his phone. "Hey, I got that, too. Creamy Dream's been sendin' me these coupons. See, I get points for a free treat when I visit their Homework Lounge on school days."

His hand was on the shoulder of a little blond girl, who tiptoed to speak into the microphone and said, "My mom says I got her addiction to chocolate, so we're going to eat here every day."

A red-faced, blond woman, clearly their mother, laughed nearby, along with a man, their dad, who was holding her hand. Darlene laughed and whispered to Leroy, "I bet her momma didn't know her baby would put her on blast today."

"To the world!" Leroy chuckled to stop himself from crying. He'd had his annual check-up yesterday, and his doctor's voice had been booming through his head all day and all night. Guilt gnawed at him.

Another reporter nearby was announcing the insidious statistics on diabetes, hypertension, and cancer affecting African Americans at a disproportionate rate versus whites. Eating too much fat, sugar, and salt was making the obesity rate rise, just like his doctor had said. The scene kept replaying in his head like a filmstrip:

"Look Leroy," his physician said, sounding just like his doctor-brother, "if you don't correct things now, you'll have to go on dialysis. Your creatinine is 4.5, which is abnormal. Your Hgb A1C is 12. That's a glycosylated hemoglobin, and it measures the history of your blood sugar. Normal is less than six. You're at twelve. The next step is hemodialysis. You're already on insulin, and you've got bad kidneys from diabetes."

Leroy felt like a child being scolded as his doctor stared at him with furrowed brows and pursed lips.

"I've been warning you for years to change your diet," the doctor said. "Now you're 44, and diabetes is nothing to play with. It causes atherosclerosis, which leads to kidney failure. You lose your eyesight. Your circulation goes bad, and you end up getting amputations—toes first, then your whole foot, then up your legs due to your poor circulation. It's not fair, but diabetes hits your ethnic group harder than others."

Leroy had confessed to his doctor that years of working long, hectic hours driving a forklift at one of the automotive factories made it hard to take time to find a healthy lunch. Now, even with his new job as supervisor of the service department at a car dealership, it was still tough-to-impossible to find a healthy, quick lunch.

And with Darlene getting the kids ready so early in the morning, dropping the older kids at their schools before heading to her job as an elementary school secretary, neither of them had time to make breakfast or pack him a healthy meal. The kids usually ate two of three toaster pastries with a glass of whole milk. Leroy grabbed something—usually a couple fast food breakfast sandwiches from a drive-thru—on his way to work.

"Plus we love to eat," Leroy confessed to his doctor. "After work I want to sit down to a good meal, not a salad or some carrot sticks. On the weekends, going out to eat is our family time together."

His doctor had insisted that the office nutritionist could teach both him and Darlene how to prepare healthy, satisfying meals and snacks for the whole family, as well as how to make better meal choices in restaurants.

Leroy had heard all of this from his own brother so many times, but never wanted to heed the warning. Their health-conscious father had echoed the same message with paternal authority, only making Leroy feel so ashamed that he avoided calling their dad on a regular basis. Now his doctor warned once again:

"Leroy, don't you realize that the reason your brother is on a crusade to end obesity is to save his own family? I mean, your brother will be testifying on Capitol Hill tomorrow and you're sitting here in my office on the verge of kidney failure because you refuse to change your diet."

Leroy shook his head, feeling sick to his stomach with fear that this time would be just like all the other times his doctor had warned him. He would feel bad right now, then find comfort in a drive-thru with a bag of greasy burgers and fries on his way home, only to eat again with Darlene and the kids.

"Look, I'll be blunt, Leroy," the doctor had finally said. "If you don't do something about this now, for your whole family, I guarantee that your three kids will be getting this same warning from their doctors—quite possibly their pediatrician."

Leroy's heart pounded with fear as his children's voices wrenched him out of his thoughts. The kids were telling the reporter their names, as were the others.

"I'm Jeremy Matthews," said the teenager with the cell phone. "I'm 19." He was chit-chatting with Kenya about their schools, where they lived, and that they were both preparing to attend Wayne State University in the fall. Leroy inhaled deeply as he realized that the Matthews family was like the Caucasian mirror image of his own family: working class, kids in public schools, three kids, and all fat.

And we're all standing in line at Creamy Dream wearing these awful blue T-shirts just to get a damned free dessert which none of us needs.

"Oh, Lord," Darlene whispered playfully, "I can feel all those calories sticking to my belly already. But ooh—" she inhaled deeply, closing her eyes with the same lusty expression that she used to have about sex, so many years ago. "Baby, do you smell that? If I had to name it, I'd call it Pure Heaven."

"Mom, it's chocolate," Kenya said, breathing in.

Leroy noticed that all three of his kids had chubby cheeks and thick bodies from head to toe. The Matthews family all had big, round bellies, with legs that were slim in comparison. He looked around at the other adults and kids: normal-weight and thin people mixed in with a whole lot of plump ones.

So many of them were wearing the tent-like T-shirts, all advertising the restaurant where they would roll out, one meal fatter than when they walked in. Leroy had a vague sense of being tricked, or lured, into a bad spot. But it all seemed so wholesome. The families, the fun, the media hype. It felt like the place to be. That whole "everybody's doing it," feeling made him enjoy being part of a movement as they celebrated the opening of the Detroit area's second Creamy Dream Shoppe.

Leroy loved how this place was making him feel at ease. He and his family were going to enjoy their food. He also liked how their neighborhood Creamy Dream shop on Livernois near 7 Mile on Detroit's west side had big chairs and booths and plenty of room to move around it. They didn't make you feel bad about being big or stuffed into your seat. The kids loved to go there to do homework with their friends, and Darlene's book club met there every month and stayed for hours.

Plus, when the shop had given out these free T-shirts, they had done away with the whole "XXL" type sizing. Instead, they picked up on the Goldilocks and the Three Bears idea. Darlene's T-shirt was "Mama Bear 1" as opposed to the "Mama Bear 5" that morbidly obese Aunt Lucille had chosen. Likewise, Leroy's shirt was a "Papa Bear 2" while the kids wore various levels of "Baby Bear."

As Leroy watched his children laugh with the other chubby kids and talk excitedly about all the chocolate they were about to eat, a terrible feeling washed through him. He was thirsty and had to use the men's room again, and had that constant, out-of-whack feeling that was only remedied temporarily by eating more. Suddenly his brother's voice rang in his head: *"You're killing yourself, Leroy."*

He could see his brother's face, with that critical-but-caring expression in his eyes as he had handed him one of the first copies of his book and said, *"You know, I wrote this book to save people's lives. But if I can't help my own family—"* Michael had run his hand over his face to wipe away tears *"— then what good is all my hard work?"*

Shame burned through him so hard, Leroy felt the urge to have a bowel movement. He and Darlene had taken the day off work to bring the kids here to celebrate the start of summer vacation. In doing so, they had refused his brother's offer to go to Washington with him—at his expense—to watch him testify before Congress.

My brother is making history for our family and everybody else, and we're not even watching it on TV. We're here getting our free dessert...

He had set the DVR, but what kind of brother wouldn't be glued to the TV to watch his own kin on an occasion like this? That bad feeling, like an emergency, overwhelmed

Leroy. *"You and Darlene are killing yourselves, and takin' down your kids with you," his brother had said with a cracking voice. "I can't sit back and watch—"*

Leroy felt dizzy. He turned to Darlene, about to say, "Let's leave!"

But the kids suddenly erupted in cheers, jumping up and down. Bewildered, Leroy saw a small army of waitresses dressed in milk-, white-, and dark-chocolate-colored striped Creamy Dream uniforms appear with trays of treats. The crowd roared with glee as they eagerly took samples of chocolate frosting-covered treats. Darlene and their three kids were among the first popping the sugar bombs into their mouths. Sweat beaded on Leroy's forehead as the smiling young waitress held the tray before him.

"It's time for your Creamy Dream, sir," she said in voice so sugary sweet he felt it would insult her if he said no. As he reached for one of the bite-sized treats, he noticed Darlene's expression as she savored the chocolate. He hadn't seen that orgasmic expression on her face in years. Since they'd both blown up, she liked to keep the lights out when they made love, which was becoming less and less frequent. They were both either too tired, or bloated, or sitting in bed eating ice cream while watching a movie before going to sleep.

Before Leroy could feel sad about how food and fat were robbing them of all the fun they used to have in the bed, the rich, sweet scent of chocolate drew his attention to the frosted treat in his hand.

"Daddy, try it!" little Keisha exclaimed.

He put it in his mouth.

Good Lord. I have never tasted anything like it…

His mind went blank, except for the party popping on his taste buds. His doctor, his brother, his worries about his family… gone. It was like the entire universe was now contained in that warm, moist, chocolate-covered fantasy inside his mouth.

He closed his eyes, savoring the sweet, creamy chocolate on his lips and tongue, hating that his first thought was, *This is better than sex.*

Chapter 6

Loathing burned hot on the skin of King Daemon as he sat facing the multi-media screen in the media room inside the Presidential Palace in the Republic of the East. His 10 Royal Brothers surrounded him in plush leather recliners facing a huge screen, as they watched a Global News Network report about fat Americans eating at a new restaurant.

"The Americans do not realize they are helping us write the script that will become the worst horror movie in the history of our planet," he said, holding his manicured, jewel-ringed hands near his chin. Dr. Wise's book sat on the 24-karat-gold-topped table beside his chair. Just minutes earlier, they had watched the surgeon testifying before Congress.

King Daemon and his Royal Brothers, along with armed security guards, sat mesmerized by the images on the screen, including a colossal gingerbread house surrounded by fat people waiting to enter and stuff themselves with sugar and fat. Three plump children appeared and the caption read: "Leroy Wise, Jr., age 13." The boy said: "I love French fries, so I'm getting chocolate-covered fries! Salt and sugar mixed together is my favorite flavor!"

The caption changed to "Keisha Wise, age 5." The

reporter turned to her. The little girl said, "I know I'll like it here 'cause I like chocolate on everything, especially my fingers. I always get it on my face, too!"

The caption changed to read: "Kenya Wise, age 18." The reporter asked, "What about you, big sister? What's on the menu for you?"

The girl smiled and said: "My mom and I are definitely going to join the Chocolate Fountain Club."

A white-skinned teenage boy named Jeremy Matthews, age 19, said, "I get a free bowl of chocolate chip cookie dough when I visit their Homework Lounge on school days. I'm in college but they make it fun here for older kids, too."

His hand was on the shoulder of a little blond girl, Bethany Matthews, age 8, who tiptoed to speak into the microphone. "My mom says I got her addiction to chocolate, so we're going to eat here every day." The screen showed the fat parents and a crowd of many more families just like them.

"Addiction," the King echoed. "That is the key word that will set Royal Tricqua free and give us the keys to the White House. My brothers, remember that word: addiction."

The screen flashed to another woman reporter: "If this current health catastrophe continues to worsen, nearly half of Americans could be morbidly obese within 10 years. Unless something radically changes, the current generation of children are predicted to have a shorter lifespan than their parents."

The King said: "The Americans killed the parents of many Tricquans. Now we will help them kill their children and all of their relatives by their own gluttonous hands."

The King squeezed his fingers into fists to stop them from trembling with rage. Hatred throbbed in his every cell; it had been written in his DNA by his parents, who blamed the US for destroying their town and killing many family members during a long-standing war that was backed by the Americans. Though the war had ravaged Tricqua, his parents had remained very wealthy, thanks to their multigenerational possession of oil-rich land. As a result, the King still lived in his family's palace.

"One day you will destroy America," they had told him *for as long as he could remember. "You have been chosen as a prophet to deliver the world from the bondage of the wicked tyranny of the United States."* But his last memory of his parents, when he was 11 years old, was of them being savagely slaughtered before his eyes by the American-led rebel forces.

Since then, the King of Tricqua had cooperated with the Americans as the President of the Republic of the East ruled the country. The King had risen to this position as part of his nation's grand scheme to deceive the Americans. In their imperialist arrogance, the Americans believed they had created a democracy here, after declaring a cease-fire with a fundamentalist resistance movement. As if this were some poor, needy third-world nation, the United States had "installed" a President and democratic system that was similar to the one that ruled in the US. The King outwardly and stealthily kept the Americans believing that he endorsed their government structure.

Their arrogance blinds them to the truth.

And the truth was that the King was *the true King* of his land, living with his many wives, children, and servants here in the opulent Palace. Across the country, his people knew that he was ordained by both his royal ancestry and by the highest powers of all creation to serve as ruler of Tricqua. Yet because the greedy Americans would always try to control them—and their oil fields—that most vile nation on planet Earth had sealed its own fate by attempting to dictate the present and future of Tricqua. That left only one clear path for the King: destroy the Americans.

By introducing their "First Amendment" blasphemy, they had opened the doors for Tricquans to criticize and condemn the Royal Family and its historic, rightful position of leadership. Now they were poisoning the native people of this great nation by bringing their lawless ways of mind, body, and spirit.

Soon, the men around him would send a very clear message to all Tricquans: those who expressed criticism through speaking, writing, or protesting would be silenced—permanently. That would create a chilling effect to show everyone that cooperation with the royal family—even under the guise of the new American-backed democratic system—was the only way to live in Tricqua.

The King would purify all Tricquans of the spiritual poisons that the Americans had introduced, and he would return his people to the pure, holy religious practices and beliefs that had been passed down by his ancestors since the beginning of time. Disobeying this edict would be punished with death.

This spiritual poison had also been delivered through the Americans' sexual music and clothing styles, as well as through technology. Computers, cell phones, and tablets in the hands of so many Tricquans had opened a global window onto sinful ways of life that would no longer be tolerated in his nation. Video games fell into the same category, as they were lobotomizing children, numbing them to violence, and making them fat by keeping them from physical activity outdoors.

The King was horrified that the Americans were inflicting their obesity epidemic onto the great people of these shores. By inviting its food companies and restaurants to do business here, under the guise of democracy, the Americans were attacking Tricquans with their fast food, packaged snacks, and processed foods in grocery stores where Tricquans now preferred to shop instead of the traditional open-air markets selling fresh fruits and vegetables, fish, grains and health-promoting teas, herbs, and spices.

The reporter's voice on the huge screen caught his attention. "…countries as remote and untouched by the global obesity epidemic are even beginning to experience dramatic spikes in the numbers of overweight and obese children and adults."

The screen showed scenes that looked familiar, including the landmarks of his nation: the spectacular mountain ranges, the beautiful tiled mosaics and ornate bell towers of the historic downtown cultural and religious monuments, and the gilded, white marble King's Palace.

"One of the most dramatic examples," the reporter said, as video showed Tricquan children eating Heavenly's burgers and fries, "is happening in the Republic of the East. Nearly twenty-five percent of the population is now overweight or obese, and what makes this especially dramatic is that a mere five years ago, as the United States began to liberate the oil-rich country from rebels, obesity was non-existent here."

The video panned restaurants and markets showing the traditional Tricquan diet of baked or grilled fish, an abundance of fresh fruits and vegetables, olive oil, whole grain breads, and rice. "But with the arrival of democracy came the standard western diet. That new diet includes a lot of fast food and snacks full of sugar, salt, and fat and is wreaking havoc on this desert nation," the reporter said, as video showed an Tricquan boy biting into a large slice of pizza and a girl vigorously licking an oversized ice cream cone.

Rage surged so violently through his body that the King gripped the carved ends of the armrests on his chair. He bit down hard and inhaled deeply, as his father had taught him.

"A true leader must control his anger and channel it with stealth precision into solutions and actions that bring his desired result," his father told him repeatedly. *"He who acts in haste and anger always loses. The victor's greatest weapons are patience, excellent timing, and perfect execution of his strategy."*

But the American woman's voice coming from the state-of-the-art sound system, and the images of the fat Tricquan children on the screen, disturbed so much that the King had to close his eyes and train his mind on discipline and control.

"Sadly, the population of Tricqua," the reporter said, "like many nations, is on the fast track to experiencing the type of obesity epidemic that is crippling and killing many Americans right now, with no end in sight."

"No!" the King shouted, opening his eyes and jumping up from his chair. "Never!" he shouted at the TV screen. His men sat frozen in their seats, watching him with wide eyes.

"The end *is* in sight," he said, picking up Dr. Wise's book. "I have read this book. This very brilliant doctor has created a plan to end the obesity epidemic. The American people are insatiable when it comes to food, and their greed for money plus their undisciplined way of life—they will never follow this Dr. Wise's advice!"

He sat down, took a deep breath, and clicked the remote, returning the screen to show Dr. Wise's hearing. The King said, "The men and women in charge of the United States of Obesity are slaves to the wealthy food and drug companies who are making billions of dollars off the sick and fat Americans who are addicted to their poisons disguised as food and beverages."

The King stood and calmly faced his trusted advisors. He clicked the remote, bringing to the screen a Power-Point presentation called: THE GLOBAL KINGDOM OF ROYAL TRICQUA.

"I have been working to formulate this strategy to return absolute power to the Royal Family of Tricqua. Not only will we remove the American presence from our country, but we will finally exact the long overdue vengeance on the United States for its centuries of bullying and dominating our entire region. Very soon, we will rule the United States and the entire world."

The King added, "My Royal Brothers, I present to you my plan for accomplishing this. And with your utmost dedication, we will rise to world dominance in a way that is unprecedented by any leader in world history." The King clicked to a screen that listed the following:

- Minister of Religious Purification

- Minister of Health

- Minister of Citizenship

- Minister of Science

- Minister of Medicine

- Minister of Royal Obedience

- Minister of Nutrition

- Minister of Propaganda

- Minister of Technology

- Minister of Logistics & Planning

"Before I begin," the King said, "I must make you aware of the superior nature of our strategy. We are not random imbeciles shoving explosives in our undergarments and boarding the cheapest flights to America. Nor are we haphazardly constructing bombs from kitchen appliances to randomly drop at a marathon. We are strategizing an intelligent, infallible, groundbreaking, and extremely stealth tactic to annihilate our enemies."

The Royal Brothers nodded in agreement.

"I have identified the problems that we must address with specific solutions, to cleanse our people of the toxic ways of thinking, speaking, eating, and living under the influence of America. To do this, I have taken into consideration all your areas of expertise and experience, and I have assigned each of you to a new post."

The men listened intently to their leader.

"First, I must say that while we lay the foundation for this revolution, we are working in complete secrecy," the King said. "No one must ever know what we are doing. As for the Americans who remain in our nation, we will continue to play along with their charade, making them believe that they are all powerful. At the same time, each of you will take the responsibilities of these positions and implement them as a duty to preserve our culture and our nation, while enabling us to claim our position of global dominance that has been preordained since the beginning of time."

The King clicked the remote. The next screen read: "Mission: Make Tricqua the world's greatest Superpower by taking over the US, installing the Royal Tricqua government, and taking dominion over the rest of the industrialized world."

The King clicked to the next screen and said, "This strategy will be achieved by executing the final two steps in a long-term strategy of domination."

He read the words on the screen:

1. *Weaken and destroy the American population by using its own gluttony; and*

2. *Trick the American people into electing our
    Presidential candidate who has been groomed
    from birth to fulfill the destiny of Tricqua to rule
    America.*

"Most of you know that we have been laying the foundation of this strategy for a very long time," the King said. "As my cousins and my brothers, we share the same blood that hungers for vengeance for our fathers, our grandfathers, our uncles and many generations of ancestors who suffered at the hands of the industrialized world."

The King took a breath as he looked from face to face of those around him. He knows unconditionally that these men share the common horrors of his memory. They each have suffered tragedy at the hands of the Americans.

"We were all young boys when the Royal Massacre occurred inside this very Palace. Our hearts and minds are seared with the horrific memories of those American-backed rebels bursting inside, lining up our fathers, our mothers, our aunts, and our uncles—and using their machine guns to create a bloody pile of death."

The King watched the men's faces as they each had a visceral reaction to recalling that day.

His own body throbbed with the pain of watching his older brothers, aunts, and uncles crumple on the white marble floor, which quickly became a red sea of blood. Very smart and stealth as a boy, he had escaped death by hiding behind a large plant, staring with horror through the leaves. He had been so stunned, he did not cry; he just longed to be with his parents, who had been grooming him to become king.

Earlier that day, his parents had traveled to a remote palace in the mountains for their annual spiritual retreat. Somehow the invaders had forced the palace security's communications director to give the king and queen a clear directive that it was safe for them to travel back and return to the palace. When they arrived, they discovered the massacre of their sisters and brothers, and stoically got to work preparing to bury them by bathing and shrouding the bodies. But the rebels surprised them, storming at them with machetes to kill them and other relatives, and left them to die.

Moments later, Daemon was standing between his parents, holding their hands, when their blood had sprayed so violently that it covered his face. He could taste it. His father's eyes widened with shock and sorrow as he looked down at the King, and the gurgle that came from his mother's throat still haunts him. When he thinks of it, a chill ripples through his body, as if he can still hear her dying noises.

As he screamed over his dying parents, the King looked up to see the murderous rebels fleeing, all wearing traditional Tricquan clothing and masks.

Out of the corner of his eye, he saw a wailing mourner come straight at the rebel, attacking him with such anger and force that his robe flew open, revealing a patch of red, white, and blue: the American flag. The King could not believe his tear-filled eyes. With his hands still on his parents as they took their last breaths, the King scanned the rebels. He could not tell one from the other as they were cloaked in identical masks and robes.

Which one of you did this to my parents? Which one of you?! How stupid of you to not kill me then, because I will find you, and one day I will kill you with my own hands.

His horror and sadness quickly turned to rage, more than he had ever felt before. In those moments, he became a man, and without his parents, he knew he had to avenge their deaths. He felt in his trembling body that he would not stop until he found the American killer.

Weeks later, after his parents and relatives had been buried, his pain and outrage merged into an underlying current of determination that ran through his entire body.

He watched televised new coverage of the massacre with his uncles, who all spoke of revenge. He learned from them that they were all under threat. As they brainstormed schemes against the Americans, the TV blared in the background. No reporter on the TV ever spoke of the discovery his uncles had made—that American soldiers had joined forces with Tricquan dissidents who were pro-democratization of the East in opposition to the Royal Family and its lineage.

As a boy, the King watched the TV, which showed a news report about a ceremony in Washington, DC, honoring General William Brewster for being the mastermind behind American dominance of this region, which included the massacre. The reporter described him as "popular" and "noble" and "the man who always gets the job done."

But the reporter said the massacre was against those

fighting against Tricqua, not the Royal Family. The young King's uncles shouted at the TV, using profanity in their outrage, and the young King knew the threat was real. As a grown man developing a strategy, the King had been watching this American General and the military since they had come to Tricqua to perpetuate the lie of defeating rebels while the US secured its hold on the oil fields and installed the new government.

But the time to kill him had not yet come.

The King wanted the murderous General to live long enough to see the Global Kingdom of Tricqua take over the US and rule the world. He reveled in the thought of killing the spirit of the arrogant American military General. Then he could carry out his plan, with much-anticipated pleasure of murdering him with his own hands.

The dramatic impact that General Brewster's death would have on the global mission of Tricqua would reverberate around the world. Watching the General on the television made every nerve in the King's body quiver with the lust to wrap his own fingers around the man's neck to avenge the crime of killing his parents.

Now, the King forced his grief and rage to subside so that he could address his men in the courageous, controlled manner that his father had taught him.

"Our Creator spared our lives so that one day we could execute a global mission to avenge the deaths of our loved ones," he said. "We will begin to do that on January 1st, the thirtieth anniversary of the Massacre. As you know, we have been preparing many people for their appointed roles in our future dominance of America and the world."

The King clicked the remote. Live coverage of the Congressional hearing in Washington, DC played on GNN. He zoomed in on one of the men on the lawmakers' dais as Dr. Wise testified before them.

"Right now, our Royal Brother is attending the hearing for the American Obesity Eradication Act," the King said, as the screen filled with the larger-than-life image of a man with light skin, and near-blond hair that was blow-dried and styled like many American men of prominence.

"As Congressman for Massachusetts, Samuel Addams is poised to run for President of the United States," the King said. "Our brother will soon launch his campaign for an election 18 months later, coinciding with the appointed time for Tricqua to reign." The King clicked to another screen, showing Skype video of Samuel Addams. "I spoke with our brother earlier today, to share this update with you."

Samuel Addams, 41, clean-shaven with white skin and intense blue eyes, spoke: "All allegiance to Royal Tricqua. Everything is on course. My constituents have asked me to vote against the American Obesity Eradication Act, so I've been promoting the idea that it's downright un-American to dictate to people what they can or cannot eat, or how much they should or should not weigh."

He laughed, as did the King and all those around him. The King could not be more pleased at his forebears' choice of the Tricqua Royal who would become President of the

United States. Uncle Sam's grandfather, El Brycka Pertussia, had been a native of Tricqua, a simple carpenter who was not affiliated with the liberation movements, the rebels, or the Royal Family. He settled in America and raised a son with the same name in the large Tricqua enclave in Detroit, Michigan. And when the next generation was born, a son named El Brycka Pertussia III, married into a white family, but stayed closed to his Tricquan relatives in Detroit and visited his family's homeland many times.

Tricquan Royals close to the family in Michigan decided that one day this second generation born on American soil would be eligible to become President of the United States. Once decided, they began to groom him from birth for his destiny to become leader of the most powerful nation on Earth, then to submit that power to the Global Kingdom of Tricqua. They named him Samuel Addams, which sounds as American and patriotic as the Founding Father who was a politician in Massachusetts during the 1700s.

These relatives made him as "all American" as possible: he attended private prep schools on the East Coast; where he excelled in crew and lacrosse; and he served as a captain and champion on the debate team. He became active in school government in elementary school and was voted class president through college, where he earned the nickname Uncle Sam. That name and reputation character-ized his attendance at Harvard and the London School of Economics. His boy-next-door looks, his wit, and his kind nature provided a constant rotation of beautiful girlfriends.

Now he was a Congressman, representing his home state of Massachusetts, where he cultivated a career in law, then politics. Married to a former Miss America, Janet Martin, with four athletic, scholarly children, he hired a family photographer to come to the house once a week to snap hundreds of candid and posed photographs that provided countless photo ops promoting his family's commitment to a healthy lifestyle.

Samuel Addams, still on the video screen, said, "You know, they don't call me 'Uncle Sam' for nothing. I gotta give it to whoever came up with that nickname, because it's subliminal, it's blatant, it's just brilliant when I hear people call me Uncle Sam. Like I *am* the government. And soon I will be. We will be. All allegiance to Royal Tricqua, my brothers."

As the video ended, the said, "Lastly, my brothers, we have a broad range of support from the many people in powerful places who are working on our behalf to prepare for our magnificent future as rulers of America."

He clicked the report to the next screen, showing a photograph of Tricqua native Gerald Blane. He, too, appeared outwardly American, with a fabricated childhood and family in Boise, Idaho. But he was raised in Tricqua, indoctrinated with the life mission to serve as a warrior who would help lay the foundation for Tricqua's US takeover.

He was born to, and raised by, an expatriate American family that defected to Tricqua after becoming disillusioned with the US. They volunteered to help Tricqua execute its long-term goal of vengeance on America; to do this, they raised their four children in the capital city, teaching them English and American ways, while programming them with philosophies that included extreme hatred toward America.

The four siblings participated in study-abroad programs throughout Europe and attended Ivy League universities in the United States. Gerald's two sisters, Cindy and Linda Blane, were trained to use their beauty to seduce their way into high-powered public relations positions in the most prominent food companies. They would ultimately prove instrumental in the King's plot. Along with their brother, Richard Blane, chief marketing executive for Golden Harvest Foods, their Caucasian parentage enabled them to pass as ordinary Americans.

"Gerald Blane is already placed in a position very close to the President," the King said. "That will enable us to have direct influence, which will help to shift the dynamics for our take-over. For that he will be handsomely rewarded monetarily and he will be appointed to a high-powered position."

The King clicked again to a screen showing a photograph of high-ranking FBI veteran Edward "Eddie" Smith. Tall and beefy with a dark brown buzz cut, the 40-year-old has a silver scar zig-zagging over his left cheek.

"While American in blood, Eddie is our brother in spirit," the King said.

Eddie had survived the single deadliest attack during the war in Afghanistan. His entire platoon, including his beautiful fiancée, died in a single blast. Outwardly, as his superiors lauded him and pinned medals on him, he pledged a fight-for-America platform.

But deep down to his core, he resented the powers that be for not valuing the little guys on the front lines. He wanted nothing more than vengeance towards the system that he blames for robbing him of the love of his life.

No one knows how deeply his hatred runs. Hailed publically as a hero for saving others' lives during his service, he wrote a patriotic memoir, *My Blood is Red, White and Blue*, which received nationwide praise. His large left bicep were tattooed with a colorful recreation of his book cover; another tattoo over his heart showed his dead fiancée's face and flowing hair. When the King's men approached him and discovered what they suspected were his true feelings, he told them they could count him in.

"Eddie will become our key contact as we advance our strategy," the King said, "assuring us access to inside information and surveillance of individuals who may try to stop us."

He looked each of his men in the eyes. "And I assure you, my Royal Brothers, nothing, and no one, will stop us from taking what is rightfully ours: The United States of America and the world."

Chapter 7

In Detroit, Johnny "Big Man" Valentine watched his brother stuff himself with fried chicken.

"Man, you can't eat a whole bucket of chicken by yourself," he said, "and biscuits, mashed potatoes, gravy, and all that pop. Then some ice cream, too? You're killin' yourself, bro!"

His brother kept eating and watching TV.

Johnny snatched the bucket up. "Stop! Control yourself, man!"

"Put my shit down!" Raynard said.

"Shit is right. That shit killed Momma. Aunt Diane is dying. And Tanya—" Johnny glanced at their sister, who was 350 pounds and feeding potato chips and red pop to her toddler, "—is on her way to death by diabetes her damn self."

Johnny was furious. His family was brainwashed to believe that taste was more important than nutrition. In fact, nutrition played no role in the thought process when anyone around him made food choices. It was all about instant gratification, and taste.

"Move out the way!" his brother shouted, because Johnny was blocking the TV.

"Man, you are such a disappointment," Johnny said. "Come out with me and make a difference. Stop killin' yourself!"

His brother glared up. "What difference does it make? I can't find a job because I didn't finish school because Momma was out trickin' and Daddy was running the streets. Nobody cared about me, and I don't give a damn about nothing but doing what I want to do, when I want to do it. So move!"

Johnny's heart ached as he glared down at his brother who was eating his way to an early grave. Having just left the gym with an extra-long workout to celebrate his 25th birthday, he'd lifted weights to maintain his buff, 250-pound physique. At six-feet, two-inches tall, he had once tipped the scales at 353 pounds. But he changed his life the day they put their mother in the ground, after watching her languish in poverty, struggle to raise three kids and save them from the life on the streets that beat her down, and comfort herself with fattening food.

The harsh reality of the city, with poor schools, violent streets, the allure of selling drugs just to buy groceries, and the accompanying plethora of problems stemming from all that, made good nutrition seem like a far-off, distant thing for other people. People on TV. White people.

Despite all that, Johnny stayed in school, unlike his siblings. During his senior year, when he was planning to go to a vocational school to become a mechanic and truck driver, this man in a white doctor's coat walked into the classroom.

"I came to speak to you on Career Day," the man said, "because I graduated from this school and I became a surgeon. I want to show you that you have the power to make a difference in the world. Now I'm on a mission to make you and our neighborhoods and everyone across America, healthier. We've got an obesity epidemic, and it's killing us."

In that moment, Johnny thought of his mother: at home, eating and watching TV. She was obese and sick, and didn't care. In fact, she expected her kids to bring her all the junk food she could eat every day. And she didn't care how they got the money to buy it.

"America is on a collision course with a public health disaster," said Dr. Michael Wise, standing in front of the classroom. Johnny couldn't believe everyone around him was giving this man respect like they'd never given anyone, especially the teacher. "If you know that saying, 'You are what you eat,' then wouldn't you rather be something natural that God made, like a crisp, juicy apple or a sweet slice of melon—as opposed to a crunchy little thing covered in fake cheese dust that was manufactured in a factory just like a car?"

Johnny's cheeks burned with shame. He had eaten three danishes from the liquor store on the way to school, all washed down with root beer. And last night he ate a whole pizza by himself. That's why he weighed 353 pounds, according to the school nurse. He had never thought about this; he just ate what tasted good and what was available.

"This neighborhood is a 'food desert,'" Dr. Wise told the class of 35 students and the teacher. "That's a term that's used around the world to describe places where good, affordable, nutritious food is not available. You can't buy fruits and vegetables at the liquor store on the corner. You can buy potato chips, hot dogs, and soda pop. But those are poison. Grocery stores with fresh produce and other healthy food don't cater to the inner city. I call this *nutritional racism*. But the same problem exists in every poor neighborhood, whether black, white, or Hispanic, or other groups."

"That ain't right," a kid in the back row said. "But what can we do about it?"

"You can do a lot," Dr. Wise said. "You can start by changing the way you eat. You'll feel better. Then you can teach by example, to help people in your families and neighborhoods make better food choices."

Johnny raised his hand. "But how can we eat better when we don't have better food?"

Dr. Wise cast a long stare at Johnny, like he saw something special about him. "Excellent question, young man." He started handing out pieces of paper. "I started a program that provides free bus service every Saturday to Eastern Market, the farmer's market downtown, where you can get all the fruits, vegetables, and other healthy foods, that you want. On this sheet you'll also find a voucher, so all the food is free. Get enough for your families. I'm also starting free nutrition classes here at the school, so you can learn how to prepare the foods in a way that tastes good and keeps you satisfied."

Johnny couldn't see himself shopping with farmers or cooking. But after Dr. Wise finished talking, he approached him alone. His whole body felt prickly with embarrassment that he was fat, poor, and ignorant about everything Dr. Wise was saying.

"I'm ready to change my life," Johnny said, only because Dr. Wise looked him straight in the eye. That gave him street cred right away, and engendered trust.

"You remind me of myself," Dr. Wise said. "I see your potential, even if you don't see it yourself. You just found yourself a mentor, young man." With that, Johnny became Dr. Wise's most eager student on nutrition, physical fitness, and a campaign to save America from the obesity epidemic.

But I can't save my own damn family, Johnny thought now, as he glanced across the room at his sister and niece.

"Tanya! Give that baby some real food!" Johnny yelled, hating the dull expression in the little girl's eyes and the fact that she struggled with terrible eczema and asthma. "Not chips and pop! That ain't food! That's garbage! Poison! Give her some better nutrition and she'll be able to breathe and not scratch her skin raw."

"Shut the F up," she said. "Go home to your wife and kids and eat all that white people food. Think you better than us because you don't eat normal like us."

Johnny wanted to scream. If he couldn't save his own family, what good was his commitment to the Food Fight Posse? He'd started it after recruiting his closest childhood friends to join the LifeQuest Movement that Dr. Wise was leading. Things were about to blow wide open, and they were ready. The Food Fight Posse not only led classes for nutrition, healthy eating, and exercise, but they were an activist group ready to make change, as Malcolm X once said, "by any means necessary." It wasn't about race. It was about humanity. And teaming up with a multiracial coalition across America, thanks to Dr. Wise, had enlightened Johnny and his crew about the civil disobedience taught by Mahatma Gandhi and Dr. Martin Luther King, Jr.

"I'm doing what I do to help us be better!" he said. "Just listen to me! That shit is poison! You're poisoning your baby!"

His sister glared at him as she popped a potato chip into her mouth and crunched loudly. Johnny shook his head and stormed out of the run-down apartment.

His drive home was slowed by a cluster of ambulances outside Heavenly's on Gratiot Avenue. People were screaming and paramedics were taking away six people on stretchers. Two of them were in black body bags. One was a kid. His first thought was that someone had shot up the place.

"Aw, man," he groaned, turning on the news radio station.

"Breaking news," the reporter said. "Six people reported either sick or dead at a local fast food restaurant as fatalities continue to rise in a national trend linking fast food to sudden sickness and death. Investigators are trying to find out if the food somehow became contaminated with a deadly toxin, or whether this is the work of a disgruntled employee who may have poisoned the food."

Johnny shook his head, pulling into the parking lot. "This ain't a coincidence," he said.

"Many of the deaths are concentrated in urban areas in the Midwest," the reporter said, "but some are reported in Texas, Florida, and Arizona. Authorities say the victims in those states had recently traveled to the Midwest and consumed fast food. Authorities tell us, all the victims had symptoms of extremely high blood sugar that caused coma and ultimately, cardiac arrest."

Johnny watched the mayhem as family members screamed and cried around gurneys loaded with sick and dead people.

"What the hell is going on?" he asked out loud. He had heard conspiracy theories that a chemical that caused impotence was put in fried chicken in restaurants catering to urban black populations. And that crack cocaine and other drugs had been deliberately put in black neighborhoods to addict and kill people, to keep the race down. Just as other conspiracy theories proclaimed that the AIDS virus had been deliberately unleashed on the gay population to kill homosexuals.

Sometimes those arguments and conspiracy theories made sense. But could something like that be happening right now? And who would do that? The scene felt surreal as TV news crews, ambulances, police, and screaming family members heightened the chaos around him.

"What's going on?" he asked a woman wearing a restaurant uniform.

"They was eatin' and just fell out," she said, looking dazed and pale, holding her stomach. "I wonder, did somebody dump some rat poison in the food. I don't know what the hell is goin' on. But I just ate here when I got to work, and I just don't feel right." A paramedic guided her to a gurney.

A few minutes later, Johnny pulled into the garage of the condo he had purchased for his family near downtown. His wife, Layna, and their two toddlers were at the kitchen table, eating an organic, vegetarian lunch of black bean soup, kiwi slices, and whole grain bread with almond butter.

"Happy Birthday, Daddy!" exclaimed two-year-old Johnny, Jr. and three-year-old Shayna.

He kissed their chubby cheeks, loving the sight of his babies looking so healthy and alert as they raised fresh fruit to their mouths and savored Mother Nature's candy. The family always ate at home, because Layna was a nutrition-ist with two degrees in food economics and nutrition. She was staying home for now to take care of the kids until they reached school age, and would return to work then.

"How's my baby?" he asked, kissing Layna's forehead.

She grasped his hand and smiled. "Still happy about our celebration last night."

Her mother had taken the kids while they enjoyed some grown folks' time to love on each other and celebrate over a candlelight dinner. Johnny had met Layna through Dr. Wise, when visiting the hospital where she worked as a nutritionist. At the time, she was still in school, and was completing an internship. It was love at first sight, as Johnny had already lost 103 pounds and had begun pumping up his muscles. He had never felt better, and her instant adoration inspired his lifetime commitment to wellness.

Now, Johnny was making a great living with his fleet of trucks that he leased to food manufacturing companies that included the Grazia family. He had met Angelo Grazia long ago, and their business dealings were all legit.

Now, he couldn't shake the images of his brother and sister poisoning themselves, or the sick and dead people on gurneys at the burger joint.

He kissed his wife and kids, then headed to his home office, where he turned on the TV to watch Dr. Wise in the Congressional hearing. That Obesity Eradication Act was a lost cause, but he had to give the brother props for his bold campaign to save America from itself. Johnny checked his phone; the outcome of the hearing would kick the Food Fight Posse into high gear. They had a meeting in an hour with Boone Davis down in Kentucky, and Carmen La Buena in California.

Johnny couldn't shake the bad feeling triggered by that chaotic scene at the fast food restaurant. And people in other states were dying, too?

Somethin' ain't right…

Johnny went online to learn more about the fast food illnesses and deaths. Something very bad was happening, and Johnny needed to figure out what the hell was going on and stop it from killing more people.

Chapter 8

America's favorite television news anchor, 35-year-old Anastasia Lee, held a microphone against a backdrop of a 20-foot banner that read *Healthy America Expo*. The event, held in Washington, DC, coincided with the Congressional hearings on the American Obesity Eradication Act. After her broadcast, she was scheduled to moderate a panel discussion with some of the nation's top powerhouses in the food and health industries.

"I'm Anastasia Lee, broadcasting live from the Washington Convention Center," said the beautiful and bubbly newscaster who was an exotic blend of her African American father and her Asian American mother. She was beloved and trusted by the nation as the "face and voice of everyone" because of her interracial heritage and family. Her husband was Irish American, and their children had blue eyes, blondish hair, and skin the color of a golden suntan. Thin, fit, and health-conscious, her wholesome image and superior broadcasting earned the network top ratings and the prestige of claiming the highest grossing advertising dollars among its competitors.

"For the first time ever, GNN is hosting this Summit on Obesity to explain how two thirds of Americans have become overweight or obese—and how we can eradicate this problem," she said, as a huge video screen next to her flashed images of obese adults and children.

Anastasia spoke in a serious tone, projecting her deep, satin-smooth voice with perfect enunciation and rhythm. Wearing one of her standard bright-colored, tailored suits, she looked picture perfect with her black, face-framing hairstyle around her light caramel complexion, exotic features, and trademark red lipstick.

"Eliminating obesity is imperative, because if this trend continues, experts say 42 percent or nearly half of all Americans will be obese within 15 years. That is a staggering figure!" Anastasia had learned in college journalism classes that her job was not to express her opinion, but to provide an objective look at every side of every story. So now, despite her concerned facial expressions that were as polished and staged as an Oscar-winning actress, her true feelings were so cynical on this topic that she had to exert extra effort to look convincing.

"We here at Global News Network are so committed to helping America end the obesity epidemic," she said passionately, "that we are devoting a major portion of our Summit to identifying solutions to get America back on track toward healthier lifestyles."

Her cameraman followed as she stepped away from the screen and strode to the center of the elaborate set. There, each expert sat in a tall, director-type chair surrounded by individual alcoves filled with images and items reflecting that person's expertise.

"Later, I'll show my one-on-one interview with Dr. Michael Wise, whose bestselling book and testimony before Congress today, inspired this GNN Summit. Now, before I introduce our panelists," Anastasia said, "I want to show a report that summarizes the obesity epidemic on a global scale."

A video began to play on a huge screen behind her. Narrated by Anastasia, the video began with overweight people in many countries eating giant portions of super-fattening food and drinking soda. Global statistics on soaring obesity rates flashed on the screen, along with figures for the corresponding diseases with medically confirmed cause-and-effect connections to obesity.

The montage zoomed in on one country, the Republic of the East, where obesity never existed before the introduction of American fast food. Statistics scrolled on the screen showing graphs and charts of the obesity rates now and projections for the next 15 years.

"At this rate," Anastasia's voice over announced, "billions upon billions of dollars are spent on obesity annually. This stems from the countless related diseases that stem from obesity. The overburdened healthcare industry and private corporations must deal with an increasingly sickly workforce. And for the first time in more than a century, today's generation of children is expected to have a shorter lifespan than their parents."

As Anastasia watched the reports, she thought about how she had sweat through a rigorous workout with her personal trainer this morning. Her demanding career, two children and a husband who is CEO of the global Fitness U. franchise of crossfit gyms and healthy lifestyle certification courses, meant their schedule was packed with family, friends, community obligations, and work-related appearances and events.

Without the nanny, the housekeeper, the personal chef at home, and the personal trainer who also owned a Fitness U. franchise, she had concluded long ago that feeding the family a healthy diet and staying in tip-top shape would be impossible. She counted her lucky stars every day, often feeling that the healthiest lifestyles that her experts talked about had become a privilege of the wealthy. The middle class, working class, and poor were too consumed with merely surviving the country's rough economic system to invest time and energy into what seemed like the frivolous pursuit of fitness and healthy eating.

Plus, she had seen the toll that a demanding career had taken on women, as she'd worked at local news affiliates in Reno, Saint Louis, and Chicago. Not to mention, it was impossible to shelter kids these days from the aggressive advertising by all the breakfast cereal companies, fast-food restaurants, and places like Creamy Dream.

Anastasia knew it was important to bring these issues front and center, but her understanding of the reality of most working Americans' lives made her doubt that anything could reverse the obesity epidemic. She had plenty of sick, overweight relatives in her own family. People she loved were addicted to junk food and sugary drinks, and they had no desire to change their ways. They were either lazy, in denial, or just too depressed about their dreary lives to find the discipline or determination to make a change.

Of course, Anastasia never verbalized her true opinions to her family, her producers, or the public. But as someone who worked so hard to get where she was—and to stay here—it was difficult to sympathize or empathize with people who seemed to wallow in negativity and the consequences of their bad food choices.

Now, hosting this program, she forced herself into the familiar feeling of robotic autopilot. She read from the teleprompter, made the appropriate facial expressions, and used her trained perfect tone and inflection to show just enough emotion. She wanted to show she was human, but not so much that she appeared biased. Even though she knew her guests were about to pay serious lip service to this very grave issue.

First, she stepped toward the alcove where a handsome, platinum-haired man sat wearing a grey flannel business suit. Surrounding him was a beautiful display of fresh fruits and vegetables, loaves of bread, cheeses, and other dairy products. Above him, the logo of his company—a bright yellow sunburst emblazoned with the words GOLDEN HARVEST FOODS—glowed under the overhead lights.

"To get us started, I have the pleasure of introducing Douglass Golden, CEO of Golden Harvest Foods," Anastasia said. "Back in 1901, his family in California started what's now one of the world's biggest food companies. Golden Harvest also owns the very popular Creamy Dream chocolate shops, as well as the first, highly anticipated Creamy Dream restaurant in Detroit. As you may know, Golden Harvest is tremendously generous by hosting community endeavors such as health fairs, awarding college scholarships, sponsoring Little League teams, you name it. This company shows it cares in many more ways than we can count."

Douglass Golden tilted his head, making his hair shift seductively, then fall back into place with movie-star quality, and smiled. As he turned to Anastasia, his suntanned skin looked like he spent more time on a sailboat than in an office, and he winked a sparkling blue eye at her like he was on a date with one of the beautiful actresses that he was rumored to be seeing behind his considerably attractive wife's back.

"Anastasia," he said, "I am so delighted to be here to talk about one of the most important topics in our country today. This topic is always near and dear to my heart, as we at Golden Harvest Foods go about the business of supplying good nutrition. So, thank you, to you and to Global News Network, for hosting this important program."

Anastasia flashed her best smile. Golden Harvest spent millions on advertising at GNN every year; her bosses had all reiterated the importance of showcasing Mr. Golden front and center, and asking him questions that would make him look good.

"Mr. Golden," she said, "please tell us some of the ways

that Golden Harvest is helping American families make healthier choices for meals and snacks."

His flirtatious affect disappeared and his face turned serious and tense. "Well, Anastasia," he began, then paused, clearing his throat before continuing. "If you walk into any of our stores, the first thing you'll see is what we call The Farmer's Market. The fresh fruits and vegetables. I mean, it is just beautiful! Succulent strawberries, bright greens of every kind, red apples and grapes, you name it, we've got it, for low prices. And you know in the department store, they've got pretty girls offering for you to test the new perfumes?"

Anastasia nodded.

"Well in our stores," he said, as the excitement returned to his face, "we've got cheerful young men and women who offer samples of sweet grapes, or chunks of watermelon, or a healthy new way to make green beans. Once the kids and parents get a taste of something they might not otherwise buy, they're more apt to toss it in the cart and make a point of buying it every time."

Anastasia smiled. "So, innovative marketing techniques are helping to shift people's tastes and preferences to healthier choices."

"That's exactly it," Golden said.

"I know it worked on my family," she said. "We shop at Golden Harvest; my kids tried the vegetarian pizza on whole wheat crust at your deli, and they're hooked!"

He beamed. "Glad to hear it, Anastasia!"

Next, she stepped in front of a woman sitting in an

alcove that read US Food and Drug Administration. The display showed colorful scenes from farms, laboratories, grocery stores, and hospitals.

"Our next expert is the very accomplished Leslie Rivers, assistant director of the National Organic Program at the US Department of Agriculture," Anastasia said. "With so much talk about organic food, GMOs, and food additives, it's very important to hear the government's perspective and how it is taking steps to protect the health of consumers."

With pixie-short white hair, sharp features, and silver-framed eyeglasses, Rivers radiated an air of authority. She wore a gray suit, sitting with her very thin legs crossed. "Thank you, Anastasia," she said. "I want to address the issue of Genetically Modified Organisms, or GMOs. These have come under criticism, as food companies grow wheat, corn, and other foods with GMO seeds."

Anastasia cast a serious expression, remembering the horror she had felt when first reading about GMOs. She had immediately ordered her family's chef and housekeeper to continue buying produce only at the grocery store that sold certified organic foods that were void of GMOs.

"Yes, you read my mind, Leslie," Anastasia said. "GMO foods absolutely top the list of consumers' concerns. Can you please tell us, where does the USDA stand on this?"

"We firmly believe," Rivers said, not moving a muscle in her grey wool suit, "that consumers have a right to know what they are consuming. As a result, food manufacturers are required to disclose whether their products contain GMOs."

Anastasia nodded, "Transparency."

"Yes," Rivers said. "And, of course, Anastasia, I want to assure the American public that the foods that the USDA allows to be sold have absolutely passed all of our stringent and rigorous tests for quality and safety."

"That's very good to know," Anastasia said, "but why are so many people afraid of GMOs, even leading protests against the companies that make the seeds?"

Rivers shook her head. "Unfortunately, the Internet enables fear-mongers with their own agendas to distribute alarming and erroneous information very quickly to a large audience."

Anastasia nodded. "Yes, one frequent theme I've seen is that consumers believe they are guinea pigs for the seed companies. No one really knows what the long-term effects are for these genetically altered foods."

Rivers vigorously shook her head. "I can assure you, based on our research, we know for certain that GMOs do not cause cancer or other diseases. In fact, by making foods immune to certain viruses, bacteria, and contamination by certain insects, many credible scientific studies have shown that GMO foods can actually be better for our health than traditionally grown produce."

Anastasia tilted her head and drew her brows together, knowing that Rivers was merely saying what she was supposed to say, which was not necessarily the truth. "This is information that people really need to hear, Ms. Rivers. Thank you for shedding light on this."

"My pleasure."

Anastasia moved to the next alcove, where she introduced a man sitting in front of a display showing children getting vaccinated, scientists working in laboratories, and hazardous materials crews working behind yellow police tape.

"Next is Roger Ramsey, a spokesman for the US Centers for Disease Control and Prevention in Atlanta," she said. "This government agency compiles the statistics that we're using as the basis for our Summit today. You may also have heard of Mr. Ramsey's wife, Wilma, who just released her first cookbook that showcases the delicious recipes she's perfected as a stay-at-home mom of five children."

"Number one on the best-seller lists right now," Ramsey said proudly, with a Southern accent. He sat perfectly poised in a dark blue suit that did a good job of obscuring the damage his wife's fattening recipes were having on his chubby midsection. With side-parted dark hair, a stylish goatee, and naturally arched brows over engaging dark eyes, Ramsey exuded charisma and charm.

"Congratulations," Anastasia said. "That leads us to a very interesting angle, Roger. I like the kind of barbecued ribs and macaroni and cheese that your wife makes just as much as anyone else, but how can we teach America to enjoy these foods in moderation while also staying active to burn off the extra calories?"

Roger flashed a megawatt smile. "That is the 64-thousand-dollar question, Anastasia. And we at the CDC are committed to a plethora of programs and educational campaigns to reinforce the importance of what you just said."

Anastasia nodded. "With my kids, for example, if we enjoy ice cream or cookies, I make sure we take a bike ride around the neighborhood or turn on music to dance. We make it fun to stay active, not punishing or chore-like."

Ramsey turned to look into the camera, aiming a thumbs up at Anastasia. "Did you hear, that, America? That's the way to do it!"

She smiled. "Roger, if today's statistics are not a wake-up call for America to aggressively tackle this problem, then what will be?"

"Well I think Dr. Michael Wise had some very good ideas in his book," he said, "that I think we can implement without the kind of policy changes and government intervention that he advocated. For example, in his book he compares overeating to smoking cigarettes. Our studies show that aggressive educational campaigns about the negative effects of smoking do deter people from lighting up. That's why the CDC is about to unveil a new educational campaign that graphically shows the negative health effects of overeating and obesity."

Anastasia nodded. Ramsey had shown her and a group of reporters the provocative commercials earlier today.

"One commercial shows a young man who lost both legs to diabetes," Ramsey said, "and while he's talking about it, the shot widens to show a half-dozen relatives in the room. Every one of them is either blind, on dialysis from kidney failure, immobilized by morbid obesity, or missing limbs. Some folks say this commercial is too graphic, but it's the truth."

"Let's hope the bold message has a positive impact," Anastasia said, before stepping toward a man sitting in an alcove decorated with bright, splashy images of happy children eating chicken fingers and fries, a thin woman in exercise wear, eating a salad, and two handsome men chowing on huge cheeseburgers.

"An extremely important angle in this dialogue," Anastasia said, "is the fast food industry, and the aggressive steps they're taking to educate consumers about the nutritional value of their food, as well as new menu items that offer healthy choices that the whole family can enjoy."

She smiled at the man who had the build of a football player with Boy Scout wholesomeness. The former college star athlete wore a pinstriped suit, red tie and crisp white shirt, with his wavy, chestnut-colored hair long on top but very short on the sides; his radiantly healthy face was clean-shaven except for a skinny, Errol Flynn-style mustache.

Anastasia doubted he ever ate the fattening food that he was paid handsomely to promote. She stepped close and said, "Meet Richard Blane, chief marketing strategist for the world's most popular fast food chain, Heavenly's Burgers."

Blane, the youngest panelist at just 30 years old, grinned. "Anastasia, I am so excited to be here to talk about what America's favorite fast food chain is doing to encourage healthier lifestyles!"

Anastasia remembered her interview with Dr. Wise, when he'd said that before most children could talk, they could identify Heavenly's logo—a halo over a burger, fries, and soda—as well as its mascot, a male angel who did magic tricks that made toys appear for boys and girls on TV commercials and in frequent appearances at children's events.

Dr. Wise had said that aggressive advertising, especially during Saturday morning cartoons, brainwashed children to associate eating nutritionally void junk with having fun, and that they carried that bad belief and habit into adulthood.

"We're glad to have you here," Anastasia said. "Obviously the fast food industry comes under fire as an easy target when we talk about obesity. So, please tell us what you're doing to counteract that."

Blane nodded. "Of course. I like what you said earlier about making it fun for your kids to stay active, without lecturing them about calories or working out."

Anastasia smiled, remembering a recent story about how posting nutritional information in fast food restaurants had failed to persuade diners to order a salad instead of a triple cheeseburger and fries.

"I know for me, if my wife tells me I should order a vegetable stir fry instead of a steak at a restaurant," he said playfully, "I don't like it. I want to eat what I want to eat."

Blane looked serious. "Our mission at Golden Harvest Foods is to make healthy eating as fun as fast food. That's why we're introducing The Enchanted Forest experience in our grocery stores. Consider it a virtual wonderland where families can step inside a beautiful space connected to the fresh produce section. We will have fairies and elves dressed in costume, offering samples of fresh fruits and vegetables prepared in a way that's fun for kids and easy for parents. This multimedia extravaganza will include an interactive, museum-type area with fun stations that challenge kids to understand calories, exercise, and how the human body processes food. It's really a revolutionary approach to food education, and we are planning some free-standing experiences as well as a traveling exhibit."

Anastasia nodded. "It sounds almost like an amusement park with purpose."

"Precisely," Blane said. "People want to be entertained. They want video and flashing lights and a fantastical experience that's not only exciting, but educational at the same time. Let's face it. Just talking about broccoli is boring. Visiting The Enchanted Forest and hearing fairies and elves talk about the virtues of vitamins and fiber is a great way to get children's attention and make them like broccoli."

Anastasia paused, thinking that was so bizarre and over the top, she wasn't sure if he was being sarcastic. But his serious expression revealed that he was being perfectly serious, so she said, "Thank you, Mr. Blane."

She stepped to the next alcove, where a man in a business suit sat before photographs of President Alexander and the White House.

"We are extremely fortunate," she said, "that presidential advisor Gerald Blane can join us today, to talk about initiatives that the White House has introduced to combat the obesity epidemic."

She glanced back at Richard Blane. "And yes, they are

brothers. Your parents must have done something right to have such successful children."

Both men smiled.

"Our sisters are the smart ones," Richard said playfully. "Cindy's a marketing executive at Golden Harvest, and Linda just took the helm at the American Restaurant Association."

Anastasia then led the panel in a vigorous discussion about problems and solutions. The whole time, she felt that it was shallow chit-chat with all the right buzzwords and no hard-hitting solutions.

"I want to conclude this portion of the GNN Obesity Summit with a report that I've compiled about what a tough battle is in store to eradicate this deadly problem," Anastasia said, holding up Dr. Wise's book. "In my next segment, we'll hear from the man himself, who's testifying before Congress as we speak. In this book, Dr. Michael Wise has outlined 20 steps that he believes the government can take to get America thin and healthy again. Take a look at this report."

The video screen behind her showed Dr. Wise in his surgical scrubs, striding across the OR at Detroit General Hospital, performing bariatric surgery. The report also addressed how technology, office jobs, video games, school budget cuts on physical education, and the introduction of high fructose corn syrup into the food chain have created a perfect storm for an obesity epidemic. The report included images of fat adults and children waddling around, eating fattening foods, and riding battery-powered scooters to grocery shop.

"So let's get our conversation started," Anastasia said, stepping toward the Golden Harvest alcove, "with the CEO of America's leading food company. Mr. Golden, can you talk about supply and demand? From a business perspective, what's more likely to sell—a convenient, low-priced frozen pizza that can feed the whole family, or an equivalent amount of fruits and vegetables that most people view as snacks and side dishes?"

Douglass Golden's blue eyes sparkled with his Southern California charm that literally got him everywhere in business, politics, and social circles.

"Well Anastasia, you've just proven why you're America's favorite news personality," he said, flashing a bright smile. "Because you just asked the million-dollar question. And I know we're all here to talk about solutions to the obesity problem, but sometimes the truth is a different story. Us Americans, we love convenience, we love our favorite foods, and we especially love feeling like we're saving a bundle in our wallets. So to answer your question—"

Anastasia wanted to shout, "No, don't!"

Because as she'd told her producers when they conceived the idea for this program, it was a waste of time to talk about ending what was already a foregone conclusion: *America had boarded a runaway train that would only stop when it inevitably crashed and burned in the worst public health disaster in world history.*

But Anastasia wasn't earning a million-dollar salary to say no to her producers, who were under pressure from the major food companies that were sponsoring this forum with very expensive television commercials that were running every 10 minutes.

No, she was earning the big bucks to look beautiful, act gracious, sound intelligent and informed, and serve as the news puppet that would help the network pull in the greatest ratings and advertising revenue.

So she smiled at Mr. Golden and listened intently as he did a charming, verbal dance around the problem, ending with an irresistible plug for his food and restaurant company that was earning billions by helping Americans get fatter and sicker.

Chapter 9

As soon as she walked through the doors of the new Creamy Dream restaurant, Katie Matthews felt all her stress melt away. The intoxicating scent of chocolate made her hectic schedule as a nurse at Detroit General feel a million miles from here. And the whimsical décor dissolved her worries about finding affordable care for her mother-in-law who had Alzheimer's. All the happy people around her, especially her family, made her forget yesterday's panic over how she and Dan would pay for a new roof on their three-bedroom bungalow in the Detroit suburb of Ferndale.

"Dan, I finally feel so relaxed," Katie told her husband. "And I got my energy back. Can't believe Suzie got me up every two hours last night. The other kids were sleeping through the night by the time they turned one."

Dan shook his head. "She's just a hungry girl. Growin'. Be glad your mom agreed to babysit, so we could come here."

"Seems like Suzie goes through more formula than the older three did put together." Katie smiled, watching eight-year-old twins Brian and Bethany, and 19 year-old Jeremy, still talking with the children who'd been in the TV interview with them.

As they entered the lobby, surrounded by people of every race, age, religion and culture, a sign said: WELCOME TO THE MELTING POT.

"No kidding," Dan said. "This place should add 'racial harmony' to their commercials. How's this?" He made a pretend broadcaster's voice and said: "Metro Detroit might be one of the most racially segregated places in the country, but not at Creamy Dream. We're all united by our common love of chocolate!"

Katie laughed. The rolls of fat on her back that had gotten bigger with every pregnancy jiggled, as did the flabby belly bulge that was encased in stretch marks and never saw the light of day. The 246 pounds packed onto her five-foot, seven-inch frame was neither healthy nor attractive, but not everybody could be as perfect as her sister Maggie and her overachieving health nut of a niece, Jeri.

Katie was so glad that her husband was able to see beyond her physical traits and love her just as she was. He'd packed on 60 pounds since their wedding day 20 years ago, and the kids had inherited their same appetites and Humpty Dumpty shape: big, egg-shaped upper bodies on slim legs.

Now, amidst all the petite waitresses in their little uniforms, Katie was so glad she was happily married. She whispered close to Dan's ear: "I can't wait to come back here for a romantic night out with you. Just you and me."

He kissed her cheek and squeezed her hand. "Give me a date and time, and I'll be there with bells on."

He was so sweet, giving her that Southern Kitchen

Comfort Foods cookbook by Wilma Ramsey as a birthday gift this morning. She couldn't wait to try the recipes, especially Dan's favorite, meatloaf.

"Mom and Dad, look!" exclaimed Bethany, pointing to a fantastical, man-made landscape of a ceiling-to-floor chocolate waterfall.

Brian ran over, staring with wide eyes. "I want to go swimming in there!"

Katie laughed. "Sorry sweetie, it's only pretend."

""We're busted," Katie whispered to Dan. She nodded toward Jeremy, who was talking with a hostess, who wore a button: TELL US IF IT'S YOUR BIRTHDAY.

"…Mom and Dad have the same birthday," Jeremy was saying. "It's today."

The waitress approached. "Mr. and Mrs. Matthews, your meal is free today. With cake, of course."

"Wow," Dan said, "I just hope you don't try to put 38 candles on it."

The waitress smiled. "No, sir, we have single number candles. A three and an eight. How's that?"

"Perfect," Dan said, casting a smile at Jeremy. "Thanks, big guy!" He turned to Katie, saying, "This place gives me so many ideas. A gift card for the secret Santa at the store for the holidays."

"Great idea," Katie said. Since the automotive supply store had extended its hours to evenings and weekends, Dan had been home less and less, thanks to added responsibilities as manager of the custom paint department. As a result, they hardly ate dinner together as a family anymore. Plus, with all the kids' activities, and her work schedule, Katie had resorted to drive-thru dinners most nights of the week. It was so much easier to just pull up to Heavenly's for burgers and fries, or stop by the kids' favorite—Taco Temptation. It was cheap, delicious, and filling. Not to mention, it allowed her to plunk onto the couch to watch her favorite talent competition shows while the kids did homework. And with the baby, the less clean-up Katie had to do after dinner, the better.

Now, as a waitress led them to a table near the African American family who'd stood in line with them outside, Dan said, "Another thing, Katie, you can pick up dessert here for your scrapbooking group next time it's your turn to bring somethin'. Just don't tell your sister. She's probably out runnin' right now, before she eats a plate of grass clippings for lunch."

Katie laughed, watching the kids hop into a huge, purple booth with a high back for privacy. Everything here was reminiscent of Alice in Wonderland, with whimsical designs on mirrors and big flowers, polka dots, knights in armor, and fun chess sets. Enormous video screens on the walls showed images of happy people eating gooey chocolate menu items.

"Before you leave," the waitress said, "you can take a tour of the performance room where we have concerts, author readings, and plays. For kids, we have the Homework Station. For adults, we have the Lounge."

Katie scanned the menu, which she had already studied

on the restaurant's website. Still, seeing it in person exceeded her wildest dreams of indulgence. For a split second, she remembered all the promises she'd been making to herself for the past 15 years. After gaining 30 pounds during her first pregnancy with Jeremy, she'd vowed to slim down. But with a new baby, and going back to work as a nurse on the night shift, it was just too hard. The same thing happened with the other kids. And during her last pregnancy, that bout of bed rest, gestational diabetes, and insulin shots, had also inspired promises to herself to slim down and get healthy for the kids.

But after the doctor said the gestational diabetes had corrected itself, Katie had gone back to her old ways. She'd start a diet, lose a few pounds, then "blow it" on cravings for sweets. She'd always say, *I'll start my diet tomorrow*. But tomorrow never came. Even though the doctor had warned that she was on track for diabetes and that her cholesterol was bordering on high.

"What's wrong, honey?" Dan asked now, as the kids chattered about what to order.

"So many choices," Katie said, feigning a cheerful tone as she remembered the disgust she'd felt this morning when looking at all the too-small clothes in her closet—and her too-big body in the mirror. She was too ashamed to ever let Dan see her nude while changing clothes or taking a shower.

Why couldn't I be naturally thin and health-conscious like my sister? Why does Maggie love to go running everyday and eat rabbit food, but I've always been the fat, lazy one?

Their kids had only become the same. The last time Katie

and Dan had taken the kids to eat at Maggie and Bill's house was years ago, when Jeremy was five, Jeri who was older, gobbled down a plate of garbanzo beans and carrot sticks, then asked for more, Jeremy had refused to eat either. Katie and Dan had stomached the vegetarian lasagna made of whole wheat pasta, but they'd made a beeline for the nearest Taco Temptation to fill poor Jeremy's stomach and their own.

Today, she still didn't understand how they had grown up in the same Midwestern, meat-and-potatoes household, yet they had turned out so differently. Katie hadn't even read Jeri's article about this restaurant. She didn't follow *The American Daily News*, anyway, and knowing Jeri, the article was probably anything but complimentary.

"Mom, look!" little Bethany exclaimed. "They named a desert just for you." She pointed to the menu. "Look, it's called Chocolate Addict's Dream, and it has everything you always eat: ice cream, brownies, cake, *and* cookies."

Katie wanted to cry. Because she had already decided that she would definitely order Chocolate Addict's Dream today. Now she couldn't wait to escape this onslaught of guilt and self-loathing by losing herself in the bliss of indulgence.

I'll start my diet tomorrow…

Chapter 10

Senator Brace Buxton was so aroused, he could hardly think straight as he entered his usual suite at the Four Seasons Hotel. He discreetly handed a folded 100-dollar bill to Pierre, the longtime concierge. Balding, clean-cut and wearing a neat black suit, Pierre was by far one of the most trustworthy men in Washington.

"Pierre, no interruptions," Brace said as Pierre slipped the money in into his jacket pocket. "Far as you know, I'm not even here. Media inquiries or otherwise."

"Certainly, sir." Pierre pointed for the room service guy to place two silver domes, two crystal glasses, and a bottle of wine on the dining table. The guy lifted the silver domes as Pierre said, "Senator Buxton, I trust that your usual lobster and crab salads appear satisfactory."

Brace eyed the huge pieces of seafood over fresh mounds of salad greens and colorful vegetables tossed in the hotel's unique champagne vinaigrette.

"Sure," Brace said impatiently. He prided himself on remembering each of his mistresses' culinary preferences. Long-time lover Lisa Jones with the FDA was a vegetarian. Janet Carlysle, new on his roster but an important ally at the CDC, could devour a steak like a man, despite her petite frame. And of course Delilah Nickson, who'd been his high school sweetheart back in Birmingham, was now the most powerful socialite on the Beltway, married to a US Ambassador. For her, the more gourmet and fancy, the better, but he didn't have to worry about a thing because she always scheduled their meetings at the Four Seasons to correspond with her events, when she could get a room under one of her lady friends' names.

Now, as Pierre and the guy left, leaving the door unlocked, Brace checked that all the blinds were closed behind the drapes. Then he dashed into the bathroom to brush his teeth and use mouthwash. In the mirror, his pants bulged with the throbbing, heavy erection that had plagued him all morning.

I hope I can last longer than a minute with that sexy girl today. Feels like I'll blow with the first thrust...

He loved it when Cindy told him how big he was. It'd been torture to watch her sitting in the front row during this morning's hearing. The way she crossed those long, toned legs with the high heels, and cast those big doe eyes up at him, then tossed that pin-straight blond hair over her shoulder, watching intently on behalf of Golden Harvest Foods as Dr. Wise had testified.

That man is out of his mind if he thinks any self-respecting Congressman will pass the Obesity Act. If anybody thought gun rights activists were outspoken and rabidly determined to maintain their constitutional right to bear arms, just let

Uncle Sam try going after their food and drinks. *It'd be a goddamned civil war!*

Brace hated everything Dr. Michael Wise stood for—a bleeding heart liberal socialist who made excuses for the masses while placing blame for every social woe—this time, obesity—on the government, then expecting one monster of a hand-out to clean up the health disaster that men and women had brought on themselves and their children.

Nobody in his neighborhood or at the country club or among their personal friends had had weight loss surgery or even allowed themselves or their kids to get more than a few pounds overweight.

Because we educate ourselves, we exercise, we take responsibility for what goes into our mouths…

The senator couldn't wait to end this hearing, cast his "no" vote along with the majority of other lawmakers, and be done with this whole ludicrous conversation.

He glanced at his Rolex watch. What was taking Cindy so long? Brace wanted her so bad, he could taste her. Tough as it was, he'd loved the anticipation of watching her all morning, knowing that he'd get to lose himself between her legs and those big, perky breasts, in a matter of hours. He did that every Wednesday morning, but today was even better, thanks to the visual build-up of seeing Cindy at the hearing.

For now, the beautiful marketing executive for Golden Harvest definitely ranked as his favorite mistress. When he was with her, while looking into those big blue eyes and watching her full, pink lips move as she talked or moaned with pleasure, the rest of the world faded away and he was lost in the pure carnal indulgence of her 26-year-old body and mind. Because Cindy loved to do things to him with her tongue that Annabelle never had viewed as something proper for a wife to do.

Plus Cindy was okay with playing by Brace's long-established Mistress Rules. Number one? No phone calls, no texts, no emails. These days, that was the first place those damn reporters looked to find evidence of scurrilous goings-on behind closed doors, whether it was for business, romance, or otherwise. Not to mention, the liberals were always sniffing around for dirt to smear conservatives.

Daddy, Granddaddy, and Great Granddaddy—who'd held Brace's seat in Congress before him—had had it easy. Back in their day, they could almost do as they pleased under the radar. Now technology let any ol' body become a spy, with video cameras in everybody's hand, just waiting to snap a photo, send it in an instant to the national media and post it on social media, all to say, "Gotcha, you darn fool!"

Today, he hadn't been able to reach his wife Annabelle for his usual pre-tryst check-in, to plant his alibi about where he'd be for the next hour. Otherwise, if she called and couldn't reach him, he'd get the third degree. And she'd been known to show up at a place or two where he said he would be. Lord help him if he had a change of venue; he'd get called all kinds of "lying scoundrels" by his Southern belle with the razor tongue.

Never should've taken Julie Sorensen on that junket to the

Bahamas last year. Some yahoo tourist had taken a picture of them on a boat, fully clothed and not even touching, but their romantic body language had been enough to set off the alarms with his wife, who'd wanted to go on the trip but was tied up with shopping for the kids' dorm rooms.

That was three years ago. Annabelle had been a self-appointed private eye ever since, after declaring that she would *"never, ever endure the humiliation of divorce. You will be at my side until my dying day, Brace Buxton, just like you promised me 30 years ago in front of God, our parents, and practically our whole town!"*

Now, Brace was too smart to let technology trap him again. That's why he'd left his cell phone back at his office; he wouldn't put it past his wife to install some kind of tracking or even listening Device in it, so she could know his whereabouts at every possible minute of the day. His staff, the maitre d's at restaurants, and of course the concierges had all been prepped on when and how to execute plan A, plan B, and plan C in response to his wife's questioning phone calls and impromptu appearances.

Little did she know, Annabelle had simply trained him to become more stealth in ways that actually enhanced his ability to advance amongst supporters and adversaries alike.

Never leave a paper trail, Son. Those were his father's best words of wisdom, whether for business or pleasure. And it was never more true than during today's ruthless climate of bipartisan malice. All an enemy needed was one wrongdoing and the evidence to prove it, and a man's career could be obliterated by one split-second upload of a picture, video, or document to all the wrong people.

They'll never get me for anything. I plan to stay clean as a whistle even after they're saying "ashes to ashes, dust to dust" over Brace Buxton, III.

That's why Brace had established a set way of doing things, in business and in pleasure. Today was a perfect example. It was Wednesday, which meant he would enjoy his standing lunchtime appointment in this suite with Cindy. If they were going to see each other on other days—out of town, or on the Golden Harvest yacht down at the marina, or up at Cindy's Hilton Head beach house that just happened to be a short jog from the Buxton family compound—then they'd confirm the details in person, right here.

Now, to save time, Brace slipped out of his clothes, hanging them neatly on the hangars that Pierre always made sure were hanging behind the bathroom door. He posed in the huge mirror, feeling quite proud of his erection that could rival any hormonal teenage boy. Then he admired his flat, toned stomach, thanks to 500 crunches every morning. He flexed his pecs and biceps, large and firm as a result of strength training four times a week at an exclusive private gym. And he was overall trim, with a lot of power and cardiovascular stamina, thanks to running and swimming.

"I look pretty darn good to be 50 years young," he said, loving the twinkle in his gray eyes. Even the few silver strands around his deeply suntanned face enhanced his appearance, as did the tiny lines fanning out from his eyes when he smiled.

For a second, he thought of Annabelle, how she never seemed to really enjoy or even want sex, even though she was always working hard to diet and stay fit in her mid forties.

If she doesn't want it, why does she care so much that I do? Doesn't she know that men need it, and we're going to get it the way we want it, when we want it, from women who can satisfy our needs—in the bedroom and in the boardroom, so to speak.

Brace smiled, admiring how his recent laser-whitening treatment had made his teeth as bright as a new bathtub. He grinned. Sure thing, that was another thing Brace prided himself on: strategically choosing his women to serve as allies to advance his many agendas in business and politics.

Cindy was no exception. Golden Harvest CEO Douglass Golden himself had told Brace that she was sharp as a tack, and would be a company vice president before her thirtieth birthday. So this dalliance with her just sweetened the honey pot of payouts that Golden Harvest supplied to its favorite ally in the US Congress.

"Me," Brace said proudly. All that money—in exchange for helping to block or pass legislation that helped Golden Harvest—had made it easy to renovate the house to Annabelle's lavish tastes, pay out-of-state tuition at the Ivy League schools of their four children's choosing, and sock away a small fortune in the Caymans for a rainy day.

"Hey big guy," called a soft, sexy voice.

Brace walked coolly out of the bathroom, led by the steel rod that aimed right at the beautiful woman in a tailored, dark suit and high heels. She took off her sunglasses, placed her purse on a chair near the bathroom, and set her eyes on the part of him that wanted her most.

"Go back in there," she said, strutting toward him and unbuttoning her pink satin blouse to reveal those beautiful D-cups hoisted up in a white lace brassiere. She tossed her jacket and blouse on the chair next to her purse, then stepped in with him. Her high heels tapped on the marble floor as she stood at the marble counter, looking at them both in the mirror.

"What 'cha thinkin' about?" she asked with a sultry tone, turning to face him and reaching down to wrap her fingers around his steel rod.

"You," he groaned.

She dropped to her knees, opened her mouth and—

"Sweet Jesus," Brace groaned, gripping her soft yellow hair and guiding her back and forth, back and forth, as his whole body tingled with pleasure.

She glanced up, then took him out long enough to say, "Somethin's got you extra excited today, huh?"

He loved the sight of her thighs spread wide, her skirt hoisted up to reveal the black lace garters holding up those sheer stockings. This girl made him feel like he'd stepped into a pictorial in a men's magazine, with a playmate who couldn't get enough of him.

Damn, I'm gonna blow my wad if she doesn't stop—

"Stand up," he ordered. She did, instantly. He didn't even have to tell her to bend over the counter or take off her bra. As his fingertips raked up the sides of her thighs, and pulled her black lace thong to one side of her firm, suntanned ass, her tits fell free, nipples hard as she cupped them and poked out her lips.

"I've been thinkin' about fuckin' you all morning," she moaned as his fingers dipped into the hot, creamy slit. "Mmmmm, yeah, just like that."

He couldn't wait another second. As the head of his dick hit the hot, wet lips between her legs, he groaned so loudly, he didn't hear the phone ringing in the hotel suite.

And once he rammed deep inside her, and started thrusting, she moaned along with him. About 15 minutes in, she shrieked—lips trembling, eyes dazed, a soft sheen of sweat down her back. Brace took that as the cue that she had climaxed, so he let 'er blow, feeling like he was shooting a darn firehose up inside her.

He groaned like there was no tomorrow. And when he stopped, he finally heard the phone ringing.

"You didn't bring your phone, did you?" he asked, remembering that she had always followed his rule to leave all electronic devices in the car or at the office for the same reasons that he did. Devices could be tracked, and those with the right technical skills could use them as microphones for spying. She also wore no perfume, at his request, and never called him by his name, lest she forget with another man and drop a hint of any kind.

"No, baby, I never do. I think that's the land line."

Brace dashed to the living room area. A red light flashed on the telephone on the coffee table. Caller ID flashed "Concierge." He picked up the receiver, but said nothing.

"Sir, forgive me for interrupting," Pierre said, "but your wife is here in the lobby, at the front desk, demanding to know your room number."

Panic prickled through Brace's lust-numbed body, blowing his orgasmic buzz like a bucket of ice tossed in his face. Cindy was at the dining room table—gloriously naked—putting a big chunk of crab into that pretty mouth of hers.

How in the world did Annabelle know he was here? Why would she think that in the middle of one of the most highly anticipated, globally broadcast hearings, he would have the gall or even desire to sneak away to do anything but serious business related to the hearing?

"If it's alright with you," Pierre said, "I can proceed with plan A."

"Yes," Brace said, hanging up abruptly. Then he went and enjoyed his lunch with his beautiful young lover.

Cindy smiled, feeding him a forkful of seafood. "Good news," she said. "Everything is all set with the Garden of Eden. We've reached out to your gentlemen friends, and my girls are more than ready to give them the thrill of a lifetime."

Lust jolted through Brace as he envisioned the girls and the millions this business would bring them both. "I couldn't have asked for a more beautiful and brilliant business partner."

"Thanks to your generous support," Cindy said, "I'm living this dream. Always thought it should be legal, anyway. It's the oldest profession in the world for a reason. Women have the sex. Men want it. Men have the money. Women want it. Quite a simple thing made so complicated by our puritanical and hypocritical world, wouldn't you say?"

Brace laughed loudly and exclaimed, "Guilty as charged!"

Then he and this young beauty chose to hit it once more, right here on the table, before they headed back to the afternoon session of the obesity hearing.

Chapter 11

WHILE THE GENERAL WAS on the phone, Calvin "Bullet" Alvarez took just a minute to chillax here with the man who'd been more of a father figure than his own dad back in San Diego.

Bullet had spent the past few years dodging bad guys on every continent, while working as a sharpshooter assassin to put more than his fair share of drug lords, terrorists, and human traffickers out of their wicked misery. Now, getting called back to the Republic of the East to finish the dirty business that he'd known was far from complete when he'd left, was the best news he'd heard.

Two weeks ago, when he'd been flown in for a briefing on his mission, he'd only seen the General briefly on the Navy ship, with a whole host of people around. Today was the first time he'd get a one-on-one with Wild Bill, the baddest dude in all the Armed Forces, and he couldn't wait to catch up. Bullet had so much to tell him, starting with the position he was offered—but didn't want—at the Pentagon. Perhaps no assignment had brought him a better feeling than the one that had earned him this offer of promotion: single-handedly taking out an international gang of pimps who were enslaving hundreds of girls and teens from around the world.

Now, as the General spoke with his wife about their daughter's stubborn and reckless determination to come here, he had the same concerned fatherly expression he'd shown Bullet years ago, when rescuing him from a bar fight in Tijuana, Mexico. The locals didn't like the young, hot-headed, Mexican American soldier who was disrespecting them on their turf by making all the pretty girls swoon.

Man, Wild Bill sure has saved my ass more than a few times…

The most important time, of course, was when he went vigilante on the drug lords. At the time, America was losing the war on drugs, in a bad way. Bullet had just gotten tired of watching them flaunt their gunpower, boats, and airplanes with the attitude that they were invincible. So after years of legitimate assignments as a Sniper with pinpoint accuracy—earning the nickname Bullet—he had decided to take justice into his own hands and save the good ol' US of A a boatload of money.

Bullet figured he was doing his duty in an even bigger way by discreetly taking down one drug lord after another. He did it while handling his normal responsibilities and relationships throughout the world, and no one had a clue how these big, bad international thugs were disappearing— or turning up dead. The diversity of settings that Bullet had chosen to deliver the fatal shots to the drug lords—in the beds of mistresses, behind the curtained booths of restaurants, on luxurious yachts, and in remote villas—had left no pattern to enable identification of the assassin.

But the last time, he got cocky, taking down a notorious bastard whose drug empire employed thousands in a small South American country. And when Bullet shot him en route to deliver his usual monthly cash bribe to the president's mansion, and the powers that be never received their money, they hunted him down real quick.

After being arrested and interrogated inside a secret military compound, they threatened to imprison Bullet with sinister hints that he would never leave their prison alive. Somehow, the Americans got wind of his intended demise and interceded. They came and paid a hefty price to free Bullet.

"Listen, here's your out," a military official told him. "We're gonna put you in the Special Forces, or we will have to open an investigation for war crimes. You're gonna work with the best Commander in the business, Wild Bill Brewster."

Of course Bullet had heard of Wild Bill and all the stories about his global prowess, annihilating evil in even the most treacherous hot spots, but never getting his hands dirty.

"You're both very good with guns," the military official said. "So consider this your match made in heaven that just saved you from a lifetime in hell down here. There's just one condition, Hot Shot. You gotta follow orders. No more vigilante, rogue, one-man-assassin-team bullshit, you hear?"

Of course Bullet had answered in the affirmative. Then as soon as he'd met Wild Bill, he knew they'd make one helluva team. And they did, earning medals and accolades for pulling off some of the craziest shit in the name of American justice that anyone would ever believe.

But right now, Bullet just couldn't relate to the conversation the General was having with his wife and daughter about their cushy life back home: running, writing, book signings, and most of all, having positive, loving relationships.

Life at my house was the complete opposite.

Born 33 years ago and raised in San Diego with Mexican American parents who were also born in California, his parents had instilled in him an aversion to marriage and family life. His mother was an elementary school teacher. Obsessed with being thin and preserving her beauty, she was always worried that Papa would leave her for a younger woman, and ultimately, he did. Unfortunately, Mom's constant dieting resulted in his younger sister battling anorexia and bulimia and nearly dying.

His father's betrayal, his mother's misery, and his sister's illness created a tense household. Calvin escaped by sneaking onto the Navy base where his father was a respected officer. Since Calvin was tall and muscular as a teenager, he would slip into the training groups.

Calvin joined the military at age 18. His natural athletic ability, competitive personality, and innate drive to do good deeds, enabled him to excel in the Navy and joined Special Forces. He was sent to the most treacherous hot spots in the world, and won many awards and medals for acts of bravery that help America, save lives, and promote global peace. He was so grateful for meeting Wild Bill very early in his career, during that high-stakes deployment in Nicaragua. Their mentor-protegé relationship led to the General treating him like a son. Though he'd never met Maggie or Jeri, Bullet felt like he knew them because he'd heard so many details about their lives. Bullet loves the General because he is honest and is one of the few men he knows who is faithful to his wife, even during long, international deployments. He speaks Spanish, French, Portuguese, Chinese, and Russian.

Now, the General hung up the phone, glanced at the Congressional hearing that was about to resume on TV, then turned to Calvin.

"Bullet, how's your family, your parents?"

Sadness washed through Bullet.

"They're both gettin' their asses kicked by all the crap they put in their bodies over the years," Bullet said, shaking his head. He still wore his helmet, and sweaty chunks of straight black hair stuck down around his ears. He ran a large hand over the dark bristles sprouting from his wide, normally clean-shaven jaw.

"Man, if we could package diabetes, it would make one wicked weapon of mass destruction." Bullet nodded toward Dr. Wise on television. "Kinda like what he's been sayin' all along. I heard him call it 'diabesity.' That's my family. I almost hate to call home anymore. Always bad news. Mom's shooting herself up with insulin, and my dad—"

Bullet bit down so hard that his jaw muscles flexed. "Man, I can't believe it. Just found out, my dad has no legs! That diabetes jacked him up."

The General's heart ached; he tapped Bullet on the back. "Oh, I'm sorry, son. That's rough. Especially for a big guy like your dad."

Bullet shook his head. "When they go, that's all the family I got. Except my sister, but she's so busy. Four kids, husband, job. But I'll tell you what, if she doesn't get a grip on herself, she'll follow in their footsteps."

Calvin shook his head, reflecting back on his family's lives. "You know, my sister almost died from anorexia as a teenager, always watching my mother do crazy stuff to lose weight and be cute. Now she's obese and diabetic, with a fat husband and fat kids."

Commercials flashed on TV, first showing thin, sexy women strutting around in jeans and high heels, to advertise lipstick. The next ad showed a happy family eating burgers, fries, and milkshakes at Heavenly's.

"You know, it's all fucked up," Bullet said. "All the actresses and models are stick-thin and beautiful, but the crap that people are eating is making them fat and sick. My dad used to get up before dawn to go running, then he'd make this juice with seaweed and wheat germ." He shook his head. "Then it's like the devil flipped a switch in both of them, and they couldn't eat enough junk or get fat enough."

The General had that fatherly expression again.

"If you ever have kids, I hope you teach them the way we taught Jeri." He glanced at the picture of Jeri and Maggie on his desk. "We taught her to defend herself with good nutrition just as aggressively as she should defend her physical safety." The General laughed. "I'll never forget, the playground bully picked on her one day. She sent him home crying. Then the boy's parents came over, complaining that my daughter kicked their son's butt. My answer was simple: your son shouldn't mess with my daughter."

Bullet laughed, wishing his dad had taken pride his every accomplishment from birth, the way the General did Jeri. Bullet had never met her, but knew everything about her. Her grades, the funny stories involving their dog, Bingo, how she dressed her Barbie doll in camo and slung G.I. Joe's gun over her shoulder, and how she'd fallen off her bike and received four stitches that formed a small, half-circle-shaped scar on her left elbow.

"Of course," the General said, "I gave Jeri a good scolding. Just because we took her to karate lessons didn't give her license to use it on the school playground. Even though I was damn proud of her for setting that little punk straight."

He laughed, and Bullet joined him, until he looked serious again.

"Son," the General said, "I hope you'll get to see your parents sometime soon. Maybe you can take a leave, go back to San Diego—"

"Nope," Bullet said, shaking his head. "Before I came back to this hellhole, I was playing hopscotch over a couple continents and climates. Putting out the proverbial fires, or at least the bastards who are starting them. After this last mission for you, when I find the evidence that King Daemon has a manifesto showing what he's really up to, I'm outta here. Already bought my ranch in Montana. I plan to spend my days fishing with my dog, enjoying the peace and quiet for once in a couple decades."

The General put his hand on Bullet's shoulder. "I want you to know, you've been like a son to me, and I'm here for you."

Bullet nodded. "I appreciate that."

"I hope someday you'll have a wife as devoted as Maggie, and kids who bring you as much joy as Jeri has given us."

"All due respect, sir," Bullet said. "That marriage and family stuff? Not for me."

The General smiled. "You're only 33. Things change."

Bullet let out a cynical laugh, chugged his water, and turned to the Congressional hearing on television. "Man, that video sure will make you lose your appetite."

The General patted his flat, firm stomach. "I'm grateful for good habits. Five-mile jog this morning, steel cut oats for breakfast. An ounce of prevention is worth a pound of cure, as they say."

"And a huge fortune's worth of medical bills," Bullet said. "What gets me is every country I visit—all the fat kids. Makes my heart hurt. They don't have a chance." He nodded toward Dr. Wise. "I hope his ideas catch on, everywhere. Otherwise, we're all doomed."

The General's expression became fatherly. "Well son, I plan to be here a mighty long time. But if I ever meet my demise and you're still around, promise me, you'll look after Maggie and Jeri, should they need you."

Bullet smiled. "I'd be happy to, long as they don't mind casting a fishing rod on the ranch I plan to buy in Montana. That's my dream. Retire. Just me, my guns, a big dog, and fishing to my heart's content."

Bullet gulped more water, then said, "Hey, besides, you're not going anywhere, for a long time."

"Absolutely," the General said. "But in this business, you never know, son. You just never know."

Chapter 12

Johnny "Big Man" Valentine stared into the screen of his Device, where Carmen La Buena stared back at him from California, and Boone Davis faced him from Kentucky.

"It don't look good," Johnny said. "My gut tells me Congress is gonna tell Doc Wise to GTFO—"

Carmen, leader of Yogis for Health, looked perplexed.

"My bad," Johnny said, "excuse me, but that's short for 'get the fuck out,' but I know you all speak love and peace all the time out there—"

"Not today," Carmen said. "We're in 'any means necessary' mode."

"Make that us, too," Boone said. "Kinder, gentler—ain't cuttin' it. It's time for war."

Johnny held up the hardcover edition of the new book, AMERICA: SHAMELESSLY FAT AND GETTING FATTER! by Jerralyn Brewster

"I need you both, and all yawl's people, to read this book," Johnny said. "Doc Wise wrote the Foreword, talking about the obesogenic culture—"

"I read the ebook," Boone said. "Then I told all 200 of us at breakfast this morning, they had to read it. We had a game day huddle at my compound. And yeah, I made everybody turn on their Devices and read that sucker from start to finish. Good summary of how it all snuck up on us—"

"Like we're about to sneak up on them!" Johnny exclaimed.

"So let's go over the logistics," Carmen said. "We've got 3,000 people across California ready to do individual guerilla attacks. This includes hundreds of food plants, restaurants, and food company headquarters."

As they discussed their strategy, Johnny glanced down at the book, which was open to a section that was especially impactful:

AMERICA: SHAMELESSLY FAT AND GETTING FATTER!

In just the past five years, the population of the United States has already surpassed the projected obesity rate for 2030. The American population is now 64 percent obese, with several of the fattest states in the South tipping the scales at 80 percent obese.

This massive shift is due to a backlash to all the talk and attempts at programs to make people eat healthier, exercise, and lose weight. Many people found it a losing battle, especially when faced with the realities of sedentary lifestyles in school and work, economic hardships that make it easier to eat cheap fast food, a mindset that getting sick is just part of life, and anger at the government for trying to control what they buy and eat.

In addition, due to the harsh realities of the economy, crime, terrorism, and worries about global warming, food is marketed and enjoyed as the ultimate comfort and escape from reality. Restaurants cater to this trend by offering decadent opportunities to "sit, eat, and be entertained" at all hours.

The overall public sentiment favors fat people who are quick to file lawsuits that they win, forcing companies to change and accommodate them.

Boosting pride in being obese is another phenomenon, as evidenced in the "no shame in my game" promotions by the fast food restaurant chain, Taco Temptation. They hired a Heisman trophy winner to say, "I got no shame in my game," before he bites into the restaurant's trademark Triple Taco, which is not only three times the size of a normal taco, but it's actually three enormous tacos stuffed and stacked into one monstrous concoction of calories.

Cooking and eating at home are equally popular. As a result, cooking TV shows are extremely popular and people go crazy trying to get tickets to be in studio audiences to win food giveaways and even Eat-Cations—vacations that make cruise ships look like weight loss camp. These food-centered get-aways at exotic locales feature chefs catering to the guests every culinary whim, around the clock.

Meanwhile, everyday life offers a cornucopia of indulgence. The food and restaurant industries—with the help of technology—have made food and eating even more of an American obsession. Here's how:

RESTAURANTS—Restaurants use aggressive advertising containing words like "all you can eat" and "Roman Feast" and "Endless Buffet." They are using the tentacles of technology to reach into every electronic Device within a certain area to titillate passers-by to eat.

As someone walks down the street, every nearby business can flash pop-up promotions, like "free chocolate!" onto that person's phone, watch, tablet, laptop, and other devices. So, that makes it extremely easy for an individual to find delicious food at every moment.

This technology—using the amped-up Internet now known as the SuperNet -- also allows advertisers to flash promotions over the GPS screens in passing vehicles. So much personal data has been collected by these companies, through legitimate and illicit channels, that advertising is tailored to each individual's Device and vehicle.

For example, when a mother picks up her children from soccer practice after school, the SuperNet knows that the kids are hungry for their favorite meal and the mother is tired from working all day.

"Hungry? Turn left at the next light and come to Comfort Café, because we'll give you half-off on all macaroni and cheese dinners if you come right now," a peppy young woman will say on the computer screen that shows her serving steaming, jumbo servings. "You're just two blocks away! And we'll give the kids a free hot-fudge sundae—"

Advertising also pops up for drive-thrus offering ice cream, cupcakes, candy/pop, and regular fast food. The GPS screen has evolved into what is essentially a television showing constant commercials for food places within a two- to five-mile radius of the vehicle.

Creamy Dream is at the forefront of such innovative marketing. On your Device, you can keep track of purchases and if you come every day for a month, you get a free purchase equivalent of $20 or your picture on the wall.

"You're just two blocks from the next Creamy Dream," the sultry female voice says, flashing a mesmerizing video of melted chocolate chips stretching as someone pulls apart one of their famous cookies.

They create a "membership" atmosphere by offering party rooms with chocolate theme parties. They have separate lounges for adults with alcoholic beverages—all with a chocolate theme and sexy finger foods—like chocolate-covered strawberries. And on Valentine's Day—you must make a reservation at the restaurant a year in advance! They also have Midnight Meal promotions and anniversary celebrations.

One of the most popular restaurants is The Comfort Café. They serve only comfort food: macaroni and cheese, beef stew, baked breads, cake, cookies and pies lasagna, ice cream, fried chicken, and butter-drenched vegetables.

While driving, 3D electronic billboards flash with obnoxious food, pop and candy ads, especially for the top-selling soda, called Crave; the most popular candy, Buzz Rocks; and the top burger place, Heavenly's, followed by Fiend Burger.

"The first 25 drivers who walk through our door will receive a free platter of cheesy, beef nachos with their meal," announces one commercial on all Devices within a five-mile range of the restaurant. "It's huge! But hurry, we can already hear tires screeching! Come get yours now!"

Of course their advertising highlights an important feature of their restaurants: "big, roomy seating to make your eating experience as comfortable as possible."

That message has become ubiquitous as Americans eat to their heart's content. Their explosive physical growth has spawned profound changes in the products and services that companies offer.

Wall Street is booming with companies that are catering to the obesity industry. Building construction is thriving because companies are renovating public spaces/accommodations in restaurants, stores, malls, sports arenas, concert venues, etc. Furniture companies are profiting because bigger, sturdier furniture is in demand.

This demand impacts every part of life, which makes many companies rich. Public transportation is being revamped with bigger seats. Amusement park rides are being built to accommodate bigger people.

HYGIENE—The whole "going to the bathroom" industry has boomed. Because it's so hard for obese people to practice good personal hygiene, and wipe themselves after going to the bathroom, the bidet has become very popular, even in public. But it's nothing like the ones used in Europe. It has a very large seat and a strong water stream that's controlled by hand with a control panel in front of the person who's sitting down. So, the water sprays up, and the spigot can be turned to aim into different cracks and crevices, then a small blow-dryer dries the area.

People also have these at home because wiping is impossible.

They also have giant bathtubs and showers. An entire industry has blossomed around obese hygiene outside of the bathroom. Absorbent, antibacterial pads can be placed between fat rolls to soak up sweat, while preventing odor and infection. Similar pads can be used under arms and between thighs to protect against painful chafing.

The sleep apnea device industry is huge, even making the masks in child sizes.

THE TRAVEL INDUSTRY—Airlines, buses, and trains compete for business by the best snacks and meals they can provide, for a price.

First class airline travelers and long-distance train travelers can order gourmet meals that are custom-prepared in elaborate kitchens in the restaurants in airports. Commuter trains and long-distance bus companies offer the same, but the meals are less expensive and less elaborate. Each one has aggressive advertising touting their "golden snack boxes" which are packed with sugar- and fat-laden junk food.

The hottest promotion for kids is one airline's pirate-themed "treasure chest" for every child passenger. Not only does the child get a pirate hat, but he or she receives a shoebox-sized, plastic treasure chest stuffed with toys, crayons, coloring books, and of course, cookies, candy, and a large snack packet containing buttery crackers, lunch meats, and processed cheese. And don't forget the cold can of soda!

Airlines sell seats by weight and the armrests are adjustable. One airline that refused to adjust went bankrupt because people complained their seats were too small and sued for roomier accommodations. The airlines also advertise "extra-large, roomy seating" on all shuttle buses and waiting areas.

The travel industry also doesn't want anyone to stay home just because they have fat-related illnesses and conditions. Hotels promote extra-large toilets, beds, showers, and restaurants with award-winning food, including entertainment-filled Midnight Meals.

Hotels also advertise sleep apnea masks. Their commercials say, "Why lug your mask on your trip, when we can provide all the comforts of home?"

Since a huge portion of the population has diabetes, which results in kidney failure and the need for dialysis, the travel industry has also gotten on board.

They now offer dialysis centers in hotels and on cruise ships! These are part of larger clinics to help travelers deal with hypertension, cancer and other obesity-related ailments. "In case you forgot your meds," the commercials say, "we'll take care of you right here! We've even got a fully stocked pharmacy in our hotel / on our cruise ship!"

ENTERTAINMENT—Movie theatres were the first to renovate with extra-large seating, more leg room and new offerings at the snack bars. They got rid of small popcorn buckets; now everyone gets a huge, buttered bucket of popcorn with a gigantic sugary drink and a jumbo box of candy, as part of the ticket purchase. They also have a "no sharing" rule on food, so everyone will feel comfortable enjoying their own enormous bucket.

FASHION—The medical industry caters to the overweight population by selling things such as:

- *Flesh-colored patches—in every shade—to cover purple skin splotches and blisters on lower legs caused by diabetes; and*

- *Stylish belts for wearing insulin pumps.*

Hollywood and the fashion industry still promote that Thin is In, and the diet industry is still a multi-billion dollar enterprise, causing people to do crazy and dangerous things to lose weight and stay skinny.

Meanwhile, fat people see victory in the fashion industry because Fashion Week in LA, New York, Paris, and Milan now include entirely separate shows for obese people, which is providing modeling jobs to plus-sized models and jobs for people in the growing number of stores selling these extra-large fashions.

THE ECONOMICS OF OBESITY—Dr. Michael Wise has warned that the obesity epidemic is affecting society in a way that is widening the gap between the haves and the have-nots. In his bestselling book, Till Death Do Us Part: A Battle Plan to Win America's War on Obesity, he wrote, "When the Kerner Commission said we were moving toward two societies, one black, one white, back in 1968 after the rebellions in Detroit, Watts, and Newark, little did we know that we were moving toward two societies: one poor, obese, and dying; one rich, fit, and thriving."

That has become true now, because a person's socioeconomic level is one of the most powerful indicators of whether they will be fat or thin, sickly or healthy. Wealth or lack thereof all increase or decrease a person's access to health care, nutritious food, exercise and education about healthy living, and this cycle begins even before concept.

As a result, the gulf between skinny people and fat people is huge, and it correlates with wealth. Why? Because the lower class fat people have only gotten more destitute when they're so sick that they can't work. In addition, poor people with no insurance who are fat and sick continue to eat highly caloric foods that lack nutritional value, and as a result they get even more sick.

The birth rate is the lowest in centuries because obese women are not as fertile, plus the diet is toxic, so they don't get pregnant or have miscarriages. Obese men have a lower sperm count with less quality sperm and they have less sex drive and less physical ability to perform the act. Plus obese people have less sex because they'd rather be eating.

Poverty and sickness have caused a drop in school enrollment. But the addition of fast food restaurants in schools, and the community center type atmosphere they have created in poor neighborhoods, has actually boosted enrollment! The fast food companies, and the Washington lawmakers who pushed for their presence in schools, actually point to this as a victory in American education. They use this as an example of how corporate cooperation with government can help everyone achieve the American Dream. The food companies offer extensive college scholarship programs for urban and rural poor students and cite this as additional evidence that their presence in the schools is a positive contribution to society.

All of this is their defense against critics who say they're feeding people food that makes them fat and sick.

NORMALIZING DISEASE AND HUGENESS— Obese America is now a place where disease is normalized by the fact that everyone is sick or has family members who are ill. That is no more apparent than the thriving diabetes industry. Dialysis Clinics that are in stiff competition for patients have created innovative lures. These include:

- *Video game competitions for the kids while they're hooked up to the machines.*

- *Magic acts.*

- *Clowns.*

- *Even a performance stage facing the dialysis chairs with a new show every two or three hours.*

- *Family movies.*

Perhaps the most unique idea is the Dialysis Bus. These double-decker dialysis buses park on a neighborhood street or in an office building parking lot, or even a campground, where they can service two dozen people at a time. Their ads say, "Don't let diabetes stop you from living your life to the fullest!"

Another advent is the Clothing Exchange in neighborhoods, schools, faith centers, and workplaces. Since people are gaining weight rapidly, this helps them save money when they need bigger clothes. People donate their smaller clothes and exchange them for bigger ones.

Likewise, department stores advertise all kinds of products for the obese world:

- *Giant baby gear—high chairs, strollers, diapers, fortified cribs.*

- *Really large children's clothing, sleeping bags, wagons, bicycles (bigger seats, heavier tires, giant tricycles for bigger kids because it's too hard to balance when obese), and heavyweight swing sets.*

- *Extra-large, fortified furniture.*

FAITH-BASED FAT—Places of worship are also pandering to the obesogenic world. Rather than sit through a three-hour service on an empty stomach, a national restaurant chain has opened Prayer Cafés inside each religious institution. Located near the front door, so they can pump the scent of fresh, creamed coffee and super-sweet cinnamon rolls, bagels, bean pies and other pastries, these cafés are decorated and stocked according to the religious beliefs. They are kosher in synagogues, halal in mosques, vegetarian in Hindu temples, etc. Prayer Cafés enable people to have a snack or even a meal before and after services, while most places also offer their traditional fried chicken meals in the banquet hall.

Johnny Valentine closed the book.

"Man!" he exclaimed to his LifeQuest partners across America. "Dr. Wise is right on point when he says we're becoming our own worst enemies."

"Let the battle begin," Boone Davis said. "Down here in Kentucky, we've been watchin' this creep up on America and it's time to stop it. Today."

"Yogis for Health are ready to rock here in California," Carmen La Buena added.

As Johnny glanced up at the Congressional hearing on TV, where those arrogant lawmakers were talking down to Doc Wise, he was ready.

"I think we're about to launch a revolution," Johnny said. "Bring it on, baby!"

Chapter 13

King Daemon was so eager to unleash the OC-8 campaign, he returned with his Royal Brothers to the laboratory to hear more about it from Dr. Braza. Together they watched a rat in the throes of an eating frenzy, as OC-8 was doing its real damage.

"The rat will only stop eating when it is too stuffed to continue eating," Dr. Braza said. "If it were a person, the same would occur. Unless the person ran out of money and could not purchase or access any more food."

Dr. Braza added that, "OC-8 contains an insulin inhibitor that shuts down the pancreas and robs the body's ability to regulate sugar in the bloodstream. As you know, the pancreas normally releases insulin when a person eats. The insulin escorts the sugar through the blood to the cells for energy. All the while, it sparks such sudden and massive spikes in rogue blood sugar, that OC-8 triggers the onset of advanced diabetes. Rogue sugar attacks organs—brain, heart, eyes, kidneys, lungs—overwhelming the body and causing cardiac arrest."

The King nodded with understanding as excitement pulsed through him.

"I have observed rats that are given very high doses of OC-8, that the reaction occurs so fast, the skin on their legs turns purple," Dr. Braza said. "It is rotten. Gangrene consumes their feet in a matter of hours. Their feet simply rot off!"

He then added, "If this were to occur in an American, he or she would be dead of a heart attack before they can even get to the hospital. I have deliberately formulated OC-8 so that it breaks down into substances that normally are present in the body. This break-down occurs almost immediately, so by the time the person gets sick, OC-8 is not detectable in his or her blood. Then, of course, it's also not found during the autopsy."

The King said, "We have already received reports of some deaths in Detroit and other cities. It is very effective and I must commend your brilliant scientific work. Now tell me more about OC-88."

Dr. Braza nodded. "Yes, I created this aggressive hybrid of the toxin. OC-88 causes the equivalent of cardiac arrest for the brain. It simply shuts down. So much sugar floods the bloodstream so fast, that the sugar literally attacks the brain tissue and kills it. When I conducted autopsies on the dead rats, their brain tissue contained so much sugar, that it had crystallized like a cube of sugar that a person might drop into a cup of tea."

Dr. Braza pointed to the rats. "Please continue observing the frenzied gluttony of the rats."

The King said, "My Royal Brothers, as we observe Dr. Braza's work in action, our Minister of Logistics and Planning can update us on his findings for the implementation of our plan for ESTABLISHING THE GLOBAL KING-DOM OF ROYAL TRICQUA."

The Minister of Planning and Logistics said, "The trial in Detroit was a success. Meanwhile, we have been conducting research and studying the best three cities to begin the campaign. We have also been analyzing which food companies should serve as our launch point." He explained that the food poisoning campaign should begin in three fast food chains in poor, minority neighborhoods in American cities.

"Little Rock, Arkansas is the fattest city in the country," he said, "and Mississippi is the fattest state. The high rate of diabetes and early death there, due to the population of morbidly obese people, would enable us to begin in a dramatic manner without drawing attention to our mission."

Then the Minister of Planning and Logistics said that he was paying particular attention to three cities that seemed ideal.

"I believe we can have the most effective campaign by first targeting the large concentrations of poor black, Latino, and white people in the ghettos of three cities: Flint, Michigan; Gary, Indiana; and Cleveland, Ohio. It would also be utilized in Detroit, Michigan. These populations are already addicted to drugs and alcohol, and they eat a diet of mostly fast food and snack foods. Few have health insurance, and they are already prone to early death due to crime, high rates of disease, and filthy lifestyles."

The King pointed to the even more frenzied eating amongst the rats. Then he said, "Have you identified which food companies would be the most opportune for introducing OC-8?"

The Minister of Planning and Logistics nodded as the other men pointed and watched the rats. "Right now we are believing that our distribution channels will have the most success through Heavenly's Burgers, Taco Temptation, and Georgia Fried Chicken. Our trials at these three restaurant chains are already underway. However, we are continuing to study these companies, with the help of our many comrades in the United States, to ensure our flawless execution of our operation when the time is right."

"Now is the time to launch our program in the three designated cities," the King said. "We will determine when to go nationwide at a later date."

Dr. Braza said, "It's very important to note the potency of these drugs. Once they are introduced, all senses become heightened so that tastes and textures are extremely pleasurable. The aroma and even visual appeal of the food is also greatly enhanced."

He said that OC-8 contained a chemical compound that both shut off the body's ability to feel full while also stimulating a wickedly insatiable hunger by flooding the body with the hunger hormone, ghrelin. That triggered the person to want to continue eating and drinking sugary soda.

"No matter the degree of an individual's willpower to fight the cravings," Dr. Braza said, "it is impossible. The addiction response is triggered so profoundly, that the person will eat himself or herself to death."

Chapter 14

Sergeant Calvin Alvarez's findings were so much worse than he ever imagined, General Brewster could hardly wrap his mind around it. Bullet had just returned from his fact-finding mission with one of King Daemon's Royal Brothers. A Royal Brother who was so furious that the King had punished him for a minor violation of palace protocol, that the Royal Brother decided to share the heartbeat of Daemon's sinister plot to take over the world.

"The bottom line is," Bullet told the General in a low voice, "is that money is changing hands between Daemon's camp and folks who are getting American military contracts. Civilians are involved. Trying to figure out who's working for who in this hornet's nest called the Republic of the East. Where lies, deceit, and double-crossing are the order of the day. "

General Brewster studied the laptop screen documenting what Bullet was saying.

"How can this go unnoticed?" General Brewster asked.

"Man, it is!" Calvin let out a long sigh. "Like I said, it's a nightmare."

Bullet explained how he obtained the information. The computer hard drives were taken from the government office of the Republic's democratically elected Vice President—who was suspected of continuing to collude with the terrorists. Then the hard drive had been taken at night and replaced with a hard drive that would appear to its owner to have been erased by a virus. Since then, the hard drivers were decoded and translated.

"Rumor has it," Bullet told the General, "that the King-slash-President has appointed this guy as his quote-unquote Minister of Propaganda. So we found a log of secret communications between this guy and several high-ranking people in the United States. Several communications make reference to the upcoming anniversary of what the terrorists call the Royal Massacre."

The General and Bullet talked about a strategy to investigate that further. This included surveillance of the men in the King's inner circle, all of whom have served in the Tricqua Army and committed atrocities that were rumored but never proven. After observing the King's inner circle visiting every home in the nation, Bullet and his men set up an undercover operation to learn what information was being obtained and distributed. Bullet said that confirmed his belief that the King-turned-President is plotting something sinister against the United States.

"The real bombshell," Bullet said, "is about Blane. As in, the guy in the president's ear. Gerald Blane. He's on the terrorists' bankroll, and deeper than that."

General Brewster felt sweat prickle over his whole body.

"If that's not bad enough," Calvin said, "Blane was actually born in the Republic. He's been groomed his whole life for a coup they're planning—"

"To take over the United States," General Brewster groaned in disbelief.

"And the world," Bullet said. "And so far, things are going as planned. I mean, Blane has President Alexander's complete trust!"

General Brewster's mind fast-forwarded to the horrific reality of Daemon's plot coming to pass. "We have to stop them. Tell me more."

"Well you're at the center of their plot," Calvin said, "because Daemon believes you killed his parents with your own hands. The Royal Massacre, as they call it, is the impetus for their blueprint for world domination. And you're the bullseye. You better believe, if I were in charge right now, I'd sneak into the Palace tonight and put an end to Daemon's plan. Then all this—"

Bullet glared at the screen. "But I figure we better go through the proper channels."

General Brewster read Daemon's manifesto on the screen. It said that Blane—though American-looking and raised by his birth family in Boise, Idaho—Blane was indoctrinated with the life mission to serve as a warrior who will help lay the foundation for Tricqua's take-over of the United States. Blane's expatriate American family had defected to Tricqua after becoming disillusioned with the US. They volunteered to help Tricqua execute its long-term goal of vengeance on America; to do this, they raised four children, teaching them English and American ways, while indoctrinating them the terrorists' philosophies that included extreme hatred toward America. The four siblings participated in study-abroad programs throughout Europe and attended Ivy League universities in the United States. Blane's two sisters worked in high-powered positions in the most prominent American food companies. His brother was a marketing executive for Golden Harvest Foods. They were selected and groomed because their Caucasian parentage made them appear completely American and therefore would rouse no suspicion.

"I have to take this to the President," General Brewster said.

"Hold your horses, Wild Bill. We don't know the extent of Blane's influence in the White House and the Armed Forces—"

"It's my duty—"

"It's your life on the line," Bullet said.

General Brewster thought of Maggie, and Jeri, and his oath to protect the United States of America.

"What I recommend," Bullet said, "is that I hand this mission over to some of my military brothers and sisters who've gone off the grid. They'd be more than happy to do what the U-S-of-A hasn't had the balls to do: obliterate King Daemon altogether. Take out Blane at the same time, and bam, done. Problem solved."

"I can't endorse that absolutely anarchistic approach—"

"Desperate times call for desperate measures," Calvin said. "Remember, Wild Bill, much as I love you, this is my last mission. I'm out. Goin' to my ranch in Montana to unplug. I won't be here to protect you. And with Daemon gone, you'll be hailed as a hero."

"I have to follow the appropriate channels of authority," General Brewster said.

"Don't let those be your famous last words, Wild Bill." Bullet shook his head. "I say this is a 'kill or be killed' situation, and we should take action accordingly."

Chapter 15

King Daemon watched as his Minister of Logistics and Planning held a video conference call in the Royal Media Room. The huge screen showed 24 squares, each with the face of an individual who was a leader in ESTABLISHING THE GLOBAL KINGDOM OF ROYAL TRICQUA.

These leaders across America had been groomed for many years, some since birth, to secretly play their appointed roles in government, corporations, education, and religious communities. Their allegiance was to King Daemon, and each possessed sophisticated communications equipment to enable video conference calls such as these to go undetected by American law enforcement and government surveillance.

Today's call was to obtain an update on the progress of getting OC-8 approved by the FDA, distributed to food manufacturing plants for the top three fast food companies, and finally served to the unsuspecting Americans who were already poisoning themselves with gluttony.

First, the Minister of Logistics and Planning called upon Chad Bluestone, a clean-cut blond man who held a top FDA position and was instrumental in the quick approval of OC-8, along with the Bakker-Elixir Laboratories representative that sought FDA approval of OC-8.

"We have all the marketing materials promoting the additive as the have-your-cake-and-eat-it-too solution to consuming fast food and not gaining weight," Chad said, as his image became bigger in a large center square on the screen, surrounded by the other 23 faces. "And they're eating it up, pardon the pun. It's really quite amazing how gullible they are. Especially when financial incentives are introduced in a stealth manner."

"Excellent," the Minister said. "Do you expect any resistance?"

"One of the scientists vehemently opposed the approval of OC-8, saying that his tests showed nothing to support our claim that the additive blocks calorie absorption," Chad said. "God rest his soul, I just got news that his brakes went out when he was driving home from work, and he didn't survive the accident."

"Very good," the Minister said. "Then approval is imminent—"

"FDA Commissioner Beatrice Donderro herself told me today that it's just a matter of paperwork," Chad said. "It's a done deal. She, by the way, expressed great joy at spending the Christmas holidays in the private villa that we're providing in Cancun."

The Minister nodded. "Chad, you will be rewarded for your excellent execution of your mission."

Next, the Minister called upon Cindy Blane, a top executive with the Golden Harvest Corporation. Her image filled the large center square on the screen.

"You are looking extraordinarily beautiful today," he said.

She smiled. "As soon as we receive the FDA certification, OC-8 will be distributed to all food manufacturing plants for Heavenly's, Georgia Fried Chicken, and Taco Temptation. That's the official story. The truth is that we have already added it to the manufacturing process. Our three test cities are already serving it. And we're just waiting to hear from you as to when we should go national and distribute these batches of burgers, fries, tacos, and chicken to our restaurants across the country."

The Minister nodded. "As eager as we are to do that, let's continue with our strategy for a test launch. Very good work, Cindy, as usual."

Cindy's image shrunk to a small square and a brown-skinned woman—whose silver hair was braided into a crown-like hairstyle—filled the big square in the center of the screen. She sat in an ornate dining room under a chandelier, and diamond-covered letters spelling BETTY sparkled on her necklace.

"Betty Jones," the Minister said. "Tell us about the safe-house network and farm facilities for recruitment and training."

She looked annoyed. "First, I told you all on the last call," she said, "send my payment a different way. The gov'ment here watches black folks different than white folks. I can't be gettin' no big EFTs at the bank like y'all do. Might as well call the FBI and say, 'Come get me.'"

King Daemon and the Ministers chuckled.

"So until I get that cash money," she said, "the way I told you I want it, you don't get to hear what I know. I ain't in this for the fun and games of it all. I got three grandbabies in college and I'm payin' room and board for every one of 'em. So—"

The Minister glared at the Finance Minister and demanded, "Have you not followed my instructions to provide Ms. Jones' payments in the method she requested?"

The Finance Minister cowered. "It will be done."

"You will be done if this happens again," the Minister said, then turned to the screen. "Ms. Jones, my sincerest apologies. You will have your payment within the hour."

"Then call me back and we'll talk," she said.

All the Ministers chuckled again, as did King Daemon, who said, "Ms. Jones, you are a very spirited lady."

"I know I got what you want," she said, "and you got what I want. That's why this works." Then she disappeared from the screen, because she hung up.

The Minister recalled how they had recruited her after seeing her on GNN. Her two sons were Army soldiers and after they were killed in combat in the Middle East, she turned on the United States for sending them to a senseless war. Her outspoken comments in the media resulted in her ultimately serving as the head of the Kingdom's national network of safe houses and farms used for recruitment and training of the growing numbers of supporters. Ms. Jones had arranged with other similarly disillusioned Americans in other states to oversee operations in their regions and report back to her on a weekly basis.

Next, a man wearing American military fatigues filled the center of the screen.

"Sergeant Green," the Minister said. "Kindly provide an update on US military maneuvers here in our country."

Sergeant Green then divulged details pertaining to the movement of troops as well as the Allies' long-term strategy for the Republic.

King Daemon seethed. But only until he began to gloat that the network he had created and groomed would ultimately enable him to finally establish the Global Kingdom of Royal Tricqua.

Chapter 16

WHEN THE CONGRESSIONAL HEARING resumed after lunch, Dr. Wise continued to testify and show video of an abdominal cavity clogged with thick layers of yellow-orange fat. He hated that several lawmakers were covering their eyes and shaking their heads. He raised his voice to command their attention and action.

"Ladies and gentlemen, this is a force more sinister and dangerous than terrorism because it has infiltrated every aspect of our daily life and culture," Dr. Wise said. "As a result, this substance has the power to destroy our world. It is our own worst enemy."

Senator Buxton noticed his disturbed colleagues; annoyance pinched his suntanned face that was framed by slicked-back brown hair.

"Foods today are manufactured in laboratories to be addictive," Dr. Wise continued, "so this enemy uses the equivalent of chemical warfare to get this poison in our bodies, where it turns into fat. As a result, it kills nearly 400,000 citizens every year. And it costs billions—"

"Excuse me, if I may kindly interrupt," Senator Buxton said, "may I please request on behalf of my fellow lawmak-

"

ers that you take down the graphic video up there? We all just ate lunch, and truth be told, it's makin' my stomach churn so much, I can't concentrate on what you're sayin'."

Laughter roared through Congress.

Rage shot through Dr. Wise with such force—from the soles of his feet up through his entire body—that his face felt hot and his ears started ringing.

How dare he make jokes while I'm talking about the biggest threat since the atomic bomb!

Dr. Wise summoned every bit of his self-control to stop the expletives that threatened to leap off the tip of his tongue. Getting into a verbal altercation with one of Congress's most powerful leaders would not advance his cause. If only he could shout the truth about Senator Buxton, how he was rumored to be receiving millions of dollars to sway his vote in favor of the "big business" that was unleashing these weapons of mass destruction on the unsuspecting American public.

"Senator Buxton," Dr. Wise said, "I prefer to keep the images up, to reinforce the life-or-death urgency of my message."

The Senator nodded. "Alright then, please continue."

"As I was saying," Dr. Wise said, noticing that the Senator was whispering to an assistant and pointing to the projection screen. "Americans are falling prey to this enemy with our eyes—and mouths—wide open, unable to escape its seductive poison."

The video screen went black. A sly smile raised a corner of Senator Buxton's mouth as he cast a mocking glance at Dr. Wise.

"It's an outrage that this enemy kills nearly 400,000 citizens every year!" Dr. Wise exclaimed, as anger amped up his voice. "Ladies and gentlemen, if another nation were attacking the people of the United States, the President, Congress, and Department of Defense would launch an aggressive military campaign to protect us with the Army, the Air Force, the Navy, and the Marines."

Dr. Wise cast a pleading expression at the committee. "Then why—*why?!*—is the government allowing this new enemy to kill more people in one year than the total number of Americans killed in World War I, World War II, the Korean War, Vietnam and the Iraq War—combined! This is atrocious!"

Senator Buxton snapped, "Dr. Wise, please keep your voice down. You have a microphone. We can hear you just fine."

Dr. Wise rose to his feet. "Ladies and gentlemen, the power is in your hands to save America!"

The chamber was still and silent as Dr. Wise said, "So what is this threat? It is obesity."

The lawmakers' expressions ranged from blank to deeply disturbed. The bill's sponsor, Senator Cheryl Simpson, looked as pained as if she'd been punched in the stomach.

"We've reached a crisis point," Dr. Wise said. "If the obesity epidemic continues at its current rate, then 44 percent—nearly *half* of all Americans—will be obese by the year 2030, and some states will have populations that are 75 percent obese!"

Senator Buxton looked bored, as if Dr. Wise were a jester, tossing balls into the air, failing to entertain the king.

That made something explode inside Dr. Wise. He had to make them hear him.

"Ladies and gentlemen, this weapon of mass destruction is killing America!" he declared. "It is not bombs, or bullets, or anthrax. It's fat! And this fat comes from excess consumption of food that's loaded with sugar, fat, and salt."

Senator Simpson nodded.

"I'm pleading with you," Dr. Wise said fervently, "to vote in favor of the American Obesity Eradication Act. It contains the aggressive steps that the government can take to stop the obesity epidemic and save our nation from sickness, bankruptcy, early death, and loss of our status as a global superpower."

Dr. Wise reached onto the table before him and held up his thick, hardcover book entitled, TIL DEATH DO US PART: A BATTLE PLAN TO WIN AMERICA'S WAR ON OBESITY.

"As you've read in my book—which remains at the number one spot on *The American Daily News Bestsellers List*—I have done the research and the work that enabled our lawmakers to write the American Obesity Eradication Act," he said. "This is a radical plan, but we're facing a radical problem. Americans won't stop committing slow suicide by food and fat, until we have aggressive government intervention to reverse this trend."

Rumbles of disapproval only intensified his determination. As did many of the people who continued to inspire his crusade to end obesity: his fat, sick, and dying family members, young and old; the growing number of obese doctors, nurses, and even nutritionists with whom he worked back at the hospital and obesity clinic; and the growing disparity between rich, educated, thin, healthy Caucasians and poor, uneducated, obese, sickly African American, Latino, Native American, and immigrant populations.

Dr. Wise wanted to shout that the American practice of slavery had set the stage for the horrific health disparities—including obesity and its related diseases—amongst African Americans. It started with diet during slavery, when enslaved people were given the least desirable remains of slaughtered pigs: feet, ears, hog maws, and chitlins, which were intestines. As a means of survival, the slaves had learned to cook these foods so well that they became traditional soul food down through the generations—and even a delicacy that whites sought to enjoy.

One thing the slave owners didn't anticipate was that they were creating an elite echelon of super athletes by "breeding" the strongest men with the strongest women. It was a horrific practice of forcing slaves to mate like animals in a barn with the goal of birthing the strongest workforce on the plantation. However, down through the generations, that practice passed down genes that created some of the African diaspora's greatest track stars and champions of the basketball court and football field. Even those who never made it into the national or global spotlight became legends in local neighborhoods and regions for their athletic prowess.

Another problem that the government had helped create was the fact that a large percentage of households headed by single black women were usually uneducated and poor. Dr. Wise grew up during the height of ADC, or Aid to Dependent Children, which provided money to single mothers. If a man were in the house, she would lose the money. As a result, this policy discouraged marriage. Now, marriage amongst poor blacks was not even part of the normal progression of life, as it was amongst educated blacks and mainstream society.

This was another factor that contributed to the obesity epidemic, because family instability, especially amidst poverty, usually resulted in the children drinking nutritionally void, sugary red pop in their bottles and eating BBQ potato chips and whatever else they could pick up at the corner liquor store.

Dr. Wise believed wholeheartedly that because government policy had helped create and exacerbate the obesity epidemic, then it should bear the responsibility for reversing and eradicating it.

Likewise, for now, Dr. Wise's efforts were colorblind.

This is not a racial thing. This is an American thing.

Even as such, he feared that it would be impossible to convince these politicians to take action against the multi-billion dollar food and restaurant industries. Making the problem even more complex was how the medical industry and the pharmaceutical companies were also earning billions of dollars by providing care and drugs to the increasingly fat-afflicted population.

Dr. Wise's mind whirled with all the factors contributing to the obesity crisis. It was no secret that the food industry lobby—including soda, junk food, fast food, agriculture, restaurants, and food manufacturers—had paid a fortune to lawmakers through lobbyists to keep things just as they were: profitable and *obesogenic*.

He looked up at Senator Buxton, and almost raised a fist. It was a joke that this committee was chaired by government's most outspoken critic of any proposals to allow the government to restrict or regulate what people ate or how they ate it.

Today is a lost cause. It's time for revolution…

Knowing that this last-ditch effort might fail, Dr. Wise had already organized a small army of citizens across America who were ready to take radical action to stop the obesity epidemic with their own hands.

As he picked up a small remote, Dr. Wise said, "Now I'd like to show you my key points in this strategy, if someone would turn the video screen back on. I have PowerPoint slides."

Dr. Wise glared at Senator Buxton, who nodded at his assistant. The projection screen lit up, showing the following bullet points, which Dr. Wise read:

- Creating a Presidential Cabinet Post for Obesity Eradication

- Creating a SuperFund to Eliminate Obesity

- Imposing a Tax on Junk Food

- Taxing or Crediting Families and Companies based on members and employees who are healthy or obese

- Implementing a Mandatory Public School Curriculum for Nutrition and Wellness

- Establishing Fat Academies

- Banning Aggressive Advertising and Marketing of Junk Food

- Putting Food Warning Labels on Junk Food

- Subsidizing Farmers to produce organic, non-GMO fruits and vegetables

- Enlisting the help of the Faith Communities

- Promoting the Healthy American Culture Campaign

- Criminally prosecuting companies for adding unapproved and/or harmful and carcinogenic additives to foods and beverages.

"Ladies and gentlemen," Dr. Wise said, "if you fail to pass the American Obesity Eradication Act, many outraged Americans are prepared to wage guerilla warfare against the billionaire perpetrators of this war on public health."

Senator Buxton stiffened and cast a hard look at Dr. Wise. "That sounds like a threat to me."

"I'm simply stating a fact," Dr. Wise responded as the people in the chamber became still and silent.

"And just who might your vigilante band of citizens have identified as the perpetrators?" Senator Buxton asked. "I'll say so-called perpetrators because this obesity problem is clearly caused by individuals' personal failure to use discipline and willpower to eat in moderation and exercise. It's rooted in a lack of taking personal responsibility for one's own health."

His every word struck Dr. Wise like a tiny firecracker; anger sparked inside him.

"Clearly," Senator Buxton said, "nobody is holding a gun to anybody's head, telling them to eat three cheeseburgers and a jumbo order of fries in one sitting."

"That is a gross oversimplification of a very complex problem," Dr. Wise snapped. "The convenience of modern life has created what I call an *obesogenic* society; we've created the perfect formula to make people fat. The term *diabesity* should not exist, but this life-threatening disease goes hand-in-hand with our culture that causes and perpetuates obesity."

Dr. Wise exhaled and said, "Senator, here's my crash course in Obesity 101. Every day, we live sedentary lifestyles made even more so by technology, then we eat highly processed fast food stripped of fiber and pumped with fat, sugar, and salt. Adults sit at desks all day at work, then go home and watch TV. Meanwhile, kids go to school where they eat high-fat, processed lunches and snacks, but no longer have gym class or neighborhood recreational centers due to budget cuts. They go home, sit, and play video games. Not only are these adults and children getting fat, they're also getting sick with diabetes, cancer, and heart di—"

"It's all an excuse!" Senator Buxton said. "You see, Doctor, from my point of view as a disciplined man who runs marathons, eats my salads, and gets my check-ups, I see this entire, so-called *obesity epidemic* as the direct result of folks' penchant for placing blame on everyone but themselves. It's about personal responsibility, or lack of it. No one is forcing people to eat like there's no tomorrow!"

Dr. Wise shot to his feet. "Senator, no one is forcing you to take millions of dollars every year from food industry lobbyists!"

The Senator stared back in shock as Dr. Wise nearly shouted: "But all that money is forcing you to consistently vote against the junk food tax, a ban on aggressive junk food advertising for children, and a bill to restrict the use of addictive high fructose corn syrup and additives that are proven carcinogens!"

Hushed comments rippled through the chamber.

"Watch yourself, Dr. Wise," Senator Buxton said. "Wild and erroneous accusations have a way of catching back up with a man in a bad way."

Dr. Wise raised his book above his head. "Every day I stare into the bellies of obese Americans. I perform bariatric surgical procedures to save them from death by obesity. But it's not enough! We need your help! America desperately needs your help!"

Senator Buxton shook his head. "You know by my voting record that I can't support anything that even hints at big government trying to restrict or regulate what our citizens eat or how they eat it."

We're done. Dr. Wise immediately knew that the American Obesity Eradication Act would be defeated. "This system is corrupt!" he shouted. "Any one of you who vote down this bill will have the blood of innocent adults and children on your hands!"

Senator Buxton hammered his gavel.

"Security!" he shouted. "Escort this man out! Now!"

Dr. Wise calmly allowed the security guards to surround him and walk him out of Congress. His supporters had explicit orders to gather for an emergency meeting if this hearing went sour. Fearing the worst outcome here in Washington, his militant underground was already prepared to begin waging guerilla war—today.

In fact, hundreds of people were mobilizing at this very moment to launch the LifeQuest Movement from clandestine meeting places in private homes, college campuses, and community group meetings—and into the world spotlight.

Johnny "Big Man" Valentine and the Food Fight Posse were about to start the Food Riots in Detroit. Boone Davis had his people primed in Kentucky. And Carmen La Buena and her Yogis for Health were about to launch their strategy in California. All while LifeQuest groups in cities and rural areas across the country were ready for action.

Dr. Wise would simply slip under the radar, and rule the revolution like a wizard behind the curtain. The bunker in Detroit was ready for him to do so, undetected by these twisted powers-that-be.

As leader of the LifeQuest Movement, Dr. Wise had led a webcast a few days ago—on a private SuperNet channel secured by military veterans who were opting out of the mainstream after feeling extreme disillusionment against the government.

Their commitment would bolster the Movement with their experience and expertise with weapons and combat. And their survivalist skills would help the Movement build secret, self-sustaining communities, similar to the Fat Academies that Dr. Wise had proposed in his book, to provide healthy sanctuaries for men, women, and children to lose weight, get healthy, recruit more to do the same, and wage guerilla warfare against the billionaires who were poisoning and killing Americans with manufactured poison disguised as food.

Now, as televisions captured what some might had considered a humiliating moment, he considered it a triumph. Because it was sparking a revolution.

And we will not stop until we have saved America from its slow suicide by food and fat.

Chapter 17

Jᴇʀɪ Bʀᴇᴡsᴛᴇʀ ꜰɪɴᴀʟʟʏ ᴍᴀɴᴇᴜᴠᴇʀᴇᴅ her dark blue SUV past the traffic jam in front of Creamy Dream. This stretch of Woodward Avenue in the bustling suburb of Royal Oak, Michigan, was always congested during rush hour, but the hundreds of cars cramming into the new restaurant's parking structure were backing up traffic for a mile, both north and south, despite a small army of police officers who were directing traffic.

It was six o'clock, and her mother's "Chat with the Author and Book Signing" was scheduled to start now at a popular Italian restaurant and banquet hall just one block north of Creamy Dream.

"A shocking ending to the contentious hearing in Congress today," a broadcaster on GNN Radio said, announcing the lead story at the top of the hour, "as Detroit surgeon and author Dr. Michael Wise is escorted out, after testifying for the passage of the American Obesity Eradication Act. This, after Wise threatened to lead a guerilla war against the food industry, which he blames for America's ever-worsening obesity epidemic."

Jeri watched chubby children and their overweight parents waddle toward the door of the new restaurant, whose sickeningly sweet aromas filled her vehicle with a syrupy smell. As she maneuvered into the line of cars in front of one of the area's most famed Italian restaurants, Cantina di Grazia, she dialed her editor.

"Shareese," Jeri said, inching under the white valet canopy. To her right was an ornate black wrought iron fence adorned with purple flowers and lush greenery around the bustling dining terrace. "I've been trying to reach Dr. Wise since the hearing ended. I need to find out what he means about 'guerilla war.' Before I left the office, I put in calls to his cell phone and his secretary at his clinic in the hospital. So far, no response. But I'll keep trying."

"Just heard from the national desk," Shareese said. "Dr. Wise and his secretary never made their plane back here. I was about to call you. No one's seen them. So we need you to work your sources here, find Dr. Wise, and get the full scoop on what he's planning. He trusts you from the other articles you've done about him."

"I'm on it," Jeri said. She hung up and called several sources, reaching none, but leaving voicemail messages. She also dialed Dr. Wise again, leaving a voice message on his cell phone.

As she inched her vehicle forward, she noticed a license plate that said CHANGE on a black Jaguar convertible ahead of her. The driver's jet-black hair was combed back, long enough to touch his collar. Tall and slim, he stood and walked around the car, wearing a crisp white shirt, yellow silk tie, and navy blue business suit. His car radio was also broadcasting a report about Dr. Wise.

"Angelo," Jeri called out the window before handing her car key to the valet. Her phone was beeping with a steady stream of news reports from all the major media about the hearing; she put it on MUTE with the intention of discreetly checking it periodically for Shareese's calls and more news during her mother's event.

"Hey, Jeri! How's the smartest girl I know?" her former classmate said, smiling as he approached with outstretched arms. "You win the Pulitzer Prize yet?"

"You're so sweet, Angelo," Jeri said as he hugged her.

"I came to see your mom tonight," he said. "My mother is raving about her new book! As you can see, our new, all-organic menu is definitely striking a chord with diners."

As they walked amongst dozens of people entering the restaurant, many were carrying her mother's book, entitled *Eating Organic for a Better You*. Angelo nodded toward slim, vibrant diners eating fresh seafood, salads, and sensible portions of pasta.

"Unlike our new neighbor," Angelo said, casting a disgusted look across the street at Creamy Dream. "That's my worst nightmare. Bein' a chubby kid, I have zero tolerance for parents who feed their kids that crap. Thank God we're upwind of them. Made me nauseous to just drive past that smell."

As they approached the door, Jeri said, "I hope my mother hasn't started yet. I'm late because of the traffic jam."

"Me, too," Angelo said. "My mom said they're starting a little late because so many people got delayed. Hey, you wrote about the doctor who testified today. Great story!"

"Thank you," Jeri said.

Angelo lit up. "Hey, that's my dad's doctor! Jeri, you'll love this. My dad finally got surgery six weeks ago. Dr. Wise says he can drop 100 pounds, like freakishly fast."

Jeri smiled, remembering how Angelo's father had been obese since the first time Jeri saw him as a preschooler when she started the Worthington School. Angelo was the same age, and they'd both continued at the school until twelfth grade graduation, though she finished two years early before heading off to England. Every year, at school events, Jeri noticed that Angelo's father would appear even bigger.

"If the owner of an authentic Italian restaurant can do it, anyone can, right?"

"Exactly," Angelo said. "Dr. Wise, awesome guy. On a mission, man! I love it! My dad is here. We're all over your mom's message about going organic—"

"Excellent," Jeri said as they entered the lobby, which was decorated with exposed brick, wrought iron, and colorful tile work around a stone fountain that sprayed water around cherubs.

"My dad," Angelo said, "he's trying to do the right thing, you know? I mean, this summer while I'm home from working on my master's in econ at Yale, I'm trying to be a positive influence for him. Plus I'm working at an investment banking firm that handles family assets. Mostly, I'm trying to be like Gandhi, and be the change I wish to see in the world. Easier said than done, considering my family's reputation."

It was no secret that Angelo's father was one of the biggest mafia dons around. That's why as a child and teen, Jeri had never been allowed to go to his house, even for birthday parties, because of the family's mafia reputation. With her father being a General, her parents were always cautious about Jeri's friends.

On top of that, Jeri's journalistic debut in middle school had earned her a few enemies, including some of Angelo's relatives.

It happened after a school field trip to a Michigan dairy farm owned by another classmate's family. Jeri was so appalled by what she saw, she went undercover there—with her friend's help—to expose the horrific conditions, cruel killing techniques, and carcinogenic contents in the animal feed that were linked to high cancer rates for humans who consumed the milk, eggs, cheese, chicken, and beef from this farm.

As her very first investigative reports that focused on the link between nutrition, health, and America's growing obesity epidemic, Jeri exposed underworld crime corruption along with the inhumane treatment of cows and chickens raised for food.

She published this on her own website, which she called "Jeri's Secret Scoop." The reports won awards and sparked a federal investigation that led to the convictions of people in the USDA, chemical companies and the farming industry. Some of Angelo's relatives went to prison.

"You've always been about positive change," Jeri said. She smiled, adding, "I saw your license plate."

"Right, change! We can all make it happen!" Angelo exclaimed, leading her toward a large meeting room whose wall of windows offered a clear view of the traffic and crowd outside Creamy Dream.

In front of the windows sat Jeri's mother, who was at a table autographing books for a long line of people. The rows of 100 chairs facing her were mostly full. Near an *hors d'oeuvres* table piled high with colorful offerings of fresh fruits and vegetables, a GNN reporter was interviewing Mrs. Grazia, who was saying, "Our restaurant has been serving Detroit for a full century now, and after I read Maggie Brewster's new book, my husband and I decided to make our menu 100 percent organic, non-GMO, gluten-free, and locally sourced. We also have a large selection of vegetarian options, including Italian favorites such as lasagna and even meatballs. We're both trying to lose weight, and like my son always says from Gandhi, we want to be the change we wish to see—"

Angelo blew a kiss to his mother.

"You've always been part of change," Jeri said. "I mean, what you helped us do in our school cafeteria was amazing."

Angelo shrugged. "Hey, with the restaurants and food distribution, it was only natural. You still friends with Lisa Silverman? Her and her flowers—"

"Yeah, she's finishing up at NYU," Jeri said. "I'm planning to visit again next month. She's getting a business degree, then plans to open a flower shop, of course."

"You two were like, out to save the world," Angelo said.

In fifth grade, when Jeri and her best friend Lisa became enraged by the unhealthy food choices in the cafeteria that served students from preschool through twelfth grade, as well as faculty and staff, they had gathered signatures from nearly all the students and parents to radically change the menus. And though the school was thriving, no money was available to pay for a healthier, more expensive food provider.

That's when Angelo saved the day. He convinced his family to donate enough money to the school to *never* have to worry about paying for the progressive new food services company that served super healthy meals, including a vegetarian menu and award-winning salad bar. They also provided enough funds to build, stock, and staff an all-hours snack bar with smoothies, green drinks, fresh fruit, and sandwiches on whole grain breads, organic pizza, and more. It was open during all breaks between classes, free periods, after school study time, and school events. Since then, the Worthington School's cafeteria had been featured in the local and national media, and was emulated by schools across America.

"Jeri, you're the one!" Angelo said. "Your book is amazing. No surprise! I mean, I've never heard of any other 13-year-olds getting hired by *The American Daily News* as a junior correspondent!"

Jeri smiled. "I hope it's the first of many books. I have so much to say, so little time to say it."

Angelo smiled, leading her to the buffet table, where he loaded a small plate with bruschetta on toasted whole-grain bread, lettuce wraps filled with low-fat pesto and vegetables, and a cluster of green grapes. Jeri went straight for the fresh-cut pineapple, Michigan cherries, and cashews.

"Hey, look how crazy it is over there," Angelo said, nodding toward the window. "The dinner rush."

Traffic was at a standstill across all five lanes of northbound Woodward. People were even standing on the grassy median, waiting to cross the street on foot.

"Unbelievable," Jeri said. "We should go give them all a copy of my mom's book—and Dr. Wise's book!"

Angelo laughed, biting into a lettuce wrap. "Mmmm, this is so freakin' good! Those chocolate addicts don't know what they're missin' over here!"

Jeri watched the crowd as she savored the sweet pineapple. "Unfortunately, my aunt and her family are probably there."

"Oh, some of my friends can talk about nothing but that restaurant lately," Angelo said. "At the office, the guys think about the whole aphrodisiac thing of chocolate. Then mix it with booze and dancing in that Lounge they're opening, and these guys can't wait to take chicks there!"

Suddenly a large presence joined them.

"Dad!" Angelo said, hugging his rotund father, who wore an enormous brown pantsuit and walked with a cane.

Jeri shook his hand. "Hi, Mr. Grazia," she said, smiling. "Thank you for hosting my mom today."

"You're so welcome," he said. "We gotta do our part to

counter all the bad stuff out there." He nodded toward the chaos outside the window, then smiled. "Every time I see your stories in the paper, I think about that time you organized those buses to take people for free down to Eastern Market to buy fresh produce." He laughed. "Even then I was happy to donate for all those community gardens you were starting."

Angelo nodded. "And exercise programs, cooking classes, oh, and that 'All Natural Foods Day' you got going in Detroit."

Jeri smiled. "Wow, you remember. No processed food and no fast food, two days a week. I wonder how many people are still doing that."

Mr. Grazia raised a hand toward the room. "Everybody here and the whole restaurant, twenty-four seven! Hey, did Angelo tell you, I got surgery?"

Jeri smiled. "Yes, congratulations."

"When I hit 388 pounds, it was do or die," Mr. Grazia said. "Dr. Wise, he was great. Couldn't believe that whole robotic surgery deal. They just drilled some holes in my gut, fed the little light and scalpel down the tubes, and boom, Lucia Grazia's legendary stomach becomes a 'gastric sleeve.' It's got me eating like a bird." He let out a hearty laugh. "Lost 25 pounds the first week."

"Wow, congratulations!" Jeri said.

"Hey, I'd be happy to do an interview, after I drop about 200 pounds," Mr. Grazia said. "Or if you're still doing community projects on your whole health and wellness kick, I'd love to help. Just call. Work through Angelo, though, keep it squeaky clean. Good for his résumé."

Angelo handed Jeri a business card. "Seriously, we really want to do more to get people healthier."

Jeri smiled. "Thank you so much."

"Ladies and gentlemen," Mrs. Grazia said over the microphone near the table where Jeri's mother was sitting. "We're so proud to introduce this bestselling author who's had such a positive influence on our family, our restaurant, and the world. Mrs. Margaret Brewster is here to talk about her latest book, which has been on the bestseller lists since it launched a month ago."

A standing ovation filled the room with deafening cheers. The crowd included: young families with children; silver-haired men and women; people who were black, white, Asian, Latino, Native American, and multiracial; Indian women in colorful saris; Mom's super-coiffed social-ite friends; a man wearing a yarmulke; hippies; women in Muslim hijabs; two guys in Harley Davidson T-shirts, jeans, and black boots; and folks in business attire, exercise clothes, and sundresses, Manolo Blahniks, and Birkenstocks alike.

Jeri clapped, beaming with pride, yet stunned by the irony that the window behind her mother provided a clear view of the crowd around Creamy Dream.

"Thank you, Mr. and Mrs. Grazia, for inviting me here to speak," her mother said. "And for all of you, it's such a joy that you're all here tonight. The news today is saturated with stories about why it's imperative that we all take control of what we put into our mouths, to save ourselves, our economy and the planet."

More people continued to enter, making the room now standing room only.

"As you know, I've written all kinds of books, 18 in all," her mother said, "including romance novels and nonfiction books about how to improve your quality of life. Right now, my upcoming 30th wedding anniversary has inspired the book I'm working to finish now, about how to keep the romance alive in a long-term relationship."

As the audience applauded, Jeri noticed sudden movement around the crowd at Creamy Dream. Dozens of people in black—carrying picket signs—were marching toward those standing in line. Their T-shirts said in neon green "LifeQuest" on the front and "Saving America!" on the back.

Oh my God, it's starting… Dr. Wise's revolution. What else could that be?

"What the heck?" Angelo whispered.

Jeri's mother continued to talk, unaware of the commotion behind her as she said, "If you watched the Congressional hearing today, you heard Dr. Wise talk about a guerilla war. Well I believe each of us, by choosing to eat organically, are waging our own food and health revolution—"

The handful of police officers directing traffic were greatly outnumbered by the people whose picket signs said: "America—Land of the Fat, Home of the Obese! No More!" and "Eradicate Obesity" and "LifeQuest Saves Lives!"

Another sign looked like the Golden Harvest logo, but

it said "Gruesome Harvest" inside a yellow sunburst and "no more GMOs."

"—just like the Grazias are doing here," Jeri's mother said. "My book includes a brief snapshot of how our daily food choices impact the big picture of our world—"

Several men and women on megaphones began to lead the protesters in a chant that drowned out Jeri's mother's voice: "Hey, hey! Ho, ho! Creamy Dream has got to go!"

Jeri's mother turned around, as the audience stood and watched the protesters—hundreds of them!—march into the crowd that was waiting to enter Creamy Dream. Then the protesters stormed inside!

"What's going on over there?" Maggie asked.

Sirens blared.

Jeri's heart pounded with the urgent need to find out what was going on, and file a report for the paper. Dashing to the lobby, she snatched her phone from her purse to call her editor; the screen said "3 missed calls and voicemail: Shareese Smith."

Jeri dialed her back, gushing, "Shareese, Dr. Wise's guerilla war, I think it's happening at Creamy Dream right now! Protesters, picket signs, police—"

Jeri hurried outside, grabbing a reporter's notebook and pen from her purse. At the same time, several police cars screeched in front of the restaurant, and officers hopped out.

"Jeri," Shareese said, "It's not just there. The Monsanto seed plant just got bombed. And in the ten biggest cities across the country, protesters in black LifeQuest T-shirts are using their own cars to block drive-thru lanes at fast food restaurants. They're also going into grocery stores, throwing buckets of paint on the aisles with candy, chips, and processed meat."

Jeri stood on the corner, watching across the street as protesters were rushing the door of the restaurant as police officers in riot gear poured out of a van, charging toward them.

"Oh my God!" she exclaimed as an officer blocked her and other pedestrians from crossing the street to get closer.

"I'm media," she said. "The American Daily News."

"Step back," the officer ordered. "It's not safe."

"Jeri," Shareese said. "They're using tear gas and pepper spray on protesters in other cities. Just tell me what you see, and I'll send it to the national desk. Your number one task right now is to find Dr. Wise, get an exclusive interview, and find out exactly how far he's planning to take this."

"Got it," Jeri said. After describing the scene to Shareese, she hung up and dialed Dr. Wise's cell phone.

"We're sorry," a recording said. "The number you are trying to reach has been disconnected."

Call his secretary… call the Detroit General PR person… go to airport now with the hope of catching him… find out where he lives and wait there… and talk to someone in LifeQuest…

Jeri pulled her media badge from her purse, hung it around her neck, then sprinted past the police officer who was blocking the street. She headed straight to the man with the megaphone to get the scoop on LifeQuest and where she could find Dr. Michael Wise.

Chapter 18

Johnny "Big Man" Valentine gripped the giant steering wheel of the 18-wheeler as it sped northwest on Gratiot Avenue through Detroit's East Side.

He didn't need to glance left or right to see the burned-out houses, clusters of obese people at bus stops, liquor stores, and boarded-up businesses. This was where he grew up, witnessing the ravages of drugs, crime, and poverty on his family and neighbors.

He hated the sight of long lines of cars in the drive-thrus of the fast food restaurants on every corner, and the men, women, and children coming and going from liquor stores where they stocked up on booze, pop, chips, and hot dogs as mainstays in their nutritionally void and toxic lifestyles.

Now was the time to strike back at a system that was killing folks by feeding them slickly packaged and advertised poison.

Johnny drove his truck faster to the major intersection of Gratiot Avenue and the I-94 freeway. There he screeched to a halt, as did 12 other semi-trucks. He hopped out, flung open the doors, and—as everyone knew to do through the

Food Fight Posse's plan that was promoted throughout the neighborhood and the city—hundreds of people flooded the streets. Food Fight Posse soldiers helped unload the massive amounts of fresh fruits, vegetables, healthy grains, nuts, and fresh meats from the food trucks that were hijacked from a food company's warehouse in Eastern Market.

The company was owned by Golden Harvest and sold all these healthy goods—along with massive amounts of junk food and other trash to urban dwellers. So, for months, Food Fight Posse soldiers had been working at the warehouse, earning trust, and strategizing this day.

Now all 48 of the company's fleet of trucks was out doing this in four locations around Detroit. Stopping traffic. And giving away huge fortunes worth of healthy food to folks in the ghettos. A similar strategy was happening in some poor white communities as well as in Mexican Town where other chapters of the Food Fight Posse were orchestrating the same plan.

Part of this war was about racial injustice, but the broader blanket of injustice toward the poor and the working class was just as much of a problem and a priority for fixing.

Johnny's heart pounded with excitement as he watched men, women, and children haul off kale, bananas, whole chickens, and sacks of oatmeal.

Media helicopters buzzed overhead. People honked their horns, screaming in rage that this major road was blocked.

But the Food Fight Posse hustled every box off these

trucks until all the food was in the hands of the malnourished masses who deserved good nutrition just as much as all those motherfuckers in Congress gave their rich kids at home.

"Food Fight Posse!" he shouted along with his soldiers. "Food justice for all!"

Chapter 19

IN KENTUCKY AND A swath of southern states, Boone Davis and his group had infiltrated manufacturing plants, working in them for months, even years, preparing for this day. These companies prepared the "Frankenfoods" that were manufactured in laboratories to create crack-addicting-like combinations of fat, salt, and sugar, so that eaters became addicted and unable to stop eating the cookies, pizzas, burgers, and candy.

"Ready, set, detonate," Boone announced into his group's network of cell phones exactly 30 minutes after Dr. Wise was booted out of Congress.

Dozens of food manufacturing plants exploded simultaneously, as LifeQuest South folks executed the plan to detonate explosives planted in the most destructive areas of the plants. This, of course, after setting off the fire alarms to evacuate the plants to avoid a human toll on the destruction.

The media was going crazy in a frenzy of coverage as all these factories burned and smoldered across the South.

In California, Carmen La Buena's group had a different approach. These peace-loving yogis took to the streets waging guerilla war on the front lines. They released live skunks inside fast food restaurants. They splattered cans of paint on movie theatre snack stands.

Meanwhile, millions of LifeQuest followers across America waged individual battles against candy stands in gas stations, vending machines, and convenience stores. Others took to social media to condemn the forces that were allowing toxic food to poison people on a daily basis.

It was war, and the food manufacturing companies were under siege.

Chapter 20

THE LEADERS OF GOLDEN Harvest Foods were watching the chaos unfold on television as they held a conference call with presidential advisor Gerald Blane.

"Tell the President to stop this anarchy!" shouted Richard Blane, marketing executive for Golden Harvest. "Where the hell are the police? How could nobody have a damn clue that this was going to happen when all these renegades have clearly orchestrated this elaborate plan to destroy us?"

"This anarchy cannot continue!" Douglass shouted. "Tell President Alexander to send out the troops to stop this multi-million dollar nightmare of mayhem."

"We're on it," Gerald Blane said. "The attackers will be stopped with a vengeance."

Chapter 21

DR. MICHAEL WISE SHOT a triumphant fist into the air as he watched the beginning of his revolution playing out on live television.

"More reports coming in from around the country," Anastasia Lee said on Global News Network, "about a radical group called LifeQuest taking credit for brazen attacks on the food industry. Our reporters are standing by live as this breaking story becomes more shocking by the hour."

"You haven't seen anything yet!" Dr. Wise exclaimed, sitting at a table inside his mobile command center.

"Lou, can you hear this?" he asked his childhood friend and most trusted associate, Lou Joseph, who was sitting behind the steering wheel of what used to be a rock band's tour bus, now refurbished with military-grade tires, engine, and bullet-proof windows. Its roof was equipped with solar panels, hidden from view, for use during extreme situations that required hiding. The bus also contained supplies of water, non-perishable food, and weapons.

"Loud and clear, Chief," answered Lou, an engineer who had served in the US Army as a truck driver and mechanic in the Persian Gulf War. He had helped rebuild this vehicle, which looked as innocuous as a family camper, with shiny beige paint and dark tinted windows. Inside, it provided sleeping quarters, two bathrooms, a kitchen, and a meeting space.

But this bus was anything but ordinary. It had a secret hiding space that sealed off with special materials that were undetectable by heat sensors and K-9 units. Prior to now, Dr. Wise had practiced many times slipping in and out of the compartment in a matter of seconds, should the bus be pulled over by authorities.

Though he'd purchased a roundtrip ticket from Detroit to Washington, he had never intended to fly back if the Obesity Act were defeated. It wouldn't take long for authorities to link him to the simultaneous assault on the companies owned by billionaires who were making Americans fat and sick. So now as the mastermind behind the revolution, he considered himself a wanted man. That's why he had taken himself "off the grid" this afternoon.

First, his look-alike decoy—tall, thin, and African American with a medium brown complexion and short black hair—had boarded a train at Union Station in Washington, DC, headed for Detroit. He even had Dr. Wise's cell phone in his pocket, so anyone tracing his steps that way would be thrown off track.

Any authorities who were following his decoy would soon be thrown off by the fact that he was actually a white man named Jed Winston. Jed was a former patient of Dr. Wise who'd worked in costumes and special effects on Hollywood movies, but returned to Michigan and ballooned up to 400 pounds. After bariatric surgery, Jed lost 250 pounds and enlisted in Dr. Wise's battle against obesity. And what better way to help than to board a train as a black man, and—thanks to the magic of makeup—get off in the Motor City as a white man? All while Dr. Wise rode undetected back to Michigan.

Meanwhile, Dr. Wise's phone and email accounts would be disconnected right about now, and all personal files and information had been removed from the small, stark apartment that he kept near the hospital. It was convenient, because most days he was at the hospital before dawn to scrub for surgery, then spent long hours checking on patients, meeting with various hospital committees and boards, and performing emergency procedures when necessary.

It also helped him save money by walking to work, where he ate most of his meals in the physicians' cafeteria. Thanks to his spartan lifestyle, Dr. Wise had saved a small fortune, which he was now contributing to the Movement, which was financed by extremely generous donations from wealthy benefactors around Metro Detroit.

Today's turn of events was the exact reason that he'd never wanted a wife or children. Somehow he knew at an early age that his life would take a radical turn, and that could not happen if he had to consider the safety, well-being, and dependency of a woman and children. His mother had died years ago, and his siblings' lives were so far removed from his that they would never be implicated for his actions.

In addition, he had left explicit instructions for each of his patients with the bariatric surgical team and clinic staff. Upon his disappearance, they would see that all of his "jokes" about having to "go underground" after writing his book and testifying in Congress were not jokes at all. He was simply preparing them to operate in his absence.

In time, he would send word to some of his colleagues and patients whom he believed were ready to join the Movement. In fact, several patients who had lost hundreds of pounds and opened their eyes to the atrocities of America's obesogenic lifestyles were some of his most militant supporters. Having escaped the nightmare of food and fat themselves, they committed their lives to saving others. And it couldn't happen fast enough.

"Tonight," the GNN anchor said, "authorities are searching for Dr. Michael Wise, who never boarded his flight out of Washington, DC this afternoon. The FBI wants to question him about any connection he may have to attacks on the food industry that began as he was escorted out of Congress today."

For the first time, Dr. Wise watched video of the two federal marshals evicting him from the hearing. He walked with his head high, his shoulders squared, and his eyes focused with determination.

The anchor said, "Committee Chairman Buxton tells authorities, he believes Dr. Wise is the quote 'evil mastermind' behind today's attacks, because during the hearing the bariatric surgeon made a direct threat and reference to guerilla warfare against the food industry."

The news replayed video of Dr. Wise's exchange with Senator Buxton about a "threat" to "billionaire perpetrators" of the obesity epidemic.

"Senator Buxton," said Anastasia Lee, "vows that authorities will find Dr. Wise, question him and bring him to justice if necessary."

Senator Buxton appeared on TV, saying: "I believe Michael Wise threatened me, my colleagues in Congress, and every food and beverage company in America. This is unacceptable and he will face the most severe consequences, up to and including the death penalty, should his treasonous behavior be proven to result in the deaths of innocent Americans."

Dr. Wise exclaimed, "They'll never catch me! Not with Lightning Lou behind the wheel, isn't that right?"

"You got that right, man," Lou said, laughing but staring ahead into the glare of late evening sun over the highway. He reached for a green apple on the console and took a bite. After a heart attack at age 30, going vegetarian, exercising daily, and giving up junk food, Lou had dropped the 65 pounds he'd packed on since they'd been lanky athletes together in high school, in the US Air Force, and at Indiana University.

"Shocking new developments right now," said Anastasia Lee, looking almost flustered on TV, "as we're just learning about explosions at eight different factories that manufacture and distribute high fructose corn syrup."

"Yeah!" Dr. Wise exclaimed. "Can't say I didn't warn them!"

"Amazingly, no injuries reported," the anchor said, "because fire alarms were set off in every factory, and employees evacuated quickly, before the explosions occurred. We are getting this report about every act of guerilla warfare waged across America. Clearly, those orchestrating these attacks engaged in painstaking planning to avoid any harm to human beings employed in these facilities and venues."

Dr. Wise grinned. "Non-violence against the innocent!"

Lou laughed. "Great strategy, Chief."

"It takes teamwork to make the dream work," Dr. Wise said. "Couldn't do any of this alone."

The news report showed an aerial view of hundreds, if not thousands, of pigs, cattle, and chickens being freed from barns and factories where they were being prepared for slaughter. "Apparently," Anastasia Lee said, "this campaign against America's food industry included sparing the lives of animals that were being raised to supply the meat industry. We're getting reports that the electronic systems at these factories were hacked, causing cages and gates to open to free the livestock. This is clearly an orchestration of extraordinary design. Coming up next, we'll talk with a cybersecurity expert about how this could possibly occur."

Dr. Wise chuckled. His friends in Silicon Valley who were ultra health conscious and passionately supported his cause were all too willing to provide the best of the best in terms of hackers and computer engineers who could orchestrate this simultaneous campaign. At the same time, animal rescue organizations were corralling the livestock into private farms where the animals would be nurtured and spared from death. Not to mention, this campaign would help save planet earth from the noxious greenhouse causes caused by the enormous production of methane gas from pig farms, which was contributing to global warming and potentially the demise of our world.

"More breaking news," Anastasia Lee said, "as authorities in ten states are confirming that dozens of trucks carrying supplies for fast food restaurant chains… have been hijacked or vandalized beyond repair. First let's go to our reporter at one of the crash sites in Minneapolis."

"That's right, Anastasia," the reporter said, standing on a road amidst the flashing red and blue lights of police cars, as six 18-wheelers laid crashed into the wall of a large industrial building. "As you can see by the logos on each truck, they were delivering supplies for Heavenly's Burgers, Taco Temptation, and Georgia Fried Chicken. Police telling us, the trucks were carjacked by armed bandits at truck stops in several states, leaving the truck drivers unharmed, but their cargo destroyed."

The anchor asked, "How did these particular trucks crash together?"

The reporter nodded, saying, "Police believe the carjackers, or truckjackers I should say, deliberately came here, hopping out of the trucks before they crashed. The bandits escaped on foot, then were possibly picked up in get-away cars."

Video showed that the building was on a remote country road.

"What's in the building?" the anchor asked.

"Authorities tell us," the reporter said, "this is a laboratory where scientists work to create the next big thing in fast food. For example, this is where the latest craze of burgers served on glazed donuts originated."

Dr. Wise laughed because even super poised Anastasia Lee couldn't hide her disgust over that one. It was only a split-second that most people wouldn't notice, but as a surgeon, he noticed everything, including that glimmer of horror in the beautiful anchor's eyes.

"So definitely a connection to the food industry," she said. "Now let's go to New York City, where movie theatre snack stands have been under siege."

A young male reporter in front of a popcorn stand splattered with green paint appeared on the screen. "Yes, Anastasia, I'm in one of several movie theatres in Manhattan where police say individuals simultaneously vandalized the snack stands before escaping into the crowds."

The anchor shook her head. "Why popcorn stands?"

"Authorities are guessing tonight," the reporter said, "that movie theatre popcorn, candy, and soda are a target because huge portions make it easy to consume hundreds, even thousands of calories, in one sitting."

Next, Dr. Wise watched a report showing tractors mowing down GMO crops in 25 states.

"So far, everything is going off like clockwork," Dr. Wise said as Lou nodded. "Your idea to set everything off simultaneously—catch everybody off guard as soon as possible after the hearing—was brilliant."

"Why thank you, Mike," Lou said, as he maneuvered over the highway through the mountains of Pennsylvania. "I'll catch the news when we get back to Michigan. Reminds me of that song from back in the day, *The Revolution Will Not Be Televised*."

"Gil Scott Heron," Dr. Wise said with a chuckle. "It's televised at least for now. But after today, they'll crack down. We'll have to go underground. Deep. Then we'll just pop up for strategic hits to show we're not going away until we make change. Big change."

Lou sang that song about how "It's been a long time comin'."

He was right. Dr. Wise and his core group of supporters had been meeting for about five years now, inspired by his work as a bariatric surgeon. He had saved thousands of lives by altering the digestive tracts of men and women. But it just wasn't enough. Obesity was both a physical problem and a mental health issue, he had concluded, because so many of his patients were using food like alcoholics drank and junkies snorted, injected, and ingested their drugs of choice. Likewise, food addicts were mentally and physically addicted to the euphoric response to eating certain combinations of sugar, fat, and salt.

He knew this because none of his patients were addicted to apples or carrots. No, they were addicted to manufactured fast food, candy bars, and chips that were deliberately created to make men, women, and children crave more and more. Not to mention, the aggressive advertising that tempted them all day and all night, served as constant lures to eat more.

As a result, Dr. Wise had concluded long ago that America's so-called war on obesity had really been a losing battle from the start.

Ordinary people don't stand a chance. And the less money and education they have, the more defenseless they are. But we're about to change that! By finally defeating the enemy within.

Chapter 22

SITTING ON HIS GOLDEN throne, the King bit down hard to control the anger that surged more violently through his body with every news report that he watched on his giant TV screen.

He turned to his Minister of Communication and ordered, "Get me an immediate video conference with our comrades in the United States. I must find out how they plan to stop this mayhem."

Moments later, the screen divided into four images: US presidential advisor Gerald Blane; future American President Samuel "Uncle Sam" Addams; FBI Investigator Edward "Eddie" Smith; and Gerald's brother, Richard Blane, chief marketing strategist at Heavenly's Burgers. (The King relished the fact that their two sisters were beautiful seductresses working in high-powered positions in the most prominent food companies; they played instrumental roles in the strategy to dominate America).

"Gentlemen," the King said, "tell me that you are in the process of stopping the chaos before it interferes with our plans in America!"

Eddie Smith said, "Almighty, I can speak to that first. The FBI is working every lead to find and stop this Dr. Michael Wise, who's callin' the shots on all these vigilantes." The silver scar zig-zagging over his left cheek shimmered as Eddie ran a hand over his buzz cut. "I promise they will be stopped. Fast."

Gerald Blane added, "Almighty, I just met with the President. He's sending out the National Guard to protect all possible targets in the food industry. Factories, restaurants, transportation, and distribution. At the same time, every law enforcement agency in America is on the hunt for these rogues. Punishment will be swift and severe."

The King nodded, but his tone was hard: "Very good, but I will not be satisfied until you have restored security and calm so that we can implement our strategy, on time, as planned, with no interference. Uncle Sam, what is your opinion?"

"Almighty, I discreetly alerted authorities as soon as I heard Michael Wise make a threat during his testimony," Uncle Sam said. "That's why the federal marshals were already on hand, to take him out, and they've been following him ever since. Thinking he can outsmart us, he hopped on a train to Detroit, and we are tracking his cell phone."

The King raised his voice: "I want one hundred percent assurance from all of you that if authorities tighten security on the food industry, it will not complicate or hinder our plan in any way."

Gerald Blane nodded. "Almighty, I can absolutely assure you of that. Myself, my brother Richard, our sisters, Cindy and Linda, and Uncle Sam, we are now on the yacht of Douglass Golden, with many of our allies who will—whether knowingly or unknowingly—assist us in our ultimate mission for the Global Kingdom of Tricqua."

The King felt the first assurance since this conversation began.

"Almighty, if I may add," Gerald Blane said, "the channels that you have already created are so far above the fray, we will be able to implement the plan seamlessly when the time comes."

The King exhaled, feeling that the men were simply telling him what he wanted to hear. Time would tell, and he would take action accordingly. "I will not rest until this Dr. Michael Wise is dead, and all of his followers stop what they are doing."

Eddie Smith said: "Almighty, let me be the first to tell you, that's as good as done from the FBI's point of view. You got my word."

"I want a photograph or video of his dead body," the King said. "With unexpected developments such as this, we cannot risk interference or delays. And anyone who tries to get in our way shall die."

Rage surged through his body, overwhelming his mind with aggressive hunger for violence and the fastest execution of his plan possible.

He stood, raising his arms, shouting: "I hereby declare that Operation Global Dominance begins TODAY! Accelerate all plans to distribute OC-8 through the appropriate channels and approvals to reach the gluttonous mouths and bellies of Americans. Take it to every city, now!"

Chapter 23

STANDING ON THE DECK of the 100-foot yacht, Samuel "Uncle Sam" Addams had never felt more excited or optimistic about fulfilling his divine mission as the chosen one to lead Royal Tricqua into global dominance. But the anger he'd just seen glinting in the King's dark eyes filled him with fear and urgency.

For 41 years, I've been groomed for this mission. I cannot disappoint the King and our people—or allow an anarchist doctor and his destructive followers to stop us!

As the lights of Washington twinkled in the distance, and the orange sunset sky reflected off the dark waters of Chesapeake Bay, Samuel savored the determination that surged through his entire body. As always, his every thought, action, and spoken words were carefully calibrated to advance his mission. Now more than ever, he did not have a single split second to waste, because things had unexpectedly accelerated.

"There you are, honey," said his 31-year-old wife, Molly, the former Miss America who would make the perfect First Lady. Looking beautiful in a white chiffon cocktail dress, with her long, auburn hair flowing in the breeze, she handed him a glass of seltzer water. Then, smiling and making her bright green eyes twinkle at him, she said seductively, "Have I told you how handsome you look when you're contemplating how to save the world, Mr. President?"

He smiled. She'd been calling him that since they'd first met a dozen years ago at a reception in her hometown of Boston, shortly after Samuel left private practice as an attorney and was elected to the Massachusetts state legislature.

"I'm going to be President one day," he'd told her, knowing that he had just cast her in the starring role as his wife in the dramatic script that was already written for his life.

Now, he kissed her cheek that was as white and flawless as porcelain. "You know me too well, Molly, always reading my mind."

Actually she had no clue about his true identity or mission, and she would not know until she was securely ensconced in the White House. Then, when the truth was revealed—if she refused to comply—her only escape would be by death, which he would gladly oblige because her ornamental role in his life would no longer be needed.

"I just checked on the kids," she said. "The nannies say everything is smooth sailing. Little Betsy's fever is gone and she's got her energy back, thank goodness."

"I knew she would," Samuel said. Their sons, ages 10 and eight, and their daughters, ages six and three, were integral to his mission, as he had been programming them to always put family first, no matter what.

Now, he watched the elite group of his allies chatter nearby, sipping cocktails and checking phones and tablets for the latest news reports about the brazen attacks on the food industry. An air of angst permeated the party, yet it was tempered by a sense of insulation and power that whatever was going on, would not prevail under the mighty forces of power wrought by the law enforcement agencies and the National Guard where necessary.

As Samuel observed his peers, he privately gloated that none had any idea that they, too, would soon become important but dispensable pawns in the dramatic demise of their beloved "land of the free, home of the brave."

Soon they will all bow to the Royal King of Global Tricqua. Of course Gerald Blane and his brother Richard, as well as Eddie Smith, were already aware, and would help tonight in planting the seeds of greed for money and power in each unsuspecting ally's mind. That would ensure a flawless transition to power.

One by one, Samuel and his Royal Brothers would pull these power players aside and set their individual game plans in motion.

"Ladies and gentlemen," Douglass Golden said, raising a champagne glass and standing beside his stunning wife amidst their 100 guests. "Welcome to our yacht, *America's Golden Harvest.*"

As uniformed waiters distributed bubbling champagne flutes from silver trays, the guests raised their glasses.

"My wife and I want to congratulate all of you for coming together on this very important day," he said, "to talk about solutions to the obesity epidemic without asking the government to dictate what Americans can and cannot eat, how much we should weigh or how we make daily choices for our families' health."

Glasses clinked loudly along with a cheer from the guests, who included Beatrice Donderro, Commissioner of the US Food and Drug Administration, and CDC Spokesman Roger Ramsey and his wife, Wilma, the cookbook author. The gorgeous Blane sisters, Cindy and Linda, were standing on each side of Senator Brace Buxton, whose pushy wife was uncharacteristically absent.

"Unfortunately, today's attacks on the food industry have taken us all by surprise," Douglass said. "Golden Harvest has activated our private security forces to stabilize the situation that, as you know, the President is handling in a very aggressive manner this evening."

The crowd was silent. Eddie Smith was at the rail, facing the water, pressing a phone to his ear, as he'd been doing since they'd ended the video conference call with the King inside one of the lower state rooms. He looked pale, and his silver scar shimmered as he bit down, causing his jaw to flex.

"Now, for those of you who want to keep abreast of the situation," Douglass said, "I've instructed our captain to stay within range of the shore so that we're close enough to the cell phone transmission towers. We've also got the big screen television tuned in to Global News Network in the Club Room, just inside." He pointed to the richly appointed room overlooking the deck. "Feel free to step in and catch up as necessary. But don't let it ruin the fun!"

Douglass raised his glass. "Let's have a toast to a peaceful, quick resolution so that we can all go about the business of making a positive impact on America!"

Samuel stood beside US Surgeon General Mabel Samuels, who tapped her glass against his and Molly's, then flashed a bright smile. A tall, slim African American who was known for her anti-smoking crusades, she had been interviewed many times in the national media in recent days about her quest to end obesity in America. She was especially eager to help minority groups that were disproportionately affected by both excess weight and the resulting illnesses.

"Mrs. Samuels," Samuel said, "I was quite impressed with your interviews this week."

Her almond-colored, freckled face lit up and her short, straight black hair blew in the breeze off Chesapeake Bay. "Why thank you, Mr. Addams. I'd be delighted for you to participate in the coalition I'm assembling to aggressively tackle this problem."

"I'd be honored," he said, nodding to his wife. "Molly can help, too. She's started community gardens and healthy cooking classes in some inner-city neighborhoods."

The Surgeon General smiled at Molly. "So nice to see you again, Molly. I saw that beautiful spread in *Town & Country*, about your program. It said you started it after you saw a young mother at a bus stop, filling her baby's bottle with cola?"

"Oh my," Molly said, raising her left hand to her heart, as her three carat wedding ring and pale pink manicure glimmered in the soft golden light of sunset. "That just about broke my heart. Here I was, driving the kids to the Smithsonian for the afternoon, after telling them no, they could not have pizza for lunch, and I thought, that little baby doesn't stand a chance! I had to do something!"

Samuel nodded. "Molly's platform as Miss America was children's nutrition and exercise."

Molly nodded. "Then after we married, I'd been so focused on our children, but I realized what I'd been learning as a mom, I could teach to others, especially the less fortunate."

The Surgeon General handed a business card to Molly. "Please, call me, so we can talk about expanding your program nationwide."

Molly smiled, shaking Mrs. Samuels' hand, just as her husband, conservative New York Senator Raymond Samuels, approached, wearing his usual seersucker suit, bowtie, and round, tortoise-shell eyeglasses. His close-cropped, white beard contrasted with his dark skin, which always looked soft and smooth, like he'd just had a facial.

"Senator," Raymond said with a nod. "Congratulations on today. Let the good doctor's Gestapo diet plan for America suffer the same demise as affirmative action and *Roe v. Wade*, what do you say?"

Samuel smiled, raising his seltzer water to Senator Samuels' tumbler of bourbon on the rocks. "I like the way you talk, Raymond."

Douglass Golden spoke again: "Ladies and gentlemen, before we enjoy a hearty buffet down on the dining deck, I want to personally thank the very talented Anastasia Lee for hosting her health summit and doing those very informative reports today."

Douglass and his wife embraced Anastasia and her husband, who stepped forward. Samuel made a point to speak with them tonight as well, to entice them.

"Thank you all for coming tonight," Douglass said. "We invite you to go down for dinner, then dancing, under the stars."

Now it was time for action. Samuel kissed Molly's cheek and said, "Sweetheart, I'll be down shortly."

"Okay, honey," Molly said, then continued chatting with the Surgeon General. "When I first heard someone use the United Nations term 'food desert' to describe our inner cities, because they lack healthy food, I was appalled—"

As the crowd dispersed and descended the two stairwells flanking the deck, Samuel stepped close to Douglass Golden. "Doug, can we chat for a minute?"

"Sure, buddy," Douglass said, flashing a smile. "Anything for my college roommate. Let's go up and check out the view."

They took an interior stairwell to the uppermost deck, which was in front of the cockpit.

"I like the view from here," Douglass said. "Wide open sky and water, as far as you can see. Makes you feel like you can go anywhere and make anything happen."

"The sky's the limit!" Samuel agreed, sharing a laugh that had far deeper meaning that Douglass would ever know. He took the symbolism of their meeting place as a good omen for what he was about to propose. "Doug, you know better than anybody that my lifetime goal has always been to become President."

"Of course," Doug said.

"Well I'm about to announce my candidacy."

"Okay," Doug said, listening intently.

"But when I consider the contenders for my vice presidential running partner, I have a very short list of men of a particular caliber that would guarantee success."

"It goes without saying, whomever you select, I'll be your biggest contributor."

Samuel smiled. "I appreciate that, Doug. And I'm hoping you'll contribute in a way that maybe you haven't considered."

"How so?"

"I'd like you to be my running mate," Samuel said, imagining it done.

"For vice president?" Doug asked, surprised. "Geez, I never thought about that."

Samuel held out a hand, pointing to the bustling decks below. "Clearly you and your wife care about politics, hosting an event like this. And of course what happens in America's top leadership affects your bottom line at Golden Harvest."

A bewildered look flashed over Doug's face.

Samuel nodded. "Look, I've thought long and hard about this. You love the spotlight, and you have the most wholesome image of any man in America."

Doug smiled.

"So what do you think about being my running mate for next year's election?" Samuel asked.

Doug gazed out at the dark water, which shimmered with the lavender glow of the last light of day. He looked back at Samuel, and his eyes glowed with excitement. "I like that! My brother Joe always wanted to take my place as CEO, and he's doing a great job as VP of Golden Harvest. I'd just have to talk with my wife. But I suspect, as much as she loves to throw fundraisers for our favorite candidates, she might just like the idea."

Samuel patted Doug on the back. "Just imagine the power we would have to shape America!"

Doug's face lit up as he looked out at the water, then up at the sky. "Count me in, buddy! Or I should say, count me in, Mr. President!"

Samuel embraced his friend, thinking, *one down, more to go.*

A short time later, Samuel, Doug, Raymond Samuels, and Brace Buxton were sitting at a table, eating filet.

"Gentlemen," Doug said, "it's important for us in the food industry to take action real quick, to show we're promoting good health in a big way. After this Summit, the defeat of the Obesity Act, and these unfathomable attacks on our industry today, we need to put even more money where our mouth is."

"I agree," Samuel said. "It's urgent."

"As long as we do it our own way," Brace said, sipping red wine. "Not by the tyrannical plan of the deranged doctor from Detroit. Christ, all hell's breakin' loose across America as we sail into the sunset." He laughed. "But in all seriousness, he's about to look like a bad guy, while we can take steps to shine in the court of public opinion."

"Yes," Raymond Samuels said. "What do you have in mind, Doug?"

"Well, I'm speaking in complete confidence," Douglass said. "With all the budget cuts threatening to impact our public school lunch programs, Golden Harvest wants to step in and save the day in a big way."

"I like the sound of that!" Samuel exclaimed.

Doug smiled, adding, "Now if you gentlemen could help me, by pushing any approval I might need through Congress—"

"Like the Bible says," Brace said playfully, "ask and ye shall receive, my friend."

Doug smiled. "What I'd like is to have Golden Harvest sponsor a healthy school lunch program like America has never seen."

The men nodded. "We'll have a salad bar and fresh fruit stand in every public school cafeteria, coast to coast!" Doug said. "Now quiet as it's kept, we're about to ink a deal to acquire the Heavenly's burger chain, and we want to use that brand recognition and popularity to implement a community center concept in the schools."

Samuel forced himself not to grin. He'd heard snippets of Doug's plan, but reading between the lines right now, he knew his friend's long-term strategy would be to own and operate fast food restaurants inside every public school in America.

That will make it so very, very easy to execute the divine mission of the Royal Kingdom of Tricqua!

"These community centers," Doug said, "will enable us to provide nutrition education, cooking classes, vegetable gardens for the kids, exercise classes, you name it."

Samuel smiled. No one dared mention that this idea was straight out of Dr. Wise's book and the Obesity Act, though he called them Fat Academies. It didn't matter. That concept was dead in the water, as the doctor soon would be.

"Now, one selling point you can share with your colleagues," Doug said, "is that Golden Harvest has an exceptional track record with this concept, as you can see by the popularity of our Creamy Dream shops."

Raymond nodded. "I have to say, they've become havens for homework and community events nationwide, especially in my district in New York City, in places where we need it most."

Samuel added, "Same with my state. All the kids love the coupons, and the special events; it just builds customer loyalty for the whole family."

Doug smiled. "I appreciate that feedback. Now our first restaurant, and the ones we're already building in a dozen cities right now, promise to do the same, for people of every age."

Brace raised his wine glass. "Somebody get me a pen so we can all sign this into law right now!"

A short time later, as the guests enjoyed cheesecake with fresh strawberries, Samuel and his Royal Brothers, Gerald Blane and Richard Blane, casually approached Beatrice Donderro of the FDA, who conveniently was speaking with Roger Ramsey of the CDC about today's attacks on the food industry.

"Enjoying yourselves?" Samuel asked.

Beatrice laughed. "I had to step away when I saw desert coming. Cheesecake has a way of overstaying its welcome by making itself at home in my fat cells."

"It sure doesn't show," Roger said playfully.

"Thank you," Beatrice said. "I didn't get to work out today, so I really have to be careful." She smiled at Richard Blane. "I have to confess, once a month, I allow myself the triple bacon-cheeseburger, jumbo fries, and strawberry milkshake at Heavenly's."

Richard grinned. "So do I!"

"I've got some exciting news that you'll be hearing about very soon," Samuel said, glancing at Beatrice and Roger. "I've been alerted of a new flavor-enhancing food additive that can help us fast food lovers win the battle of the bulge." Samuel patted his flat, rock-hard stomach, which hadn't contained fast food since college when he'd noticed how late-night pizza was thickening his waistline.

"Do tell!" Beatrice said.

"Well, we were given a tour of the new facility for Bakker-Elixir Laboratories in Maryland, and one of the scientists I've known for ages pulled me aside to divulge something called OC-8."

"Never heard of it," Roger said as he and Beatrice shrugged.

"Nor have I," Beatrice said, looking puzzled. "What is it?"

Samuel said, "The scientist said OC-8 stands for Obesity Controller, with the number eight being for infinity, because it has infinite power to do exactly what we've been talking about: ending the obesity epidemic."

Roger's eyes widened. "So, what's in this stuff?"

"Apparently," Samuel said, loving their rapt attention, "this brilliant team of scientists from around the world has extracted all the best ingredients from superfoods—like chia seeds, acai berries, and some kind of green tea from China that melts body fat."

Beatrice and Roger listened intently as Richard looked on.

"Apparently, when all these ingredients, which are mixed with a heavy dose of antioxidants, are added to burgers, fries, fried chicken, tacos, even pizza, they do something to block the negative effects of the sugar, fat, and salt in the food."

Beatrice lit up. "Sounds like a miracle!"

"The perfect elixir," Roger said with an awed expression.

"Miracle elixir, absolutely," Samuel said.

"Side effects?" Beatrice asked.

"Right," Roger said. "If something sounds too good to be true, it usually is."

Samuel shook his head. "No, my very trusted friend, the scientist at Bakker-Elixir Labs, said OC-8 actually staves off weight gain, diabetes, cancer, and heart problems caused by cholesterol."

Roger looked puzzled, as did Beatrice, as he asked, "Why have we not heard even a whisper about this, until now?"

Beatrice shook her head. "Certainly someone at the FDA would have mentioned it."

Samuel laughed. "You should see your faces! I said exactly the same thing to the scientist. And he said until OC-8 is officially patented, the international team has been under the strictest orders to keep it confidential. They even had lawyers draw up non-disclosure agreements."

Roger nodded. "I can believe that."

"Honestly," Samuel said, "this could be the greatest discovery of modern science."

"Are you kidding?" Beatrice asked. "If folks find out they can have their cake and eat it too, so to speak, this will take the world by storm."

Samuel smiled, as did Richard, who said, "You can't imagine how excited we are at Heavenly's. I mean, Americans are going to keep eating fast food, no matter what obesity statistics are released by the CDC. So, assuming the FDA approves this additive, you'll literally be helping us all do our part to reduce obesity."

Roger nodded. "From a PR perspective, you won't have to advertise it that way. This is great. Because as soon as you say 'healthy' or 'vitamins' or start naming exotic ingredients, people lose their appetite, thinking it won't taste good."

"So, when can we expect this to come to the FDA for approval?" Beatrice asked.

"Now that, unfortunately," Samuel said with feigned regret, "my scientist friend could not say. He said the clinical trials are still going on, to make certain that OC-8 has no unexpected or adverse side effects."

"Better to get it right, than rushed," Roger said, casting a smile across the crowd at his wife. "Soon as it comes out, Wilma will want to add this OC-8 to every fattening recipe in her kitchen!"

Samuel laughed, loving the ease with which he would get Americans to swallow the royal poison.

Chapter 24

King Daemon sat on his throne, watching news coverage of Dr. Wise's Congressional testimony on the giant TV screen. Around him gathered his Royal Brotherhood, while his Minister of Health handed each man a copy of Dr. Wise's book.

"This contains the blueprint for us to use to make our nation the healthiest in the world," the Minister of Health said. "The brilliant gentleman on television right now, in Congress, is begging for his leaders to hear his plea to save Americans with the plan in this book. They will ignore him. But we are listening. We are going to use his strategy to reverse the obscene problems of overweight and obesity in our country, because the Americans brought their disgusting fast food and slovenly habits here, and we will return our citizens to excellent health."

King Daemon nodded toward the Minister of Propaganda, who handed a spiral-bound booklet to each man and said, "Our plan is called ESTABLISHING THE GLOBAL KINGDOM OF ROYAL TRICQUA, and we are distributing it to every person in the Kingdom. Every man, woman, and child is obligated to participate in a strategy of global dominance that begins in the home."

King Daemon nodded. "We are implementing our aggressive, anti-obesity plan based on Dr. Wise's book and the American Obesity Eradication Act that the Americans are too gluttonous and money-hungry to follow. I charged our Minister of Health with translating the book into our language, and representatives from the Royal Palace is going to distribute this booklet to every home in the nation. The policies will be enforced by our Minister of Royal Obedience." The King nodded to that minister.

"We are telling every family that it is their duty to our Kingdom to study this plan and implement it," said the Minister of Royal Obedience. "Those who disobey will face imprisonment and possibly death. These punishments will include events reminiscent of public floggings, hangings, and beheadings of centuries gone by. Of course we will be instilling fear in the families by describing how those who disobey this plan and engage in American-style gluttony would be fatally punished."

The Minister of Royal Obedience paused. "And what is the punishment? Everyone from an entire neighborhood would be gathered at a secret location to witness it. The offender—whether a child, a woman, or a man—will be forced by soldiers to consume a massive amount of fast food, sugary drinks, and processed snacks. Since children are not exempt from this punishment, parents will be responsible for making sure that boys and girls follow these rules, or their children will die by their own hands. The person being punished will be forced to eat and drink until death occurs."

King Daemon interjected: "Be reminded, gentlemen, that you are not exempt from this policy, nor its punishments. Your wives and children must also be obedient or they will suffer this fate. Our Minister of Obedience has a video to demonstrate how that could happen."

The GNN reports stopped playing on the giant screen and video began showing Kingdom soldiers entering a home, confronting a fat family, and proceeding to demonstrate each family member—grandparents, the mother, father, and two children—being forced to eat to death. The sounds of screaming and suffering finally stopped echoing through the palace media room and a chilling silence fell over the Ministers.

"Portions of this video will be shown to families to demonstrate the importance of being obedient to our Kingdom's weight loss regimen," said the Minister of Propaganda.

"We must follow this plan until every Tricquan achieves a healthy weight once again," the Minister of Health announced. "Specifically, we must return to the wholesome foods of our country's ancestors: fish, lean poultry, fresh fruits and vegetables, grains, beans, and natural oils. Eating fast food and processed snacks is hereby prohibited. Daily exercise is now required for everyone. Health and nutrition classes will be introduced in schools, in addition to healthy meals. All technology and media that fill the Tricqua citizens' minds with American-style trash—including music, video games, television shows, Internet propaganda, social media garbage, magazines, and books—are now prohibited and punishable by death."

The Minister of Propaganda nodded. "Citizens will be permitted to enjoy wholesome programming on Republic Media via radio, television, and controlled Internet. Since the Americans are monitoring this, our television is modeled after the slick programming format of Global News Network."

King Daemon smiled. "I am making certain that Republic Media is the main propaganda tool to trick the Americans into believing that I, as the democratic President, am running a country that conformed to the Americans' vision in every way. This way it appears that we are participating in their charade by pretending that we are adhering to their democratic and bogus government, so they will not suspect we are doing anything other than that."

The Minister of Propaganda nodded. "While our citizens were grateful for the Americans' help in liberating the country from the rebels, many believed that Tricqua never would have been taken over by the rebels if American-backed soldiers had not been involved in this region for the past several decades. So when it came to loyalty, most Tricquan hearts honored the King. This is simply a natural progression that makes it easy to implement our plan in secrecy, and to ensure absolute cooperation."

The Minister of Royal Obedience added, "Fear is a great motivator. We anticipate that families will immediately began to lose weight and follow healthy lifestyles, causing the rates of overweight and obese children and adults to plunge very quickly. We will monitor every citizen, and weekly weigh-ins will be conducted in homes. Fast food restaurants will be forced out of business. Sedentary behavior will be punishable, especially for children."

With GNN playing again on the big screen, the Minister of Propaganda pointed to Dr. Wise looking angry during a report about the Congressional hearing. "Just as he speaks of needing a cultural shift to change behaviors, we are going to do the same here. We are introducing anti-American words to our popular language that make being fat and unhealthy an extremely shameful trait. We are going to use 'USA' as a synonym for 'fat.' So the ultimate insult will be to tell an overweight person, 'You're so USA!'"

King Daemon relished all of this: "While the American people are getting sick and fat, we will make the Republic of the East the world's healthiest country, very quickly. And we will give new meaning to the term 'suicide bomber.' The Americans are setting off bombs of food and fat inside their own bodies. We are simply providing a more explosive bomb. And this will allow us to dominate America and the world."

Chapter 25

THE FIRST LIGHT OF dawn cracked through the steel-gray clouds over Detroit as Lou steered the bus through the black wrought iron gates of a run-down mansion. It sat on the periphery of a Detroit neighborhood long celebrated for its mini-palaces built by auto barons and bootleggers.

"We made it," Dr. Wise said, wide awake with adrenaline. They couldn't be too careful; the media had just reported what Lou had learned by phone. Someone had tried to kill the decoy on the train. Shots were fired into his sleeping berth, but the decoy fired back, then escaped out the window as the train slowed to stop in a small town in Ohio.

Now, the bus passed under the portico, past an overgrown backyard and crumbling fountain.

"They started working on the interior," Dr. Wise said. "This place will make a perfect LifeQuest Academy. Teaching people how to live, not make themselves sick." Dr. Wise stifled a pang of disgust that neither schools nor American culture were doing enough to help people truly transform their lifestyles to value health over the instant gratification of toxic food choices and sedentary behavior. It infuriated him that he would have to operate the Academy under the guise of a cooking school. "Can't open soon enough!"

"I hear you, Doc," Lou said as he drove toward a large carriage house. Though it looked ancient and crumbling, its wide, high door opened with the push of Lou's remote control, and the bus drove inside. Once the door closed behind them, the interior of the garage became an elevator shaft that took them 1,200 feet below the surface of Detroit, to its vast and historic salt mines, whose tunnels contained 100 miles of roads and covered 1,500 acres.

Two operational elevator shafts existed in Detroit that were fully functional for the mining of salt that continues today. However other secret shafts—such as this one—were built to serve those with less legitimate intentions, such as transporting illegal alcoholic beverages.

The LifeQuest Movement had obtained maps of the tunnels, and had navigated routes connecting this entrance to the headquarters in a nondescript warehouse building near the Detroit River. Now, in the tunnel that was wide enough for three buses to drive side-by-side with plenty of overhead space, Dr. Wise looked out the window at the rough-hewn walls of salt and occasional piles of salt boulders.

"Man, this place is fascinating," Dr. Wise said. "Perfect for the bunker and the LifeQuest Headquarters."

"We'll be there in 15 minutes," Lou said, focusing forward as the headlights provided the only light in the dark tunnel, and their route glowed green on the military-grade, undetectable GPS display in the dashboard. "It's good to have friends in high places. I just hope they stay loyal, don't fold under pressure, and keep everything classified for the long haul."

Dr. Wise could consider nothing less than his network maintaining the utmost secrecy. Otherwise a whole lot of people would be going to prison, and that would allow food and fat to continue killing Americans, with no end in sight.

A short time later, the bus pulled into a smaller tunnel and a gate closed behind it. Then two metal sliding doors opened beside the bus, and there stood two young, African American men in dark jeans, Timberland boots, and tight-fitting, black athletic shirts emblazoned with the LifeQuest logo over their big muscles. Each had an AK-47 automatic rifle strapped over his shoulder.

"Welcome back!" said brothers Hank and Henry, who had lost 150 pounds each after undergoing bariatric surgery a few years ago. The deaths of their morbidly obese parents had inspired them to take action to save their own lives. Now, as bodybuilders with college degrees in nutrition—along with their streetwise expertise with weapons—they had committed to the Movement to save others.

"Please come in, Dr. Wise, Lou," said older brother Hank. Henry closed the gate behind them and pushed buttons on a shiny new panel on the wall.

"You two look as healthy and strong as ever!" Dr. Wise said, welling with pride over their incredible transformation. "Everything going according to plan?"

"Better," Hank said. "Although as far as security goes, when we got the call about the decoy, and the FBI hunting for you, we cranked it up to Level Three. Not takin' any chances."

A panel in the wall slid open to reveal the Control Room. As sleek and modern as a spaceship cockpit, it featured a wall of video monitors showing dozens of areas throughout the warehouse, the surrounding exterior grounds, the 20 sub-basements, and the salt mine tunnel that provided the most discreet entrance to HQ.

"Welcome home," said Security Chief Shane Browne, who stood and stepped forward. With a platinum buzz cut and blue eyes exuding both compassion and a hardcore fighting spirit, she flashed a bright smile. Her black, long-sleeved LifeQuest shirt hugged the impressive muscles in her arms, shoulders, and abs. A holster held an automatic handgun at her hip.

"I definitely put the right woman in charge of security," Dr. Wise said. "You are looking more buff than when you did the bodybuilding competition last year."

"Gotta say, Doc, the fitness center you built here is out-standing," she said.

"You can thank the Grazia family for their generous donation to outfit our exercise equipment and activity rooms," Dr. Wise said, nodding toward the half-dozen staff members who stood at attention to greet him. Each had a chair and a workstation to monitor communications, logistics, inventory, weapons, and other areas.

"Come in," Chief Browne said, "I want to show you all the upgrades to the control room while you were away." She pointed to the largest screen that was surrounded by many smaller ones.

"We can zoom in on any space in this facility," she said, touching a screen to show a close-up of guards flanking the entrance to the auditorium where men, women, and children were entering to hear Dr. Wise speak. The guards held automatic rifles while other LifeQuest staff members used small devices to scan the wristbands of every person entering. This included the 250 people who lived here thus far, as well as supporters who were allowed entrée for this morning's meeting.

Chief Browne touched the screen, whose live images corresponded with what she was saying. "Here's the salt mine entrance, a 360-degree view on the exteriors of the mansion, and here at the warehouse."

The video screen showed what looked like an abandoned warehouse on Detroit's industrial waterfront. Not a single car or person was visible on the glass- and garbage-strewn lot around the warehouse. Then a blue truck appeared. A metal gate rose over a huge garage door, and the truck entered the warehouse.

"Our sensors can provide video tracking for any person or vehicle here in the LifeQuest HQ," Chief Browne said as video switched to the interior of the warehouse. The truck rumbled over the cracked cement floor, past rusty poles and weeds, to a cement wall that opened to reveal a freight elevator. The truck drove in, the doors closed behind it, and the brick wall gave no indication that it was hiding an elevator.

"We can monitor the entrance," Chief Browne continued, "all 20 sub-basements, all residential, common, and classified areas of the facility, as well as the upper floors of the warehouse. You can see we've also got cameras in the classrooms, the garden, the fitness room, the dining hall, the auditorium."

Dr. Wise felt a jolt of confidence that all of the planning he and his leaders had done over the past five years was being implemented now. That included their eight levels of security, with One being the lowest, and Eight being "Defense Under Attack." The goal was to keep this underground network secret for as long as it took to reverse and eradicate obesity, and that would take years.

"I'm still concerned about people coming and going, and being followed," Dr. Wise said.

"So were we," Chief Browne said, touching another screen. "That's why we built this entrance in Eastern Market. The warehouses and stores there are so busy with trucks and customers coming in and out, LifeQuesters as well as our delivery folks can enter unnoticed through here."

The video monitor showed Zeke's Barn, a fresh produce market and restaurant whose exterior stands overflowed with colorful fruits and vegetables beside an outdoor café where people were eating, and a delivery truck customers streamed in and out of the front door, and a delivery truck exited through a double-wide garage.

"Johnny Valentine used to work there," Chief Browne said, and once he got the owner to join LifeQuest, the owner showed him a tunnel from bootlegging days during Prohibition, and we connected the dots." Video showed a tunnel and doorway where several people were exiting a van and entering yet another pair of sliding metal doors into LifeQuest HQ. "We're getting more and more supporters every day. And thanks to our friends in Silicon Valley who rigged this room with the highest-tech devices to evade detection, along with the expertise of our military veterans, I think we are going to win this battle, Doc." Chief Browne shook his hand. "Honored to help you accomplish this mission, Sir."

Dr. Wise's guarded optimism spiked to all-out excitement when he stepped into the auditorium a few minutes later. Cheers and applause exploded from hundreds of people in the Greek-style amphitheatre. They stood on 10 wide tiers that formed a descending semi-circle around a stage.

Dr. Wise raised his arms and said, "Thank you" several times as he walked down to the stage, where a woman in a LifeQuest T-shirt placed a microphone in his hand. "Thank you," he said, amplified with static. "I want to thank all of you for pulling off Day One of the Revolution!"

The people—every race, age, religion, and size—erupted with applause once again. Dr. Wise's leaders stood on each side of him.

"Outside, the sun is rising on a new day," he said, "and this is the dawn of a healthier future for America. So you could call this a pep rally, but you'll also be getting your marching orders for the next six months."

The audience became quiet as Dr. Wise said, "You may have heard the President talk about how the National Guard was rolling out to protect the types of places that we put out of commission today. Factories, restaurants, distribution sites, et cetera."

Throughout the audience, Dr. Wise saw many of his benefactors or their representatives. They included CEOs of private companies that were enduring tremendous financial strain from an increasingly obese and sickly workforce. Many of them had read Dr. Wise's book and attended his lively lectures around town. Then, as the Congressional hearing had approached, they had called and visited Dr. Wise to say that if the Obesity Act were defeated, they would provide generous financial backing to implement and sustain as many of the points in his book as possible. That offering had opened the door for Dr. Wise to invite them to support and/or participate in the secret, underground LifeQuest Movement.

Among them was his new patient, Lucia Grazia, whose son Angelo now sat in the audience, wearing a dark hoodie. Dr. Wise loved that the notorious mafia don wanted make a positive impact on the world while also losing the weight that would have killed him with sleep apnea, high blood pressure, diabetes, and heart disease.

"To all of our benefactors," Dr. Wise said, "this is a revolution. It won't be quick, and it won't be easy. But your support will help us endure for the long haul, because that's what it'll take to save lives and eradicate obesity for the next generation."

Dr. Wise turned to the men and women standing beside him, then he told the audience, "I want to introduce you to our leadership."

Dr. Wise looked at the tall man in military camouflage to his left. "This is Peter Glass, a retired Army General. I've known him since the third grade here in Detroit. I've trusted him with our short-term and long-term strategic planning." Dr. Wise handed him the microphone.

"Thanks, Mike," said Peter, whose deep, booming voice had a rapid-fire cadence. "Now, as you know, last night, someone tried to kill a man they thought was Dr. Wise. The FBI is after him, because authorities are trying to figure out, 'What the hell just happened?'"

The audience laughed. "We really blind-sided them, all across the country. And I confess, I'm stunned to report, that not a single person in the LifeQuest Movement was arrested today while performing our first anti-obesity initiatives."

Cheers exploded from the audience.

"That's the good news," General Glass said. "The bad news is, authorities will be looking for us, especially in the coming weeks. So we have to stay low, and only discuss the Movement through communication methods that you know are secure. No email, social media, hand-written notes or letters, or conversations on phone lines at work or unsecured lines."

Dr. Wise added, "I can't say I'm glad we're here, because if it's come to this, we definitely have a big problem to solve across America. But I am glad that we all have the guts to do something about it."

He explained that the LifeQuest Movement was utilizing the Obesity Eradication tactics from his book within commune-style communities that included organic farming and schools. Integral to the Movement were aggressive weight loss programs that included nutrition and health education, exercise programs, and leadership training. He was also teaching people to retrain their brains about standards of beauty, especially the "bigger is better" attitude amongst African Americans.

"This is a revolution on every level," Dr. Wise said. "In addition to our profound disruption in the food industry, we are campaigning to change cultural beliefs about health and beauty. Big is not beautiful if it's unhealthy. Fat acceptance is not acceptable. Therefore, our allies who remain out in the open are using social media to campaign against these skewed viewpoints to make everyone see that healthy is beautiful. Healthy is sexy. Vegetables are vogue."

The men and women facing him cheered.

"But leave no doubt," Dr. Wise said. "This is war!"

Johnny Valentine, his wife, Layna, and their two children, were in the front row, now living here in the LifeQuest HQ along with other Food Fight Posse members and their families. Dr. Wise remembered how far Johnny had come, and pride welled inside him.

"Federal soldiers are after us," Dr. Wise said. "We could be prosecuted for malicious destruction of property. We are fugitives. And thankfully our military veterans who've joined the Movement along with our Silicon Valley supporters have outfitted this compound with military-grade technology that makes us undetectable by our enemies. This will allow us to continue doing the work required to end the obesity epidemic in America!"

Everyone in the tiers shot to their feet and cheered.

"We must all execute the utmost vigilance for our safety and secrecy of what's going on here," Dr. Wise said. "More and more people are joining the Movement every day, and we've opened more underground housing centers for intake, detox, and nutrition education across the city and across America. Much work lies ahead, and I want to thank all of you in advance for your unwavering commitment to the cause."

Dr. Wise scanned the crowd, praying that all of their lives would be spared as they worked to save the lives of millions of others. He felt a chill. *I'm a wanted man. Lord help me win this war on obesity—and defeat the enemy within—before they take me out...*

Six Months Later
Chapter 26

IN THE GNN NEWSROOM in New York, Anastasia Lee stood in front of a screen splashed with a huge graphic that said: "Obesity Backlash!" She inhaled deeply to calm her anger about what would be broadcast over the global airwaves for the next 30 minutes.

"Good morning, I'm Anastasia Lee. Welcome to a special edition of *America Now*. Today marks the six-month anniversary of the Congressional hearing that defeated the Obesity Eradication Act, and the subsequent attack on the processed food industry."

A photo of Dr. Wise testifying in Congress appeared on the screen. "Dr. Michael Wise is a wanted man, accused of orchestrating a multi-billion-dollar attack on the food industry that occurred immediately following the hearing. However, the author, activist, and founder of the LifeQuest Movement may be dead—"

Video showed a man who looked like Dr. Wise being shot during a raucous protest outside a manufacturing plant for GMO vegetable seeds. "Authorities believe this man—who collapsed under a hail of bullets at this protest where four people died—was Dr. Wise. The man vanished into a vehicle and authorities have no information about whether he survived and if he did, where he might be. Efforts to find him in his hometown of Detroit, where the LifeQuest Movement is believed to be headquartered, have proven unsuccessful."

Anastasia turned to another camera and said, "While Dr. Michael Wise and his underground LifeQuest Movement had intended that their guerilla warfare on the food industry would inspire Americans to make healthier food selections and lose weight—" Anastasia stifled a cough—"their brazen attacks have actually caused a backlash against healthy lifestyles."

A montage of video showed: Angry drivers pulling away from Heavenly Burgers, Taco Temptation, and Georgia Fried Chicken restaurants emblazoned with signs on the windows saying, "Closed due to attacks on our manufacturing facilities, trucking fleets, and restaurants."

Movie theatres giving away free popcorn, candy, and soda, to lure droves of movie-goers back while their snack stands were rebuilt, bigger and better.

And gun-toting National Guard members standing at doorways to fast food restaurants as well as Creamy Dream, both its flagship near Detroit, as well as its eight new restaurants in cities across America.

As the video played, Anastasia said, "Many Americans were so outraged about the disruption of their food supply, they vowed to eat out more to support the industry that was under attack by Dr. Michael Wise and the LifeQuest Movement. For this special report today, I interviewed a number of leaders on this topic, and here's what they had to say."

The screen showed Anastasia interviewing US Congressman Brace Buxton. "Senator Buxton, talk about how public sentiment has taken a sharp turn against any type of government regulation on food, advertising, weight, and lifestyle."

He looked as impeccably groomed as usual, in a crisp blue suit, white shirt, and red tie, as he said, "Anastasia, what you're seeing is an affirmation that the men, women, and children of America believe that neither the government nor some radical activist group have any place at their kitchen tables. The government takes a 'hands-off' approach when it comes to dictating what Americans can put into their mouths. This is the hottest issue of our time, and it's a victory for our citizens to maintain their freedom of choice. After all, America is founded on the principles of life, liberty, and the pursuit of happiness. We must always fight to preserve that."

Next, video showed Anastasia interviewing Congressman Samuel "Uncle Sam" Addams.

"Congressman Addams," she said, "you announced your bid for the presidency, and you want to promote healthy living, you said, without quote-criminalizing obesity-unquote. What does that mean?"

The Congressman nodded and said, "That was a reference to the radical and absurd proposals that Dr. Michael Wise made in his book and during his testimony six months ago. He proposed imposing legal regulation on how much people should weigh, and he even wanted to impose penalties on corporations whose work forces do not conform to his radical viewpoint."

Anastasia asked, "Then what, as president, would you propose as the solution to this problem that is actually costing corporations money by having to care for an increasingly sick and sluggish workforce as obesity rates escalate?"

"It starts in the schools," Addams said. "Well I wholeheartedly endorse the campaign that has already begun to be implemented by Golden Harvest Foods to help cash-strapped public schools. They are revolutionizing the school cafeteria experience by transforming them into safe havens of good food, wholesome activities, homework centers, and gathering places for the entire community. And—"

"Full disclosure here," Anastasia said, "your running mate is Douglass Golden, CEO of Golden Harvest Foods, which also owns the top three fast food chains. Is it true that you intend to facilitate government contracts to replace public school cafeterias with Heavenly's Burgers, Taco Temptation, and Georgia Fried Chicken?"

Addams shook his head. "That's the propaganda that my opponents are spewing to discredit my intentions and my integrity. That is a blatant conflict of interest. Our intent is to introduce healthy food options in some of America's hardest-hit communities—in our inner cities and rural areas alike. These community cafeterias will ensure that children get three square meals every day, along with a feeling of safety and security."

Anastasia's skin crawled. Something about Addams was so slippery, even more slippery than Buxton. But these were the leaders and the newsmakers, and her producers insisted that their opinions be heard. The same went for the next interview.

I hate giving screen time to these people.

GNN had tried without success to find Dr. Wise or anyone from the LifeQuest Movement to interview them about how they planned to eradicate obesity without the government's assistance. But even the network's Pulitzer Prize-winning investigative journalists had failed to find him or anyone who would talk on camera or even admit any affiliation with the organization. Likewise, Anastasia had heard whispers at a cocktail party that Silicon Valley billionaires and mafia dons alike had joined the Movement, but again, she had nothing to substantiate these rumors.

Anastasia felt that she was part of the problem by amplifying voices of people who were not part of the solution. *Sometimes I think I should join that Movement, because these money-grubbing piranhas are leading Americans' health to hell in a handbasket.*

She inhaled deeply as the image of a black woman with perfect make-up, movie star hair, a designer dress—and an obese body—appeared on the graphic screen behind her.

"Next, I interviewed the popular comedienne, Maya Mink, who is on her own crusade to convince America that big is beautiful," Anastasia said. "I visited her on the set of her popular sitcom, *Mama's Blues*, about a single mother who dreamed of being a blues singer, but is instead struggling to raise three teenagers in the ghetto. When I visited, Maya was preparing for a photo shoot to promote her new talk show."

Video showed Anastasia in Maya's dressing room, where the actress was modeling a red sequined evening gown with a dramatic feather boa neckline. As she twirled in the three-way mirror, running her hands with long acrylic red fingernails over her plump stomach and hips, Maya said, "Girl, I am as bad as I wanna be!"

Anastasia laughed. "That's your motto on the show, and to the women of America."

"It sure is, honey," she said. "I am a five-foot-five, 300-pound, black-diva-queen, and I want every big girl and woman out there to feel just as confident as I do. Skinny women like you—" she did a body-scan of Anastasia "—can't understand what I'm sayin'. Y'all too busy running to the gym and eating rice cakes. But guess what, there's a reason I've been on the covers of every women's magazine out there. Big is beautiful. And the average woman can relate to what I'm saying."

Anastasia refused to endorse this idea, but she had to be tactful. "Maya, what is your response to the reality that obesity causes health problems, including diabetes, hypertension, cancer, and even early death?"

"All my numbers are good," she said. "Including the number of fine men who want me. Black men don't want to hug up with a clothes hanger, honey. They want us to have some meat on our bones. And honey, when it comes to the behind, you can never have too much booty."

Anastasia looked pensive. "Do you think you're fooling yourself into thinking that being overweight could possibly be healthy?"

"Oh, honey, no," she said. "Girl, we need to fatten you up! Look like you'll blow away in the wind!"

"Do you ever wish you were thinner?" Anastasia asked.

"Oh, no, sweetheart," the actress said. "My attitude is, I just don't try anymore. I'm done tryin' to live on carrot sticks and lettuce. I exercise, and all my numbers are good at my check-ups. It's possible to be big and healthy, too. So I'm gonna continue to be bad as I wanna be for as long as I damn well please."

Maya headed to her make-up chair, where two stylists began doing her hair and make-up.

"Tell me about your plans for the future," Anastasia said.

"Well, on top of my sexy clothing and lingerie line for big women, I'm planning to open a chain of restaurants called, of course, Bad As We Wanna Be!" she said with a laugh. "Our motto is, 'Welcome to America's Most Delicious Melting Pot,' because our menu lets you go around the world without leaving the table. You can eat every kind of ethnic food in one spot. I'm hiring Thai people to make the Thai food, and Mexicans to make the Mexican food, and some Italians to make the pasta, and of course some black folks to make the soul food, so every bite will taste like you just earned a new stamp on your passport, without leaving town. And no, Anastasia, you won't find any calorie counters here. Our food is full-fat and fabulous."

The videotaped interview ended and Anastasia's report cut back to the TV studio, standing before a large graphic of a smiling woman wearing an apron and holding a pie.

"As you can see, the backlash against the war on obesity is taking many voices, and many forms," Anastasia said. "Next, my report takes me to the South."

Video showed Anastasia standing beside the woman with the pie in an upscale country kitchen.

"I'm here with Wilma Ramsey in the Mississippi home she shares with her husband, Roger Ramsey, spokesman for the Centers for Disease Control," Anastasia says. "Wilma's wildly popular cookbook, *Wilma's Down Home Southern Kitchen*, has inspired her future plan to open a cooking school, her TV show will begin airing next month."

Anastasia glanced at all the grease bubbling on the stove, the basket of biscuits steaming on the counter, and the peach cobbler baking in the oven. *You couldn't pay me to eat any of this*, she thought while smiling at Wilma.

"Everything looks so delicious," Anastasia said. "Wilma, tell me, why do you think America loves the foods that you prepare?"

Wilma, with her Southern accent and grandmotherly floral print dress over her plump body, said, "Well, I think when life is rough and bitter, we want something soothing and sweet to make us feel better. Sometimes the economy is tough. We may face uncertainty or deal with grief or loss of a job. Divorce. Our sons and daughters have been overseas fighting in wars. So when we're stressed out, we turn to the comfort foods we enjoyed as a child. Macaroni and cheese; stew; cobbler, cake and pie; fried chicken, of course; candied yams; grilled cheese; and buttermilk biscuits with honey."

Anastasia nodded. "But what about all the information your husband presents from the CDC, about eating a healthy diet?"

Wilma sampled a biscuit and smiled. "Well, I always say you can enjoy this food in moderation. We have a home gym upstairs, and we like to take a nice stroll around the property here. My husband hunts, so he gets plenty of exercise out in the woods. But the average person doesn't want to sit and count calories at Sunday dinner. You just want to relax and enjoy yourself. We might indulge one of my home-cooked meals on a Sunday, then have lighter meals during the week."

Wilma offered a piece of fried chicken to Anastasia, who politely declined. Then Wilma started mixing cake batter. "You know my favorite saying is, 'Everything goes better with butter and brown sugar!'"

After that segment, Anastasia interviewed someone from America's biggest pizza chain, Pizza King, who said their most popular item was called Meat Monster Jam, which was topped with double cheese and five types of meats.

"Sales of Meat Monster Jam have doubled in just six months," the spokesman said. "Whereas when we introduced our low fat cheese pizzas, it was a disaster. People want real cheese with the traditional taste and texture of cheese. And that includes the fat."

After that, the report included a visit to a men's clothing store chain that launched an advertising blitz aimed at taking the shame out of being a big man. Anastasia concluded her special report with video of an 800-pound woman, sitting at a kitchen table and eating a huge platter of pancakes, bacon, and eggs.

"Some people are literally so fed up with hearing that they should exercise, eat in moderation, and maintain a healthy weight that they're doing the opposite—in the extreme," Anastasia says. "Tomorrow on my HEALTH IN AMERICA segment, I'll introduce you to this woman in America's fattest city, Little Rock, Arkansas. Rachel Jones says she wants to become the world's fattest woman, so she does nothing but eat all day long."

Video shows the woman eating a pile of syrup-drenched pancakes while her three obese children devour enormous slices of pizza, each washing it down with their own liter bottles of sugary soda.

"Neighbors have asked Child Protective Services to remove her children because she is putting their lives in danger by encouraging them to become obese, which can lead to dangerous health problems," Anastasia said. "What are your thoughts? I invite you to log onto the GNN website and share your opinions. Should a parent be charged with neglect for allowing children to eat junk food to excess and become obese?"

As she stood in the studio and commercials signaled that her special report was finished, Anastasia was consumed by a bad feeling. Why were Americans allowing their appetites to blind them to the dangers of obesity? And what would happen if this trend continued? She thought of her children… and their children.

I have to do more to save them from this terrible trend…

Chapter 27

JERI BREWSTER WAS AT her desk, making phone calls and taking notes on a story summarizing the dramatic changes in the United States since the "food riots" that started rumors that Dr. Michael Wise was dead.

I think he's very much alive, and I'm going to find him! She was considering an undercover investigation by disguising herself and infiltrating the LifeQuest Movement where Dr. Wise was rumored to be leading a militant underground network.

She had tried to contact him on the same cell phone number that she had when he wrote the Foreword for her book. But that line was disconnected and she had been unable to reach him. The Movement included people from every walk of life who were united with the common goal of getting and staying healthy. Yet the underground was so secretive and stealthy, even Jeri had yet to find credible confirmation of its existence and location.

I have to find him! I have to hear his vision on how to reverse the terrible tide of backlash against efforts to reduce obesity. I have to broadcast his message in the paper and everywhere!

Now, having watched Anastasia Lee's disturbing report, Jeri flipped through the articles that she had written over the past six months, chronicling the many dramatic changes that have occurred in the United States.

The first article described Anti-Terrorism Technologies, and how the US government implemented a requirement for every man, woman, and child to have a computer chip implanted inside their left wrist. Trademarked as the SafeChip, it could detect whether an individual was carrying explosives. The chip enabled the government to track every person on US soil. Farmers received a special SafeChip, as well as authorization to possess fertilizer, which could be used to make explosives. Travelers to the US had to get a temporary chip that monitored their time and helped the government enforce their departure when their visas expired. The chip in children also eliminated the need for Amber Alerts because any missing child could immediately be located by his or her chip.

To accomplish this massive monitoring system, the government rigged the nation's satellite system as well as surveillance towers on earth with the high-tech advent of Raman Spectroscopy. It had the ability to scan a whole city in microseconds to determine activity. The Raman Spectroscopy system could identify any individual, anywhere, by picking up on the unique "chirp" or "ping" and electronic fingerprint assigned to each person. This would be useful for detecting bombs or explosives. In addition, the government had portable Raman Spectroscopy devices that enabled a federal agent to track individuals from cars, airplanes, helicopters, boats, and even on foot.

Of course the ACLU, liberal politicians, and every other civil liberty group protested the mandatory introduction of the chip. But the government determined that it was justified in the name of saving Americans from terrorism. That had proven correct, as the country had not suffered a single incident of terrorism on American soil since the chip's introduction.

Many Americans, however, had exemption from the SafeChip. Those included: many high-ranking military personnel; individuals with no history of mental illness, terrorist ties, criminal record or activity that the State Department considered radical; as well as journalists, elected officials and law enforcement personnel. However, Congress was likely to pass a bill very soon that would expand the requirement of a SafeChip implantation to every person in the United States, with no exemptions.

Those who refused the SafeChip risked a $10,000 fine and prison sentence. Many of the first who were forced to receive a chip were individuals living in the United States who were born elsewhere. Since it occurred in conjunction with the passage of laws around immigration reform, this mandate sparked outrage, even riots in communities with large immigrant populations.

Criminals had replicated the military's anti-chip muzzling device that blocked the chip's ability to emit a trackable signal. As a result, criminals were engaging in high-tech bank robberies; possession of such devices carried a sentence of life in prison.

Jeri was extremely suspicious when the lead presidential candidate made the SafeChip a major tenet of his campaign. With tremendous fanfare, Massachusetts Congressman Samuel "Uncle Sam" Addams announced his bid for the Presidency. Something about that man was so plastic, but Jeri hadn't quite pinpointed it. A story about him was percolating in her mind.

Coinciding with the advent of the SafeChip was the aggressive marketing of the "Device," a combination of a cell phone, tablet, and computer. Its microphone could be worn as a tiny, earring-type device that also took photographs, recorded video and processed information about the individual to ascertain location, nearby businesses, weather conditions, and much more.

The Device was programmed to its owner's biological data, so it would only work in the possession of its owner. In addition, the Device was programmed to know his or her preferences on every level. Because it was tapped into the SuperNet, the network that took the Internet to a supersonic level, it enabled advertisers to aggressively target individuals, anywhere.

Jeri viewed all of these stories as connected. The common theme was that money-driven powers—including companies and government leaders—were robbing individuals of privacy and freedom, leaving them to make choices in an environment that promoted and even celebrated unhealthy lifestyles.

She glanced over print-outs of other stories that she'd written about the changing world since Dr. Wise's disappearance. Each one emphasized the importance of the revolution that he was leading. Perhaps most disturbing was what was happening in schools.

FAST FOOD CHAINS TRANSFORM CASH-STRAPPED SCHOOL CAFETERIAS AND COMMUNITY CULTURE: ARE THEY HELPING OR HURTING?

by Jerralynn Brewster

The American Daily News

Popular fast-food chains claim they are coming to the rescue of public schools by taking over cafeterias and creating family-oriented community centers offering breakfast, lunch, and dinner for families and people in surrounding neighborhoods.

"Heavenly's is our saving grace," said Detroit Public Schools Superintendent Jane Reynolds, standing in a bright, clean community room as children and tutors do homework after school while snacking on milk and cookies supplied by Heavenly's. "Our families are simply loving the transformation that the food industry is so generously providing."

Cindy Blane, chief marketing officer for Golden Harvest Foods, which owns Heavenly's Burgers, said the company's altruistic relationship with schools is grooming young people for success by providing mentors, college scholarships, sponsorships for team sports, and even field trips to visit museums and college campuses. "We are pioneering new territory with a long-term strategy for students' success. Our innovation is actually cultivating better relationships between parents and children, and it's making our young people excited about education. We are extremely proud to partner with our public schools and communities across America."

Parents praised the support as well. "My son can't wait to get to school in the morning and have his Superhero Cereal & Sausage Breakfast with his friends," said mother of three Rose Neale. "His grades have improved because he likes to stay after and work with the tutors. I think the cookies help."

Or are they hurting? Critics of the fast-food fix for public schools say the companies are infiltrating a sacred space to brainwash children and parents with what looks like a goodwill endeavor, but is actually a ploy to get people hooked on their unhealthy foods.

"This is an obscene abuse of power as wealthy corporations exploit the financial vulnerability of public schools and the children and parents who are part of those communities," said Mick Bates, founder of the nonprofit Save Our Schools organization that protested the fast-food outlets inside schools. "This is

a set-up for children to become hooked on fast food, and by eating it every day, sometimes three meals a day, including weekends because these so-called community centers have weekend programming for kids and families, the children are being poisoned and condemned to being unhealthy, overweight, and having shorter lifespans than their parents."

In addition, the food companies are also accepting federally-funded food stamps at the cafeterias in schools, a measure that Senator Brace Buxton supported.

Under the new partnership with food companies and schools, all public school children receive an eBooklet of coupons for the fast-food chain in their school. They have enough coupons for breakfast and lunch during the day, then additional passes to bring their entire families back to discounted and sometimes free meals for school-night dinners, snacks, and even weekend meals. The restaurant keeps its dining area open and has made it friendly for kids to play and do their homework while their parents hang out in a lounge with big-screen TVs showing sports events and movies. Of course, "study snacks" are offered along with treats for the parents.

The fast-food restaurants in schools are part of the most popular international chains: Heavenly's Burgers; Georgia Fried Chicken; Taco Temptation; and Pizza King.

Next, Jeri glanced at the article about how schools and colleges were adjusting to the obesity epidemic by providing larger desks or simply long rows of tables with bench-style seating. She'd written a similar story about how the auto industry was adding features to vehicles to cater to the obesogenic world. The article said, "Seats are advertised as 'roomy and comfortable' with 'ample leg room' and 'plenty of breathing room behind the wheel' to accommodate big bellies. Roofs are higher because sitting on thick layers of fat makes a seated person 'taller.'"

Another article described how the obesity epidemic was eliminating bipartisan blocks on Capitol Hill. "Amazingly, the obesity epidemic has been the unifying factor to rid Capitol Hill of bipartisan blocks between Republicans and Democrats," the article said. "Turns out, the huge fortunes being made from the food industry, pharmaceutical companies, and the healthcare industry are lining the pockets of money- and status-hungry politicians as if an oil boom were occurring on US soil."

Jeri wanted nothing more than to write a series of articles about these topics from the perspective of Dr. Wise—how each item could be stopped and reversed. But first she needed to find him, and write an insider's story about how the LifeQuest Movement was working to save America from its love affair with food.

Chapter 28

Katie Matthews feared she was truly addicted to chocolate. She couldn't stop thinking about it, and she wished she could spend every minute eating it. But she couldn't. She had to take care of the kids, her husband, her full-time work schedule, the house, her Alzheimer's-afflicted mother-in-law, and serving as president of the scrapbooking club. Oh, and figuring out how they could finance a new roof. Plus Katie was getting the kids ready for two weeks away at a science camp as a school field trip. That would be a much-needed break for her and Dan, even though paying for camp had cut into their savings for the new roof.

As did the costs of eating out and buying bigger clothes, as she'd had to do for the kids recently. All their school clothes from last year were too small, because they were growing taller and wider.

She'd also noticed that Dan had recently purchased three sets of work pants and shirts, two sizes bigger his last. He hadn't told her, but she of course had made the discovery in the laundry pile. She didn't have to buy new nurse's scrubs to accommodate her recent weight gain because she was still wearing the super roomy ones she'd bought as maternity wear *five years ago.*

She felt so ashamed about that—especially when one of the skinny nurses had quipped, "Katie you're such a fertile turtle! When's baby number five due?" Katie had laughed it off, but all she wanted to do was eat chocolate to soothe her shame and hurt feelings. She hadn't even shot down the rumor-in-the-making that she was pregnant.

So now, after leaving work and before picking up the kids from aftercare at school, before she headed home to make dinner, Katie couldn't have been happier.

She had a full 30 minutes to indulge her obsession at Creamy Dream's drive-up, take-out service. They made it so convenient! All she had to do was touch the app on her phone, choose what she wanted, drive up to what looked like a gingerbread house garage, pull in, roll down the window, and one of the waitresses would come to the window with her order.

She didn't even need to exchange money, because the app was preloaded with money from her bank account. She loved how it felt so private; nobody could see her in a drive-thru line. More and more restaurants were taking the shame out of eating, and that was such a relief.

Plus, even though somewhere in her mind she knew she had to transfer money onto the restaurant app, it almost felt like she was getting this treat for free because she didn't have to handle money. She never had to see the receipt either, reminding her of her indulgence. That removed even more guilt over spending money that should have gone into savings.

Meanwhile, Katie didn't love the idea that her kids' school was chosen to test the fast-food companies' proposal to take over cafeterias. At least she'd know that the kids ate a hot meal that they liked. Half the time they said the school cafeteria food was so bad, they just threw it out and bought chips and pop out of the school vending machines anyway. The same went for days when the cafeteria tried to serve a "healthy" meal like salads with grilled chicken.

Katie was so overwhelmed, she checked this off as one less thing she'd have to worry about. Even better was the fact that as the pilot school in this new program, the meals would be totally free for the entire school year!

Maybe the money she and Dan saved on school lunch money could be use for the new roof...

She pulled her vehicle into one of the parking spaces in the back of the Creamy Dream parking lot to enjoy her Chocolate Addict's Dream. And that helped her forget everything but the orgasmic tastes and textures on her tongue.

Chapter 29

General Brewster had a very bad feeling about returning to the Republic. He'd been re-assigned to Washington, DC for about five months, ever since his private meeting with the Joint Chiefs of Staff occurred shortly after the historic attacks on the food industry.

The Joint Chiefs granted facetime after the General's numerous attempts to speak directly with US President David Alexander were declined, even when the President came to the Republic to visit the Allied troops.

"I have information that shows the United States is in grave danger," General Brewster had told the Joint Chiefs, before divulging what Sergeant Alvarez had discovered, including that presidential advisor Gerald Blane was a terrorist.

The Joint Chief of the Air Force let out a robust laugh. "General!" he exclaimed. "Sounds like you need a mental health check. Your hypothesis is preposterous—obviously the result of bogus intelligence."

A short time later, as the President spoke to the troops on the base, Blane confronted General Brewster in the men's bathroom.

"Hey, Wild Bill, I'd be careful with that creative propaganda of yours," Blane said with a threatening glint in his eyes. "Wouldn't want you to choke on your own words."

"If anybody goes down," General Brewster responded, "it'll be you."

That afternoon, the General said goodbye to Bullet, who officially retired.

"Remember to help my daughter if she ever needs you," he told his protégé.

"Anytime, anywhere," Bullet said, "for all you've done for me, Wild Bill. I've been saving for this dream for a long time. Montana. Just me, my dog, my guns, and as much hunting and fishing as I can manage."

The General chuckled. "You'll be back. You're a soldier. You'll miss the action."

"No, sir," Bullet said, looking the General in the eyes. "You take care of yourself."

The General hugged Bullet and said, "You're like a son to me. Don't you forget it."

"Got it," Bullet said.

An hour later, American military officials arrived at the General's office and told him he was being reassigned to the Pentagon as part of a campaign to scale back Allied presence in the Republic, now that democracy had allegedly been restored. He was escorted out so abruptly, he did not have time to clean out his office in Trykka.

While in Washington, the General made it his mission to prove Blane was a spy and a terrorist. Through his many excellent relationships that he had cultivated over the years on every level of the military, the General arranged for surveillance of Blane. Not only was the presidential advisor using the White House as his personal playground by abusing his full access to the most sacred chambers, but he was also having an extramarital affair with a French actress. They'd met at the White House Press Corps Dinner. The General had credible sources who had also seen Blane engaging in inappropriate relationships with rogue agents in the FBI and CIA.

Just as the General was ready to present his and Bullet's findings to the President during a meeting that was finally granted, he was ordered to return to the Republic for a two-week mission to gather intelligence about a suspected terrorist cell. The General was well aware that his list of enemies was long and growing longer, both in the Republic and in the Pentagon. All the while, he would be required to provide daily briefings to the Intelligence Committee via live video conferencing. Having waited this long, he vowed to reveal his findings to the President in two weeks, upon his return.

If, by the grace of God, I do return to American soil alive.

Chapter 30

As Jeri Brewster walked across a gravel lot behind an abandoned warehouse on Detroit's riverfront, she had never felt so frustrated about reporting a news story.

Where is Dr. Wise? And where are the LifeQuest Movement's headquarters?

She had a feeling that it was hiding in plain sight, and she was determined to find it. She didn't believe he was dead. She believed he was alive and well, and running his revolution right here, right now. But where?

One of her sources had said he was operating in an underground bunker that was undetectable. But if thousands of people were part of LifeQuest, living in commune-style compounds throughout the city, how could they not be detected while coming and going to the HQ?

Suddenly on a road leading to what appeared to be an abandoned warehouse, she saw a flashy car. A metal gate opened and the vehicle entered. Its license plate said CHANGE. Angelo Grazia! That's it!

Jeri dialed him. "Let me in with you," she said flatly.

"Jeri?" he asked with a laugh as she watched the metal gate close behind his car.

"Let me in."

Silence. "I can't. Not today. Meet me later. I'll explain." He hung up.

Jeri lit up with an idea. Somehow she would go undercover and pose as a LifeQuest recruit, with the newspaper's help in obtaining a fake identity and background check, and get an inside view of the Movement. She tried reaching her editor Shareese by phone, but got her voicemail. She texted. No response. So she got into her car and sped back to the newspaper offices.

"You're going!" her Shareese, declared as Jeri hurried in.

"Yes!" Jeri exclaimed; Shareese must have read her text message. Any other assignments could wait. "I figured out how to do it. I just need a new identity that can clear the LifeQuest background check that I heard about."

"Wait," Sharese said, furrowing her brow. "What are you talking about?"

"You said I'm going. *Undercover.*"

"No, I meant you're approved to go to the Republic of the East."

Jeri sighed and took a deep breath. "Six months ago, I was excited about that assignment. Now, the real action is here! All I want to do is dive into the LifeQuest Movement and report about how it truly could stop the obesity epidemic and restore Americans to wellness." She shook her head. "They are like a day late and a dollar short."

"Well the powers that be have made their decision," Shareese said. "You're going."

The trip to the Republic had been delayed for six months due to a State Department warning that things had gotten so tense there, that non-combat American journalists were told not to travel. Then she realized that maybe the required credentials to enter LifeQuest would take just as long as her trip to the Republic. Plus, she'd get to see her father. He'd been in Washington five months and she'd only seen him three times when he came home to visit her and Mom, who was traveling a lot to promote her book.

Now, as Jeri dialed her father, she glimpsed her article in today's paper sitting on the desk. Her story was about how anti-obesity backlash was opening the door to rapid, reckless weight gain for masses of adults and children. She had interviewed the Michigan Democratic Congresswoman who had sponsored the American Obesity Eradication Act. The lawmaker said childhood obesity rates would only get worse if fast food companies were allowed to hijack school cafeterias.

"Jeri," her father answered.

"Dad, you sound tense."

"It's tense over here."

"I just got my assignment," Jeri said. "I'm coming in a few days to do a story about how American ways are fattening the people there."

"Don't come," her father said. "Things here are not as they seem."

"It's my assignment," she said, "and I asked for it."

"Coming here is asking for trouble," her father said. "If Bullet were still here to watch over you, that'd be another story. But he retired to his ranch in Montana, and I'm—" Static.

"Dad?"

"—who to trust... It is very precarious—"

"Dad, you worry too much! Remember, you're the one who's always telling me, 'The pen is mightier than the sword!' I have to do my job; it's my calling to write stories that affect the whole world. Now, I'll see you on Wednesday, and I want to go to lunch with you at that amazing Mediterranean restaurant by your office."

"—don't come. It's a snake pit over here—"

"Dad, I'll see you soon. I love you."

Six months ago, Jeri's assignment had been to explore how American foods were making people in the Republic overweight and obese. Western ways were causing the country's once-impressive health statistics—thanks to the benefits of the traditional Mediterranean diet—to backslide after American fast-food chains being introduced along with video games that promoted sedentary lifestyles for children. For her story, Jeri was going to reference the World Health Organization's latest report about obesity rankings among children in countries around the world, with the Republic showing the fastest and most dramatic increase.

Since then, however, a dramatic decrease had occurred. In fact, the Republic was on its way to achieving a zero obesity rate by: enforcing food rations; forcing residents to adhere to a healthy diet; fining companies whose employees are overweight; taxing and jailing families if any members were two hundred pounds overweight; and teaching a strict nutrition curriculum and exercise program in schools.

And where had they obtained the blueprint for their zero-obesity population? From the pages of Dr. Michael Wise's book, which outlined the defeated American Obesity Eradication Act. Jeri's colleagues had discovered that King Daemon and his Royal Brotherhood had translated the book into their language and given a copy to every citizen. Their philosophy was: "We will make it the law to be healthy. As America gets fatter and sicker, our nation becomes stronger and healthier."

Hand in hand with this was something that one of the newspaper's undercover reporters had discovered: the Republic of the East's secret national doctrine was all about hating America, so they brainwashed the people to think that to be gluttonous, fat, and lazy is to be American. They actually had a slang word for fat: "USA." In addition, they used English words like freedom and liberty to mean "slovenly" and "gluttonous."

As much as she wanted to stay in Detroit to track down Dr. Wise, Jeri's stomach fluttered with excitement to report how the Republic was using the American doctor's blueprint to radically transform its increasingly obesogenic culture to help citizens achieve healthy weights and wellness.

"Wow, this is really dramatic," she said. "My story will be a wake-up call for Washington to finally hear what Dr. Wise is saying, and see that his strategy can have fast, positive results."

Chapter 31

King Daemon smiled as his Ministers reported the dramatic weight loss success that they were monitoring in the households of the Kingdom.

"Only a few families who were obese continue to require a weight loss plan," said the Minister of Health. "Other than that, today's weigh-ins reveal that we have had 98 percent compliance with our plan. Sadly, we have had to enforce punishments on two percent of the population that failed to lose weight or that reverted to gluttony, fled from mandatory weigh-ins, or committed other acts of defiance."

The Minister of Obedience nodded. "Those who were punished serve as reminders to others that this is not a short-term experience. This is the destiny of the Kingdom, and must be maintained forever."

King Daemon looked at the Minister of Propaganda, who said, "We are delivering financial bonuses to every household that has exceeded our expectations in terms of quick weight loss and strict adherence to our rules, which include daily exercise."

"Very good," King Daemon said.

The Minister of Propaganda clicked a remote and a video started on the big screen, showing a GNN report about how "the Republic" was showing the world that they were a utopian democracy where citizens were treated with equality and respect, students were high achievers, and the country's manufacturing industry was producing one of the world's most popular Devices. The report also said that "the Republic" was doing good deeds around the world by: feeding children in Africa; providing shelter for refugees from war-torn countries who were then provided education and job-training; and donating emergency relief to far-away countries during natural disasters.

"The Kingdom is cultivating a reputation as a global leader with educational, manufacturing, and humanitarian endeavors," said the Minister of Propaganda.

The GNN reporter, however, added, "Despite this progress, the Republic of the East remains under surveillance by the United States and its Allies due to past atrocities, including genocide and deadly acts of terrorism."

"They will eat their words!" Daemon shouted. "Get me Eddie!"

One of the Ministers pointed to the screen with a remote and FBI comrade Eddie Smith appeared. He reported about the benefits of its many contacts with the US military. The Kingdom had obtained from these contacts the latest technology that enabled them to track any person in America as well. They also had the decoding devices that helped them penetrate any shields that individuals attempted to use to de-activate their SafeChips. However, it was a constant challenge to obtain the very latest, because the Americans were continuously upgrading the technology to provide barriers to intruders and terrorists.

"We will remain three steps ahead of any adversary, anywhere on the planet," the King exclaimed. "In this twisted web of lies, the American intelligence knows the truth about what is happening in our country. Tell me that the investigative spy work done by General Brewster and his young sidekick is harmless!"

The King glared at the Minister of Military Affairs, who looked startled and said, "We have made our financial contributions to various members of the US military and government. I am confident that our many points of power within the enemy camp will keep the General in check until we have our way with him."

King Daemon nodded as the Minister of Communications aimed a remote at the screen and three more faces appeared in a live video conference: FDA leader Chad Bluestone; the Bakker-Elixir Labs representative; and Linda Blane, head of the American Restaurant Association.

"Tell me that everything is going according to plan," King Daemon ordered. All four people nodded.

"If I may go first," Linda said, "it's all smooth sailing on our end. We've promoted OC-8 in a way that makes every restaurant and company to add it to their recipes, when the time is right. For now, the fast food companies are all in."

"Very good," the king said.

"We've got shifts working overtime to meet your demand, to manufacture enough OC-8 for now and in the future," said the Bakker-Elixir Labs representative, who never showed her face on video. "And we are succeeding."

Chad nodded. "Green light here at the FDA. All systems go."

"Yes," Linda said, "and we've received assurance from our representatives in high-ranking executive positions in the food companies—specifically Heavenly's Burgers, Taco Temptation, and Georgia Fried Chicken—that OC-8 was added to all food being supplied to the three chains' stores in the inner-city areas of: Flint, Michigan; Gary, Indiana; and Cleveland, Ohio."

King Daemon stood and raised his arms, causing the sleeves of his red robe to form a circle around his tall frame. "All of you! Join me in claiming success as we activate our plan to annihilate the Americans, elect a Royal Tricquan to the US Presidency, and assume dominance over our most despised enemy. Then we will take over the world."

Chapter 32

In his office overlooking the service department at the car dealership, Leroy Wise ached with guilt over the fact that his brother was possibly dead. Leroy felt even worse as he believed his brother may have died for a cause that Leroy couldn't embrace, because he refused to give up his favorite foods. He was savoring every bite of his lunch: a big plate of Georgia Fried Chicken with mashed potatoes and gravy, two buttered biscuits, and candied yams. He was also watching the TV on his desk and observing his staff through the window in his office overlooking the entire garage.

"Investigators are still working to confirm whether Dr. Michael Wise did, indeed, die during a protest that—" Leroy stopped chewing. He sobbed for several minutes as the news report continued: "A story now about how some pediatricians' offices are purchasing bigger scales to weigh obese children." The candied yams tasted so good, they helped dull the pain of Leroy's emotions. But glancing out at the garage, and seeing so many overweight men, women, and customers, only filled him with doom. The news report showed children as fat as his own.

How could I be happy that Heavenly's is serving breakfast, lunch, and snacks at the kids' school?

Since their school was participating in a promotional pilot program, lunch would be free for the whole year, and that would save him and Darlene a boatload of money. Plus the community center that Golden Harvest Foods added to the school seemed like a good, safe place for the kids to stay every afternoon, and even on weekends. While Leroy Junior was on a health kick inspired by his athletic prowess, and chose to abstain from fast food, Keisha had never been so happy to attend school and do homework.

But am I being just as reckless with her health as I am with my own? Because I'm definitely paying the piper now. On a dialysis machine.

Leroy dreaded stepping onto Detroit General Hospital's mobile dialysis unit, known as the "dialysis bus," that came to his workplace to accommodate employees from the dealership and surrounding companies. *This is what I get for ignoring all the warnings from my brother, our father, and my doctor.* And Kenya. Ever since she joined the LifeQuest Movement, she was a constant critic of his and Darlene's unhealthy lifestyles. *Lord, that girl is the food and fat police, prosecutor, judge, and jury.*

"I deserve it," he said aloud. "I didn't listen. Leroy reached for his soda pop and took a long swig. He couldn't wait to dig into that slice of cherry pie that he got free because today marked his tenth punch this month on his

George Fried Chicken rewards card. As he ate, a truck pulled into the garage. It was one of the guys, just returning from Flint, about an hour north of Detroit, where he picked up a new vehicle.

Slim Jim Wiley was a low-ranking porter who'd been working at the dealership for about 10 years. Heavyset, high-school educated, about 30, supporting three small children and their mother, who called him her "fiancé" for as long as Leroy has known him, he'd been a hardworking and popular handyman. But today when he pulled up in the dealership truck with the vehicle on the flatbed, he looked ashen. He exited the truck and came to Leroy's office.

"Boss, I don't feel right," Slim Jim said, plopping his 250-pound bulk into the chair facing Leroy's desk.

Sweat covered Slim Jim's round face. He was gripping his chest.

"Aw man, this ain't right," Slim Jim groaned. "I never get sick."

"You drink or eat anything different?" Leroy asked.

"Naw, just my usual when I drive. A couple energy drinks, couple tacos—" Slim Jim's brown face turned even more gray. "Oh, man, my chest—"

Leroy grabbed the phone and called 911. He thought about the training everyone had gotten for the defibrillator. Was Slim Jim having a heart attack? Leroy was about to run into the hall and call for help, but Slim Jim slumped, then slid on the floor, his eyes and mouth wide open.

"Oh, Lord, no!" Leroy shouted. Other employees rushed in. They helped Leroy lay him flat.

"He's not breathing," said one of the mechanics, a former paramedic. "No pulse, no heartbeat." He administered CPR until the ambulance arrived.

But Slim Jim was dead.

Chapter 33

Guarded by retired General Peter Glass, who was holding an automatic weapon and wearing military gear, Dr. Michael Wise stood in front of the amphitheater in the LifeQuest Headquarters as hundreds of people faced him for a weekly assembly.

"Rumor has it that I'm dead," he said, causing the men and women to laugh heartily as Hank and Henry, along with other armed guards, lined the perimeter and the entrances at the top of two main aisles.

"The grim reality, however, is that a lot of people want me dead," Dr. Wise said. "All this backlash against the anti-obesity movement is a nightmare. It makes our work even more difficult. The good news is, more and more people are joining our underground resistance movement. In fact, as of today, we now have 53,875 people across America who are officially part of the LifeQuest Movement."

Three people walked onto the stage with him, and the audience applauded.

"These heroes don't need any introduction," Dr. Wise said, "but I am so proud that Johnny Valentine of Detroit, Boone Davis of Kentucky, and Carmen La Buena of California are here with many of their team members for a strategy session." Dr. Wise turned to them. "You've been instrumental in launching our revolution, and keeping it going for the past six months. It's been rough. Dodging surveillance and arrest has been the biggest obstacle. But thanks to our underground network across America, and our dedicated military veterans who know how to get around undetected, we're having great success. And for that, I want to thank you."

After the applause subsided, Dr. Wise said, "I now want to invite a very special man, a patient of mine, onto the stage, to show the dramatic power of change, physically and philosophically. I want you to meet Luciano Grazia and his son, Angelo."

Both men stepped on stage.

"This man is the salvation of the world," Luciano said, putting his arm around Dr. Wise. "I've lost 104 pounds since he performed my bariatric surgery 8 months ago. And I've never felt better. My son Angelo and I, we believe in what you're doing here. You've got our support one thousand percent, along with the support of a lot of our friends in high places."

The audience exploded with cheers.

Luciano's eyes glistened as he looked at Dr. Wise. "You saved my life," he said. "Whatever you need, I'll support you on that. If you got a problem with anybody, just come to me and we'll take care of it."

The men hugged, then Luciano pointed to Angelo.

"You need anything, Dr. Wise, just work with me through my son."

Angelo then said, "We are the change! And together we can change the world!"

Everyone cheered so loudly, it felt like they'd blow out the walls. Dr. Wise thanked them, then said, "Now I want to give an update on what's happening."

He felt encouraged by the eager faces and prominent individuals who sat before him. But how many were possibly spies? Undercover agents masquerading as LifeQuest seekers? Had anyone been slick enough to trick their way through the strenuous application and screening process to enter this compound? He kept a steady eye on Hank and Henry, who would alert him with a signal and anything were suspicious.

"As you know, the primary goal of the LifeQuest Movement is for all residents to achieve optimum health through good nutrition and exercise," he said. "Followers are committed to bringing others into the community to save their lives and grow the Movement. Ultimately, we want to return people across the country and world to enjoy healthy weights, vitality, and longevity. Now let's bring Layna Valentine up to talk about how she's overseeing our Life Academies."

Layna stood beside Dr. Wise, as Johnny beamed with pride from the front row.

"Thank you, Dr. Wise," she said. "I just returned from visiting three of our 200 Life Academies in every state across America. These are hidden, commune-style communities where obese children, teens and their parents can go to lose weight and become indoctrinated, essentially reprogrammed, to lose weight, change their thinking and eating habits, and experience a rebirth as a healthier person who can then help others do the same. I visited Life Academies in Detroit, Saginaw, and Flint. Each Academy has a community garden where the families grow their own fresh produce."

A video screen behind Layna showed images from the Academies.

"Thanks to our many benefactors," she said, "the families live and learn without having to pay tuition. Also thanks to our high-tech donors, many of these communities are totally 'off the grid' and rely entirely on solar- and wind-powered electricity. Like us, many have dropped out of the mainstream and don't plan to return until what we're doing here becomes the norm for society."

"We can make it happen!" Dr. Wise exclaimed, welling with pride as the audience cheered.

"People are trying to infiltrate the Movement," he said. "We have to be on the lookout for imposters. They want to come in here, see what we're doing, and shut us down. Not to mention, the feds want to take us out, as do countless companies that hate us right now."

He glanced around at the somber faces. "The future of our country depends on what we do here. If we win, America wins. If we lose, then the people we know and love will continue their slow suicide at the kitchen table and in the drive-thru lanes."

Chapter 34

Kenya Wise was so furious as she sat with her family at the dining room table, she was trembling. She wanted to explode with orders to her parents and little sister about how to eat healthier foods. She scanned their heaping servings of fried pork chops, au gratin potatoes from a box, and salad drenched in ranch dressing. Except... Leroy Junior was eating what Kenya had taught him to prepare for himself: an all-organic plate of broccoli, brown rice, and black beans.

"You should all be eating what Leroy Junior is eating!" Kenya pleaded. "Mom, why are you serving heart-attack-on-a-plate for dinner tonight?"

"Hush your mouth, girl!" her mother spat. "This is what your father asked me to make."

Kenya glared at her father, who was forking down the fattening food with gusto. "Dad!" Kenya said with an accusatory tone. "How was dialysis today? Don't you see how wrong it is—that there's a dialysis bus that comes to your job and our neighborhood because so many people need it!"

He cast his eyes down as his daughter persisted: "How do you feel that your brother may be dead and you wouldn't even support him when he went to Congress to save America? Uncle Michael might have died knowing he couldn't even save his own family!"

"Kenya, enough!" her mother shouted.

Kenya crossed her arms. Leroy Junior continued eating, but Keisha just stared at her big sister with wide eyes, looking too afraid to pick up her fork.

"Mom!" Kenya exclaimed. "Why are you still feeding this fattening food with all the grease, sodium, and chemicals to our family, when you know better? The refrigerator is full of processed lunch meats. They're carcinogenic! They cause cancer!"

Her mother glared. "Kenya, you will not play food police with me!"

"Somebody needs to!" Kenya shouted back. "You need to lose weight, too. And so does Keisha, who weighs much more than a 10-year-old is supposed to weigh. I know she's your partner in crime, when you go eat beef and cheese burritos in Mexican Village, followed by baklava in Greektown!"

"Shut up!' Keisha yelled tearfully. "Don't call me fat!"

Kenya glanced at Leroy Junior, whose sudden growth spurt over the summer had helped him slim down. Now 13, he was nearly six feet tall and solid muscle. As a result of his commitment to athletics, and being under the influence of Kenya's constant dialogue about nutrition and health, Leroy Junior seemed destined for the NBA, because basketball was his favorite sport.

Kenya smiled at her little brother. "Junior, I am so proud of you for refusing to eat Heavenly's in the school cafeteria!"

He smiled. "Thanks for packing my healthy lunch, Kenya."

"Those boys still teasing you?" she asked.

Leroy Junior forked up some broccoli and brown rice and smiled. "Remember the guys who were saying, 'Why are you eating that rabbit food, dummy?'"

Kenya nodded. "When they saw me become a beast on the basketball court and get promoted to the high school Junior Varsity team as an eighth grader, they asked how they could get as ripped as me! 'Not by eating French fries,' I told them. Now they bring a lunch like I do, even though the school doesn't like it."

"They used to call your uncle 'Little Fatty Michael,'" Leroy said. "Just like you, he hit a growth spurt, started playing sports, and slimmed down. Michael was always saying he thought the barbaric act of breeding the strongest slaves had created a super race of black athletes."

"Nobody is superior," Kenya said. "But we should all follow his example."

"I just don't see how some radical, Black Panther-type underground movement could possibly make a difference against the government and big business," Leroy said. "If you want to run off and join the revolution—"

"Come with me!" Kenya pleaded. "Since I became a vegetarian, I feel so much better. But it cost me my boyfriend. That jerk said I 'lost *the* booty' and Aunt Evelyn told me I look 'sick' and will never get another man. She's the one who's sick with diabesity! Why is that even a word? Don't you all see how insane this is? We *know* better! So we have to *do* better!"

"Kenya—" her mother said with a pleading tone. "I'm worried about you going there. You're a college student. You can't jeopardize—"

"I can't jeopardize the future of my family and America by *not* doing something!" Kenya exclaimed. "The LifeQuest Movement is the solution! They have everything arranged, so I'm not detected, coming and going. Jeremy—you know, my boyfriend that I met at Creamy Dream back when we didn't know better!—and I go to the Wayne State campus together. Then he goes to his family and tries to talk some sense into them while I'm here doing the same."

"Mom, will you still take me back to school tonight?" Keisha asked. "They're having free—"

Kenya glared at her sister, whose inhaler was on the table and whose elbows were scabbed over. "You need to get some exercise, not go to school for free snacks. That Heavenly's community center in the cafeteria is so bogus! The government lets them take over public school cafeterias so they can hook entire families on their junk. Keisha, you can barely run to the bus stop. I guarantee if you eat better, you'll get rid of that eczema, asthma, and lactose intolerance."

Keisha burst into tears and ran away from the table.

"Are you happy now?" her mother snapped.

"No, Mom, I'm not happy at all. What did your doctor say at your checkup this week?"

Her mother cast her eyes down and almost whispered, "I'm pre-diabetic."

"Mom!" Kenya exclaimed. "Is that enough to convince you to give up your favorite foods and stop worrying that if you exercise, you'll 'sweat out' your expensive salon hairdo? Or do you plan to join dad on the dialysis bus someday?"

Kenya crossed her arms and shook her head. "Why do people have to wait 'til tragedy strikes before they can make a change?"

Mom glared and said, "LifeQuest is really turning you into a militant something-or-other! Tone it down at the dining room table, young lady."

Kenya shot to her feet, trembling. "I can't tone it down, Mom! I am so disgusted by the way we've all fallen prey to the food industry's campaign to get us addicted to food, fat, sugar, salt, grease, chemicals! I just want you all to know right now, I'm moving into the LifeQuest headquarters. I can't sit back and watch it kill my parents!"

Leroy Junior looked confused. "What's LifeQuest?"

"Uncle Michael started it," Kenya said. "It's a place where people are learning how to be healthy so we can all live a long time and be happy."

"Where is it?" her mother demanded. "It sounds dangerous. I don't want you—"

"I'm grown, Mom. You should come with me. We should all go."

"Stop!" Leroy shouted. "Stop, now!"

Everyone froze and stared at him. He looked sad, and emotion cracked his voice as he said, "Kenya, if you want to move there, you have my blessing. I don't want you to end up fat and sick like me. Will you be able to communicate with us?"

Kenya nodded, hating the defeated look in her father's eyes as she said, "Yes, I've already gone through the screening process. So has Jeremy Matthews. He's going with me. His family is exactly like ours, even though his aunt and cousin write about healthy eating. He—"

"Are you going of your own volition?" her father asked.

Kenya crossed her arms, rolled her eyes, and huffed, "I have my own brain!"

"Young lady, show some respect!" Mom snapped.

Kenya huffed. "Yes, it's my decision. If you're not part of the solution, you're part of the problem. And the problem is right here in our house."

Her father grimaced, then said, "I'm changing my ways. Today. Slim Jim died in my office today. Heart attack. Said he'd just eaten fast food. They found Taco Temptation wrappers in his truck, and some empty cans of energy drinks."

Leroy buried his face in his hands. "Nobody dies from eating tacos. Something about today—"

Her mother dashed around the table and stroked Dad's shoulders. "Oh baby, I'm so sorry."

He looked up at Kenya. "I want you to come back here and teach us everything you learn at LifeQuest."

Tears of relief filled Kenya's eyes as she joined her family in a group hug around her father, who began sobbing.

Chapter 35

Johnny Valentine stood in the Emergency Room at Detroit General Hospital, staring at his brother, his sister, and his baby niece. All three were on gurneys. And all three were dead.

"A neighbor heard them screaming for help," the paramedic said, "and by the time we got to the apartment, they were all unconscious. Looked like a regular day, no signs of foul play. The neighbor said they were just sitting around eating Heavenly's—"

Johnny remembered the scene outside a Heavenly's about six months ago when six or seven people mysteriously died. "When will the autopsies be done?" he asked. "Something isn't right."

"I'll find out and let you know," the paramedic said.

Johnny thought about who to call to report the bad news. Their mother was dead. Hadn't heard from their father in years. Didn't even know where he was. So he headed to LifeQuest HQ and met with Dr. Wise, Boone Davis, and Carmen La Buena.

"I think somebody's waging their own war in the drive-thru lanes," Johnny said. "My brother, sister, and little niece are dead. Possibly from eating Heavenly's."

Dr. Wise looked perplexed. "What's the connection?"

"I heard about some folks in Flint talk about people dying," Johnny said, "and all they did was eat a hamburger."

"Maybe somebody is doing that to sabotage our Movement," Boone said, "to make it look like we're taking a turn in our campaign to punish anyone who eats fast food."

"Could be a lone wolf type thing," Dr. Wise said.

"I think it's more than that," Carmen said. "My cousins in Cleveland were telling me a story like that. The problem is, the people involved were also on drugs and caught up in other high-risk behaviors, so the coroner blamed their crack pipe, not their fast food meal, as the cause of death."

Johnny shook his head. "We gotta find out what's going on, and stop it."

Chapter 36

INSIDE A HOTEL BALLROOM at the annual Midwest Coroners and Medical Examiners Association's conference, people representing several hundred counties gathered to discuss trends in death.

"The opioid crisis is definitely public enemy number one right now," said Association President Alicia Violet, sitting on a panel with three other medical examiners. "In Wayne County, where I'm the coroner for Detroit and several surrounding suburbs, overdoses top the list for cause of death."

After a spirited discussion about current trends, President Violet looked out on the crowd and pointed to a microphone in the center aisle. "We'd like to hear questions and comments about what's happening in your counties."

The first man to stand at the microphone said, "Hi, I'm the coroner in Gary, Indiana, and we've noticed a lot of deaths by sudden cardiac arrest, even in children. The only common denominator is that all the victims had fast food in their stomachs. Most of them come from poor, urban neighborhoods where that's just what most folks eat. But we can't find anything else to pin as cause of death besides cardiac arrest. I'm wondering if anyone else has noticed this trend."

President Violet gazed out at the crowd. Three people stood and headed to the microphone.

"I'd like to echo that," a woman said. "I'm the medical examiner in Cleveland, Ohio, and at first we wanted to blame the high risk lifestyles these individuals were living. Drugs, alcohol, homelessness, prostitution, obesity, etcetera. But then we got three kids. All dead from cardiac arrest. We tried to tell the media, but they blew us off. The kids were poor. Their parents were not exactly model citizens—"

"That's unfortunate," President Violet said. "What do you surmise might be happening here, if anything?"

"Well we saw the toxic water in Flint, Michigan," said the Cleveland medical examiner. "There could be some kind of toxin that's leaching into the water, the air, the food. Maybe even a virus caused by a mosquito that hasn't been discovered yet. We have nothing conclusive thus far. But it's definitely something we're watching."

A man stepped to the microphone. "I'm from Toledo. Same story. Not a coincidence that we're all witnessing the same trend."

President Violet looked pensive. "Tell me, were you able to identify exactly what these individuals had eaten?"

All three speakers remained at the microphone.

"Fried chicken, tacos, burgers," said the man from Gary as the others nodded.

President Violet looked perplexed. "Hmmmm. Would you mind writing up something that I can share with my colleagues in the other regional coroners' organizations, and the national group? This kind of thing isn't a story until someone who matters becomes a victim."

Chapter 37

FDA Commissioner Beatrice Donderro was exhausted and hungry after a long day of meetings in Cleveland, Ohio. As her driver took her back to her hotel, where she could hopefully get a good night's sleep before a morning flight back to Washington, DC, they passed a Heavenly's.

"Oh, I shouldn't," she whispered. But she was quite hungry, having spent the dinner meeting talking and listening to her colleagues, as opposed to eating much of the tasteless chicken that was served. Then she realized with great glee that she had yet to indulge her weekly burger splurge. And she had spent 30 minutes on the treadmill in the hotel fitness room this morning.

I earned it!

"Jake, let's pull into the drive-thru."

"This isn't the best neighborhood—"

"Are there any other Heavenly's on the way to my hotel?"

"No," he said.

"Then let's please stop," she said. "But don't tell anyone about my guilty pleasure. This is strictly classified information."

"My lips are sealed," he said, as they pulled into the glow of neon lights.

"I want a triple bacon-cheeseburger, jumbo fries, and a strawberry milkshake," she said, feeling less guilty about this caloric indulgence when she remembered that Heavenly's was one of the restaurant chains that would be using the calorie-blocking additive called OC-8 that she had approved.

Excitement surged within her as she anticipated her guilt-free treat. She was also eager to test it out. Would she really be able to eat highly caloric foods and not gain weight? If so, this would revolutionize the food industry! And she wouldn't have to worry about "wearing" her weekly indulgences when she donned a bathing suit on vacation in Cancun in just a few months.

"Oh," she said, inhaling deeply as her driver handed her a white bag and plastic cup. "That smells heavenly!"

"Thus the name," Jake said playfully.

Minutes later, they were at the hotel, and she couldn't wait to put on her pajamas and savor every bite of bliss.

"I'll pick you up at nine for your ride to the airport," Jake said.

"I'll be ready." Beatrice smiled, excited to wake up guilt-free after her nighttime treat.

Chapter 38

Anastasia Lee appeared on TV screens around the world: "Breaking news this morning, as FDA Commissioner Beatrice Donderro is found dead in a Cleveland hotel room. No foul play is suspected. GNN has learned the apparent cause of death is a heart attack."

Chapter 39

King Daemon was furious as he watched continuing coverage of Ms. Donderro's demise with his Royal Brothers and Dr. Braza.

"Her death will be investigated!" King Daemon exclaimed. "Assure me that this substance, this OC-8, will not be detected and traced back to us. Otherwise, our campaign will fail!"

Dr. Braza looked pale, but remained composed. "I assure you, Almighty, that I conducted many, many tests, and with each death, no trace of OC-8 was found in the rats' systems."

"But it was not tested on humans!" King Daemon accused.

"Actually, Almighty," Dr. Braza said, "the many deaths in the three test cities have proven its effectiveness, with no reports of OC-8 being detected."

"That we know of!" Daemon shouted.

"Almighty," said the Minister of Propaganda, "I assure you, our many contacts have been monitoring the media and other channels, and they report that these many deaths have raised no suspicion."

"Yet," King Daemon said, turning to Dr. Braza. "I will kill you with my own hands if this campaign fails."

Chapter 40

General Brewster sat in his office in Trykka, dreading the idea of his daughter showing up today to report about the Republic of the East's ailing health status. Her allegiance to her calling as a correspondent for *The American Daily News* was as fierce as his to the American military.

He smiled slightly, feeling proud of his daughters' values, but still worried about her safety here. He would have felt a lot better about it if Bullet were still here to serve as her bodyguard. No soldier had ever been as efficient and effective as his younger protégé.

I trust him like a son. I trust him with my daughter's life.

General Brewster couldn't wait to return to the United States, meet with the President, and provide the information that Bullet had obtained for him and that the Joint Chiefs had called bogus.

Meanwhile, the General's many years of service had resulted in trusting relationships with Republic natives who continued to provide him with insider information. Today, one of his informants appeared in his office, disguised under a wig, sunglasses, and scarves. Inside, he removed them to reveal he had been beaten. He handed the General a flash drive, all the while looking over his shoulder and trembling.

"I am a dead man," the messenger said. "You must take this. Save us all."

The General took the flash drive.

"I'm taking you to get medical care," the General said.

"No," the man said. Then with one haunting glance back, he ran from the office.

General Brewster was overwhelmed by a sinister feeling as he sat at his desk and plugged the flash drive into his Device. On the screen of his computer tablet appeared the heading: OC8: THE UNITED STATES OF TRICQUA.

If he thought what Bullet presented was bad, this was beyond belief. But the black and white words were real on the screen. This document outlined how the terrorist leadership of the Republic of the East planned to use a food additive toxin called OC-8 to poison and kill American men, women, and children. While killing off the population, they were also grooming a seemingly perfect American candidate for President. Their plot also included many people in the top levels of government who were either being duped or blatantly bribed, in addition to many people who had been groomed by the terrorists from birth or childhood to help overthrow America. These people were in the White House, FDA, CDC, FBI, and executive offices of major food companies.

The flash drive contained many documents explaining how this would work, including their plot to poison Americans through fast food with a toxin called "OC-8," which stood for "Obesity Catalyst 8," with the number eight representing infinity. It explained how scientist Dr. Braza had been working to perfect the toxin for many years, and how it would be passed through a contact at the FDA as a flavor enhancer, then sold to American food companies through a network of people who were colluding with the King and his men.

As the General read, he was horrified to learn that OC-8 contained a chemical compound that both shut off the body's ability to feel full while also stimulating a wickedly insatiable hunger by flooding the body with the hunger hormone, ghrelin. That triggered the person to want to continue eating and drinking sugary soda as fiendishly as a drug addict craved more drugs. Meanwhile, during this eating frenzy, OC-8 was doing its real damage by accelerating diabetes, heart attacks, and death.

This is a matter of national security. I have to get this to President Alexander. If that means climbing in his bedroom window at the White House in the middle of the night, I will get it to him. The Fate of America depends on it. On me.

No one below the President would do, as his prior attempts to report corruption had been met with disbelief and retaliation. Terror consumed General Brewster. Had anyone followed the messenger?

I need to get out of here. My life is in imminent danger. Maggie… Jeri…

She would arrive any minute. His phone rang. "Jeri" flashed across the screen. He inserted his earpiece and answered, unable to stop the shakiness in his voice.

"Dad, what's wrong?"

He gripped the flash drive, as his brain spun out a plan. If he told her not to come here, she would do just that. *And when I leave, they'll follow me…*

"Dad?!"

He put the flash drive in a small, blue ceramic box on his desk that Jeri made in third grade. Chunky clay letters on top said DADDY. He wrote a sticky note, then wrapped the flash drive in it, and put it inside the box, which sat beside his favorite eight-by-ten framed photograph of himself with Maggie and Jeri on vacation in Hawaii. His heart ached as he said, "Jeri, honey, I have a gift for you in the blue box on my desk."

"Dad, you don't sound right. What's wrong?"

"Just a little indigestion. I love you."

"I'll be there within thirty minutes," she said, "but you should go to the doctor. Can you breathe okay?"

He wiped sweat on his brow. He glanced back at the pretty box on his desk, alongside the family photo of him, Maggie, and Jeri.

"Yes, honey, we'll have lunch—"

Boom! An explosion shook the building. The window was intact, but debris—and the messenger's body—blew up into the air outside his third-story window.

The phone line went dead.

Two men burst into his office, and everything went black.

Chapter 41

Terrified Jeri Brewster arrived at her father's office in the US Embassy as quickly as possible. She had already heard about the bombing in front of the building, so she snuck in the back of the building and sprinted up the staircase to his open office.

Blood streaked the desk. His computer was gone. His safe was open. She opened the blue ceramic box, finding a bunch of yellow sticky notes scribbled with his handwriting and wrapped around a flash drive. The note said:

"Jeri, take this to the President. But first, go to Calvin 'Bullet' Alvarez at 44 Ranch Road, outside Billings, Montana. He'll help you. Then go to Dr. Wise. Jeri, DO NOT GO HOME. Do not call. Go to Ibraham. I love you and your mother, Daddy." After that, another note said, *"If you're reading this, run far and fast."*

Jeri plugged the flash drive into her Device and quickly glimpsed the Terrorists' plot to use obesity to overthrow America. She was so horrifically captivated by what she was reading, that time seemed to stand still. Her mind reeled forward over the possibility of these terrorists actually executing this mission on innocent Americans. Her heart was pounding with fear, along with panic over what might have happened to her father. Was he dead?

She needed to call her mother, but her pulse quickened at the need to escape from here. Still, she could not stop reading the nightmare that King Daemon had crafted for the United States and the world.

Suddenly bullets whizzed through the office. Dust and debris flew as the gunfire struck the walls. Jeri, gripping her Device and the flash drive, shoved a file cabinet aside to reveal a wall grate. She yanked it off, and, just as her father had shown her for such an occasion, escaped through a secret tunnel.

Fearing her father was dead and that the same people wanted to kill her, she ran into Ibrahim's house. She carried a small, backpack-type travel bag containing her Device, energy bars, a bottle of water, toiletries, and a few changes of clothing. She also had the flash drive and note from her father tucked in her pocket.

"My father told me to come to you," she said. "Do you know where he is?"

Ibrahim's eyes glowed with fear. He cast his gaze downward and grasped her hands, saying, "All we can do is pray. Let's go."

They hopped into Ibrahim's truck. He threw a bag onto the seat with them. "Open it, and wear that," he said. Jeri retrieved a wig, sunglasses, and a long, brightly colored, hooded gown like the women in the Republic wear. She was completely disguised as he drove her to an industrial shipyard on the sea.

"Your father told me many years ago that if you showed up under circumstances like this," Ibrahim said, "to put you on this ship. You will be taken care of."

Jeri's mind was spinning in a thousand directions. Was her father dead? Were they being followed? Could she make it to the Bullet and the President? Would she survive whatever was about to happen on that huge, rusty cargo ship?

"Is it going to the US?" she asked, only half-trusting Ibrahim. Double-crossings were so common in war-torn regions. Could he have betrayed her father? She had no choice right now.

"Jeri," Ibrahim said. "You will be safe. The men on this ship owe your father their lives. They will take you to New York." He pointed to rows of large, wooden crates. Most were gray; Ibrahim instructed her to climb into the single blue one. As she did, he waved for the dock workers and closed the lid but did not lock it.

"They will carry you to a special area for fragile cargo," Ibrahim said.

Through a small hole in the crate, she watched Ibrahim walk away. He got back into his truck. And it blew up.

Shaken and terrified, Jeri took deep breaths to stay calm. If Ibrahim were being watched, then certainly their enemies knew her location. So it was no comfort when the man who moved her crate under Ibrahim's direction later opened it, and said, "Come with me, you have a private room on the boat for your comfort and safety."

She was suspicious, but did not want to spend the next two weeks living in a crate. So she followed him, always ready to fight. He led her—still wearing the clothing that Ibrahim provided—to a windowless room that contained a bed and small bathroom.

"I will bring you food," he said. "I knew your father. I have been working with the resistance for many years."

Jeri had no choice but to believe him, and was grateful for the hiding place as she headed back to the United States, where hopefully she would be able to execute her father's orders by going to Bullet, then the President.

During the transAtlantic journey, thanks to electricity to charge her tablet, she read the entire document, which listed all the individuals who had been groomed from childhood for specific roles to execute this mission. It also revealed the positions in America that had been bribed to collude with the terrorists' plan without knowing they were working for the terrorists, who used layers of people to shield their evil enterprise.

She was horrified to read that, as part of their plot, King Daemon and his terrorists invited people from every nation that hated America—to come to their country to become indoctrinated in this plan and share in the ultimate glory of bringing America down and sharing the resources. So they had assembled an evil band of America haters from every continent—leaders and regular citizens alike—to create a diverse genetic pool from which to pull spies. The manifesto stated that the terrorists used a secret online network that they called the SuperNet to lure random individuals and groups from around the globe.

King Daemon's so-called Royal Brothers had been doing this for several decades, since the Allied invasion of their country and the assassination of their tyrannical government leaders who had been responsible for atrocities against everyday citizens, including children. The manifesto said that King Daemon and his team crafted a plan of attack against Americans as they watched the obesity rate spike, and they were inspired by Dr. Michael Wise on television many years ago when he became an outspoken proponent of reducing obesity in America.

All the while, people of every ethnicity went to Tricqua and had babies that were indoctrinated to carry out the mission hatched in Daemon's traumatized, boyhood imagination. To the outside world, Tricqua looked like a global melting pot with the world's lowest infant mortality rate, lowest obesity rate, and subsequently the lowest rates of cancer, heart disease, and diabetes.

Now Jeri was reading that it was actually ground zero for a plot to destroy America and to rule the world.

"I have to stop them!" she exclaimed. Her thoughts spun on fast-forward, in a desperate attempt to visualize finding Bullet.

What if he's not at his ranch? What if he's on the other side of the world on a mission? What if he's dead? Why can't I go straight to the White House and tell the President as soon as I get off this boat in New York?

In the truck, Ibrahim had told her that it would dock in Brooklyn, and that he had followed her father's instructions to contact Jeri's good friend who owned a flower shop.

"You will be picked up in a flower truck," Ibrahim had said. "The crate will be loaded off the boat and into the truck. She will be waiting for you."

Jeri feared that her father was dead, and that his warning "do not go home" meant that her mother was in danger, too.

"I have to shake this emotion," she declared. She closed her eyes and focused on her military training, which until now had enabled her to channel all emotion to execute a mission. She took some deep breaths, and shifted herself into military mode, channeling all her brain power into her mission:

- *Get Calvin "Bullet" Alvarez to help her.*

- *Take this evil manifesto to the President of the United States.*

- *Go to Dr. Wise in Detroit.*

She hoped that Angelo Grazia would help her gain access to Dr. Wise inside the LifeQuest headquarters.

Now she understood that her mission was a matter of national security, and she had to act on that above all else. She had no idea how she would find Dr. Wise when her previous attempts had failed, but she was certain that her desperation would help her find a way.

Chapter 42

As the ship approached New York City, the man who had brought her to this small room and delivered meals and water, even allowing her out for fresh air one day, arrived to announce it was time to get in the crate and disembark from the ship.

As Ibrahim had promised, the crate was lifted onto a flower truck, which rumbled away from the shipyard and stopped. Suddenly the top of the crate opened, and Jeri squinted to adjust to the light.

"Lisa!" she exclaimed. "We've got to stop meeting like this."

"Jeri, oh my God, this is like a bad movie," said Lisa Silverman, a Detroit native who attended New York University and now owned a flower shop in Brooklyn. "If you had told me in third grade that someday I'd be rescuing you from a wooden crate after some guy across the ocean calls me, I'd be like, you are crazy, girl."

Jeri loved the feeling of her feet now on American soil. But she still didn't feel safe. And how in the world would she get to Montana? If only she could go to the newspaper officers in New York City.

"I want to go to the office but that's probably too obvious," she said, knowing that her editors could—through the paper's correspondents on the White House Press Corps—get the manifesto to the president directly and immediately. But her father had told her to go to Bullet first for a reason. And based on the infiltration of American government by American-looking impostors who were working for the enemy, that created an environment where no one could be trusted.

Jeri trusted her father's leadership and intuition. So rather than risk exposure—and perhaps death—which would put the entire nation at risk, she decided to stick with her father's plan.

"I need to hopscotch my way to Montana," Jeri said, sitting amongst bushes and plants in the truck, as her friend drove through a rough neighborhood as opposed to taking main streets. The area was totally desolate except for fortress-like blocks with fencing, boards, barbed wire, dogs, and "enter at your own risk" signs.

On one corner, a lady carrying a bag of vegetables exited a run-down building. The friend says, "That's Life-Quest center. I heard they have schools and gardens and all kinds of things happening in there. You'd never know from the outside. But this one, a retired cop who used to come into my shop started it after his whole family died. Nobody bothers them here in no man's land. I think the government thinks these people are so far gone, why bother."

On other corners, people were loitering around liquor stores whose signs announced "Liquor - Food - Cigarettes." On the sidewalk, an obese mother with little fat kids were walking and eating potato chips and drinking fluorescent orange pop. They passed a Heavenly's burger joint that's packed with people. Billboards advertising diabetes products adorn bus stop shelters.

When they reach the flower shop's greenhouse, Lisa served hot soup, salad, and fruit.

"I figured you'd be starving," she said as Jeri devoured the food. "Oh my God, were you like, sleeping in that crate for the whole trip? I had no way to reach you, all I could do was go on what Ibrahim said. Obviously your Device was turned off."

Jeri nodded. "My father showed me how to deactivate the location tracker on my Device if anything like this ever happened. I hope this worked. If not, it already has military coding, so it can't be tracked. I want to call my mother so much, but I can't."

"I can," Lisa said, pushing a button on her steering wheel to activate her phone.

"No!" Jeri shouted. "I don't know who's watching her, or bugging her phone and internet, and it could put you in danger."

Lisa's eyes widened. She did not make the call.

"My Device is equipped with a special military shield that lets me make phone calls in case of emergency," Jeri said, "but I don't know if whoever got my dad can tap into it. So I'm not going to risk calling my mother."

The women rode in silence as Jeri fought fears of whatever might have happened to her father, and what could be happening to her mother.

Chapter 43

KING DAEMON'S MINISTER OF Surveillance scanned three screens before him, each showing a map of Brooklyn, New York; a green grid that would indicate a voice spoken into a phone, tablet, or computer, and numbers dancing in a continuous formation that would create a string of digits if or if call were made to or from Jeri Brewster or her parents.

"The girl is in the truck on Flatbush Avenue," the Minister of Surveillance said. "Her Device is still sending out a ping, so we can track her position. Unfortunately we are only hearing snippets of dialogue because the microphone is either blocked or malfunctioning."

"Make it work!" Daemon ordered through taut lips. "And tell me, does she have our information?"

The minister responded, "We are quite certain that she retrieved it from her father's office before he was—"

"I want her dead now!" Daemon shouted. "Dead!"

Another screen lit up on the panel before them. Their FBI confidant in the United States appeared and said, "Almighty, we have him here."

General Brewster was pushed before the camera, bruised and tousled, but alive and looking defiant.

King Daemon's eyes burned as he glared at the man he hated most on planet earth. "Were it not for my desire to kill you with my own hands, you would be dead right now," Daemon said through trembling lips. "I have waited my entire life to get my hands on you and avenge the murder of my parents and the destruction of my country!"

"You will not win," General Brewster said with all the authority of a man commanding legions of soldiers awaiting his orders.

"You have no power!" the King shouted. "You are as good as dead!"

"If you wanted me dead, I would be," he said.

"I want you to watch me kill those you love, and destroy your country, before I decide your dying day," Daemon said.

General Brewster stared back with an unblinking, defiant expression as men spoke Tricquan in muffled tones around him.

"Get out of my sight," Daemon spat.

The General was shoved off camera, and the FBI informant appeared.

"Get his wife to me, here, now!" Daemon ordered.

The man on camera bowed. "It will be done, Almighty."

"And get his daughter to me, here, now!" Daemon said, envisioning the pure ecstasy of killing the General's wife and daughter before his very eyes.

Chapter 44

As Jeri climbed onto a semi-trailer truck full of orchids bound for Montana, her friend Lisa gave her a hug and said, "Be safe. Fortunately it's summertime, so you don't have to worry about freezing to death."

When the truck stopped in Ohio, the driver asked Jeri, "Wanna go in the convenience store to use the ladies room and get some food?" She agreed.

Pop! Pop! Pop!

Jeri froze. Gunfire in the men's room left no doubt, the driver was dead.

The women's restroom door flew open. But Jeri had already escaped through a window. She ran through a corn field, coming to train tracks, and a stationary train. She hopped on, and took a seat as if she had just walked from another car.

She also plugged in her Device on the train and used a special secret app to make tickets so she could anonymously take the train without being detected. Eating an energy bar from her backpack, she studied the route to Montana.

When Jeri finally arrived in Montana, she hitched a ride on the back of a semi-truck, unbeknownst to the driver, on

Interstate 90. Then she hopped off when she reached the destination, according to GPS on her Device.

It was early evening as she hiked down a long, dirt road through thick woods. Finally she reached a clearing around a log cabin. She knocked on the front door. No answer. She walked around back to a deck overlooking a stream surging over rugged rocks, with a gorgeous mountain view. She knocked on the sliding glass doors. No answer. She tried one. Locked.

She remembered how her father said that Bullet was always talking about how much he loved to hunt and fish, so she headed for the stream. Wishing she had her gun now and throughout the death-defying odyssey that got her here, her heart hammered with anxiety about walking through the woods alone.

There he is. Thank God! It's Calvin.

A muscular man wearing a white tank top, jeans, and hiking boots straddled the rocks with a pole over a calm expanse of the stream which surged loudly. A big dog stood beside him. Both their backs were to Jeri, and they were focused on something.

"I got it!" Calvin exclaimed, standing with his back to Jeri.

The dog barked and wagged its tail, eagerly watching the line strain while Calvin yanked up on the pole. Jeri stared in amusement, loving how his muscles rippled as he attempted to pull the fish up and out of the water.

Despite the anxiety of moment, and the urgency of her mission, Jeri couldn't stop a hot sensation from surging through her body. *Damn, he's gorgeous!* The muscles on his broad shoulders and arms flexed, and his back tapered down in a V-shape to a waist belted in black leather that matched his boots. His faded jeans were filled out oh-so-nicely over his muscular behind, and his long legs were slightly bent as he struggled with the fish. She hadn't seen this man since she was a little girl when her father introduced—

Stop it, Jeri! I'm not here for romance. I'm here to save America—and my parents.

And judging by the gun strapped to Calvin's belt, he did not want unwelcome visitors.

He yanked a giant fish from the water.

"Yeah!" he shouted. "Check out that baby!"

The dog barked up at the huge fish dancing in the air, throwing droplets of water everywhere. Bullet turned to bring the rod, the line, and the dangling fish over the rocks as he stepped down.

He was grinning, staring at the fish.

Until he saw Jeri.

He froze—about 20 feet away, just staring with laser-sharp intensity.

Jeri stared back, hating that her heart was racing. Was it because he could open fire on her—an intruder on his land in the middle of nowhere? After all, he had killed a lot of people around the world, and had made a boatload of enemies.

He might think I'm an assassin. He hasn't seen me all grown up. Even the pictures on Daddy's desk were of me as a little girl, and since Bullet retired, he wouldn't have seen updated photos.

"Bullet, it's me, Jeri."

He stared, not looking convinced. At all. The dog growled. In a split-second, Bullet dropped the fish in a giant bucket, put his hand on his gun, and stepped toward her.

"Jeri who?" he demanded. "What are you doing here?"

She stepped toward him. "I'm—"

He wrestled her to the ground. But she slipped her legs and arms around him the way her father had taught—and pinned him down. Until he flipped her over and held her down.

"Bullet! It's me, Jeri Brewster! Wild Bill's daughter! He disappeared in the Republic. Gave me a note to find you!"

"Prove it!"

She pulled out the note as the dog growled.

"Dragon! Quiet!" The dog stopped growling. "Tell me the name of your dog when you were eight years old," Bullet said. "And your favorite candy."

"Bingo was our dog. I always chose grapes over candy."

"Favorite toy?"

"Barbie in camo."

"Show me the scar," he ordered.

She pulled up her sleeve to reveal a small half-circle on her elbow.

"How many stitches?"

"Four," she said.

He let her up from the ground. "Shit. I knew I shouldn't have left him! What happened to your Dad?"

"I don't know, but he left me a few things and said find you. To help."

"Help what?"

"Save America, and—"

"I was in that business," he said with a chuckle. "Twenty years in. Now out. Out to stay. Talk to me about fishing or running the trails with Dragon here, and we're good."

"My father said you would help me. That you promised him."

Calvin shook his head. "Look, I knew your dad and he talked about you so much, I felt like I knew you. And yeah, he told me to look after you—"

Pop! Pop! Pop!

Bullets pinged off the rocks.

Calvin grabbed Jeri's hand and they ran into the woods with Dragon.

While running, he asked, "Where are your Devices?"

"I deactivated them," she said.

"No such thing. If somebody wants you, those things are a dead give-away. Who's after you?"

"People in the Republic of the East. And probably people in the Pentagon."

"Shit."

"Follow me!" he whispered as they sprinted through the woods. At the base of a hill leading to a mountain, he moved a rock, pushed a button, and a small door slid open.

"Hurry," he said, entering, then closing the door behind

them. "My bunker has electromagnetic deflectors, so your Devices can't be detected." They entered a room containing guns and ammunition.

"Come in here," he said, leading her to a room with a sofa, chairs, and video monitors showing three black SUVs driving around his property. "Who the hell are these goons?"

"Like I said, the feds who are working with Daemon—"

"I shoulda wiped him out when I had the chance," Bullet said, shaking his head. As video showed one of the SUVs heading toward a large fence, Bullet pressed a button. Something exploded under the truck, which disappeared in a fiery explosion.

"One down, two to go," he said, watching the other vehicles on his property.

"Tell me more about what's going on," he said, maneuvering knobs and watching the screen as if he were playing a video game. "Hey wait, where's your Mom?"

"I don't know," Jeri said, "and I haven't called out of fear they might detect me."

"I have an idea," he said, as the second SUV exploded on the screen. "But first, show me what we're working with here." She activated her Device to show him the manifesto on the flash drive.

"Dad told me to find you first, then take this to the President," she said. "Tell me how I can do that."

He cast an annoyed glance at her and snapped, "You're the journalist here. Call one of your sources or somebody in the White House Press Corps."

"I don't trust anybody," she said.

"Smart," he said.

"Tell me the most clandestine way to get to the President," she said, "without tipping off the wrong people."

"Impossible," he said, "especially since these guys are on Daemon's payroll."

"OK then let's start over," she said with a hard look. "My father would only have sent me to you because you can make this happen."

He laughed. "Listen, it's nice to be thought of like that, but—"

"But nothing! He also said to go to Dr. Michael Wise, the obesity doctor in Detroit, to alert and mobilize the underground. His LifeQuest Movement is all over America."

"So is Daemon's network," Calvin said. "You wouldn't believe how they've infiltrated places you'd least expect.

"Dr. Wise," he said. "Good guy. I got a lotta buddies who joined." He glanced at a rack of free weights in the corner. "You can probably tell I'm a health and physical fitness fanatic. A lot of my relatives are sick or dead from food and fat. So I'm "in" on the philosophy of the mission, but I sure wish you had picked somebody else."

"Daddy picked you—"

His expression softened. "You think he's still alive?"

"I can't allow myself to think anything but that."

"If those bastards hurt one hair on his head, I will personally—"

Jeri smiled. "I take that as a yes, you agree to help me get to the President."

He looked surprised.

"Excellent! I knew you'd honor your promise to my father. The doctor. The President. Done." She smiled.

"You're not making this any easier by being so darn cute." His eyes filled with adoration.

"Puppies are cute," she snapped. "You can call me a bad ass; you can call me a soldier; you can call me a warrior." She picked up a gun, fired, and shredded the bull's-eye on a paper target.

He grinned. "Oh hell yeah!"

"Or you can call me a bad ass."

"I'll call you Jeri," he said, intrigued.

"I'm here on business, so treat me as such."

"Deal," he said, pushing a button to blow up the third SUV as it approached his log cabin. "I think we should spend the night down here until we know the coast is clear in the morning, because somebody is gonna come looking for the fallen comrades littering my property."

Bullet prepared a healthy dinner in a small kitchen, and they ate while watching Global News Network with the anchor Anastasia Lee, who said:

"Tragic news tonight about a well-respected Army General who helped bring democratic stability to the Republic of the East. Tonight law enforcement officials reporting, General William 'Wild Bill' Brewster has been reported as missing since his assignment in the Republic, it may be associated with foul play and he is presumed dead."

"No!" Jeri screamed. "I don't believe he's dead!" She scrambled to find her Device. "I have to call—"

Bullet snatched it away. "You make a call, and you're next, sweetheart."

Anastasia Lee's voice caught their attention. "This just coming into the GNN newsroom. More tragic news involving General Brewster. Police now telling us, his wife—best-selling author Margaret Brewster—disappeared from their suburban Detroit home today. Police say the 55-year-old had just filed an article for *Women's Daily News*, and was speaking on a video conference call with her editor in New York when masked men wearing black abducted her. Authorities are now analyzing the video to identify these men, and whether they're affiliated with a terrorist organization."

Jeri sobbed; Bullet put his arms around her and stroked her head.

The news anchor continued: "Investigators added that the couple's only child, award-winning journalist Jeri Brewster, is apparently the next target. Police tell us, scrolled across the living room wall in red spray paint in the Brewster's home was the message: DEATH TO DAUGHTER."

Jeri watched in disbelief as her photo appeared on the TV screen. "Even more shocking news to this already tragic story," the anchor said, "Jeri Brewster has apparently disappeared while on assignment for *The American Daily News* in the Republic of the East. Her editors report that they have not heard from her since she called several days ago, at the exact time of the bombing outside the US Embassy there."

Anastasia Lee added, "American investigators both in the US and in the Republic of the East say they have been unable to detect any signals from Jeri Brewster's phone. Authorities believe her life is in grave danger."

Jeri sobbed. "They killed my parents! Dad had a lot of enemies. People in the Department of Defense, the Pentagon, the White House. Who did it?"

Bullet hugged her. "Jeri, I got your back now."

Chapter 45

AS KENYA WISE AND Jeremy Matthews watered kale and lettuces in the indoor organic farm at LifeQuest, he gazed down at her and said, "Didn't know we'd be able to save the world and fall in love, all at the same time."

Kenya smiled as the big leafy greens danced under the spray of water from her watering can. "There's nothing I'd rather do," she said. "Being here, with you. I just wish our families would join us. It'd be nice to save the world, *including* the people who mean the most to us. I mean, Dr. Wise is my uncle, and my dad didn't even read his book."

Jeremy looked disturbed. "Do you believe the rumors that the government may someday raid and destroy this place?"

Kenya shrugged. "We can't let fear stop us. My mother was hyped about this being dangerous. But it's the only way we can save our families."

"Our families," Jeremy said sadly. "I'm trying to do a high-pressure sale on my family to join us here. I was so angry that I grew up in such an unhealthy environment, but when you're a kid, you just eat what your parents give you. And if they're not informed, or willing to be healthier, the kids are doomed."

Kenya shook her head. "Case in point, we met at Creamy Dream with our families. I want my little sister here, now! I'm praying that my family with really commit to changing."

"Same here," Jeremy said as they stepped into an aisle between dozens of raised garden boxes that covered the entire upper floor of the former warehouse building. The lighting was specially designed to simulate sunlight; skylights would be too risky, Dr. Wise had said, due to surveillance tactics by the government.

"Now we need to pick cilantro," Kenya said. "I love the guacamole the chefs make in the dining room." They walked toward the rows of herbs and stopped at the cilantro. Their job was to deliver it to the industrial kitchen for the cooks as they prepared meals for all LifeQuest residents, who assembled every evening at six in the dining hall.

"The detoxing herb," Jeremy said, as they picked the first bunches and put them into a basket. "I learned about the medicinal qualities of herbs during our health sciences classes at Wayne State. Then when I read Dr. Wise's book, I just had this epiphany about food and health. Going vegan changed everything. I've lost 35 pounds since we met. And Kenya, oh my God, you look amazing! Not just on the outside, but because I can tell, you feel better, and you're radiant from going vegan."

Kenya smiled, but her heart felt sad as she remembered her boyfriend breaking up with her, shortly after she joined LifeQuest and began losing weight. She had dated him all through high school, and he was always talking about how much he loved her "big booty." Losing it meant losing him. *"I can't hang with skinny," he'd said. "Or all that weird shit you eat now. Looks like you cut the grass and put it on your plate with some damn beans, like you're too poor to buy some meat."* He just wouldn't listen when she talked about nutrition and better health. How many other girls and women are maintaining unhealthy weights out of fear that they'll lose their boyfriends or husbands for such shallow and hazardous reasons?

"It makes me so mad!" Kenya exclaimed. "How people put taste, appearance, and pleasing others before their own health. How can we reach people who aren't trying to hear our message?"

"Like Dr. Wise told us," Jeremy said, "they either have to get a wake-up call by getting sick, or they get inspired by seeing how much better all of us are looking and feeling."

Suddenly a half-dozen kids came running into the farm, dashing past the raised garden boxes.

"There's Kenya and Jeremy!" they exclaimed.

One girl clung to Kenya's shirt. "Can we pick some strawberries?"

"Miss Kenya, what time does your dance class start tonight?" another girl asked.

"Yeah!" three other kids cheered. "Can we do those spinning moves again?"

Kenya smiled. "Of course! We'll do extra spinning moves, just for you, starting at eight o'clock because it's Friday and you don't have school tomorrow." She was so honored that her uncle allowed her to teach dance classes to adults and children to help them learn fun ways to stay active. She gazed at the children, feeling an overwhelming need to protect them and teach them how to live healthy lifestyles and teach others by example. "Right now, you can help me and Mr. Jeremy pick cilantro and help us take it to the kitchen."

Suddenly a half-dozen little hands joined the action, picking the aromatic stems and leaves.

"Man, I love this!" Jeremy said. "You all are awesome! Everybody! Tell me your favorite ways to eat cilantro."

"Salsa!" one boy said. "No, my aunt makes the best green chutney!" Another boy shoved some in his mouth and exclaimed, "I like it this way!" The other kids laughed.

"Excuse me." A deep voice startled them.

They turned around. There stood a man who resembled Dr. Wise, only older.

"Grandpa?" Kenya asked.

"Kenya?" he said, dismayed.

Behind him stood Henry and Hank, who said, "He wanted to check out the garden before his meeting with Dr. Wise."

Kenya checked out her grandfather, looking all academic in his tweed jacket, bowtie, and cap. He even had a battered leather shoulder bag with a tag that said Harvard University. She did not feel anything warm and fuzzy toward him because she had not seen him in years and felt that he was a snob, hiding out in his distant ivory tower, never visiting his sons.

He never sees my dad, and he didn't even go to Congress to support my uncle.

"Dad?"

Her uncle's voice made Kenya turn to see her uncle approaching and staring in disbelief at her grandfather.

"Dr. Wise!" the children cheered.

He hugged his father. "Wow, I never thought I'd see this day."

"I'm here to help you now," her grandfather said.

Instant forgiveness flashed in her uncle's eyes and warmed Kenya's heart.

Chapter 46

DR. WISE STARED AT his father in disbelief as they sat on a bench amidst towering tomato plants in the indoor farm.

"Son, I want to apologize for not supporting your testimony in Congress," Professor Wise said. "I was up for a prestigious chair at Harvard Law School, and the powers that be in academia were closely linked to those in Washington. Those particular individuals in Congress who were opposing you were actually once students at the University and are now huge benefactors. I was afraid that by supporting you publicly, I would lose my opportunity for this Chair, which comes with a significant sum of money and the prestige and ability to speak at conferences around the globe, not to mention high-profile book deals with my publisher in New York."

Dr. Wise stifled a pang of anger at his father's admission.

"I was putting profit before principle, something I taught you never to do," his father said. "For that, son, I apologize with every cell in my being."

"I forgive you, Dad, and I can understand," Dr. Wise said.

"Now I want to support you in every way that I can," he said. "I actually retired and want to join LifeQuest. I've been advocating your message here since you were a boy, in our own family, but folks wouldn't listen. Now your brother Leroy—"

"We can work on him together," Dr. Wise said. "Then we'll save Evelyn from herself, too."

"Your sister," the elder Wise said, shaking his head. "As for the LifeQuest Movement, I want to contribute my legal expertise in any way that might be helpful. And if you need assistance in writing a curriculum for re-education, I'd be honored."

"We'd appreciate that," Dr. Wise said. "I have to admit, I'm really shocked that you're here."

His father put a hand on his back and said, "Son, I have to confess, what really snapped me back to my senses was hearing news reports that you may have died. I'm so proud of you! Now put me to work!"

Chapter 47

Inside his bunker, Bullet watched Jeri sleep fitfully. Something about her overwhelmed him with the desire to protect her and love her. He wanted to wrap his brawn around her and hold her while she slept, but held back. He thought of Wild Bill.

Can't mess up my promise to help her by getting my heart involved…

The next morning, they left the bunker in a bullet-proof SUV, with the goal of driving to Michigan to find Dr. Wise. They departed on a dirt road through the woods.

Ping! Ping! Ping!

Gunfire struck the vehicle, and fallen trees created a roadblock up ahead.

Bullet veered a sharp left into a secret underground tunnel.

"What's this?" Jeri demanded. "Where is this tunnel going?"

"It's a survivalists' compound commune operated by my ex-soldier friends," Calvin said. "I don't trust 'em one bit. They went to the dark side. Government informants about the LifeQuest Movement, and Daemon's terror cells operating out of farms and factories and houses in this part of the country. But our options are slim right now."

Jeri turned around. The tunnel behind them was black. "Yeah, we ditched whoever was chasing us."

Calvin stopped at a guard station. The door opened, and Tuck Jones, a renegade soldier with many more than nine lives, stepped out, flashing a grin and a gold tooth. A few other guys, sitting near the booth on motorcycles, nodded.

"Bullet's back!" exclaimed Tuck Jones.

No, I'm not coming back to you bastards who went to the dark side. All Calvin wanted was to hide out from Daemon's goons and take off as soon as possible.

"Hey man," Calvin said. As Tuck approached, he immediately knew something was not right.

"Hold on," Calvin told Jeri.

Calvin gunned the motor and the SUV sped in reverse—just as Tuck pulled a gun and shouted, "You're not welcome here, motherfucker!" Calvin quickly spun around the vehicle and exited the tunnel, returning to another part of the dirt road. Then they heard a terrible crunching sound.

"What's that?" Jeri said. "The tires?"

"Yeah," Bullet said.

Ping! Ping! Ping!

"We gotta run or we're sitting ducks," Calvin said. "Ready?"

They ran for their lives. Bullets were flying. Men were literally jumping out of trees, all around the SUVs whose tires were shredded by spokes hidden in the road by the terrorists.

Calvin's former military friends—who must have seen the commotion on their surveillance cameras and wanted to protect their turf—shot automatic rifles at the men, and the men shot back with equal fire power. Jeri, wearing her backpack that contained the flashdrive, her laptop, and her phone, dove behind a rock, shooting one gun and pulling a second one from her belt holster.

Suddenly a man fell from a tree, his ankle attached to a rope, and shot at her upside down. Before he could shoot her, Jeri made sure he didn't survive the stunt. Suddenly two motorcycles roared up; Calvin nodded to Jeri that they were safe.

Jeri hopped on behind one man; Calvin got on the second bike. They sped away into the forest. Within minutes, they arrived at a bunker operated by one of his ex-military buddies.

From there, they were transported in an RV to Northern California, not far from the LifeQuest Movement's West Coast arm, which was operated by Carmen La Buena and her Yogis for Health. Today Jeri and Bullet had met with Carmen, who promised to help them reach Dr. Wise in Detroit. But getting back across the country while evading Daemon's henchmen was proving increasingly difficult.

While Calvin talked in the adjacent room with his friends, Jeri remained in the windowless bedroom, fuming.

We have to make it! People are dying!

Jeri flipped on the TV news and heard yet another story about people dying after eating fast food, even though investigators had found no source of contamination.

I have to do something. What if I never make it to the President? What if Daemon kills us first? Then the killings will continue… No! I'm going to write this news story right now, send it to Shareese and the publisher of the American News, and do an old-school journalistic exposé.

She could not risk another American life being taken while she attempted to follow her father's directive—a seemingly impossible one—to reach Dr. Wise and then the President.

She glanced at the door; she could hear Calvin in the nearby meeting room with his military buddies, talking strategy and reminiscing about war stories. They weren't planning to leave for three hours; that would be just enough time to excerpt the manifesto and email it to her editor and publisher. A surge of adrenaline shot through her as she wrote the headline: FAST FOOD DEATHS REVEAL DEADLY PLOT TO KILL AND CONQUER AMERI-CANS By Jerralyn Brewster.

With two guns on the table beside her laptop computer, she typed nonstop for an hour, and didn't pause until she heard Bullet enter—

It's not him. The hairs on the back of her neck stood up.

She could still hear him and his buddies talking in the other room. She grasped a gun, just as a man dove toward her. She rose from her chair, which hit the hard floor loudly. He knocked the gun from her hand. And she flipped him to the floor. Pinned him down on his back. Sitting on his stomach and pinning his arms over his head with a painful twist, she ordered: "Tell me who you are, who sent you, and what you want."

Pure evil shot up from his eyes as he refused to speak.

Calvin shot into the room, pressing a gun to the guy's head. His buddies followed, while others searched the property for more invaders. They found none, but Jeri and Calvin were driven to another safe house where Jeri resumed work on her report.

"No," Calvin said. "When Wild Bill gives an order, there's good reason for it. You don't know if the publisher is in bed with those maniacs around the President. They could squash the news, snuff you out, and there goes America…"

"No!" Jeri insisted. "I can't risk more Americans dying while we play hide and seek with terrorists!"

"Jeri! The number of Americans who might die between now and us executing this mission as instructed, compared to the number of Americans who might die if this information is never revealed, is astronomical. You know that."

She stood to glare up at him. "I know that we've dodged death more times than I can count in recent days. I can't risk—"

"I can't risk anything happening to you!" He cast a tender look down at her and said softly, "Jeri, this has become more than a mission from Wild Bill. I want to be with you forever—"

Jeri's glare softened into a gaze. For a split second, she forgot about everything but the love radiating down from his face. The air around them seemed to crackle with electricity as they stared into each other's eyes for a long moment that promises much more than either is willing to say right now.

"Show me the gun range," Jeri said. "We need to practice."

He laughed. "G.I. Jane, you stole my heart. Now let's go see who's got the best shot."

Chapter 48

IN THE PALACE MEDIA room, King Daemon sat with his Royal Brotherhood, reviewing the progress of their plan.

"Our reach is growing exponentially every day," said the Minister of External Operations. "We have networks of cells throughout the United States. Our many training posts include farm houses. Fortunately for us, our financial backing from our brothers in like-minded countries is music to the Americans' ears. It is relatively easy to go to farmers who are poor and need money."

The giant screen showed video of Kingdom representatives meeting with the naïve farmers, who had no idea that providing support to these networks would ultimately hurt them.

"You can see," the Minister of External Operations said, "these networks have been able to set up surveillance with sophisticated equipment, at these locations to monitor just about any type of activity. They have been able to infiltrate law enforcement agencies as well."

Video showed law enforcement officers meeting with the Kingdom's employees. "This is why we've been able to detect every move of the girl and her boyfriend."

Chapter 49

Jeri gripped her backpack containing everything she needed to show Dr. Wise and the President so the deaths would stop. She was so exhausted by this cross-country trek that was just one death-defying moment after another.

Now all she wanted was eat a good meal at this diner attached to a gas station and continue to the next safe house, hopefully getting them closer to Detroit. A TV in the diner aired disturbing news reports about more people dying after eating fast food, as well as new numbers about the obesity rate spiking in the wake of Dr. Wise's Congressional testimony and the defeat of the Obesity Eradication Act.

As Jeri ate with Calvin, and his friends kept watch outside, they believed that they were evading surveillance for the time being.

"They got us," Calvin said. "We gotta go."

Jeri knew not to question Calvin, because she felt it, too. Because of their skill set, they recognized danger and had a six sense how to react in difficult situations.

Now, they were tipped off by too much activity outside of the diner. They both slipped out of the diner through the back kitchen. They stealthily gained the upper hand on a group of goons that have surrounded the diner. They took them out, one by one, without creating a sound or any commotion. A stabbing, a wire across the throat, and a broken neck, they escaped the goons and were on their way.

A few hours later, they reached a farm house that seemed unoccupied. Bullet's resources and network of former military men, had mapped out this place for them to rest. It was fortified, but again the terrorist network uncovered their hiding place. But the terrorists did not realize how fortified this place was. One goon approached the farm house, only to trip over a wire that sent him sailing through the air on a tree limb upside down. A second goon tried to approach the farm house, but met a hatchet that seemed to have sprung up through the ground. He was dead before he hit the ground. Bullet and Jeri exited through an underground tunnel and caught the third goon, who suffered a knife blade through his neck. They escaped and returned their journey to get to the President.

Time after time they evaded the terrorists and always seemed to be one step ahead.

Chapter 50

At 3:00 a.m., Jeri and Calvin were driven to the next safe house, in a mountainside home in Arizona, as part of a plan to fly them to Detroit on a private plane owned by one of Calvin's Marine buddies who was involved in international business deals.

"You saved my ass in Afghanistan," the guy said, opening the back door to his huge, log cabin home as Jeri and Calvin stepped inside. "Now I'm saving yours. And your pretty lady-friend." His suntanned friend had Hollywood good looks and wore expensive-looking loafers, jeans and a business shirt that showed off his buff physique.

"Good to see you, Chuck!" Calvin said as they hugged.

"Same here, man, you look good," Chuck said. "Listen, you must be exhausted. Get some sleep. We fly out in exactly 12 hours. The third floor is all yours. And don't worry, this place is more secure than Fort Knox."

A woman with a gun belt around her slim-fitting mini dress escorted them up to their suite and said, "Use the Devices to order whatever food and drink you like, and our chef will prepare it and deliver anything you desire."

Jeri hardly noticed the expansive space or the luxurious décor as she sat at a table and pulled out her laptop and started typing.

"What are you doing?" Calvin demanded.

"I'm writing the story of the century," she said. "The millennium. If we get to Dr. Wise and the President, then I'll save this for a series in the paper and the book I'm going to write. But if we don't—"

Calvin closed her laptop. "We will!"

She tried to open her computer. He pressed it down.

"Stop!" she ordered, attempting to pry his fingers off. He squeezed tighter. She bit his wrist.

He let go. And burst into laughter.

She cast an angry look up at him, crossing her arms, seething.

"Jeri," he said softly. "Let's just relax and get some sleep. We have a big day tomorrow."

She pursed her lips at him. All she wanted to do was get back to her keyboard and write the story that could potentially save the nation if Daemon killed her first.

Chapter 51

CALVIN HAD NEVER FELT more love toward another human being. It was so strong, he could taste it, and all he wanted to do was make Jeri feel safe and peaceful, for once. He wanted to make her forget all about this nightmare where they were being chased across America by crazy gunman sent by a terrorist, while she thought her parents were possibly dead.

But she was so fiery and passionate about doing the right thing above and beyond the call of duty.

"Jeri," he said, picking up a Device from the table. "Let's order some food."

She sat with her arms crossed, staring straight ahead. He put his hand on her shoulder, expecting her to push him away. She grasped his hand. Then stood up.

One look into her eyes and he knew that she felt exactly as he did. They stared for a long moment, then he pulled her close, and pressed his parted lips to hers. The sensation of hot velvet came to mind as his thoughts melted under the heat of their kiss and the electricity pulsing between their bodies. He pulled her closer.

She jumped up, wrapping her legs around his waist, pressing her breasts into his chest, and holding the back of his neck as they devoured each other with their mouths. He carried her over to the king-sized bed, which was made of lacquered, redwood stained logs and covered with plush white linens and pillows.

As passion fused them into one, their fears and crisis-mode existence melted away, and he could see in her eyes that she too had escaped—if only temporarily—into nirvana. He hated that it wouldn't last, because they could very well die at any time.

"If we make it alive out of this insane mission," he vowed, "we are going to have this, you and me, in our own private paradise, for the rest of our lives. I promise."

Jeri smiled up at him as a tear rolled down her cheek.

Chapter 52

Finally, after a jet ride that ended on a private airstrip near Detroit, and a transport in an ambulance, Jeri and Bullet reached the LifeQuest Movement headquarters in an abandoned-looking warehouse by the river.

The ambulance pulled into an empty first floor whose cracked cement floor had weeds growing through it. The vehicle stopped beside a very modern-looking elevator, where they were greeted by a young woman named Kenya and two physically fit men with guns.

"Come this way," she said, leading them onto the industrial elevator that descended many stories. It stopped at a floor with no number. Kenya punched in an electronic code to open the elevator.

I have to do a story about this! Jeri was so excited. First that she was seeing this rumored place with her own eyes. Second that she was about to meet with Dr. Wise, which put them one step closer to getting to the President. Hopefully.

"I'm taking you to Dr. Wise in his office," Kenya said as they passed a very impressive gymnasium where young kids and teenagers were working out vigorously. They were in various stages of physical fitness, from obese to Olympic-looking athletes.

"These students are excelling in their public schools with good grades and in competitive sports because they are getting excellent nutrition and training here," Kenya said. "They run faster, train harder, get good grades, and are very focused. Not to mention, they're like nutritionists in training."

Hank, who was following Kenya, Jeri, and Calvin along with Henry, laughed and said, "You couldn't pay them to eat a French fry or a Heavenly burger."

"I like that as superior athletes," Kenya said, "they're serving as role models to inspire other teenagers and kids to follow healthy lifestyles and to recruit their families to participate. They have to be careful, though. Some of these kids are so good, but coming from areas that are so bad, they're being harassed. They're winning competitions and scholarships to college, and not everybody likes that. Some people have the attitude if you come from an urban wasteland—or rural wasteland out in other parts of Michigan—you should stay there, become obese and just die there."

After walking a long corridor, Kenya said, "Next we're coming to the big studio where I teach dance classes to adults and children."

Another elevator ride took them down to another floor, where a huge garage door opening onto a salt mine tunnel was opening to allow a modified bus to enter. Then

LifeQuest staff helped extremely obese people exit the bus, very slowly. Kenya led Jeri and Calvin alongside the group, which went to the detox clinic.

"Here we help people detox from sugar, junk food, and a generally toxic diet that's literally killing them," Kenya said.

Jeri cringed, thinking, *More than you know.* She was astounded by the ghoulish expressions and hellish moans and groans of people who sounded like they were quitting heroin.

"Next, I want to show you the indoor farm," Kenya said, as they walked past a dining hall that was serving super healthy food. "The school, dormitory, and residences are on other floors. We also have classrooms where people of every size shape and race are learning about nutrition and how processed foods poison the body and cause early death."

Jeri's mind spun a mile a minute, recording every detail that she observed. In the hallway, she saw a young man who looked familiar.

"Jeri?" he exclaimed.

"Jeremy?" she responded. "Wow, you have really slimmed down!"

He put his arm around Kenya. "I see you've met my partner in creating a better world, starting with ourselves and our families."

"How's that going?" Jeri asked as they approached the organic farm, where Dr. Wise was waiting at the door with a man holding a rifle.

"Jeri Brewster," Dr. Wise said, extending a hand. "Nice

to see you again."

"Thank you for seeing us," she said.

"This is my niece, Kenya Wise, my brother's daughter," Dr. Wise said. "I am so proud of her and Jeremy. The two of them are like pied pipers for the kids to dance and play in the gym, then work in the gardens and make lunches with the fresh produce."

Kenya and Jeremy beamed.

Do you mind if we meet in the farm?" Dr. Wise asked. "Walking the aisles amidst all the organic produce helps me get my exercise and keeps my brain sharper. "I agreed to meet with you because I liked the responsible way you write your stories, and the articles you wrote after interviewing me about my book. I'm sorry about your father. I respected him a lot, and I hope his story has a happy ending."

Dr. Wise cast a suspicious look at Calvin. "Who's your friend?"

"Sergeant Calvin Alvarez, sir," Calvin said. "I had the pleasure of working with General Brewster for a good part of my entire military career."

Dr. Wise led them into the fruit tree grove and, still walking briskly, asked, "So tell me how can I help you?"

Jeri began to explain the crisis.

"I'd heard rumors at King Daemon had used my book as a template to beat America, and I suspected that's why they ranked number one in health," Dr. Wise said. "But the Republic of the East is an extremely secretive country and no proof was ever leaked of what they were doing. It might look like they're the ideal model for the United States to follow, but I'm afraid it's much more sinister than that."

"You're right," Jeri said. "In fact, it's part of their master plan to take over the world, starting with the United States. I'll show you exactly how." On her Device, she showed the Doctor the terrorists' plan.

"Exactly as I predicted," he groaned. "Only worse!" Looking distressed, he walked faster. "They cannot win!" He spoke into a speaker on a mini Device on his wrist. "Code Genesis! All leaders report to the auditorium immediately."

"What's going on?" Jeri asked.

"Follow me," Dr. Wise said.

"Listen, doc, we're here on urgent business," Bullet said with an annoyed tone. "If you're about to call an assembly—"

"The fate of our country is in our hands right now," Dr. Wise snapped.

"Right, and we need *your* help!" Jeri exclaimed. "My father said I have to get this to the President, and that you can help."

The doctor abruptly turned a corner and briskly strode down a long corridor.

"Good luck," Dr. Wise said. "The President is surrounded by people who are motivated by money. The heavy toll of health care for obesity and its related diseases is pennies compared to the money the food industry is making by hooking people on their processed poison."

"I have to get to the President," Jeri said with a glaze in her eyes as if she hadn't heard what the doctor said. "That's what my father said. I have to get to the President."

"They'll kill you first," the doctor said.

"Already tried, several times," Bullet said.

"I guess that's why Pops sent her to you," the doctor said. "I'm certain you were followed here, so I'll have to see you out another way."

"Wait, you have to help us!" she said.

"I am helping you. I'm taking you to the only person I know who can get you where you need to go."

"And who would that be?" Bullet asked.

"General Will Marcus," the doctor said. "He's one of the only people the President trusts when it comes to this issue."

Bullet shook his head. "Get us to him and we're all done for. General Marcus sold his soul to the devil about 20 years ago. Daughter was dying of cancer. Some big food industry pimp comes along, pays for some miracle cure, and he's had his head way up the food industry's ass ever since." Bullet cast a hard look at the doctor. "Is that the best you can do? I thought as leader of the underground, you'd have more juice than that."

Dr. Wise got in Calvin's face and said through pursed lips: "Then I will take her to the President of the United States myself."

Calvin laughed. "If you had pull like that you wouldn't

be hiding out in this inner city rat hole."

"Excuse me!" Jeri said. "There's no room in this equation for your testosterone-driven power plays. Now I need you both to focus and help me figure this out. Doctor, how can you get me to the President?"

The doctor cut her a hard look and asked, "Don't you have media friends in Washington?"

"I don't have any friends right now. The second place the terrorists went looking for me was at my job. After they kidnapped and possibly killed my mother."

The doctor's expression softened to sympathy.

"Time for Plan B," he said. "My father became friends with the President at Harvard Law School. They're in touch. I rarely do this, but I'll ask my father to arrange a meeting."

Calvin crossed his arms and said, "So you're hiding out here, but you can get face time with the Commander in Chief. Right. This sounds too easy."

The doctor shook his head. "Jeri, my father has admired your parents, then you as a journalist, for a long time. If I tell him that you have information that is paramount to the survival of the United States as we know it, he will listen."

"The FBI is looking for her, and believe me, not all those dudes are trustworthy," Bullet said. "How can you tell your dad it's her without saying it's her?"

"We have special communications codes; I'll proceed accordingly."

Bullet cast a suspicious stare that softened into a nod.

"Okay."

"Thank you, Dr. Wise!" Jeri said.

"Don't get too excited until we see what he can do," Bullet snapped. "Let's go."

"No, stay here," Dr. Wise said. "Our LifeQuest centers have been fortified with materials that shield them from satellite, radar, and other surveillance equipment. So here inside, the terrorists can no longer track you. One step outside, there could be snipers firing on the door to the Underground."

Later, Dr. Wise dined with Jeri, Calvin, and his father.

"We are going to do everything in our power to help you reach the President," said Professor Wise.

"I second that," Dr. Wise said.

Later, Jeri and Calvin sat in the front row during a LifeQuest assembly in the amphitheatre where Dr. Wise addressed hundreds of people, many of whom Jeri recognized and wished she could write about this. For now she was recording it in her mind and notes for future use.

"We knew things would get tough," Dr. Wise said, "but things are happening on a global scale that are beyond my scope of imagination. For now, our greatest threat is government attempts to infiltrate and conduct surveillance. If we get too powerful, too successful, that's when they'll crack down hard. So we have to be extra careful about who can join and what degree of access they can have."

A short time later, Dr. Wise met with his close circle of leaders. And it was only to them that he shared the fact that they were stockpiling weapons and supplies.

"It'll be a small-scale World War III," he said, "a real showdown, right here in Detroit. Not only do we have the government out to get us, but now we have the King of Tricqua, because Jeri Brewster discovered their plot. And they see us as an obstacle to what they want, so they want to take us down, too."

Chapter 53

As HIS TOP ADVISORS in the United States appeared on a video conference call on his giant screen, King Daemon was furious.

"This LifeQuest Movement is a direct threat to their mission!" he shouted, surrounded by his Royal Brotherhood. "The more people who refuse to eat fast food, the fewer people the Kingdom can kill with OC-8. Why have you not squashed this movement like a beetle under your feet?"

Eddie Smith spoke first: "We have plans to annihilate them very soon."

"Do it yesterday!" King Daemon ordered. "And why have you allowed the girl and her boyfriend to escape us over and over? How many incompetent imbeciles do I have working for me? You should all be hanged on live video!"

Richard Blane spoke next: "Our OC-8 campaign is proceeding smoothly, and while the inner-city deaths of poor minorities have been reported by the media and authorities, especially since Beatrice Donderro of the FBI made headlines, no one has been able to prove any of the many conspiracy theories born of this experience."

"I feel we are delayed," the King said. "I blame the General's daughter and his protégé, the soldier. They are attempting to interfere with the King's royal destiny. It's time to accelerate the pace. I believe we should add a large city with an easily dispensable population. Add the city where the girl and the wise doctor are hiding: Detroit, Michigan. We must be thankful to Dr. Michael Wise for providing a blueprint for us to save our nation from the gluttonous ways of America. But it is time for us to stamp him out before his growing movement can save more the Americans. That would only interfere with our mission. And that is unacceptable."

The King recommended that smaller doses of OC-8 be added to the food in the restaurants in schools.

"If children start dying quickly, it will spark an investigation that could jeopardize our plan," he said. "Make sure we administer only enough OC-8 to the children in schools so that they gain weight rapidly, and meet their demise through the natural evolution of quick-onset obesity and related diabetes, cancer and cardiac arrest."

Chapter 54

Nurse Katie Matthews had never seen so many bizarre cases involving high blood sugar, soaring blood pressure, and sudden death as a result. During the past two weeks, she had seen 36 people in the Emergency Room with these symptoms.

Most of them were indigent; fast food was a staple of their diets. They were young and old, male and female, and mostly black. They all reported a general malaise.

"It feels like glass in my stomach," her patient said. "Ever since I ate Taco Temptation last night. Then I got light-headed and fainted."

Another patient came in with a stomach that was literally ripped from the inside because he had eaten so much.

"He couldn't stop," his brother said while the man was wheeled into emergency surgery. "He said he just felt this overwhelming hunger and I think he ate three large pizzas and downed it with a gallon of pop. The only reason he stopped eating was because I literally pulled a gun on him and said I'd shoot him if he didn't get in the car and come here with me."

After him, another person came who had literally eaten himself to death. The flesh on his belly was split open. The doctors were astounded that someone could keep eating beyond the pain threshold of being so full.

"I kept telling him to stop," the man's wife cried to Katie. "But it was like he was possessed and kept saying he was still hungry, and he kept eating."

The man's autopsy showed crystallized sugar in his blood, his extremities, and in his brain.

One of the coroners, who was Katie's childhood friend, told her that he was attending a conference of coroners, and these same conclusions were reported across the state. Sugar crystallization in organs, in blood, and in brains. Sudden onset of sickness and death amongst indigent people who consumed a lot of fast food.

"We are working on pinpointing the source of the food that these individuals are consuming," he said. "This is a very sinister trend that we do not believe is coincidental, but we cannot report to the media until we confirm the source, because we do not want to cause panic."

Katie felt panicked, because her family loved fast food. So did she. In fact, she had just scarfed down five tacos at lunchtime along with a hot fudge sundae from the Creamy Dream drive-thru.

She was so ashamed. And now afraid that perhaps she and her kids and her husband could end up sick and dead like the folks she was seeing in the ER.

Katie couldn't shake these nightmarish images when she

went home. She was extremely disturbed that their twins, Brian and Bethany, were packing on weight at an alarming rate. Seemingly overnight, they had outgrown their clothes. Their faces were as round as the moon, and even their fingers and toes were chubbier.

Just today, she noticed that the youngest, five-year-old Suzie, was also getting pudgy through the middle.

"Dan," she said, while cleaning up the empty pizza box from dinner, "we really need to do something. All of us. I just don't know what. If I can't stick to a diet longer than a few days, how do I expect the kids to?"

Dan shrugged, still sitting at the table with a tall mug of beer. "I'm at a loss myself. I mean, maybe we should ask Jeremy. He's connected to that whole movement that's helping people lose weight and—"

"No, the underground thing sounds scary to me," Katie said. "Militant people in the inner city. Guns. At least that's what I've heard—"

"Jeremy has a very different spin on it," Dan said, "and he's been there. He tried to tell me, and get me to go there. He says it's safe."

"Can we find a happy medium," Katie said, "getting healthy without being radical militants?"

Brian and Bethany ran into the kitchen. "Mom, Dad, we want to go to school tonight. Heavenly's Homework Lounge is having a contest. Whoever wins the spelling bee wins a free chocolate sundae!"

Katie and Dan exchanged a concerned expression.

While she wanted to feel excited that her kids were asking to go to school, it was for the wrong reasons. She pointed to the bowl on the table. "We're going to do something different tonight. Your brother Jeremy brought over these delicious green grapes from the farmer's market."

The kids poked out their lips and crossed their arms. "We don't like fruit! We want ice cream!" They stomped around the kitchen, shouting, "Ice cream! Ice cream! Ice cream!" Suzie ran in and joined them.

Bethany shouted, "Why do we have to eat grapes if Mom gets to eat chocolate brownies in bed at night?"

Katie's cheeks burned with embarrassment. But ever since her sister had been kidnapped and possibly murdered, the General had disappeared, and Jeri had vanished, the only way Katie knew to cope with her shock and grief was to eat sweets. They made her feel better in the moment, and once she was stuffed, they created a numbing sensation on her mind, body, and broken heart. Then the sugar high became a crash, which had a sedative effect and made her want to just go to sleep and forget everything. But she couldn't. She had a full time job as a nurse, a husband, four kids, and a house. So she'd eat more chocolate for a quick boost to power through laundry and cleaning, only getting fatter with every bite.

"And Dad, you eat potato chips, not grapes!" Brian shouted.

"Silence!" Dan yelled. "Kids, I hate to say this, but it's time that we all cut back on ice cream and treats. We need to be like your brother Jeremy, and start eating more fruits and vegetables. Let's go for a bike ride."

Chapter 55

The women were so beautiful, Senator Buxton didn't know where to look first.

The brunette with big tits. The blond with the juiciest ass he'd ever seen. The redhead with lips that looked like candy. The twins with diamond-studded nipple rings. The petite Asian girl with a serpent tattoo on her back, its blue-green tail snaking down to her crack.

"Cindy," he said, "you have outdone yourself."

The women—all two dozen of them, were posing around the room as just as many CEOs, legislators, and other high powered men perused the goods by making small talk and eyeballing their bodies.

"The Garden of Eden is exceeding my expectations in terms of excellence in products and services," he said.

"And profits," Cindy added. "I can hardly recruit new girls fast enough to keep up with the demand. And how brilliant of you to suggest that we operate under the innocuous guise of a sports supply company, that looks legitimate on all of our gentleman customers' credit card bills."

"Their wives will be none the wiser," Brace whispered

with a sly smile. "I think you and I should celebrate in private after this little mix and mingle."

This was a monthly event where Cindy provided the girls, and Brace provided the male clients, so that they could go "shopping" for new playmates in a private, secure space. All transactions were handled discreetly, and the company even arranged for the hotel rooms and made travel plans for the mistresses to travel with the men, undetected by secretaries, wives, and media.

Brace gazed at Cindy, who was so beautiful he couldn't think straight when he looked into her big blue eyes and thought about the thrill of fucking her. But this was a business deal, too. He was making millions on this venture with her, and so was she.

"We need to expand into major urban centers across America, then into Europe," he said, watching a Brazilian girl with luscious curves sit on a Congressman's lap. He nuzzled his nose between her huge tits, and Brace's dick throbbed. *I need to try her out sometime. That girl is hotter than July in Texas.*

"Cindy," he said, "let's map out our strategy for expansion. I think you and I just struck gold."

She smiled, then kissed his mouth passionately. "Let's do it. I am all in."

Chapter 56

THE GIRL AND HER boyfriend had all but disappeared from surveillance, and King Daemon was on a rampage.

"What kind of idiots are you?" he screamed at his top aides in the United States on a live video call. "You have yet to kill the girl who stole my manifesto. Now everyone will suffer. Push OC-88 through the proper channels, and begin serving it in cities across America!"

He summoned Dr. Braza to stand before them and provide a refresher of the drug. "OC-88 is hybrid of the toxin that causes the equivalent of cardiac arrest for the brain—it just shuts down," Dr. Braza said. "So much sugar floods the bloodstream so fast, that the sugar literally attacks the brain tissue and kills it."

"I say slow your roll," Eddie Smith warned. "Now the media is picking up on this, because coroners are reporting that they're performing autopsies that show brain lobes that contain so much sugar, they crystallized like rock candy. The same crystallization was also found in other organs and solidified arteries."

Linda Blane nodded. "On a more reassuring note, we have key individuals who are making sure that inquiries and reports meet as many roadblocks as possible, that Freedom of Information Requests about autopsies are delayed or denied, and that evidence even disappears. We are working very diligently to cover our tracks."

Samuel Addams looked anxious. "Fix this! I can't have this blow up during my presidential campaign! All of you, fix this! I'm so mad, I want to kill the girl and her boyfriend with my own hands."

Chapter 57

CALVIN CAST AN AFFECTIONATE glance at Jeri as she slept on the plush sofa inside his friend's private jet. She looked so peaceful, nestled in the cream-colored leather chair, as the plane hummed at 35,000 feet above their troubles.

All hell was breaking loose with the terrorists' food poisoning plot, and they couldn't get to Washington, DC fast enough. If everything synchronized on cue, their allies would help them get to the President and save the world in one fell swoop.

Calvin's gut cramped.

Nothing is ever that easy.

Sometimes surprises happened to either make it easier, or in most cases, make it harder. Or damn near impossible.

Jeri shifted, letting out an agonized moan as a grimace tensed her face. Her eyes didn't open; she was having a bad dream. She had already been through so much, and now the weight of the world was literally crushing down on her.

The shock of her parents' disappearances, and now shouldering the burden of getting to the President to stop Daemon, all while being pursued by snipers at every turn… was a nightmare on every level. Except in Arizona. Making love with Jeri was by far the most beautiful experience of his entire life. Now, Bullet ached down to his soul to get through this alive and unscathed, so that he could spend the rest of his life in that magical euphoria.

But first we have to go through hell to get to that heaven…

His heart pounded with anxiety as he checked the electronic screen attached to the wall of the airplane cabin. They were just 40 miles out from Washington. Since his neighbor engaged in international business that took him into rough parts of the world, this plane was equipped with a military-grade shield to deflect any kind of detection devices that the terrorists might be using to track them.

Likewise, he had just installed on his Device a new "inferno wall"—which was a much tougher version of the typical "firewall" security systems on computers. He had done the same with Jeri's Device.

Calvin sent a digital note to his team that would be assisting with the plan to kidnap the President of the United States. Getting him alone, away from the crooked team of terrorist colluders around him, was the only way for Jeri to share the information that could save America and the world.

Calvin typed a note to all of them; they were traveling with their teams to DC now in a variety of vehicles that included trucks, campers, and airplanes.

He addressed the note to: Johnny "Big Man" Valentine of the Food Fight Posse; Boone Davis from Kentucky; Dr. Michael Wise of the LifeQuest Movement; and Carmen La Buena of the Golden Lotus Yoga Studio in California.

Dr. Wise could not risk traveling to Washington. Instead, the plan was to transport the President to Detroit, for safekeeping until everything blew over.

All the vehicles were in place, including what looked like an 18-wheeler truck emblazoned with adorable color photos of the cutest puppies anyone had ever seen. That was the logo for a popular, eco-friendly pet food company whose mafia-linked owner was a major contributor to the Movement. The truck's interior was designed like a plush studio apartment, so the President would travel in luxury, comfort, and most of all, absolute security.

"On schedule," Calvin typed. "White House visit today at 15:00 hours. Departure at 16:30."

Bullet had already confirmed the strategy for his and Jeri's arrival. His military buddies would pick them up at the hangar in rural Virginia, where they would get into a van and disguise themselves as White House staff. Their credentials were ready, and their clearance was authorized. Once inside the White House, they would attend a Cabinet Meeting, after which Bullet and his military buddies—all serving as Secret Service agents—would whisk the President into a service elevator.

Down into the secret tunnels they would go, winding their way under Pennsylvania Avenue until they reached the stairwell that led to a utility shed in a nearby park. There, they would emerge, and the truck would transport them all back to Detroit, where Dr. Wise's super secure bunker would serve as Command Central for America's Commander in Chief to take control of the United States and stop the killing.

Bullet's heart pounded with excitement. With the help of Dr. Wise's father, his military contacts enabled him to set up the meeting in the White House. This sounded like the craziest spy movie science fiction plot ever. But it was really happening.

And we're going to kidnap the President of the United States to make it happen.

That seemingly horrific offense paled in comparison to the alternative: allowing the terrorists to continue killing Americans and to ultimately take over the nation and the world.

It will be worth every risk.

Bullet chuckled. He'd done some crazy, outrageous shit in his life. This was right on par with breaking into presidential palaces, drug lords' bedrooms, and heavily armed militia camps in some of the most hellacious armpits of the world.

The White House will be a piece of cake compared to what I've done! I'm gonna make Wild Bill proud…

He started to smile, until he glimpsed beautiful Jeri sleeping peacefully once again. Fear for her safety surged through him like ice water in his veins. And worry that Wild Bill was dead made his heart ache for her and for himself.

He trusted me with his daughter's life. That's by far the biggest job I will ever have…

A successful conclusion for all parties involved would be his only option.

Chapter 58

As Johnny "Big Man" Valentine rode in the back seat of the SUV, he peered through the black-tinted windows at one of Washington, DC's most notorious ghettos: Anacostia. His DC Food Fight Posse partner, Jamal, was driving them to a meeting with the local crew before everything went down at the White House.

"This is the downtown area," Jamal said as they stopped at a red light at the intersection of Good Hope Road and Martin Luther King, Jr. Avenue. "We got dudes comin' from all over town, like Barry Farm, Naylor Gardens, and Washington Highlands."

Johnny watched a fat little boy waddle across the street beside an obese woman on a scooter. The child's yellow T-shirt was smudged with dirt and orange fingerprints, because he was eating a bag of fake-cheese-covered-junk. His shoelaces flopped back and forth as he struggled to keep up, hold onto the scooter, and eat all at once.

"Man," Johnny said, "I feel like I'm lookin' at myself when I was a kid. That was me. And my Momma."

The mother drove her scooter with the boy in tow to a Taco Temptation near the corner. They stopped in front and stared at the neon green words that were spray-painted across the glass-walled façade of the restaurant: "DO NOT EAT THIS POISON!" Below that, it said: "Closed by the Food Fight Posse."

"We're the new sheriff in town," Jamal said proudly. "The health department wouldn't do nothin'. They said there's not enough evidence to link all the dead people to the restaurant, but to us, it's clear as day. So we took the law into our own hands."

"We did the same thing in Detroit," Johnny said. "What about Heavenly's, Georgia Fried Chicken, and King's Pizza?"

"Heavenly's is still open," Jamal said. "They got like, an army of security guards. So we had to take to the streets ourselves and warn folks, enter at your own risk. If they won't believe those places are killing us, then—"

"We're about to stop it all," Johnny said.

"Man, it's fucked up, "Jamal said sadly, proceeding through the intersection.

Johnny marveled at how here in the 'hood, it looked, smelled, and felt just like the eastside of Detroit where he'd grown up and now lived. Though the architecture of brownstones was different than the free-standing houses back in the D, it was the vibe, the people, here and in every urban center in America, that captured his heart.

The beautiful beige, brown, and black faces all exuded the same strength, resilience, and indomitable spirit as folks back in Detroit. But, just like at home, their eyes radiated the same desperation, sickness, and lack as the "have-nots" in a world ruled by the "haves." The tragedy—no, the crime—of it was that the "haves" had the power to change it all, and they were just down the street on Capitol Hill, and in all the wealthy communities throughout Washington and in the surrounding states.

"When we get through," Johnny said, "it ain't just about stopping folks from eating poison. It's about flipping around the entire system so the 'have nots' can be equal and even with the 'haves.' We need everybody to have a chance to live a good life. Is that so hard to ask?"

Jamal let out a chuckle. "Time for asking is over. It's time to just start taking. Take back our health. Take back our 40 acres and a mule. Take back the right to be healthy and live in a safe place."

"Amen to that," Johnny said.

A few minutes later, Jamal pulled into a garage behind a four-story, cement building with a storefront and apartments above. From the garage, they headed up to a large, open space where several dozen Food Fight Posse leaders from across the region were gathered.

They stood and applauded as Johnny entered.

"Today some of the wildest shit you ever heard is gonna go down," Johnny said. "What I need all yawl to do, is stay ready. We might need you to come to Detroit, if things get outta hand."

"You got us, boss," one guy said as others nodded and said, "Yeah!"

"The Food Fight Posse's gon' win this," Johnny said. "We gotta save our people, or it's over."

Chapter 59

As Dr. Michael Wise strode through the hallways of his complex, deep beneath Detroit, his wrist Device glowed with a tiny blue light to indicate that he was receiving a message. He touched the gray screen, which glowed with a text from Calvin Alvarez, saying that he and Jeri were on schedule.

This is it. Do or die. God help us.

Adrenaline surged through Dr. Wise as he passed through three separate security chambers that required a retina scan and voice analysis to enter.

"How's it coming?" he asked the crew that was putting the final touches on what would become the bunker hideout for the President of the United States.

"Come on in," the lead construction worker said.

Dr. Wise stepped past the plush living quarters, through a titanium sliding door that opened, and into a room that looked like the cockpit of a spacecraft. Video screens, computerized panels and keyboards and telephones cast a futurist blue hue over the stainless steel surfaces.

"The most important aspect of this is security and zero detectability by the most advanced surveillance equipment anywhere," Dr. Wise said.

"Sir," the man said, "our lead tech security guy, the one you met who used to do this stuff for NASA and the Pentagon, he did the final check on everything that he designed himself. You better believe, this is as good as it gets."

Dr. Wise always listened to his gut. Right now, it was telling him that the technological infrastructure to support the President was in place. Now his greatest worry was the human trust factor. All it would take was for one person with malicious intent to compromise this entire operation.

Fear knotted his stomach.

"Dr. Wise," said one of his assistants, hurrying toward him. "The trucks with today's shipment of ammunition have arrived. We need you to inspect everything."

Minutes later, Dr. Wise was in the garage, watching men and women unload four trucks full of guns and bullets.

"I don't think World War III will need this much gun power," said Angelo Grazia, wearing a business suit and sunglasses. "But we'll be ready. That's for sure."

"Tell your father and everyone else," Dr. Wise said, "I can't thank them enough. They've helped me build this place and get ready for the show-down in ways that are so far above and beyond, it's unreal."

"Like I always say," Angelo said, "my Dad is trying to do the right thing. He's got the power and the money and the friends in important places to do it, so here we are. Helping you save the world. Be the change, baby!"

Dr. Wise shook his head. "Hopefully we'll all still be standing—"

"My Dad doesn't lose," Angelo said as a rocket launcher was carried off a truck. "And you can see, he doesn't mess around."

Dr. Wise chuckled. "This is war. And we have to win."

Chapter 60

IF THESE FOLKS DIDN'T stop bickering, Boone Davis
was about to go off. His wife Lynette was being sweet as
pie about the sweltering conditions inside this little apartment where they were waiting for everything to go down
this afternoon.

But Ginger was pitching a hissy fit, and Tate was trying
to calm her down, as usual. And none of them were takin'
too kindly to being in here alongside two dozen northern-
ers who also happened to be black, Hispanic and from the
inner-city.

"Good Lord," Ginger said, "it's hot as hell in here. Why
couldn't yawl have at least gotten us an air conditioned
place to stay?"

"Honey," Tate said, "I told you, this is a military operation we're runnin' here. It ain't about the Ritz Carlton. It's
about savin' America."

Ginger rolled her eyes and dabbed her sweaty forehead
with a cloth as she sat on the sofa.

Beside her was Lynette, who was on the phone with the
guy in charge of the caravan to Michigan. A lot of vehicles
were involved, and Lynette's experience in EMS dispatch

back in Kentucky made her the perfect person to coordinate everything now. If everything went according to Plan A, they would proceed with the President in his vehicle, while everyone else rode to the D in a hodgepodge of cars, vans, trucks and campers.

If all hell broke loose at the White House this afternoon, they'd dispatch a whole different set of vehicles for rescue and anything else that might be required.

Lord, don't let it come to that! Boone thought about all the people in his family and in his town—and now across America—who had died from obesity and the fast food poisonings. He couldn't believe people were still eating that crap, even though the anecdotal evidence made it clear that somebody had spiked America's burgers, pizzas, fried chicken and tacos with a deadly toxin. But the restaurants and food companies of course were still claiming that it was a coincidence, and too many idiots believed them, at the cost of their own lives.

Boone exhaled loudly. Soon this would all be over and this revolution would be won. America would be a safe place to live in a healthy new way.

We'll fight to the end, because if we don't, they'll kill us anyway...

Boone stood close enough to Lynette to massage her shoulder as she continued on the phone.

"Hey yawl," said a young black fellow with the Food Fight Posse outta Detroit. "Lunch is comin' up."

Two more black men came to the door with large boxes containing a healthy mix of salads, sandwiches, stir-fries, and fruit. They placed the food on the table and everyone ate. Except Ginger, who eyed the guys suspiciously and crossed her arms.

"Where'd this come from?" she demanded.

As Boone reached for a salad topped with grilled chicken, he was about to explain that Jamal Jordan's wife owned a nice restaurant here and that he and Lynette had visited last night for dinner and to discuss today's plan with Johnny Valentine.

But Carmen La Buena looked like he wanted to make a teachable moment, as he was always saying, out of this here situation.

"Ginger, my dear friend," Carmen said, wearing her usual flowy clothes with a ponytail and sandals. How that woman always stayed so calm was the greatest mystery on earth. Her voice was always soft and her face was always as peaceful as if life were just one nice walk in the park. She wasn't even sweating like everybody else.

"You must be grateful for the bounty that is provided," Carmen said. "You must trust that the divine is always blessing you with abundance."

Ginger glared at the food. "I don't know where it came from or who touched it."

Carmen offered her a box containing a whole grain sandwich, bursting with vegetables and chunks of turkey. "Once we engage in our strategy this afternoon, it may be a long time before the next meal, dear friend."

"Eat, girl," Tate ordered, glancing at Lynette, who was devouring stir-fried broccoli and brown rice. "This ain't no time to be persnickety about food."

Why they had to drag that she-devil along—

Boone stopped himself. Nobody could be left behind in Kentucky. The feds and whoever else were too hot on their trail to risk being separated right now. That's why their entire group of 400 people had dispersed to various parts of the Midwest, positioned to go to Detroit to fight, when and if the time was right. And the way things were looking, it wasn't a matter of "if" anymore. And "when" would be sooner, rather than later.

The tiny blue light at the right corner of Boone's wrist Device glowed. He touched the center and the gray surface lit up with a message from Bullet. According to schedule, he and Jeri would still be in the plane, about to land.

"Excuse me, my friend," Carmen told Ginger, who reluctantly began eating. She read the message, then exchanged a quick glimpse with Boone, who nodded. He pretty much inhaled his lunch, just to fuel up for what promised to be one helluva long night.

Chapter 61

CALVIN HAD A BAD feeling as the plane touched down in Washington. He couldn't put his finger on it, but he could put his finger on the triggers of the multiple guns strapped to his body and in his bag.

Hopefully he was just in overdrive and hypersensitive as a result.

As he and Jeri stepped off the plane inside the hangar, a dark-windowed SUV was waiting nearby as planned. Nothing looked unusual; all the people working on planes around them appeared legitimate.

But it didn't feel right.

"Wait," Calvin said as they strode toward the vehicle. The driver stepped out. It was his buddy, as expected. But something still—

Tires screeched.

A silver Porsche 911 Carrera sped toward them.

Bullet reached to grab Jeri.

Two men ran from under the plane they had just left, grabbed each of her arms, and—as the Porsche screeched to a stop—threw her inside.

The car took off like a bolt of lightning.

The two men who had snatched Jeri tried to run. Bullet grabbed one of them with each of his huge arms. He threw them in the back seat of the SUV. His buddy took off behind the Porsche.

"Where the fuck are they takin' her?" Bullet demanded, pinning them to the seat with one of his knees in each of their laps. They punched at him, but he smacked them so hard, they sat still.

Bullet turned around. He glimpsed the Porsche zooming over the tarmac as the plane was approaching. It swerved, then sped over a field.

"I'm on him," Bullet's friend said. He hadn't seen George since their mission in Nicaragua, but this wasn't the time to talk. All that mattered was that George was an extraordinary driver.

Plus, George had instructions on whom to call if anything unusual went down. Boone Davis, Johnny Valentine, Carmen La Buena and all their people were waiting for instructions on what to do in a variety of worst-case scenarios.

As the vehicle roared over the tarmac, then onto the field, George said, "I got a full tank of gas, an engine that could compete in NASCAR, and tires that can't go flat. We got those motherfuckers."

Bullet spun back to face the men. "Tell me where they're goin'!"

The men, who were Caucasian and wearing blue, zip-front jumpsuits with the Racer Aviation logo, glared back in silent defiance. Bullet shoved a gun into one of the men's throats.

"Tell me!"

"Kill me and you'll never know," the other guy smirked.

"Who are you with?" Bullet demanded.

"Your worst enemy," the other guy said.

Bullet punched him in the nose. It bled, and the guy groaned, grabbing his face.

"Shit!" George exclaimed. Bullet turned around as the Porsche zipped up a little ramp behind a big trailer truck. A metal gate closed, obscuring the Porsche.

"Oh hell no!" Bullet tied the two guys to each other.

George sped up to the truck, which was now on a two-lane highway flanked by fields.

"I got the front, you got the back," Bullet said, opening the sunroof.

When the SUV was side-by-side with the cab of the truck, Bullet stood in the sunroof, climbed out, and leaped onto the side of the truck. He stood on the silver step outside the driver's door, and grasped the vertical handle behind it.

At the same time, George maneuvered the SUV behind the truck, in case they tried to get away by opening the back and driving away with Jeri in the Porsche.

Bullet banged on the window, tried to open the door, and thought about climbing on the hood. He also aimed a gun directly at the head of the man in the driver's seat. But he ignored the whole situation, as if Bullet and his gun weren't even there.

Bulletproof glass, no doubt. The truck kept going for miles. It came to a bridge, crossed a river, and proceeded into a wooded area. Bullet held on. Then it proceeded down a long dirt road, kicking up clouds of dust, before finally pulling into a warehouse-type building. Inside, a half-dozen men with big guns surrounded the truck. Bullet stepped down. He put his hands up.

The back door rumbled up, the Porsche pulled out, and the men carried Jeri, unconscious, toward him.

"Take one last look before she dies," said the big, swarthy man with a thick accent who was holding her. "She is going on a long plane ride where if the King does not kill her with his own hands, she will join his prized stable of whores."

Bullet used all his strength to pull away from the men restraining him. Until someone clicked a gun at his head. He would be no use to her if he were dead. Equally painfully in his heart and mind right now were the fact that they wanted to hurt and kill the woman he loved, and by losing her, he would fail to honor his pledge to Wild Bill. And the United States would fall to its enemies.

At the moment, he was on his own. George and the SUV were not inside the warehouse. He was more useful outside than in, as long as these goons didn't trip him in the woods.

The man held Jeri's limp body in front of Bullet. Her right cheek was bruised. Her skin was pale. Her arms and legs and head hung as if she were a rag doll. The man pressed his lips to Jeri's exposed neck, then looked up at Bullet with a delighted expression. "Mmmm," the guy said, "the King will savor the triumph of plundering his enemy's sacred spaces."

This was the worst moment of Bullet's life. Fighting with a gun to his head would get him killed. Letting that man take his beloved Jeri and precious charge to the enemy would kill him in another way.

Chapter 62

GEORGE HAD BOTH GUYS strung up in an abandoned farmhouse, using his favorite truth-telling technique. These guys were no different than any other man who'd always had a way of cooperating when situations involved introducing sharp objects to certain areas.

Even if these guys and their ringleaders were world-class terrorists, they were several rungs below George's elite training and ability.

The truck that had pursued him when he turned around fled the warehouse, had fallen for the tree-toppling trick. All George had to do was shoot down one tree along the wooded road, and it toppled right in front of the bad guys' vehicle. So they couldn't follow him.

Plus, anybody trying to leave the warehouse would be stuck until somebody took a chainsaw to the five tree blockades that George left along the road.

Meanwhile, George had activated a variation of the back-up plan with a team of guys who'd been on call near the hangar. The only thing that could disrupt the plan would be for those motherfuckers to kill Bullet and Jeri.

Not on my watch.

Chapter 63

Jeri awoke in horrible pain. It felt like an ax was lodged in the top of her head, which was throbbing beyond belief.

Where the hell am I?

Suddenly the super-fast images of being snatched from Calvin's grasp in the airplane hangar… thrown into that car… driven out—

I was kidnapped!

This little room spun. It was sort of a lounge, with plush black furniture and a low table. A little radio was playing horrible, hard rock music with a pounding base beat and ear-screechingly high guitar chords.

Where's Bullet?

Her heart pounded even harder than her head.

The King. She had heard one of those men say, "The King."

"Oh my God," she gasped. "Daemon's people got me!"

She told her body to leap up from this couch and knock down the door. But her body didn't move. It felt heavy. Immobile.

I was drugged…

Chapter 64

BULLET COULD FEEL IT. Something was about to go down.

Flanked by two armed goons, he was tied to a pole in the warehouse, which was empty except for the truck that had transported the Porsche in here. Jeri was in a room somewhere behind a bank of offices along the far wall.

About six men were in this building. A few were arguing in Tricquan, which Bullet comprehended with perfect clarity. They were disagreeing about how to transport Jeri, now that their road was blocked by fallen trees. One wanted to call in a helicopter; another wanted to wait for the tree cutting service to clear the road. Both plans would delay their flight to the Republic, which would make Daemon furious.

Meanwhile, Bullet could think of nothing but what was happening to Jeri. He felt sick at the idea of those men doing more than just kissing her neck. He balled his fists, overwhelmed with the urge to kill anyone who hurt a single hair on her head.

Boom! Boom!

The metal grate that formed the garage door crashed in. A military tank—yes, a military tank!—rolled in.

Hell, yeah!

A dozen men in fatigues and helmets—with guns blazing—bombarded the warehouse. Faster than the captors could realize what was happening, these snipers took them out, one by one, in quick succession.

Pop! Pop! Pop!

The soldiers untied Calvin, who had only one thought: saving Jeri.

Chapter 65

Jeri heard the gunfire, and prayed that her rescuers were shooting her captors, and not the other way around. Where was Bullet?

Bullet holes pierced the dingy walls of this little office where those grimy men were holding her captive. Her hands were tied behind her back; she squirmed and tugged to free herself, constantly watching the gunfire shred the drywall, spraying her face with dust.

The door burst open.

An American soldier in fatigues, holding a huge assault rifle, charged in, followed by Calvin. He dove toward her.

The soldier used a knife to free her hands.

Calvin scooped her into his arms and, under a hail of bullets from a terrorist who suddenly appeared at the door, and fell just as quickly under a spray of the American soldier's gunfire, they sprinted through the garage.

The gate was open, and a military tank idled beside a helicopter.

Bullet lifted Jeri into the chopper, and it took off.

Chapter 66

I CAN'T BELIEVE WE'RE inside the White House.

With her head still throbbing in pain, Jeri was sitting just a few feet behind the President in the Cabinet Room. He was seated at the long oval table with his back to the French doors that opened onto the Rose Garden. Jeri was in a chair between the American flag, and one of those doors, which were adorned with long, gold draperies.

"These mass deaths by fast food have reached a crisis point," the President said, facing the Vice President across the table. Expressions of dire concern reflected back at him from his two dozen Cabinet Secretaries around the shiny wooden table.

"And while our investigators have found the chemical cause of the problem," the President said, "the perpetrators of these heinous acts remain a mystery."

Jeri, wearing a dark business suit and a visitor's badge that identified her as part of the Department of Homeland Security, glimpsed Presidential Advisor Gerald Blane through her large, black-framed glasses. With make-up over her bruised cheek, she was certain that he would not recognize her under this shoulder-length, black wig. Nor would he recognize Bullet, who looked gorgeous, disguised as a black-haired, eyeglass-wearing Secret Service agent, compliments of one of his friends from a mission in Somalia.

Why didn't anyone else pick up on that SOB's scurrilous vibe? The sight of Gerald Blane made the hairs on the back of Jeri's neck rise as if she were in a haunted house. Because he was pure evil.

She glimpsed the huge, gilt-framed portraits of George Washington, Thomas Jefferson and Theodore Roosevelt around the room. What would they say about that despicable terrorist who hated America, sitting here at the pinnacle of power, duping the President and his Cabinet?

Jeri wished she could stand up and shout the truth right now. But she couldn't risk Blane or anyone else who was close to the President to stop her.

I've waited this long. I can make it one more hour.

She glanced at Bullet, whose eyes glimmered ever-so-slightly in a way that was almost celebratory. He, too, was anticipating the long-awaited moment when they could tell the President what was going on.

"I'm convinced," said the Agriculture Secretary, "that this is a campaign by a disgruntled worker in one of the companies that makes a common ingredient in fast food. Somebody with an ax to grind, and the scientific know-how to do something about it."

The President shook his head. "That's a valid theory, but our evidence is showing it's a much more sophisticated plot—"

"Mr. President, if I may interject," Gerald Blane said with his usual demeanor and silky-smooth voice. "I'm leaning toward the report given to me by Beatrice Donderro at the FDA that says the illnesses and deaths have occurred as a result of the organic and unintentional break-down of a substance as commonly used as MSG—"

"Not so!" shouted Myrtle Nettles, the head of the Department of Health and Human Services. "I'm tired of hearing you try to diminish the horrific impact of this crisis, Gerald! You've been accused of bias because of your family's interest in the fast food industry, and I'm afraid your behavior of late is proving that true."

Blane cast an empathetic, almost charming look at her, but violence glimmered in his eyes for just a split second. "I'm sorry, Madam," he said, "but my beliefs are rooted in strong empirical evidence—"

"So are mine!" she snapped. "I'd appreciate if you would appreciate this deadly problem as something dire that requires immediate action to stop it."

As Blane launched into a diatribe to undermine Ms. Nettles' concerns, Jeri's heart pounded. This type of argument could rage on for hours. But she and Bullet needed this meeting to wrap up as scheduled, in exactly 52 minutes. Only then could they execute their perfectly orchestrated plan with every player in place.

I can't believe we're going to kidnap the President.

As soon as this meeting was over, Bullet and three Secret Service agents who were in on the plan would escort the

President ostensibly to the Oval Office. But they would actually proceed down a secret stairwell to a basement room leading to a tunnel that few knew existed. The tunnel led to another hidden room in a nearby building, where a truck would be waiting for Jeri and Bullet to whisk the President away from his traitorous staff. Inside the truck, Jeri would divulge the truth to the President.

And once they reached the safe house near Richmond, Virginia—a cottage owned by the General's college room-mate—they could proceed with the second phase of their strategy to save the American people and its government from the enemy within.

Oh my gosh, what would Dad say about all this? Actually, she knew. He would be damn proud that she was taking matters into her own hands to fulfill what was possibly his final assignment for her.

Her heart skipped a beat. She felt sick.

Dad… where are you? Are you alive? Are you safe?

Jeri felt that her father was still alive. Then she wondered if her hope were so strong that it convinced her of what she wanted to believe. She glanced down as tears burned her eyes. She reflected back on how this had transpired, and all the horrific moments that had occurred, starting when she found the note and flash drive in his office.

This is our last shot. We'll either succeed today, or die trying…

Panic prickled through her. What if something went wrong? What if she wasn't able to finally tell the President?

What if they got caught, or had to delay their plans once again? It would take weeks or longer to orchestrate yet another plan to get this close.

"Mr. Blane," Ms. Nettles snapped, "I reject your vicious verbal assault that brings into question whether your allegiance for big business is stronger than that of the health and well-being of the American people."

Jeri stared at the back of the President's head as he sat in a shiny brown leather chair. He was literally one step away from her.

I have to do it now… I can't risk another delay…

She gazed across the room at Bullet, who was looking at the President and pressing his finger to his earpiece, which was attached to a coil that went into his suit jacket. His face remained stern as he scanned everyone at the table, and the people seated behind them.

"We're treating this as a matter of national security," said Defense Secretary Shepherd Jones. "We've long discussed the vulnerability of our infrastructures, especially the possibility of spreading deadly toxin through the water supply. It makes sense that a terrorist—whether domestic or international—would choose the cheapest, easiest available, and popular food—to kill mass numbers of people."

"All due respect, sir, but that's a wild theory," Blane said, shaking his head. "If you saw the security protections that have been put in place in the food industry since the Dr. Michael Wise hearings, and the Food Fight riots, and all the other wackos who want to make war on food—"

"Those groups, however lawless they may seem, are trying to save people," said Health and Human Services Secretary Nettles. "I can't believe they'd be behind—"

Blane narrowed his eyes at her. "I didn't say they were behind anything. I'm saying the industry has become extremely stringent and secure since they came on the scene."

Those two exchanged a contentious look that could have set the air on fire.

"To put speculation to rest," the President said, glancing toward the doors as they opened, "we are going to hear from the lead investigator from the CDC."

In walked a bespectacled Asian man in a white lab coat. His spray of short hair was the same color. Flanking him were a plump woman with her auburn hair pulled back in a bun, and a young blond man whose appearance was an odd cross between All American football player and card-carrying Mensa member.

"CDC Assistant Director Roger Ramsey himself has personally supervised their investigation," the President said as White House IT staffers escorted the scientists to a laptop where they inserted a flash drive.

Jeri wondered if they were going to provide more propaganda for the President and this Cabinet Meeting, because Roger Ramsey was linked to some of the shady characters in Blane's terrorist plot. And his wife, the top-selling TV chef and cookbook author, Wilma Ramsey, was hardly an ally of Dr. Wise with her line of "Wilma's Down Home Southern

Kitchen" cookbooks, cooking schools, products, and even a national restaurant chain of the same name.

"Ladies and gentlemen," the lead scientist said as video showing lab rats eating fast food appeared on a large white screen that drew everyone's attention. "We are now about to reveal the truth about what is killing innocent Americans right now."

Suddenly Jeri realized that this room—not the kidnapping plot with Calvin—would be the perfect opportunity to reveal the truth to the President and ALL of his key Cabinet members. Her information would be free of whatever propaganda or lies that the CDC person was being forced to present. Or if his team's information were inconclusive about the source of the poisoning, his presentation would really be a waste of time.

I have the truth! As if she were adjusting her blouse under her suit jacket, she discreetly reached into her bra and pulled out the flash drive, which she gripped. Her heart pounded with anticipation as boldness pumped adrenaline through her like rocket fuel.

Oh my God! Here's my moment! I can commandeer that laptop, plug in my flash drive, and reveal the truth now!

Jeri shifted in her seat. All she'd have to do was announce, "I know the answer!" and dash over—

I'm gonna do it. Why risk the whole kidnapping scheme when I can just—

She glimpsed Bullet. His face was stiff but his eyes were screaming, "No!" She loved that they vibed so passionately that they could communicate without words. But right now, that was more of a curse than a blessing.

Because I really want to just do it right now. I've waited long enough. We've been through so much. And with every day, every minute, thousands of people have died.

Jeri watched the lab rats on the screen as they devoured burgers, tacos, and pizza.

"We replicated the deaths that Americans are experiencing," the lead scientist said, "with lab rats." Everyone in the Cabinet Room was captivated by the video as the rats consumed massive proportions of food compared to their body size.

"You can see that substances in the food are highly addictive," the scientist said, "so that the rats are unable to stop eating when they clearly would have reached a point of fullness."

Jeri's insides were jumping with excitement. She didn't need the CDC to explain what was going on. She could do it herself with a PowerPoint presentation made by the terrorists themselves!

Dad would tell me to take the bull by the horns and just do it now! She could hear him loudly and clearly right now, in her head, repeating one of her favorite quotes by Mark Twain: "Courage is resistance to fear, mastery of fear—not absence of fear."

Courage. Jeri's whole body surged with courage. Her mind spun over how she would take action without revealing herself in a way that would cause Blane to have her arrested or even shot right here, right now.

"Why didn't all the rats die?" asked Myrtle Nettles.

"Good question," the blond scientist said. "The answer is that they did die. But not immediately. Instead, toxins in the food rapidly induced diabetes, so that within a few hours, the rats' blood was so saturated with sugar, our autopsies revealed that the rats' brain tissue had literally crystallized with sugar."

The HHS Secretary shook her head in disgust. "I don't understand how this could happen."

"If in fact this is a terrorist act," said the Homeland Security Director, "it is brilliant. Fast food contains so many additives, from so many sources, it would be extremely difficult to trace the origin or the perpetrators."

The red headed scientist shook her head. "Actually," she said, "we believed that, until we isolated an ingredient in this food that is only manufactured in Russia and China. These substances are banned in the United States, forever denied by the FDA."

The lead scientist nodded. "The only way for these toxins to make their way into the American food supply is for someone to disguise them as something else. Which is exactly what has been happening—"

"This sounds like a monstrous conspiracy," the President said somberly. "Tell me how we find and go after whoever's behind this." He looked to the Secretary of State, who was sitting beside the Vice President, directly in front of Calvin.

Jeri could not stand it another second. She had the answers, and these people had the power to do something about it. Determination and boldness surged so strongly inside her, she shot up to her feet and declared, "Mr. President, I can tell you exactly how."

The President turned around, with an expression of both shock and intrigue. Jeri met his eyes. She could feel Blane and Calvin both staring at her with equal intensity— for opposite reasons.

She was acutely aware that her actions during the next few minutes could cost her life—but save America. But if that were the price that needed to be paid to stop Daemon from conquering the USA and the world, then it would be an honor. In fact, in the split second that Jeri realized this, she was so convinced, that her entire body tingled with goosebumps. It was not a question.

This is not about me. It's about America and the world.

She pulled off her wig, took off her glasses, and held up the flash drive.

"Mr. President, I'm Jerralyn Brewster, the daughter of General William Brewster."

As gasps erupted throughout the Cabinet Room, the President's unblinking stare at Jeri was serious and shocked, but not suspicious.

"During my father's last day in the Republic," Jeri said, "he obtained a document from King Daemon that details his sinister plot to kill Americans and overthrow the American government, by killing our population with poisoned fast food."

The President shook his head; cynicism clouded his face.

Jeri's heart pounded. *This is it. He's going to have the Secret Service tackle me and escort me out.* She refused to look at Blane, who would certainly have her followed, kidnapped, and killed. Calvin's stare was boring two holes through her, but she didn't dare meet his gaze. He was probably furious but—deep down—proud of her boldness to seize this opportunity.

"If this is true," the President demanded, "why have I never heard about this?"

"Because my father was kidnapped and possibly killed, and he left a note with instructions to get this to you," Jeri said, holding out the flash drive. "I've been trying for months to get around some of your gatekeepers who are trying to block you from knowing this information."

Shocked whispers and gasps filled the room with a low chatter, while the Defense Secretary piped in: "This sounds preposterous. The stuff of a spy thriller, most certainly. But not really by any stretch of the imagination."

"Mr. President," Blane snapped, "clearly this woman is in blatant violation of protocol. We have neither the time nor the desire to entertain the wild conspiracy theory of someone who sneaks into this meeting in disguise—"

"Let her speak!" Myrtle shouted. "We have neither the time nor the desire to let people keep dying if someone can tell us the culprit! Mr. Blane, your blatant protectionism of the food industry at the expense of public health is an absolute disgrace! It is treasonous!"

The President ignored them both as he stared at Jeri with a perplexed expression. He studied her face; a look of recognition softened his stare.

"Jerralynn Brewster," he said. "Your father was, is, a good man. Show me what's on the flash drive."

Jeri could feel Calvin's angst as she strode to the laptop, where the scientists removed their flash drive and handed her the clicker. She inserted her flash drive.

Her hands were shaking with excitement, relief, and fear as the screen showed the title page of King Daemon's Power-Point presentation entitled, ACHIEVING OUR DIVINE DESTINY: THE GLOBAL KINGDOM OF OLYMPIA. Beneath that, it said, "How the Royal Kingdom Will Dominate the United States and the World."

"This can't be!" someone exclaimed.

"My God," the Defense Secretary groaned.

As worried whispers and outraged comments erupted from the high-ranking officials around the table, Jeri clicked to page one.

"Mr. President!" Blane said, quickly stepping toward Jeri. "I believe this woman is posing a security threat to you and all of us right now, by disrupting this meeting—"

"Mr. Blane," the President said, shifting in his chair so he could continue to read the screen. "Sit down. I knew her father. A good man. My gut tells me, she's authentic and has good intentions."

Calvin stepped between Blane and Jeri and said, "Sir" in a tone that meant, *Step back motherfucker.*

"For the record," Blane said, "I believe she is not a credible individual. The beginning of her presentation looks as questionable as an alien abduction or sightings of Bigfoot. Conspiracy theories perpetrated by quacks."

The President nodded, and a second Secret Service agent stepped toward Blane and escorted him to his seat.

Jeri's heart pounded. She just needed a few minutes to divulge this information. It seemed like things were going to work out better than she could have ever imagined!

She'd always envisioned herself revealing the truth to the President by whispering to him in some shady hallway. Now she was actually standing in the Cabinet Room in the White House, doing a Powerpoint presentation!

It almost seemed too good to be true—

"Holy shit!" gasped the Secretary of State, staring wide-eyed at the screen.

Shocked gasps punctuated the silence as everyone began to read the screen. It said: "Mission: Make The Global Kingdom the world's greatest Super Power by seizing the USA, installing the Global Kingdom's government, and taking dominion over the rest of the industrialized world."

The King clicked to a new screen and said, "This strategy will be achieved by executing the final two steps in a long-term strategy of domination." He read the words on the screen:

1. Weaken and destroy the American population
    via its own gluttony; and

2. Trick the American people into electing our
    Presidential candidate, Samuel "Uncle Sam"
    Addams, who has been groomed from birth to
    fulfill the destiny of the Global Kingdom to
    rule America.

Jeri clicked to the next page. Under a heading called
"Objectives," it showed a dozen bullet points:

- Groom and position a team of Royal Brothers
  who look, sound, and act American.

- Position them to infiltrate the highest heights of
  American government, including an unbeatable
  candidate for the office of the President of the
  United States.

- Use American obesity epidemic as the weapon
  of mass destruction to kill Americans by their
  own gluttonous hands.

- Develop OC-8 food additive to induce diabetes
  and cardiac arrest.

- Use ingredients that dissolve into innocuous
  and undetectable substances during digestion.

- Infiltrate proper channels at the FDA to approve
  OC-8 for use in fast foods.

- Use relations within the American food industry
  to convince companies to purchase and aggressively utilize OC-8 in fast food restaurants in

several urban centers, where deaths of minorities and poor people will go unnoticed due to high rates of crime, illness and drug use.

- Gradually expand distribution and use of OC-8 in fast food restaurants in higher socioeconomic communities across America.

- Prepare more aggressive diabetes- and death-inducing OC-88 for use when the campaign accelerates.

- Provide financial incentives to collaborators in high-ranking government positions who facilitate implementation of this plan.

- Orchestrate victory for Presidential candidate Samuel "Uncle Sam" Addams.

- In the Royal Kingdom, force the population to revert back to: traditional healthy foods; active, low-tech lifestyles; and morally pure music, movies, and entertainment.

- Indoctrinate the population for the Royal Kingdom with propaganda that instills entitlement for world domination into them and the next generations.

- Impose criminal penalties that can include death for anyone who defies this edict.

- Maintain the appearance of complying with the American government's presence in the Royal

Kingdom until all Americans on Royal soil are killed.

"This is war!" exclaimed the Defense Secretary. "This means there are enemies in our midst right now, around you, Mr. President. I demand a full investigation, immediately!"

The President looked stunned. He cast a probing stare at everyone around the table, starting with Blane, whose face glistened with sweat.

"And once we confirm the source of this," the Defense Secretary said, "we have to take it to the International Tribunal. I'm certain our allies will be more than eager to assist us in bringing Daemon to justice."

"How could we not know about this?" demanded HHS Secretary Nettles. She turned to Blane, then the CDC scientists: "Why haven't you discovered the root cause of this conspiracy? Are you on the terrorists' bank roll, too?"

The scientists vehemently shook their heads. "No, no, we were trying to explain! We are innocent."

The President raised his hands like a referee. "This is not the time for finger-pointing or making accusations. It's time to confirm this information and if it's true, take action to stop Daemon in his tracks. No more Americans will die, and for those who did, their families will be vindicated."

The President turned to Jeri. "Tell me exactly how you obtained this information."

She nodded. "My father's messenger, Ibrahim, who had worked for the Americans for years, obtained this report in the Republic. Ibrahim was killed immediately. And my father was kidnapped."

The Vice President, looking pale as he sat beside the Commander in Chief, nodded. "Wild Bill sent me a communication, albeit encrypted, after he was kidnapped. It hinted at something like this."

Jeri cast a desperate look at the President and the Secretary of State. "My mission here today is for me to tell you about this terrorist plot that's killing Americans as we speak. My plea is for you to take immediate action to save the people who are eating poisoned food right now—and stop Daemon and his team of conspirators—who are being led by someone in this room—"

Dread filled the President's eyes as he stared back at Jeri, then glanced around the room. Everyone sat frozen, looking at him with perplexed expressions that attempted to announce, "It's not me!"

Blane wore a skeptical countenance that projected pure disdain at Jeri. She glimpsed Calvin; he stood poised for action, as if he knew Blane were planning some kind of sinister strike.

Suddenly a deafening alarm blared. In a flash, Secret Service agents closed in on the President like a huddle of linebackers. Calvin was among them.

"Emergency!" announced a recorded female voice as red and silver lights flashed from tiny boxes on the ceiling. "Evacuate now! Emergency! Evacuate now!"

The rumble of feet on the floor accompanied a calm but urgent rush to the doors. Jeri reached to snatch the flash drive from the laptop. But Blane's hand beat her to it. His fingers wrapped around it as he cast a threatening look down at her.

"You're as good as dead," he said loudly enough for her to hear over the alarm. His evil tone and the hatred in his eyes made the hairs on the back of her neck stand.

"You're as good as burning in hell," she snapped back. She jabbed her index finger into a nerve point in his wrist; his fingers reflexively opened.

The flash drive fell on the floor. As she bent to snatch it up, his polished black leather loafer stomped on it. Confident that the commotion around them would provide a good cover, she punched his kneecap. His leg jerked backward. He grunted, and bent over to clutch it.

She grabbed the flash drive, then slipped away, following Calvin and the group of men who moved like an amoeba engulfing the President. As they proceeded into a back hallway, the Secretary of State put his arm around her, and for a moment, she felt comforted by what seemed like his protective gesture.

But as she looked up at him in appreciation, something sinister glimmered in his eyes.

Oh my God, he's in on the plot, too…

He narrowed his eyes at her and ordered, "Give me the flash drive."

Jeri gripped it so hard, her fingernails pierced her palm. At the same time, she slipped through the cluster of security, standing behind Calvin.

Her thoughts fast-forwarded into what might come next. Now that the truth was out, Blane would want the President's head. He and his cohorts would also launch a campaign to discredit what the entire Cabinet had read on the screen.

He's going to kill me, and discredit me as a crazed conspiracy theorist with a wild imagination.

Jeri's heart hammered as she hurried behind Calvin into a narrow hallway.

And everything went dark.

Chapter 67

IN A HAIL OF gunfire, Calvin tackled the President. He had to save the Commander in Chief's life because America and the entire world depended on it.

As soon as this gun battle ended, he would drag the President into the secret tunnels and into the truck that awaited a few blocks away on Pennsylvania Avenue.

A half dozen bogus Secret Service guys—the foot soldiers of King Daemon and his terrorist faux Americans—surged toward them, flashing silver and black guns of every size.

Jeri stood in front of Bullet as he shielded the President, who was beneath him on the floor. He had done the same in the hallway of the White House, when the Secretary of State had pulled a gun on the President, aiming straight at his face.

The Secret Service agents were quicker, blasting the Secretary of State down in a split second before he could even pull the trigger. Now he was dead, and the President was under siege yet again.

As the men began to shoot—bullets pinging off the black metal walls—one of Bullet's buddies handed Jeri an AK-47.

She aimed at the bad guys. She thought of her parents, and terror washed through her. Were they dead? Hurting?

She pulled the trigger, shouting, "Time's up, you terrorist motherfuckers!"

Two men fell; the others kept shooting.

Bullet was so big, his entire body covered the President, who was cowering on the floor. Thank God all three of them wore helmets and flak jackets. Bullet aimed his gun past Jeri and popped two of the bogus agents.

The deep rumble of automatic gunfire echoed off the hallway walls. They had to get to the panic room, but bullets were pinging loudly in every direction. Suddenly, six more guys wearing fatigues ran into the hallway, surrounding Gerald Blane, who shouted, "Kill them all!"

"Oh hell no!" Bullet yelled, aiming at Blane's solar plexus. "I've been looking forward to this."

The President peeked up. "Let me have the honor!"

"You are a stupid, spineless puppet," Gerald spat toward the President.

"Step back!" Jeri shouted.

The terrorist soldiers continued shooting toward Jeri.

If Bullet weren't so terrified of Jeri getting blown to bits right now, he'd let himself feel damn proud of what a good shot she was. So far she'd mowed down a bunch of dudes, and—

Pow! Pow! Pow!

She sprayed them all and they toppled like dominoes. Overwhelmed with pride and love, Calvin almost smiled.

Damn, a few hours ago, she was kidnapped and knocked out. Now she's got guns blazing like the best G.I. Jane she can be.

As a result, the only man standing was Gerald Blane, who drew a silver handgun and aimed it at the President. But with a flash of silver and a spray of red, the gun went flying—as did Gerald Blane's right hand.

"That's my girl!" Bullet exclaimed, awed at her shooting skills.

"You bitch!" Gerald shouted, staring in shock at the blood gushing from the fleshy stump that was his wrist. His severed hand laid—fingers up—on the black floor.

"Step the fuck back," Jeri said, stepping toward him. She picked up his hand, because it contained his biochip that would be used by White House investigators, the FBI, the CIA, police, and Daemon to track Blane's whereabouts. Without lowering the gun, Jeri put the bloody hand in her suit jacket pocket.

"Give me my hand!" Blane screamed. "I need a tourniquet!"

"Do it," Bullet said, looking around to make sure no one else was coming. "We need him to tell us everything, so we can save more people from dying."

Jeri looked down at Bullet, her face a mix of rage, extreme excitement, and shock. The gun remained aimed at Blane.

As Bullet rose, so did the President, who glared at Blane. "You are the most despicable piece of shit! How could you betray me and the American people?"

Ghostly pale Blane was whimpering and staring down at his bloody stump, trying to stanch the blood with his left hand. "Help me!"

Jeri pulled a piece of heavy tape from her pocket. "Sit down!"

Blane slumped to his knees beside one of the dead terrorist soldiers. Blood on the floor soaked into his gray pants. Bullet aimed a gun at Blane as Jeri knelt beside him with the roll of tape. She placed the tourniquet a few inches above his jagged skin, flesh, and bone.

"You are pure evil," Jeri said, as she wrapped the tape until the blood stopped gushing. "Evil!"

The President groaned, grabbing his leg as he tried to stand. He did not take his furious glare from Blane, who gripped his wrist.

"After you tell us how to stop this war on Americans," the President boomed with authority and rage, "you will be executed for the most heinous acts of treason ever committed on American soil."

Blane glared up at the President. "If you think I'm going to tell you anything, you're dead wrong."

"Get up!" Bullet shouted, aiming his gun down at Blane. "We gotta get out of here."

The President grimaced when he tried to step toward Blane. He gripped his right leg. "Damn, something's wrong."

Bullet exchanged a look with Jeri. With the slightest nod, he conveyed instructions without words. She immediately stepped to the President.

Bullet towered over Blane and said, "Get up, scumbag."

"My brothers will find me and kill all of you," Blane threatened, standing. He was pale, and glistening with sweat. Blood speckled his white shirt and darkened his pant from the knees down. He swayed, woozy from blood loss.

"Shut up and walk this way," Bullet ordered, directing with his gun for Blane to move toward the darker end of the tunnel.

"Our Founding Fathers are turning over in their graves," the President said with a disgusted tone as he glared at Blane. "That the likes of you and your cohorts could stoop to such horrific depths of evil—"

"Shut up!" Blane spat. "You are as much to blame as anyone for being an arrogant, invincible American. No one will believe the accusations you're trying to make against me. My people have already launched a campaign to show that you are the monster behind the fast food poisonings."

"Let them try!" the President shouted, balling his fists and surging toward Blane. Jeri pulled him back.

"Let's go," she said. "We don't know who's coming down here. We gotta clear out."

The President glared at Blane and said, "The truth always prevails, and it will now more than ever."

"I said go!" Bullet spat, pushing Blane so hard that his head jerked back and he stumbled forward.

The tunnel was dark and smelled of blood and death. Bullet's heartbeat pounded in his ears, but it did not block the sound of the President's heavy breathing.

"My God, I don't know who the hell to trust," the President exclaimed with wide eyes.

Bullet was disturbed by the profound angst haunting the President's eyes. Man, he looked so different than he did on television. At events and press conferences, he was always so perfectly coiffed, impeccably dressed, and confident. Now he looked like he would shit his pants—if he hadn't already.

"You can trust us," Bullet said deeply as he glimpsed up at Jeri. She was grasping the President's arm, helping him walk as he gripped his leg.

"I hope it's just a bad bruise," Jeri said.

"Ssshhh," Bullet said, glancing toward the light glowing from an overhead chute about 50 yards ahead. Holding out his arm to make Jeri and the President stand still, Bullet strained to decipher a tapping sound, then shook his head. "Just dripping water."

"My people are coming," Blane threatened. "To kill you all so we can usurp the power from people who don't deserve it."

"Shut the fuck up!" Bullet glared down at him. "The only reason we're keeping you alive is for you to tell us what's going on. But not until we get to the safe house."

As they proceeded through the tunnel toward the lighted chute, Bullet strained to hear the slight sound of footsteps or voices that could signal another ambush.

"How come nobody ever told me about this tunnel under the White House?" the President whispered in a tone that sounded like he was trying to distract himself from the horrific reality at hand.

"They were sealed off," Bullet said. "My buddy was the contractor who did the job. And he kept the only key. Until the traitors infiltrated the most sacred—"

"Americans are the traitors to the world," Blane spat. "So it's easy to infiltrate where murderous, power-hungry whores are wallowing in greed and bowing to the glory of money."

"Shut up!" Jeri shouted.

"Oh my God," the President gasped, staring wide-eyed at Jeri. "How many people did you say died? And how long have you been trying to get to me? We could have saved so many people if—"

"No, please stop," Jeri said. "We can't change that. But we can change things now. We just have to get the backstabbers away from you—"

The President's face paled as he glared at Blane. "My senior advisor! Blane, who are you? What kind of animal are you? Inflicting a murder plot on innocent Americans?" The President shook his head. "Who are your partners in crime?"

Blane stared back with a blank expression.

"Tell me!" the President shouted. "Tell me who's on your team of killers!"

Blane spit in the President's face.

Bullet punched Blane in the stomach. "Do that again and I'll blow off your other hand."

The President groaned. "Tell me I'm having a nightmare on the set of the worst spy movie ever—"

"It's real," Jeri said, pulling him along. "Sorry."

"I need you to call a few people," the President said.

"Ssshhh," Bullet ordered, signaling everyone to freeze. He had to assume that they were all crooked, and that they were looking for Blane as their leader, with the goal of duping or even killing the President.

The real danger now would be for them to put poisonous gas in this tunnel or to toss a grenade down here. They needed to get out of here as quickly as possible, but the President was limping.

Hopefully he could climb the ladder in the overhead chute; that was their only escape. If they were to venture into the end of the tunnel where Blane and his commandos had come from, they could meet up with more terrorist soldiers.

Suddenly a crackling sound—like a lighted wick on a stick of dynamite—echoed through the tunnel.

"Get down!" Bullets shouted. They all hit the floor.

Flaming objects the size of baseballs whizzed over them. A chemical burning smell filled the air. Another round flew past. Then Bullet noticed, they were being shot from inside the chute. They had no other way out.

We are dead ducks right now.

Chapter 68

RAGE SURGED THROUGH KING Daemon as he sat with his Royal Brothers, watching live video on the giant screen here in his media Throne Room.

"It is complete mayhem!" Daemon shouted. "The Americans are making complete mayhem on our streets! They have turned our people into wild animals!"

Video showed a young boy tossing a Molotov cocktail into the window of a celebrated restaurant on the city's once-bustling square, which was now barren. Smoke filled the air. Men and women ran back and forth like banshees, tossing rocks and bottles at soldiers. Gunfire rang out. Six infidels fell to the ground. Puddles of blood spread around them.

"Almighty," said the Minister of Defense, "we have captured and executed four of the traitors who conspired with the American instigators to spark this civil war. Their bodies are hanging in the market square—"

Video showed three men and a woman, all wearing western-style clothing, hanging upside down on meat hooks that merchants typically used to display and sell livestock.

"The individuals," the Minister of Defense added, "were instrumental in providing the Americans' financial backing, weapons, and propaganda to the insurgents."

"Find the rest of them," Daemon ordered. "I'm certain there are more. This is retaliation for the disappearance of the General—"

King Daemon squeezed his bloodshot eyes closed. His fingers tingled with the desire to kill the General with his own hands, slowly, methodically. But it was not yet time.

"Find all the instigators," King Daemon said. "And kill them all to wipe out this virus of insurrection."

"It's bigger than we think," the Defense Minister warned. "The current President in the United States wants to perpetuate unrest here, then squash it in time for the election, so he can look like a hero to the world."

King Daemon watched the screen as a small boy wearing traditional clothing ran across the square. He threw himself onto one of the bloody corpses of the insurgents.

"Momma!" the boy screamed. "Momma!" Blood covered his face as he screamed up at the sky.

King Daemon flashed back to the moment during his childhood when the Americans had killed his parents, and they laid around him, slumped in pools of blood. Pain and sadness stabbed at his heart as he became entranced by the boy, mourning his mother. His mother, who was fighting against the Kingdom for the Americans. The King's sympathy turned to ice.

"Turn it off!" Daemon screamed. "Now!"

He glared at his Brothers.

"The Americans have instigated a civil war on our land, and I blame all of you!" he accused. "You have failed the Republic and you will all be assassinated by my own hand unless you can stop the senseless bloodletting on our streets!"

"Almighty," insisted the Defense Director, "we are working right now to create peace in our country. All of our men, our soldiers, are working to make sure that peace prevails by the Holy Day next week."

"I want it now!" Daemon shouted. "If you fail, I will slaughter all of you and your families. But I will keep your wives and daughters for my own pleasure."

The Defense Director put his hands in a prayer position. "Almighty, I beg of you, please believe that we have been fighting the Americans at every turn. We have been countering their efforts to create chaos in our land, but instilling terror in our residents."

A high-ranking military officer nodded as fear glowed in his eyes. "We have even executed individuals who have been seen talking to American soldiers, to send a message—"

"Your message was not loud enough!" Daemon yelled. "You must go into the streets right now. Tell all the people to stop fighting each other. Stop fighting the war that the Americans caused so that they can say we failed at keeping peaceful relations in our country."

The Brothers immediately gathered their things and

stood around King Daemon, awaiting final instructions. His nose flared as he spoke in a deep, sinister voice.

"If I am outraged about what is occurring on our land," Daemon said, "I am incensed about what is failing to happen in America."

The men listened as terror tensed their faces.

"Your failure," Daemon accused, "and the failure of your Brothers in the US to find the girl and her Mexican soldier, are the most despicable examples of incompetence that I have ever seen!"

The Defense Minister shook his head. "King Daemon, we have her exact location. She is in Virginia right now. Inside a small home—"

"Why haven't they killed her?" King Daemon demanded, envisioning images of her pale face and blond hair in the latest surveillance video that his men had provided. "Why has a stupid girl been able to evade our assassins?"

"She and her bodyguard are very clever," the Defense Minister said. "When we catch them, we should force them to work for us."

"When we catch them," King Daemon said, "I will kill them both with my two hands. In front of her father! Find them!"

As the king's voice boomed through the vaulted chamber, the men cowered.

"Go kill all Allied troops in our country."

The men nodded.

"Now," Daemon said, "as for the lawless animals who are the people in our own country, you must alert our military to kill anyone suspected of colluding with the enemy. Go make the streets run with blood to prove your point if you must."

As the men bowed and departed, King Daemon glared with disgust.

"Call my scientists," he ordered one of the guards. "Tell Dr. Braza and his team to bring me the latest information about our campaign to kill gluttonous Americans."

The guard immediately touched his Device, which glowed with the image of Dr. Braza.

"Come to the Throne Room right now," the guard said. "King Daemon would like to hear the latest statistics."

Minutes later, the scientist entered, carrying a computer tablet. He sat beside King Daemon and said, "The Americans are coming close to solving the mystery of what is happening. My source at the CDC has told me that investigators sent by the President have been demanding to see toxicology reports—"

"Provide false ones!" King Daemon snapped. "Tell our Brother at the CDC to provide reports that will lead the President and his pathetic Cabinet on a wild goose chase to nowhere, as the Americans say. And implement the next degree of our campaign."

"Yes, sir," Dr. Braza said. "Brother Blane has been on alert to hear instructions on this. He has repeatedly told me that the American President and his men—"

"I don't care!" King Daemon seethed. "Do not mention that man. He is as good as dead. He is as insignificant as a fly. And he will die. You are dismissed."

As the scientist departed, Daemon turned to his Assistant. "Get all our Brothers in America on a video conference. Now."

Moments later, the huge screen in the Throne Room divided into four squares showing live video of: future American President Samuel "Uncle Sam" Addams; FBI Investigator Edward "Eddie" Smith; and Richard Blane, chief marketing strategist at Heavenly's Burgers.

"Where is Gerald Blane?" King Daemon demanded, furious at the sight of one quarter of the screen blank where the man closest to the US President should have appeared.

"He's missing, Sir," Eddie Smith said.

"Tell me you have found the girl!" Daemon shouted.

"We've got her under surveillance in a cottage in Virginia—"

"Under surveillance is not good enough!" Daemon yelled. "I want to hear that you have caught her, confiscated our document, and that she will be arriving at my feet as soon as an airplane can fly across the ocean."

Eddie Smith nodded. "I anticipate you'll be hearing that from us by sundown. The problem is—"

"Do not tell me problems," Daemon snapped. "Tell me solutions."

"I've got a beautiful solution for you," said Uncle Sam. "My presidential campaign is beating all of my opponents, including the current President, in the polls. You are looking at the next President of the United States. Which means the good ol' US of A will soon be ruled by the Global Kingdom of Tricqua."

"That is the only good news I have heard on this day," King Daemon said. "We must let nothing interrupt our campaign."

Chapter 69

Kenya Wise and Jeremy Matthews kissed passionately amidst the tomato plants inside the LifeQuest HQ's farm in Detroit. They were supposed to be harvesting vegetables, but they were so excited to see each other, they could do nothing but kiss.

"I missed you so much," confessed Jeremy, who had spent the past week at a compound in northern Michigan, helping train men and women for the upcoming showdown. As a nutrition therapist, his role was to teach people how to eat foods that fueled their bodies for maximum health and performance, especially during times of high stress and exertion. "I never want to spend a single night away from you, Kenya."

She kissed him with all her heart and soul. "I hated being away from you. And I have news."

Jeremy smiled. "You convinced your parents to join the Movement, and bring the twins?"

"Close. It's about family. Ours."

Jeremy's eyes widened. Pure joy spread across his face. She lifted her shirt, and put his hand over her flat, toned belly. He held it there, and placed the softest kiss on her lips.

Then, in a split second, Jeremy dropped to his knee, took her hand, and said, "Kenya Wise, will you marry me?" She gasped. Tears filled her eyes. And she said yes.

Chapter 70

CINDY BLANE BENT OVER the table in the Four Seasons as Senator Brace Buxton frantically unzipped his pants and rammed inside her.

"Fuck, I missed you, girl," he groaned, bending over her as he thrust like his life depended on it. "I can't stand the thought of some scoundrel putting his hands all over you."

Cindy moaned as if she were enjoying this, and to distract him from the kind of possessive rant that he'd been prone to unleashing lately.

"Tell me I'm the only one," he demanded with a gruff tone. "Tell me!"

Cindy rolled her eyes. She wanted to say, "*You're the only old, arrogant motherfucker I needed to help me launch my Garden of Eden business in grand style, with the most powerful men in Washington and corporate America as my clients.*"

Instead, she let out a sultry moan and said, "Oh Brace, you're so big, so hot, why would I want anyone else? Of course you're the only one."

She even gyrated her hips in rhythm to his thrusting to make him think he was pleasuring her.

He's prospering from me—that's for damn sure.

Cindy was making hundreds of millions of dollars with her Garden of Eden escort parties and its online counterpart, SuperStar Sporting Goods and Services. She had expanded nationwide and even provided services to major international destinations, with the most popular being Paris, Rome, London, Monaco, the Caribbean, and Cabo San Lucas, Mexico.

She would love nothing more than to say, "Sayonara, motherfucker," to Brace Buxton, but she still needed him for a variety of reasons. First, he was the wrong person to have as an enemy. His tentacles of power extended into the highest echelons of the world's political, social, and business elite. Second, his ego was so enormous that bruising it would provoke a wicked wrath that could destroy her. Third, he was very close to her boss, Douglass Golden, who could very well become the Vice President of the United States.

He was still the power behind Golden Harvest Foods, and now that Cindy was a Vice President, she needed to maintain the excellent rapport that she enjoyed with Douglass on more levels than anyone needed to know. Not only did her Garden of Eden provide him with extramarital entertainment, but she and Douglass indulged occasional trysts that were extraordinary.

Cindy's sister, Linda, was providing bold, innovative leadership as president of the American Restaurant Association. And inspired by her personal preferences for pretty, young women, Linda had helped Cindy develop an extremely discreet, niche market for the Garden of Eden:

wealthy businesswomen who wanted to meet beautiful female escorts in a setting where the truth about their sexual orientation would never be revealed or jeopardize their reputations and power in the corporate world.

And since Brace Buxton was wildly, vehemently opposed to gay marriage, gay rights, and even boys wearing pink, and was one of the Hill's most powerful opponents of the homosexual agenda, Cindy knew better than to ever reveal this aspect of her business.

So, until circumstances made it acceptable and safe for her to break relations with this man, she would continue to bend over this dining room table or lay on the bed or do it in the bathtub during their Wednesday lunchtime trysts here at the Four Seasons Hotel in Washington, DC.

"Oh do it so good, Brace," she moaned as he smacked her ass. She hated it when he did that. But most men got off on hearing the palm of their hand whacking a woman's behind. It was pure dominance. It was actually violent. But she just didn't care. All she had to do was think about how her nine-figure bank balance could potentially grow to make her a billionaire before her fortieth birthday.

"Oh Brace, I don't know what I'd do without you," she said with a sultry tone. "You're the best!"

He smacked her ass, hard enough to make it sting. "If I find out you're fuckin' anybody else, there'll be hell to pay."

Her sexy laugh belied her rage. He had no right to threaten her like that.

"So you're gonna leave Mrs. Buxton and marry me?"

she cooed, knowing damn well that would never happen. It would be her worst nightmare. But it would appease his ego to believe she wanted him like that.

"I just might," he said, groaning and thrusting faster.

Anything a man said in the pursuit of sex, in the midst of it—and especially on the verge of orgasm or during an orgasm—had no value or truth. He wouldn't even remember it an hour from now. It was pure pillow talk. Fantasy. Bullshit.

"Oh, Brace, if I could wake up and fuck you every day like this," she lied as he reached around to grab her tits while he thrust harder, "I would be the happiest bitch in the world. Fuck me harder! I just can't get enough of you."

With that, he shot his wad, and fortunately, he was done. She couldn't wait to get in the shower to clean him off of her. As far as she was concerned, these meetings constituted "working" to build her billion-dollar empire.

Brace Buxton was just a pawn in her game, but she had to keep making him believe he was the king.

Chapter 71

Katie Matthews had had enough. Dan's two heart attacks and his refusal to lose weight were a personal attack on the family. She felt like he just didn't care enough about them—to care about himself.

"Dan, if you don't put that damn burger down," she scolded as he sat down at a TV tray to watch the car racing programs that he'd recorded, "then I'll take it from you. If you watched the news instead of race cars all night long, you'd know that people are dying from some mysterious toxin in fast food."

He glared at her, reaching down to pick up the burger and take a giant, defiant bite. His big belly bumped into the TV tray, making his orange soda almost spill from the tall glass.

"I don't believe that for a single minute," he said, eyeing the burger in the lustful way that he way he used to look at her body when they were newlyweds. "First of all, the people who are dying are indigent, inner city types. Already sick, on drugs—"

"Not true. Three kids in Bloomfield Hills died, and 25 people who were all professionals got sick and died after eating at Taco Temptation." Katie shook her head, watching her husband commit slow suicide, bite by bite. "You're setting the worst example for our kids. That's why our son ran off to join LifeQuest, because you're so disgusting. Such a disappointment."

Dan took a giant bite of the burger and moaned, closing his eyes as he chewed loudly.

"Mmmmm," he said, with his mouth full, "this is so good. I don't taste any toxins. And I feel fine. I think the government is just trying to scare people—"

"You feel fine?" she snapped. "You drag around here like you weigh 500 pounds, and soon you will. Your belly is so big, it looks like it's going to pop. And you eat constantly. Dan, you are addicted to food."

She reached to grab the food out of his hands. He gripped the burger and shot a hand back to her. His fingers jammed her arms; his fingernail scratched her skin and it bled.

Katie burst into tears. "You have become a complete pig, literally and figuratively. You have never made a mark on me! Ever! Dan, I vowed to be with you in sickness and in health. But I can't. I'm giving up on you, because you've given up on yourself. You weigh 300 pounds or more. Your cholesterol is through the roof. And you're diabetic. They made up a new word for people like you. Diabesity. Pathetic, because you brought it on yourself!"

Katie glimpsed herself in the mirror over the fireplace. Thanks to her plant-based diet, she had dropped 40 pounds, and she couldn't remember when she felt this good.

"Jeremy—our son!—has helped me get control of myself and cleanse my body. You haven't even noticed that I've lost weight or that I'm exercising and meditating. Jeremy taught me how to replace chocolate with cauliflower, burgers with broccoli, and chips with grilled chicken. All my numbers are in a healthy range, and I haven't had this much energy since we were teenagers."

Dan was devouring his food and not looking at her. He was as consumed by the French fries, burger, and pop—with an apple pie awaiting him for desert—as a crack addict might be consumed by filling his pipe.

"You're acting like a drug addict," she accused. "The kids ask why you don't play with them anymore. And I—"

Katie sobbed. She was no longer stuffing down her feelings with food, so now the emotions surged up and out.

She hadn't been to Creamy Dream—nor had the kids. She packed their lunches every day so they did not eat from the Heavenly's that had replaced their school cafeteria. And she had been secretly visiting Jeremy in the Movement that had once terrified her.

Despite her rage at Dan right now, as he watched TV and gulped his greasy death wish as if she were invisible, Katie wanted to take the kids and run out the door. And that's exactly what they were going to do: join Jeremy and Kenya at the LifeQuest HQ in the warehouse district near the Detroit River.

She was amazed that it was so different than her original assumptions about it. Her image of the Movement had been rife with frightening stereotypes of militant, gun-toting black people in the inner city.

But after visiting Jeremy, she discovered that the reality was anything but. In fact, during her first visit, she discovered that the order and good will of the place was so overwhelming, she didn't want to leave. Taking Jeremy's nutrition seminars in the auditorium there, along with cooking classes, had been extremely helpful. But the real change had come from the counseling she had undergone with a board-certified psychologist who was trained to help people overcome "emotional eating."

"We use food the same way as alcoholics use drinks, and drug addicts use drugs," the psychologist had explained during a lecture where people of every size, shape, background, age, and socioeconomic status had gathered to learn. "We use food to deal with our emotions. Some people eat when they're happy; others eat when they're stressed. For some, food is a sedative. And for everyone, it's the centerpiece of celebrations. Think about it: birthday cakes, wedding cakes, ice cream and cookies as rewards for good behavior, dinner parties to mark anniversaries and such."

That lecture had been Katie's "aha moment," because she had never been conscious of just how she "used" and "abused" food.

"The terrible difference is that an alcoholic can vow to never drink again," the lecturer had said. "The drug addict can promise to never use drugs. But food addicts still have to eat three times a day or more."

In addition to lectures, Katie had also gotten one-on-one therapy with the psychologist, to address the specific reasons why she used food as a drug. She had realized that she also used the resulting fat and depression as an excuse to avoid living life to the fullest. For example, she'd wanted to take a yoga class with the other nurses at the hospital—it was offered during lunchtime—but she'd always felt too fat and out of shape to do all those poses in a mirrored room full of fit women.

Now she did yoga almost daily, at the hospital as well as at home in the evenings, while Dan plopped in front of the TV and ate for hours, stuffing himself with junk while watching garbage that filled his mind with nothingness.

Katie had also succeeded at getting the twins to lose weight, simply by slowly introducing more vegetables and fruits while gradually removing processed foods, fast foods, and high-fat snacks and fried items from their diets. After awhile, they started asking for baked fish and colorful salads because they enjoyed helping her prepare them. They even took weekly trips to Eastern Market, purchasing fresh vegetables from the farmers while beholding the beautiful cornucopia of people and produce.

All of this made the sight of Dan tear at her heart. Her therapist had repeatedly said during lectures that nobody could help a food addict but himself or herself. "Intervention works for awhile," the counselor said, "but sooner or later, the addict finds his drug and gets back to his old habits."

"Bethany!" she called. "Brian! Let's go!"

The twins, now nine years old, came bounding down the stairs. Four-year-old Suzie followed.

"It is time to go see Jeremy?" Bethany asked excitedly.

"Yes," Katie said, saddened that Dan had not noticed the two suitcases in her hands, or even that the kids had entered the room. Instead, he aimed the remote at the TV and turned up the volume as he popped a French fry in his mouth.

Brian ran up and hugged his father. "Bye, Dad! We get to see Jeremy!"

Dan hugged all three kids at once, and kissed their foreheads, leaving shiny spots from the grease on his lips. "Tell him I said hi, will ya?"

Katie blinked back tears. She was certain that the shock of waking up tomorrow to discover that they were leaving for good, would spur him to action to save his own life and their family.

I hope. Good God, I hope so...

A short time later, armed guards allowed them to pull into the garage at the warehouse downtown Detroit that had been transformed into an entrance to the Movement's underground headquarters. Greeting them was not just Jeremy, but adorable Kenya as well.

Both were beaming like the sun. Katie knew immediately: *They're getting married.*

The looks on their faces gave it all away, and Katie' couldn't have been happier. She'd seen this coming for a long time, ever since Jeremy had joined the Movement and began talking about the girl he'd met at Creamy Dream.

Now, though they were both only 19, they shared an apartment here and were devoting their lives to this mission that was saving lives and the future of America.

Every time Katie saw a story about how the obesity rate was declining, even ever-so-slightly, she smiled with pride that her son was helping to make that happen. Still, so much work remained, with the likes of her husband sitting at home right now, stuffing his face with poison.

"Mom, your apartment is ready," Jeremy said as he took their suitcases from the car. "Two bedrooms. I hope the kids don't mind sharing. We've got your work all set up as a nurse to work with our morbidly obese residents who have extreme health problems. And the kids can start school here in the morning."

Bethany, Brian, and Suzie hugged their brother. "Do we get to grow vegetables in school, too?"

"Of course," Kenya said. "Fruit, too."

As the kids ran toward the elevator, Bethany asked, "Can we go check on our green beans?"

"Yeah!" Brian exclaimed.

"Mom," Jeremy said, as they took the elevator up to the vegetable garden. "You're going to have a new name soon."

"What's that?" Katie asked, enchanted by the sight of the kids picking beans and eating them.

"Gramma," Jeremy said proudly. "And mother-in-law."

Katie shrieked with joy. But that meant Dan would be Grandpa and father-in-law. Would he live long enough to see that day?

Chapter 72

DAN WAS ALONE AND wanting to get up and go to bed. But he couldn't stop eating. Something inside him was making him crave more and more food. Fortunately, he had stopped at the grocery store and stocked up on ice cream, cookies, and candy bars.

Plus he had bought five dinners from Heavenly's, which he'd kept out of view from Katie. He was so glad she was gone with the kids. When they got back, maybe he would talk about changing his eating habits. But for now, this was the best way to relax after a hard day at work.

It was challenging to get up and out of the chair. He felt so sluggish, and his brain was moving in slow motion, except for the thought that he wanted to eat, and eat, and eat.

Everything seemed to taste extra good, and he couldn't get enough. So he went to his car, retrieved the extra bags of burgers, popped them in the microwave, and spread his feast on the table while he watched the 11 o'clock news.

Five burgers, five fries, a half-gallon of ice cream, a jug of pop. His stomach was hurting. But his urge to eat was stronger. He was almost numb from the food, and he just kept shoving it in. In. More.

"I can't stop," he cried mid-bite. He really could not stop. He felt possessed by the urge to eat. So he kept shoving it in, shoving it in.

He was breathing hard. Sweating. Heart pounding. Chubby fingers grabbing food.

Then he felt a sting on his stomach. He heard something rip. The skin on his abdomen turned red and purplish.

He felt drunk. Vision was blurry.

What's going on? I can't…

His mind was fog.

He glanced down and saw a red blur on his T-shirt. Somewhere in his intoxicated mind he knew that he had eaten himself to death.

A horrible pressure on his chest made it hard to breath. He heart was struggling.

Somewhere in his mind it registered that he had just busted his gut himself from the inside out.

But his forehead hit the table, and he was dead before he could really comprehend the horror of his final moments.

Chapter 73

Leroy Wise forked up some mixed greens and savored the garlic-basil extravaganza on his tongue.

"Darlene," he said, "I never thought I'd see the day where I'd enjoy eating rabbit food. But, baby, you can *make* some salad!"

Darlene smiled. Her cheeks were slim, and her eyes appeared bigger, since she'd lost so much weight. She still had a good 30 pounds to go, but for awhile there, she'd been looking like a hot air balloon that was nearing the bursting point.

"I want cheese on my salad," demanded nine-year-old Keisha.

"Yeah, with ranch dressing, like at school," Leroy Junior said.

"Your salad already has dressing on it," Darlene said. "My special homemade vinaigrette with olive oil and spices. And we don't need cheese."

Both kids frowned for a moment, but devoured their salads. Darlene and Leroy shared a furtive smile.

"Kenya says big things are about to happen in the Movement," Darlene said as she brought a platter of baked tilapia and quinoa to the table, then served healthy portions for everyone. "Big, big things."

"Such as?" Leroy asked. "Michael didn't mention anything when we saw him last."

"Didn't have to," Darlene said. "His expression and the look in his eyes spoke volumes. That man knows something—"

"My brother has always been serious like that," Leroy said, savoring the fish. "When can we see Kenya?"

"Tonight or tomorrow," she said. "As soon as possible."

"Let's go tonight," Leroy said, grateful that he had mended his relationship with his brother. He also felt good about the fact that he was finally heeding his brother's warnings about losing weight and having a healthier lifestyle.

Watching Slim Jim die in the service department had been the turning point for Leroy to finally heed his brother's and his doctor's advice to lose weight. He, too, still had a good 30 pounds to go, but he sure was doing better and feeling better than back in the day.

The *fat* and *getting fatter* day. Sure, he and Darlene still splurged, calorically speaking, on the occasional favorites like macaroni and cheese, meatloaf and gravy, and peach cobbler à la mode. Leroy's saving grace was that Darlene had learned how to put her recipes on a diet, as she liked to say, by preparing their favorite foods with lower-calorie ingredients.

"Yay!" exclaimed Leroy Junior. "We get to see Kenya!"

"I want to see those soldiers at the door again," Keisha added. "They're cool."

Leroy enjoyed the rest of the meal, but he was worried. Darlene was right. His brother had looked more intense than usual. Plus all the news reports about folks dying after eating fast food, had him worried that something far more sinister was going on. Whoever could orchestrate something so evil, and get away with it for so long, had to have a lot of power and inside access.

And the fact that it wasn't being stopped meant someone in a high place was reluctant to do so, for whatever reason. He remembered an Emergency Preparedness presentation at the dealership, years ago, about how, since 9/11, authorities were worried someone might try to poison the water supply.

He'd also been worried about a conversation he'd overheard the last time they visited Michael underground.

"We just got another shipment of guns for the showdown," one of the armed young men in the garage had said to another. "You're talkin' the battle to end all battles!"

Kenya was right in the thick of it. She and Jeremy were as happy as they could be, making a difference in the world. Leroy didn't mind that they were living together. They would probably marry one day, and that would be fine. Now Leroy just prayed that the anticipated gun battle wouldn't stop that "one day" from coming.

"As soon as we finish our meal," Leroy said, "let's go see Kenya."

Chapter 74

CALVIN, JERI, THE PRESIDENT, and Gerald Blane jumped down a trapdoor in the tunnel's floor. They found themselves in another tunnel, this one lit by a strip of tiny white lights along the ceiling.

"Today is just full of surprises," the President said with a tone of relief. "My senior advisor is conspiring with a terrorist to destroy America, and there's yet another tunnel under the White House that I didn't know about."

"This way," Calvin said, guiding him toward the small pink light that his team had put in place to guide them.

"Take me to the hospital!" Blane shouted. "Where are we going?"

"Wherever I point this gun," Jeri responded.

Calvin wanted to smile and shout, "That's my girl!" But he was quiet as they practically ran through the tunnel. At the end, a metal grate opened and they were whisked up a staircase, into a utility shed, and into the back of a landscaping van.

"You can't get away with this," Blane threatened. "You are being tracked every step of the way. My people will catch you and destroy all of you. Starting with her." He pointed at Jeri. "Slowly and painfully."

Jeri pressed the tip of her gun into his cheek. "You're not really in a position to make threats right now, you stupid bastard."

Calvin bit his lip to stop smiling. He loved watching G.I. Jane in action. Made his dick hard.

Jeri gave Blane's severed hand to Boone Davis, who put it in a cooler full of ice. He gave the cooler to Tate, who got into another vehicle.

"Give me my hand!" Blane screamed. "My biochip—"

"Is on its way to Florida," Bullet said. "After we copy it to make decoys that will keep Daemon and your other co-conspirators on a wild goose chase for a long time."

The van took off, and they were taken to an underground garage beneath an office building. There, Calvin escorted the President into the back of a large truck whose trailer was outfitted like the most luxurious celebrity tour van.

Inside, the key players on Calvin's team were assembled, as planned. He and Jeri and the President were greeted by Johnny Valentine, Carmen La Buena, Boone, and Lynette, who inspected Blane's wrist.

"Bring him back here," she said, directing him to the kitchen table. "I'm a paramedic. I can fix him up for now."

"I need a real doctor," Blane protested, casting a condescending look at Lynette. "A surgeon. This isn't sanitary. I could die."

Lynette proceeded to bandage Blane's wrist.

"He'll make it to our next stop," she told Jeri, who stood over Blane with her gun to his head. "They can stitch him up there. Hopefully he won't be dead from an infection by then." She winked.

Once Calvin determined that Blane was secure, she escorted the President to the back chamber, which was sound proof and secured by a powerful lock system on the door.

"I need to go back to the White House," the President insisted. "You can't just take me away. I have a wife, a family, a country to run."

"All due respect, sir," Calvin said, "but we're saving your life. We knew your Senior Advisor was out to get you, but the Secretary of State was a surprise. No telling who else has a mark on your head."

The President shook his head. "Where is my family? If I'm not safe, they're not safe."

"They are," Calvin said with a reassuring tone. "My military buddy, George, is personally watching them right now. They've been escorted to a safe house in New England."

"I need to call them," the President said. "I have no phone. No Device. They need to know that I'm safe."

"You can communicate with them when we arrive at your secure bunker, which is undetectable," Calvin said.

"Where?"

"The safest place on earth," Calvin said. "Detroit."

The President's eyes widened. Then he laughed heartily.

"You're very good at what you do, Calvin," the President said. "And a comedian on top of that—"

"I speak the truth."

The President stared long and hard at Calvin as the

truck pulled away. "They'll follow us," he said. "The high tech surveillance capabilities we have today mean no one can evade detection, anywhere on earth. Especially the President." He held out his right hand and pointed to the tiny blue square on the back of his hand, just below the knuckle of his pinkie finger. "My biochip has a special presidential tracking element—"

"It's been reprogrammed," Calvin said. "The original data was copied three times, and we used it to create three decoys, which we'll send off, one at a time. The first one is heading to Florida right now, with Blane's hand. Anybody tracking it will eventually realize it's bogus. Then we'll send the second decoy to Oregon. The third one, if necessary, will go to Texas."

"What about all of you, this truck, your Devices?" the President asked.

"Same deal," Calvin said. "We've got military grade shielding on everything. Daemon's been pursuing us for a long time, as we've crisscrossed the country, trying to get to you. He failed. We know what we're doing."

The President shook his head. "I don't know who or what to believe. And with my Secretary of State trying to kill me today—" he sighed in disbelief.

"We're taking you to see Dr. Michael Wise," Calvin said. "He's got an underground compound where you'll be safe to serve as Commander in Chief, totally undetected by the world. We've installed military grade technology for you to communicate in any way necessary, and no one will be able to determine where you are."

"Dr. Michael Wise," the President said. "His father and I became friends at Harvard. We've been trying to infiltrate the Movement for a long time." Revelation flashed in his eyes. "I guess that is the safest place, if the President's people couldn't even get in."

Calvin smiled.

Then the President said, "Calvin, go get Jeri. I want you and her to tell me everything you know. I want to see everything that's on that flash drive."

Chapter 75

THIS WAS THE MOMENT Jeri had been envisioning ever since she'd read Daemon's plan to conquer America. She was face-to-face with the President of the United States, showing him the terrorists' sinister plot on her Device. They were sitting at a table in the secure chamber as the truck raced toward Michigan.

"I need to mobilize a team to strategize how to defeat them," the President said. "But I don't know who to trust. Who to call—"

"My father told me to get this to you," Jeri said. "And he told me to find Calvin to help me. In doing that, Calvin has assembled a team for you."

The President looked at Calvin with a questioning expression.

"Some of the team is on this truck," Bullet said, "Everyone is committed to the cause for the right reasons, and they're committed to fight to the death. We've got more ammunition than the Department of Defense stockpiled in Detroit, and some of the best minds in the military—"

"Who?" the President asked.

"We'll tell you names and credentials when we get there," Calvin said. "We'll also brief you on the strategy of what's about to go down."

They turned on a television mounted to the wall. Anastasia Lee appeared on GNN. "In this unprecedented turn of events in American history, the President of the United States has been kidnapped from the White House."

Video showed the President's photograph. "Investigators are telling us that this occurred a short time after an imposter at a Cabinet Meeting commandeered a PowerPoint presentation, set off a fire alarm, and attempted to shoot the President as he was being escorted out."

A photo of Jeri—the one published in the national newspapers after the disappeared—flashed on the screen. "Police say this woman, Jeralynn Brewster, is the suspect in the assassination attempt on the President's life today. She is also suspected of masterminding a kidnapping plot involving a number of criminal individuals connected to the militant Food Fight Posse."

Jeri watched in disbelief. "I don't know if I should laugh or cry," she sighed. "That is pure propaganda. Lies."

A photo of herself with her father appeared on the screen. "The suspect is the daughter of General William 'Wild Bill' Brewster, who disappeared recently. His stellar record for installing a democratic government in the Republic of the East was tarnished when investigators discovered he had taken bribes for—"

"Turn it off!" Jeri shouted. "I won't listen to them smearing my father's reputation and legacy!"

Calvin changed the channel.

Another national news network was running a tally of all the people who died of suspected food poisoning after eating at fast food restaurants. "The total rose to 25,000 people today," the anchor said. "Investigators believe that the number is probably twice or even three or four times that, because many of the victims have become ill over time, and are afflicted by other health problems related to morbid obesity. So their sudden deaths may be attributed to causes such as diabetes, high blood pressure, and even cancer."

Jeri turned to the President and said, "Our top priority at this moment is to stop the killing. We need to take swift action to shut down the fast food restaurants so all the people who refuse to see the danger—including the public schools where Heavenly's burgers has replaced the cafeterias."

"Then we need to go all the way up the food chain where the toxin is coming in," the President said. "We need the FDA, the CDC, the food manufacturers, we need them all informed and involved."

"That's the tough part," Jeri said. "A lot of links in the chain are corrupt. They're the ones who've enabled this whole plot to unfold. They're colluding with Daemon and his mad scientists—"

"I've always wanted to just blow up his Presidential palace in the Republic," the President said.

Calvin let out a robust laugh. "So have I!"

The President looked surprised, and they shared deep laughter.

"I'm a Navy Seal," Calvin said. "Worked with Wild Bill in Trykka for years. Did more ground work in the Republic than I care to remember. Rough place, but I think we really made a difference. Now it's gone back to hell in a handbasket."

The President nodded. "My personal opinion is that Daemon instigated the civil war himself, just to make it look like America failed to install a democratic system that they didn't want anyway."

"Bingo!" Calvin said. "Now he's trying to play war games on American soil. It ain't happenin'."

"I agree," the President said, "but without the ability to communicate, I feel powerless."

"You'll be able to communicate with the Vice President once we arrive in Detroit," Calvin said. "We've also implemented a strategic campaign to educate people about the dangers of continuing to eat fast food. We can brief you on that when you arrive."

The President buried his face in his hand and let out a distraught sigh. "I'm in shock. I can't believe the people closest to me are the ones behind this. Or that this terrorist campaign has been going on..."

Lynette entered with a dinner tray for the President. She set it on the table in front of him.

"For now," Calvin said as the three of them left him. "Enjoy your dinner, and get a good night's rest. You need to be ready for the revolution."

Chapter 76

KING DAEMON'S ENTIRE BODY shook with rage.

"They have kidnapped one of my most important men in America!" he shouted. "Find Blane! Find my Brother!"

He was standing in the center hallway of the palace, surrounded by the 10 men of his Royal Brotherhood.

"You imbeciles!" he screamed as his golden robes fluttered under his raised arms. "How did you let this happen? Get Eddie Smith back."

In an instant, the Minister of Communications had Eddie Smith on live video on a giant screen as the King led his men into the Throne Room.

"What is going on?" Daemon screamed, standing before the screen. "Where is the President? Where is Blane?"

"He's got the President," Eddie said. "We're tracking them in a vehicle that's heading south from Washington along the Atlantic coast. The vehicle's navigation system has Key West, Florida as its destination."

"Capture them!" Daemon shouted. He turned to his Communications Minister. "Get me Blane on the screen."

"Almighty, we have tried many times. But we cannot

reach him. No one has seen or heard from him since the Cabinet Meeting ended in disaster."

That set off another explosion of rage inside Daemon. "How did the girl get into the Cabinet Meeting to reveal our plan? How did the President get away? This is the most inexcusable, incompetent—"

"Almighty," Eddie said, "our intelligence has reported that the girl is dead. So is her Mexican boyfriend. They were both shot after the girl compromised our plan."

"I will not be defeated by a girl, whether she is dead or alive!" Daemon screamed. "A girl who has escaped my reach too many times to count. A girl who caused the killing of my men. A girl who has compromised my entire operation. A girl who is threatening to block me from ruling the world!"

Eddie shook his head vehemently. "Almighty, she is no longer a risk. She is no longer an obstacle or a problem—"

"I will not rest until you bring me her dead body!" Daemon screamed. "Bring me the dead body of the girl. Wrapped in the loving arms of her dead boyfriend."

Chapter 77

Dr. Wise felt a burst of adrenaline and nervousness as he stood in the control room inside the LifeQuest HQ.

"There's the van," said Security Chief Shane Browne, pointing to one of the many video monitors showing dozens of areas throughout the warehouse, the surrounding exterior grounds, the 20 sub-basements, and the salt mine tunnel.

Dr. Wise watched the monitor as the van rolled up through the lighted tunnel and approached the high security gates leading into the HQ basement garage.

"I never imagined the President would be coming here," Dr. Wise said, "but this is what it takes. We have to win this."

One of Dr. Wise's assistants entered.

"Double delivery," Chief Browne said, pointing to a convoy of three large trucks following behind the van.

"That's the Grazia family's special delivery," Dr. Wise said. "Enough ammunition for World War III. Whoever imagined a mafia family's good deed literally would be converging on our revolution headquarters alongside the President?"

Dr. Wise's assistant nodded and said, "All the bedrooms are secure. And the parents are ready."

As the deep rumble of the metal garage gates rising down the hallway filled the room, Dr. Wise felt electrified by what was happening. "That girl is in for a big surprise. The surprise of her life!"

"Dr. Wise," Chief Browne said. "The weapons training for all residents is set for today at five."

"Good," Dr. Wise said. "We don't know when it's going to go down, but we do know it's coming. Especially with our new guests here. We have to be prepared."

Dr. Wise dashed into the hallway, flanked by security guards armed with automatic rifles, down the hall, and into the garage. A long line of LifeQuest soldiers—male and female, young and old—filed past him, awaiting arrival of the weapons cache on the trucks emblazoned with the Grazia Food Distribution logo on the sides.

The van stopped, the doors opened, and out stepped Calvin Alvarez, Jeri Brewster, the President, and presidential advisor Gerald Blane, whose hand was bandaged.

"Mr. President, welcome," Dr. Wise said, feeling a twinge of resentment that the President had not spoken up in support of the Obesity Eradication Act during the Congressional hearings.

I bet he supports my mission now!

Wise thought as he shook the President's hand.

"Where am I?" the President asked.

"Twenty stories below Detroit," Dr. Wise said. "You entered through the salt mines. These tunnels go all over the city. This one leads to our LifeQuest headquarters, which is safer than the Pentagon for you right now."

"I appreciate the protection while I sort things out," the President said.

Two hulking guards with guns stood beside the President.

"They will escort you to your room where you can shower and get comfortable," Dr. Wise said.

The guards escorted the President away.

Jeri hugged Dr. Wise. "Finally, we made it! Now we have to stop the deaths. We have to get the restaurants to stop serving the poison that's killing people."

"We will," Dr. Wise said. "Come in, let's get to work."

Calvin hugged Dr. Wise. "We made it. We still got a long way to go."

Dr. Wise turned to Jeri and said, "Before you do anything, I need you to come to my conference room."

"Sure," Jeri said.

"Hey, everybody!" Angelo Grazia shouted as he jumped out of the cab of one of the big trucks. "Time to unpack the motherload!"

Other men began unlocking the trucks' cargo areas, and rolling down ramps. The LifeQuest soldiers—men and women, young and old—lined up and followed instructions to begin unloading the ammunition.

Angelo shook Calvin's hand and said, "Hey, dude, glad to meet you."

Dr. Wise approached, patting Angelo's back. "Angelo, I can't thank you and your father and your associates for donating so many weapons, ammunition, vehicles and other supplies for the movement."

Angelo shook Dr. Wise's hand. "It's our honor and privilege. A lot of the families came together to donate resources and manpower. We can't watch our beloved country get smacked down by a terrorist bully—or anybody."

Calvin jumped on the back of the truck and greeted the mafia soldiers who were manning the delivery.

"This is like Christmas," he said, checking out all the military-grade fire-power that included automatic weapons and rocket launchers.

He picked up a huge gun, looked through the viewfinder, and cocked it loudly. Meanwhile, soldiers for the Movement came up to the truck to receive their assigned weapons, while a stream of soldiers unloaded the goods and carried them inside HQ.

"This will be one helluva showdown," Bullet told his ex-military buddies who were amongst the crew. "Never thought I'd get so close to the apocalypse. It's our job to stop it. Right here in Detroit."

Angelo came around with a clipboard. "We've got dozens of truckloads like this coming in at all the warehouses across the city right now, and into all the chapters across the country."

Chapter 78

Inside the Palace War Room, King Daemon sat on a golden throne facing a wall-sized video screen showing a map of the world. His top military officials sat around him as the Royal Commander of Military Domination used a red dot to point to Detroit, Michigan, in the United States. He zoomed in on the map, which focused on a brick warehouse building near a river.

"The President, the girl, the soldier, and Dr. Wise are all at the LifeQuest bunker in Detroit," he said. "And we believe that the evil General may be there. Having everyone in one spot will facilitate our ease of destruction."

King Daemon seethed. "Bring them all to me now. I want to kill them all with my own hands. And we will keep the doctor alive so that he can help us further implement his anti-obesity plan here in Royal Tricqua."

The Royal Commander of Military Domination clicked his red pointer at another spot on the map, across the city of Detroit. Then he zoomed into what became a white-gray tunnel lit by headlights.

"Our soldiers are racing through the salt mines of Detroit as we speak," he said. "These tunnels connect to the LifeQuest Movement's headquarters in the warehouse where our targets are sleeping right now. It is only a matter of time before our tanks reach the bunker."

King Daemon nodded. "I want to watch it live. I want to watch it all unfolding before our very eyes. They attempted to block our plan, but here we are, ready to dominate."

Chapter 79

Jeri followed Dr. Wise and Calvin into the Life-Quest conference room.

Jeri screamed. There in front of her sat her parents at the table. She threw herself into their arms and sobbed.

"You're alive!" she cried. "Oh, thank God, you're alive!"

After long minutes, her father said, "I was kidnapped in Trykka, but escaped thanks to an Tricquan soldier whose family I saved years ago. He returned the favor by smuggling me out in a soldier's uniform, and got me on a military plane back to the States. I've been traveling under the radar to get here. Then your mother showed up. We both prayed that you'd eventually make your way here."

Jeri stared at her mother, whose cheek was scarred and she was much thinner and pale. "What happened?"

"When they came for me at the house," Maggie said, "I was on the phone with my editor. Actually a video conference call. I didn't know what had happened to your father, other than you and he could not be reached. I was a wreck! So, these guys, they took me to a house. I don't know where it was. They made me talk to King Daemon, who told me all the terrible things he was going to do to us."

Her mother sobbed.

"I was kept in a room. Then one night a woman came into the room," she said, "and I couldn't believe it. She woke me up and said, 'Ssshhh, I'm taking you out of here.' She was a young woman from Asia, and I don't know how she fit in with the terrorists, except I think she was disillusioned by what they were doing. She actually drove me here to LifeQuest! She's lived here ever since. All I know is, she was an angel, and she saved my life."

Jeri hugged her mother and they sobbed.

Chapter 80

As soon as Congressman Buxton got wind of the disaster at the White House, he booked a flight for the Bahamas. He had offshore accounts, and he needed to lie low until everything calmed down.

He instructed his staff to tell any inquiring media representatives that he had fallen ill with pneumonia and was hospitalized in a private room, unavailable for interviews. He knew too much and needed to keep his distance from this scandal to preserve the long-term legacy of the Buxton family and his own immediate future.

"Sweetheart, how are you?" he asked, turning to Cindy in the seat beside him on his private jet.

"I'm good, baby," she said, laying her head back and closing her eyes. "Took care of all the books before we left, so the sports website is operational but our other services are on hiatus. Too many of our clients are under scrutiny with the fallout of the White House craziness, so we are officially closed for business until further notice."

"Not too long," Brace whispered, nuzzling her ear. "Just long enough for a little holiday in a different type of heat."

He was so glad his wife and kids were on a different plane, heading down to their home in the Exumas. Cindy would have her own place nearby, so Brace could sneak away any time to enjoy the fruits of his labor and the birthright of all Buxton men: a hot mistress.

Despite his excitement, he seethed inside at the reality that corruption had struck America on such a profound level, and that it could jeopardize life as he and all Americans knew it.

Chapter 81

Life Quest HQ Security Chief Shane Browne kept constant watch over the monitors showing the people they were protecting from global malice: the President of the United States; Jeri Brewster; Calvin "Bullet" Alvarez; General William "Wild Bill" Brewster; his wife, Maggie Brewster; and Dr. Wise. Each slept in their rooms, under the watchful lenses of security cameras, and under the protection of two armed guards outside each person's bedroom door on the top security 8th floor sub-basement.

"Chief Browne," said another guard who was watching a wall of monitors showing every entrance to HQ, as well as the streets and salt mine tunnels leading to the warehouse and sub-basements. "Our monitors are detecting a rumble."

Suddenly four military tanks appeared on the screen, rolling toward HQ in the salt mines. Chief Browne zoomed in on the vehicles.

"Attack!" she ordered.

A frenzied pace took over the Control Room, as officers communicated with the LifeQuest Defense Force.

"Mobilizing tanks," one officer said as video showed six

LifeQuest tanks departing from their stations within the salt mines, and rolling toward the invaders.

"Move our charges to the safe chambers," Chief Browne ordered.

"Our signals show these are not U.S military," one officer said. "They're Daemon's goons."

"Spray!" Chief Browne commanded.

One officer pushed buttons on a control panel, causing a blue mist to rain on the tanks. They slowed but did not stop.

Everything became a fast-moving blur as Chief Browne scanned all the videos showing the President, the Brewsters, Dr. Wise, and Alvarez being moved into the Safe Chamber. At the same time, she watched the LifeQuest tanks and the invaders' tanks moving toward each other.

The floor and walls rumbled.

"They're getting closer," an officer said.

On the screens, the dark tunnels lit up with headlights racing toward each other.

Dr. Wise burst into the control room.

"What's going on?" he demanded as two soldiers stood by him.

"Dr. Wise, please go to the safe chamber," Chief Browne said. "We are under attack."

"I'm staying right here," he said, pointing to the monitor showing the President, the Brewsters, and Bullet safely ensconced in the safe chamber. Other monitors showed guards armed with automatic weapons on all 20 sub-basements as well as the upper floors of the warehouse, instructing the men, women, and children to remain inside their rooms to shelter-in-place.

"Is it US military or the terrorists?" Dr. Wise asked.

"Don't know yet," Chief Browne said.

Boom!

The control room shook.

The monitors lit up with red light.

"They fired on our tanks!" an officer said.

"Attack!" Chief Browne ordered.

Red flashed on the screens.

A deep rumble shook the room as the LifeQuest tanks fired back.

"They're close enough for us to hear," Dr. Wise said. "We need to take 'em out now! We have two thousand people here! Including the President! Now!"

Suddenly the screens turned pure red.

The blast shook the control room like 6.9-magnitude earthquake.

"Who's getting who?" Dr. Wise demanded as the officers attempted to communicate with the tank drivers.

Booooommmmm! Booooommmmm! Booooommmmm!

The walls shook.

And a cloud of dust sprayed up at the cameras monitoring the tunnel.

An alarm blared.

"Breach!" Chief Browne declared. "Defense Plan A!"

A monitor showed dozens of armed LifeQuest officers running through the hallways and guarding the residents' doors three-deep. A small army assembled outside the safe chamber.

"We've gotten this far," Dr. Wise said. "Nothing can stop us!"

Boom! Boom! Boom!

The lights flickered.

The monitors hissed with snow-static.

The room went dark.

Chapter 82

As the floor and walls vibrated each time a loud *boom* went off, Jeri sat between her parents, watching Calvin pace the room. The President sat in a chair flanked by two soldiers holding automatic weapons.

"We have to get out of here!" Calvin declared to the guards. "We are sitting ducks! If they blast through the entrances, we are done!"

"Orders," the guards said. "We have to protect you here. No one can get inside."

"Then how do you explain the demolition blasts all around us?" Calvin asked.

"Being underground, sounds are amplified," the guard said. "Relax."

"I can't fucking relax when you've got a room full of people who are the only ones who can literally save the world from the terrorists' poison!" Calvin shouted, lunging at the guards. "Let us out!"

A guard pointed a gun at Calvin and said, "Stand down, soldier. We got this."

Boom!

The lights dimmed. Then the room was cast into darkness.

Chapter 83

Johnny "Big Man" Valentine commandeered his souped-up 18-wheeler into the salt mine tunnel.

"Dr. Wise said it was in this area," he told the guy in the passenger seat who was holding the rocket launcher controls. "We're gonna give those motherfuckers the surprise of their life."

Two more trucks sped behind him.

Suddenly the tunnel, lit only by their headlights, turned dusty. Fire burned orange and red in the dusty cloud filling the giant tunnel.

Pop! Pop! Pop!

Johnny screeched to a halt in front of two crashed tanks and two others that had rammed into each other. Men and women soldiers were peeking out from behind the smoking vehicles. A giant hole gaped in the wall, where one of the tanks had rammed it. Soldiers wearing camouflage adorned with the Royal Tricqua flag were running through the hole, into the LifeQuest HQ.

LifeQuest soldiers opened fire on them.

Johnny couldn't fire on them because he would hit LifeQuest folks.

He pushed a button to open the back gate on the truck. Three dozen Food Fight soldiers ran full speed ahead toward the gaping hole.

Johnny ran first, leading them as their tactical helmet lamps lit the way.

Chapter 84

Jeri was terrified. It was pitch dark. Bullets were flying in the hallway. And all they could do was wait. Was this US military sent to kill the President? Would she and her parents be killed along with him? Or were they under attack by Daemon's people?

Who could save them?

The soldiers had pressed them into the corners while they stood at the door, guns drawn in the darkness.

Bam!

Complete chaos exploded in the hallway. Gunfire. Screaming. Rumble-blasts.

Jeri was sure they would die.

They had no escape. They were 20 floors below the earth's surface, and two sets of bad guys were after them.

Bam! Bam! Bam!

Someone was pounding on the door with such intense force it slammed in.

Dusty air poured into the room. Red lights flashed.

Deafening bursts of gunfire rang out.

Jeri's mother was crying.

Her father was comforting her while also exclaiming, "Goddammit, why did they take my weapon?"

In the dusty shadows, Calvin snatched one of the soldiers' guns and opened fire on the men bursting into the room. Several fell, but not before some of their shots landed on a few of the guards as they ran into the safe chamber.

Jeri's heart pounded: they were yelling in the Tricquan language.

Daemon's people got us here!

How did the find us?

Jeri understood the words. One of the men exclaimed the word for president. Then another said assassin-soldier. Girl. Mother.

They came for the four of us. They got us. And we are as good as dead.

Chapter 85

DR. WISE FINGERED A panel on the wall, knowing that he could switch on the generators and get some light in the control room and throughout the entire LifeQuest HQ.

He imagined the men, women, and children feeling totally terrified right now, while this gun battle and whatever else was happening unfolded around them.

Ah, there it is!

He flipped the switch, expecting the relief of light.

Nothing happened.

It was still dark.

He could hear the pound of footsteps and men yelling in the language of Tricqua outside the control room.

The door burst open.

A soldier opened fire.

Guards fell.

Chief Browne fell.

Dr. Wise pressed against the wall.

One of the invaders yelled as another pressed a gun to Dr. Wise's temple and pulled him into the hallway. Dr. Wise coughed on the gun smoke and dust amidst the deafening chaos of gunfire. Deep rumbling. Explosions. Screaming.

Dr. Wise envisioned Daemon taking over the United States and the world.

I am a dead man... and this is the apocalypse.

Chapter 86

Johnny Valentine just wasn't havin' it.

No way was he going to allow those terrorist mother-fuckers to mess this up. No, not after all that Dr. Wise had done, and not after all the LifeQuest Movement was doing.

They just messed with the wrong dude. Food Fight Posse in the house!

Another truck rolled up with Carmen and Boone and their soldiers, all armed and assembled behind Johnny and his fight-ers. Adrenaline surged through his every cell, propelling him on foot, automatic rifles slung over both shoulders, with maga-zines strapped to his flak jacket, pistols strapped to each leg.

He ran with superhuman strength into the dust, the gunfire, and the flashing red, as the salt mine floor rumbled beneath his boots.

His soldiers followed behind, all armed and ammo'd up like him.

Suddenly, as he was about to enter the blast hole into the LifeQuest headquarters, one of the enemy soldiers lunged at him.

Johnny looked into the eyes of the terrorist. They were void of emotion. Void of anything except pure evil. In the dim light, they were like glassy brown windows into hell.

This motherfucker came all the way from the other side of the world to get stomped in Detroit.

Time stood still as the gravity of the moment struck Johnny's soul. He had set out on this mission with his Food Fight Posse to save black folks from the system that was keeping them in poverty, in prison, and poisoned by toxic "food."

His group was up against the American food manufacturers and the US government entities that allowed them to sicken American citizens. And now a terrorist group on the other side of the world was battling the government along with the writer who was trying to save the day with her Army General daddy, the Special Ops boyfriend, and her mother, the author.

This is some twisted shit, but we're about to save the day— Detroit style!

The split-second analysis stopped as pure instinct for survival kicked in.

Johnny didn't even want to waste a bullet on this evil motherfucker who had the nerve to stare him down here in the salty bowels of the D. And now the dude looked like he thought he could shoot a brotha. Johnny simply held his gun with both hands, horizontally, and bashed that motherfucker out of his misery.

Johnny stepped over the terrorist's dead body as his posse ran alongside him. They knew where to go, and what to do.

"Five minutes," he said into the dusty air, "and we're out. Done."

Chapter 87

Footsteps, gunfire, smoke…

It happened in a flash in the darkness.

Jeri punched, clawed.

Her mother was screaming.

Her father was fighting.

She couldn't see them.

She could feel and hear them.

And Calvin was fighting. Thuds. Slams. Pounds.

The sound of someone slumping to the floor.

"Calvin!" Jeri screamed. "Mom? Dad!?"

"Oh, no," a man groaned.

It was the President.

"Where are you?"

The gurgle of blood mixed with a cough—the sound of a man dying from internal bleeding after being shot—let Jeri know that the President was mortally wounded.

Suddenly more men surged into the room, all yelling in Tricquan.

An arm went around Jeri's neck. The man smelled of cigarettes, and in his jerky seizure of her body, her feet lifted from the floor.

"I got the girl," he grunted in his native language. "Daemon is going to kill you with his bare hands."

He swung Jeri in front of him, her back to him. Jeri kicked back and stomped his knees. He dropped her.

She had to find her mother. Where was her father? Where was Bullet?

Metal pressed into the back of her head. A hand grabbed her neck.

She froze.

In the dim, smoky light, Bullet rose from the chaos. He was holding a giant automatic rifle, aiming it at the guy who was pressing the gun to Jeri's head.

Suddenly the terrorist dropped.

And Johnny Valentine appeared, lit by a light on his helmet. It illuminated the President, bleeding on the floor. Her mother was crouched in the corner. Her father was lying beside her.

"Dad!?" Jeri fell to her knees beside her father, checking his pulse. "Dad!?"

Chapter 88

Dr. Wise sat in a chair in the control room as the terrorist pressed the gun to his head. The terrorist soldiers had shot and killed everyone in the room; their bodies were crumpled and slumped in various positions on the floor and on the desk-like control panels.

"Get up!" the terrorist ordered. "We are taking you to King Daemon."

Dr. Wise slowly stood, terrified that the gun would go off and kill him right then. He was overwhelmed with hopelessness. All that work. All the people committed to the cause, and working so hard to change America for the better. Now this. Done. Finished. Wasted.

He rose, contemplating a quick move that would enable the captain to go down with the proverbial ship.

Had the invading terrorist soldiers killed the President, Jeri, Bullet, the General, and Mrs. Brewster?

Dr. Wise squared his soldiers.

I will survive this. And assess what's going on. I'll go along to get along for now...

He stepped into the hallway, where something burning near the blasted hole in the wall cast a red glow over bodies on the floor. He knew some of them were his people. Dead for the cause of trying to save lives.

"In 24 hours," the terrorist said, "you will be the new Minister of Health for Royal Tricqua as we embark on Plan B to take over America."

Sour vomit rose from Dr. Wise's stomach. Like a reflex, he shook his head. And the man cocked his gun.

He can just take me out right now…

Dr. Wise shook his head. Couldn't stop.

The cold metal pressed harder into his temple.

A deafening blast…

A flash of red.

Dr. Wise stood, stunned.

He lifted his hand to his head, expecting to feel a gaping mess of brains and blood.

"Doc!" Johnny Valentine shouted. "You okay?"

What was happening? Dr. Wise glanced down. The terrorist was on the floor. Blood oozed from a hole in the middle of his forehead.

Dr. Wise touched his hair. Ran his hand over his whole head. His temples were intact.

I wasn't shot. The terrorist's gun went off, when Johnny shot him.

Johnny was holding a smoking pistol. Then he shouted, "Let's go!"

Chapter 89

General "Wild Bill" Brewster sat in a room in the Pentagon, orchestrating Operation Daemon. He and the team of top military leaders watched a giant screen as US Air Force planes flew toward King Daemon's palace.

They were about to write the final chapter on this nightmare. Thankfully, the President had a happy ending, as he was recovering well from the bullet wound to his throat that, had it been a few millimeters closer to his artery, would have been fatal.

Officials were weeding out the corrupt people around the President, and installing legitimate leaders who supported the President's commitment to enacting the Obesity Eradication Act.

As America's new Surgeon General, Dr. Wise was busy implementing new programs in schools and communities to teach healthy living to aggressively reduce the obesity rate.

He was using his own brother and sister-in-law, and their children, as the poster family for his cause, showcasing how they had all dramatically changed their eating habits and the health status. Maggie's sister and her children had also joined the cause, volunteering alongside the Wise family to inspire people with their radical transformation. They used Dan's tragic death as an example of all that could go wrong when food addiction consumed a person's mind and body.

Meanwhile, in Montana, Jeri and Bullet were planning to marry, and were now living on Bullet's ranch, where Maggie was staying for the time being. Jeri was writing a book about what happened, while Maggie was composing a series of articles for *The National Journal* about their ordeal.

Johnny Valentine, along with Boone and Carmen, were instituting Health Academies across America to teach men, women, and children how to eat healthy foods, exercise, and practice meditation and yoga.

Now, General Brewster felt grateful that he had so quickly recovered from the mild heart attack that he had suffered in the LifeQuest headquarters during the terrorists' ambush. He was back to normal, and had even taken a long run this morning around the Washington Mall.

"Ready," the President said, as everyone in the room watched the monitors.

US Air Force planes dropped bombs on King Daemon's palace.

The aerial views showed each missile striking the massive structure, which crumbled, smoked, and burned.

"Our soldiers are on the perimeters to ensure that no one escapes alive," General Brewster said. "The rubble will be torched. They are done. Forever."

Chapter 90

King Daemon watched his palace burn as a satellite camera beamed the live images to this remote Siberian castle. He was surrounded by his Royal Brothers here, and his wives and children were safely ensconced in the residential wing under tight security. Here they were taking refuge from the expected retaliation that the Americans would inflict. They were so predictable. So stupid.

He could almost taste the delicious thrill of someday killing the evil General and everyone associated with him. Especially the girl who exposed OC-8 and brought the Royal Tricqua's mission to a pathetic halt.

"Bring me Dr. Braza," King Daemon ordered one of his guards. "I want a full report on our next plan to destroy America."

THE END

Biography
Michael H. Wood, FACS

DR. WOOD IS THE Director of the Bariatric Surgery Program at the Detroit Medical Center (DMC), Harper University Hospital and is Clinical Professor of Surgery at Wayne state University.

He is board certified by the American Board of surgery and has over 25 years of surgical experience with an extensive background in weight loss surgery and advanced laparoscopic surgical procedures. He has performed over 6000 weight loss surgical procedures and has devoted a large portion of his medical career to the study and treatment of obesity and weight loss strategies. His clinical interests include minimally invasive surgery (laparoscopic and robotic), performing a host of different types of bariatric surgical procedures. He is an active member of the American Society for Metabolic and Bariatric Surgery and a Fellow of the American College of surgeons.

Dr. Wood has authored many articles related to obesity and bariatric surgery. He has a passion for treating obesity and its disease processes; including physiologic consideration, dietary factors in gastrointestinal disease, and strategies for prevention of obesity. He has received research grant funding for the study of the effects of endogenous opiates on gastric acid secretion. He is co-inventor of the patented Sapala-Wood Micropouchclip_image002.png gastric bypass procedure. His collaboration includes, colleagues in the Division of Endocrinology, Wayne State University, studying the differential gene expression of inflammatory cytokines in the fat cell.

Honors and Awards

Best Doc. Inc. , Hour Magazine, Detroit Michigan.; Faculty Researcher Award, Wayne state University; Theodore McGraw Clinical Faculty Teaching Award, Department of Surgery Wayne state University; Best Author Award, Journal of Obesity Surgery; Michigan health and Hospital Association, Physician Leadership Award for outstanding community service, to make name a few.

Biography
Elizabeth Ann Atkins

ELIZABETH IS A BEST-SELLING author, actress, TV host, and an award-winning journalist who uses a multimedia platform to inspire people to unlock their infinite potential and live with passion, prosperity, health, and happiness. Her 2019 spiritual memoir, *God's Answer is Know: Lessons from a Spiritual Life*, provides the launchpad for her global intuitive teachings.

Elizabeth's desire to empower others springs from a trailblazing matrix of colorblind love and courage from her mother, an African American and Italian judge, and her father, a former Roman Catholic priest who was English, French Canadian, and Cherokee. They taught her to challenge the status quo by writing innovative ideas to *edu-tain* people.

With a master's degree in Journalism from Columbia University and a bachelor's degree in English Literature from the University of Michigan, Elizabeth has written over 20 books, including novels *White Chocolate, Dark Secret* and *Twilight* (with Billy Dee Williams).

Elizabeth has ghostwritten books for executives, prominent government and civic leaders, physicians, a surgeon, an intuitive medium, a family that triumphed on NBC's The Biggest Loser, an insurance agent, and a quadriplegic man who lived his dream to become a record company CEO. Her novellas about empowering women to overcome abuse and identity crises were published in *My Blue Suede Shoes: An Anthology* and *Other People's Skin: An Anthology*.

Elizabeth runs Two Sisters Writing and Publishing with her sister, the young adult author Catherine M. Greenspan. Together they have published over twenty books, including an annual anthology of short stories by international writers who won the Two Sisters' ongoing short story writing contests.

Elizabeth is a health and fitness enthusiast whose 100-pound weight loss was featured on Oprah.

Elizabeth co-hosts a weekly television show, MI Healthy Mind, which promotes wellness by shattering stigmas around taboo topics such as mental illness, addiction and abuse.

She is a popular writing coach whose PowerJournal™ program teaches people to enrich their lives with journal-writing. She has taught writing at Wayne State University, Oakland University, Wayne County Community College District, and at national conferences.

As a speaker who promotes human harmony, Elizabeth was previously represented by the American Program Bureau. She rouses ovations by reciting her autobiographical poem, "White Chocolate," and has spoken at Columbia University, the University of Michigan, GM's World Diversity Day, Gannett, 100 Black Men, the NAACP, and many other venues.

As an actress, Elizabeth plays a major role in the feature-length film *Anything Is Possible*, nominated for "Best Foreign Film" by the Nollywood and African Film Critics Association. She composed an original screenplay, *Redemption*, a gritty drama about a Detroit gangster and a writer. And Elizabeth plays a 1950s journalist in the international shipwreck drama, *Are The Passengers Saved?*

Elizabeth has been a guest on Oprah, Montel, NPR, Good Morning America Sunday, The CBS Evening News, and many national TV shows. After writing her master's thesis about mixed-race Americans, her work appeared in *The New York Times*, *The San Diego Tribune*, *Essence*, *Ebony*, and many publications.

Her *Detroit News* articles on race were nominated for the Pulitzer Prize, and she wrote a biography for the Presidential Medal of Freedom tribute for Rosa Parks.

Elizabeth runs, cycles, lifts weights, does yoga, journals and meditates to cultivate a joyous and peaceful mind, body and spirit.

Books Published By Two Sisters Writing and Publishing

A.M. Total Being Fitness Journal: A different kind of journal
Anthony Moses

Broken Hearts: Like Mother, Like Daughter—A Spiritual Call For Equality In Health Care
Alma G. Stallworth, PhD

"CLEAR!" Living the Life You Didn't Dream Of
Herman Williams, MD

Confessions of a Plastic Surgeon: Shocking Stories about Enhancing Butts, Boobs, and Beauty
Thomas T. Jeneby, MD

Dark Secret (Previously published by Forge)
Elizabeth Ann Atkins

The Dr. Sanchez Books on Raising Healthy Children—Baby's First Year: A Survival Guide For New & Experienced Parents (Forthcoming)

> Eduardo M. Sanchez, DNP

The Energy Within Us: An Illuminating Perspective from Five Trailblazers

> Joyce Hayes Giles
> Carolyn Green
> Rose McKinney-James
> Hilda Pinnix-Ragland
> Telisa Toliver

God's Answer is Know: Lessons from a Spiritual Life

> Elizabeth Ann Atkins

Legacy of a Lawmaker: Inspired by Faith & Family

> Alma G. Stallworth, PhD

Let the Future Begin

> Dennis W. Archer

Lifted: A Journey from Trauma to Triumph

> Mike Ritter

The Making Point: How to succeed when you're at your breaking point

> Master Sgt. Cedric King

My Name is Steve Delano Bullock: How I Changed My World and the World Around Me through Leadership, Caring, and Perseverance

Steve D. Bullock

The PowerJournal™ Series

PowerJournal: A 28-Day Challenge - Workbook #1

PowerJournal: A 28-Day Challenge for Weight Loss - Workbook #2

PowerJournal: A 28-Day Challenge for Making Big Decisions - Workbook #3

PowerJournal: A 28-Day Challenge for Spiritual Awakening - Workbook #4 (Forthcoming)

PowerJournal: A 28-Day Challenge for Discovering Your Purpose - Workbook

#5 (Forthcoming)

Elizabeth Ann Atkins

Catherine M. Greenspan

Remembering and Forgetting: A spiritual journey

Lin Day

The Triumph of Rosemary: A Memoir

Judge Marylin E. Atkins

The Veronica Series
Veronica, I Heard Your Mom's Black
Veronica Talks to Boys
Race Home, Veronica
Grace Under Pressure (Forthcoming)
Sally's Indoor Fiesta (Forthcoming)

Hey, Jude, Is that White Lady Your Mom? (Forthcoming)
A Girl Named George (Forthcoming)
Have You Seen Debbie? (Forthcoming)

Catherine M. Greenspan

Two Sisters Writing and Publishing Short Story Anthologies

Two Sisters Writing and Publishing First Annual Anthology: Featuring International Writers

Two Sisters Writing and Publishing Second Annual Anthology: Featuring International Writers (Forthcoming)

Catherine M. Greenspan

Elizabeth Ann Atkins

We're Standing By

Al Allen